Praise for *Savvy She...*

"Taj McCoy has created a protagon... ...
determined, and perfectly imperfect. I ador... ... journey and
couldn't get enough of her ride-or-die friends. This one's a treat!"
—Mia Sosa, *USA TODAY* bestselling author of *The Worst Best Man*

"One can't help but root for Savvy Sheldon as she comes into her own.
Taj McCoy's entertaining debut is filled with heart, humor, and loads of
feel-good vibes!"

—Farrah Rochon, *USA TODAY* bestselling author
of *The Dating Playbook*

"An enchanting love letter to the power of self-care. McCoy's sparkling
debut is a warm, witty, relationship-powered story that will leave
you grinning and rooting for the characters. It is a perfect blend of
mouthwatering food and soul-nourishing resilience."
—Denise Williams, bestselling author of *How to Fail at Flirting*

"Savvy goes on one heck of a self-love journey post-breakup and I was
cheering for her the whole way. Add a steamy romance into the mix and
my heart sang as I tore through this book. This feel-good, empowering
romcom will blow you away, guaranteed."
—Sarah Smith, author of *Simmer Down*

"McCoy delivers heat and laughs in this uplifting debut. Readers are
guaranteed to root for Savvy's empowering journey towards self-love and
success. Because with hilarious friends and a sexy new love interest, the
destination will be well worth it."
—Charish Reid, author of *(Trust) Falling for You*

"Sexy, sumptuous and superb. Funny with fantastic characters and a lot
of heart. Taj McCoy takes us on Savvy's journey full of self-realization,
self-love and self-empowerment with a graceful poise, making it hard to
believe this is her debut!"
—Catherine Adel West, author of *Saving Ruby King*

SAVVY SHELDON FEELS GOOD AS HELL

Taj McCoy

mira

mira™

Recycling programs
for this product may
not exist in your area.

ISBN-13: 978-0-7783-1184-3

Savvy Sheldon Feels Good as Hell

This edition published by arrangement with Harlequin Books S.A.

For questions and comments about the quality of this book, please contact us at
CustomerService@Harlequin.com.

Mira
22 Adelaide St. West, 41st Floor
Toronto, Ontario M5H 4E3, Canada
BookClubbish.com

Printed in U.S.A.

To Ma and Pop, who taught me that hard work pays off.
To Uncle, my childhood hero.
To Chantal, because my victories are hers, too.
To Ka-Ton, for refusing to accept my excuses.
Thank you for being my village.

SAVVY SHELDON FEELS GOOD AS HELL

1

"Shit!" Savvy whispered. A bubble of bacon grease popped on her arm, and she jumped back. Rubbing away the grease, she turned down the white knob on her gas stove to calm the crackling bacon, flipping the thick slices of applewood-smoked goodness with a pair of tongs. *Crisper this time.*

Other than her occasional muttered curses, the only sounds in the house came from the sizzling on the stove and the deep hum of a cranky old refrigerator. The kind of hum that kept you guessing whether it actually still functioned. Tugging on the door, she ducked her head in to pull out baby portobello mushrooms, fresh spinach, and a red bell pepper from the crisper. She grabbed Gruyère cheese, a carton of eggs, and a pint of fresh strawberries, closing the door slowly to avoid its signature creak.

Savvy skillfully ran her chef's knife through mushrooms, peppers, and onion more slowly than usual. She took great care not to wake the man sleeping down the hall. She eyed the black silk camisole and lacy short set hanging nearby, and a shiver of excitement ran down her spine. She looked down at Jason's old basketball shirt, a relic from some college intramural tournament that he and his boys played in. *Not exactly a seductive look.* Whoever those guys were that enjoyed women with their hair tied back and no makeup on, Jason was not one of them.

She separated egg yolks from whites and tossed the veggies into a heated omelet pan, adding handfuls of fresh spinach as they softened, then the beaten egg whites a moment later. Using a handheld cheese grater, curls of Gruyère sprinkled onto the omelet, slowly expanding and flattening into a melty pool.

Savvy had moved into her childhood home eight months ago, right after Mama moved to San Jose with her new husband, leaving it empty. Very little had changed in the house since her childhood. Carpets still covered pristine hardwood floors, and plastic runners lined the hallway leading to the bedrooms. Dingy from years of wear and tear, the edges of the runners were yellowed with age. Mama's house, with its floral decor, took clutter to hoarding levels—she never threw anything away.

The faded yellow paint on the walls, dry and peeling, reminded Savvy of the lists of contractors Mama had given her, tucked between the milk crate and the French press. She intended to renovate the house to make it feel more like her own, but work was too busy to take on a project. The teakettle hissed hot steam, and she snatched it from the stove before whistling interrupted the morning quiet. Boiling water cascaded over finely ground Kona coffee, the aroma carrying just enough caffeine to raise her energy level.

After peeking over her shoulder, Savvy reached into the oven and grabbed a slice of chewy bacon from the tray. *If it's eaten straight from the pan, it has no calories. These are the Bacon Rules.*

Sliced strawberries and cubed mangoes with a chiffonade of fresh mint joined the omelet and crispy bacon, making for a colorful, drool-worthy presentation. Savvy ran a paper towel around the rim of the plate before capturing the aesthetic for her IG Story.

She kicked off her slippers and lifted the enormous T-shirt over her head before realizing with a flash of embarrassment that the kitchen curtains were wide-open. She rushed to shut them, stubbing her toe on a loose piece of tile and yelling silently into the morning. Once she regained her composure, she slipped the camisole over her head, sucking in her breath and running her fingers over the slightly taut, black fabric. *Don't overthink it, Savvy.* With her silky cream kimono robe with pale pink peonies framing her sexy new pj's and Jason's meal on an enameled wooden tray, she shook out her hair one last time and headed down the hall.

"Good morning, Baby, I have breakfast for you," Savvy cooed softly as she reached the doorway.

Jason opened his eyes slowly, rolling toward her onto his side as he yawned. "How long you been up, Savs?" His beard was flattened on his left side from being pressed into the pillow. He smoothed a hand over the crown of his head, flattening the top of his fade, then grabbed his phone before turning to look at her. Jason took in her attempt at seduction, his deep voice thick from sleep. "What you got on?"

Dammit. "Just something new. I thought you'd like it. I was up for maybe an hour?" she lied. *More like two.* "Couldn't get back to sleep, so I thought I'd surprise you." Setting the tray on the nightstand, she stole a quick kiss.

"I taste bacon on your lips." He dug into his plate, shoving bacon and mango into his mouth at the same time. His hooded eyes chastised her before returning back to his meal.

How does he even taste his own food eating that fast? She sat down next to him with a bowl of fresh fruit, resting her pedicured toes on the edge of the bed frame. "What do you have going on today?"

"Need to stop by my momma's after she gets out of church, go home and walk Ginger, and then play a couple of pickup games with the fellas. What's on your plate today? You cookin' tonight?" He crunched through his bacon with enthusiasm, moving half of his omelet onto a piece of toast.

"I need to check on my uncle before I go shopping for some work clothes. You could come over for dinner later."

He grunted, looking up from his omelet on toast, cheeks threatening to burst. "What you cookin'?" he repeated.

She rolled her eyes as she fixed her mouth to give him options, but her phone pinged.

Jason hit her with a side-eye, shaking his head. His mouth bursting with food. "Is that who I think it is?" His voice peaked, like a kid three seconds away from a tantrum.

Grabbing her phone from the nightstand, Savvy eyed him carefully. "Yes, Babe, it is." Her voice calm, she scrutinized the request from her boss. He needed data about insured millennials to present to a new insurance client, and she'd forgotten to incorporate that into her presentation slides.

"He's interrupting quality time, Savvy." Jason stood, bare chested in basketball shorts, his deep voice booming with displeasure. Athletic, but not overly muscular, he ran his fingers over his flat stomach, stretching his long limbs, as she pounded away on her phone's keyboard with her thumbs. "Why am I just waking up on Sunday morning, and you're already working?"

Shit. "Just one sec, Jay, I promise." Biting her lip, she ran through report data in her head to pinpoint the figures her boss wanted. She'd always had a good memory for numbers. She typed her response as quickly as her thumbs allowed, noting that she would be in the office for a few hours in the afternoon if he had any additional questions. Jason didn't need to know that last part. "There, see? Done." Savvy smiled up at him, willing him to sit next to her.

He did. "I don't know anyone else who is okay with their boss interrupting their weekend. He can't just wait till to-morrow?"

"Well, I'm not working now…" Nuzzling his shoulder, she traced her fingertips down his back. "You know, Babe, I was hoping that we could…you know." The kimono robe slipped suggestively, exposing her shoulders.

Jason avoided eye contact as he handed Savvy his empty tray. "You ain't got time for all that, Boss Lady." Tsking, he shook his head, making his way to the bathroom. The sound of a shower curtain being shoved aside and water raining from the showerhead followed. As steam spread across the bathroom mirror, he called out to her, "You should prob-ably see if you can take them clothes back. Fit's too tight."

Savvy set the tray down on the bed next to her, then stood, wrapping the kimono tightly around her middle. Shoulders rounded, she returned to the kitchen with Ja-son's empty plate, helping herself to another slice of perfect, chewy bacon. *So much for quality time.*

Jason left as Savvy showered, calling out to her that he'd come back for dinner. After getting ready, she pulled con-tainers of last night's leftovers out of the fridge and shoved them into a heavy cloth grocery bag. Baked chicken breasts with sautéed mushrooms covered in a marsala wine sauce. Parmesan and asparagus risotto. Mixed greens with grape

tomatoes and a mason jar of fresh lemon and shallot vinai-
grette. After grabbing her purse and a sealed envelope from
her desk, she walked out into the sunshine. The sky swirled
a perfect blue, a breeze ruffled through the treetops, kissing wind chimes on her neighbor's porch. A good-looking
Black man in dusty jeans, a torn T-shirt, and work boots
walked by with a beautiful chocolate Lab. He raised a hand
in greeting as they strolled by, and she nodded in response.

Her surroundings changed from lush greenery to con-
crete skyscrapers and industrial buildings as she navigated
south on the 5 freeway, past Downtown LA. Spotting USC
on her right, she threw a strong side-eye at the home of the
Trojans. *Bruin blood for life, baby.*

Big brick buildings blurred into dilapidated warehouses
and older residential neighborhoods. Exiting at Century
Boulevard, she steered toward Uncle's house, which he'd
inherited from Savvy's grandparents, since Granny and Pop-
Pop had already bought the Los Feliz house for Savvy, her
mom, and her brothers. Mama complained that Uncle's place
was an old money pit, always needing repairs, but Unc and
Savvy loved that house.

Pulling up in the driveway, she took in the dip in the
roof that Uncle described on the phone. He'd sunk the last
of his savings into the front porch when the steps needed
replacing. The upkeep crept up faster now, but there was no
letting go of Granny and PopPop's most prized possession.

Whenever she needed money in college, Savvy'd called
her uncle to avoid stressing Mama, who worked hard to put
three kids through school. Unc helped whenever he could,
treating her like the daughter he never had. Now, with the
stability she found at work, Savvy reciprocated as often as
she could, while still building a renovation fund for her
own house.

Walking up the steps, Savvy looked through the screen door into the sitting room. "Unc! Where you at?"

"Now, why do you always have to holler like you ain't got no home training?" Uncle's husky voice rang with amusement. He leaned hard against a crutch, swinging open the screen door for her to walk through.

Savvy grinned at him, planting a big kiss on his cheek as she walked past. "Any home training I received was undone by a certain someone." In her childhood, Unc had been her hero; he helped to raise her and her brothers when their dad took off. Ma's older brother, Uncle Joe, always came by to check on them. When money ran short, he stepped in and made sure they never without.

"Mmm-hmm." His smile twitched at the corners of his mouth. "What you up to today, Baby Girl?"

Inside, her uncle's security uniform hung on the back of a chair in a plastic cover from the dry cleaner. A retired police officer, he'd taken on part-time work as a night watchman for an office building in Inglewood. On his limited retirement pay and meager income handling security, making ends meet had been a challenge, especially after he got injured on the job. At the time, Savvy had shaken her head at his explanation. "They vandalized the side of the building—of course I chased after them." *Who did he think he was, Usain Bolt?* Unc sprained his ankle running after the vandals, and, under doctor's orders, had to take time off until he could put full weight on his foot.

Savvy waved her bag of food containers at him, carrying it into the kitchen. She put the containers in the fridge and placed the sealed envelope on the Formica countertop; she had written "ROOF" on the front with a Sharpie. "I'm supposed to run an errand, but I think I'm just going to go into the office for a few hours. How was your week?"

He stood in the doorway, rolling his eyes. "I'm bored. I want to be back at work, but they want me to be off the crutches first."

"I support that decision."

"Yeah, well. Ain't got much to do, other than checkin' in on Mabel."

Her eyebrows shot up. "Miss Mabel, huh?" Mabel Winslow lived across the street from Savvy's grandparents' house most of her life. Like Unc, Miss Mabel grew up in her house. She'd moved away when she married, but returned after a bad divorce to help care for her parents. When her parents passed within a month of each other, they left Mabel the house and their golden retriever, Samson. A smile curved across her lips. "You've been jonesing after Miss Mabel since I was in high school. Tell me you finally asked her out."

Uncle Joe shook his head, fighting a smile, his upper lip curled slightly with amusement. "I'm a gentleman, Baby Girl."

"Uh, gentlemen go on dates, Unc." She winked at him, coaxing laughter.

"We ain't there yet. I just stopped by to see how she's doing. You know she was in that car accident a couple weeks ago. Tweaked her back."

"Is she okay?" She leaned against the counter.

"Says she is, but I think she might need a couple rounds of physical therapy. Doesn't hurt to make sure she's fully recovered."

Savvy eyed her uncle. "Sounds like somebody can dish advice he isn't willing to take…"

He tsked, pursing his lips at her. "Thank you for the help with the roof, but listen, Baby Girl. You workin' too much. And you should be putting this money toward your own house."

She rolled her eyes, following him into the den, where his favorite leather recliner faced a big-screen TV. "You are forever saying I work too much. And I want to help, Unc."

He sat gingerly, leaning his crutch against one of his armrests. "You need a vacation."

"You know I work the way I do because of what I learned from you and Mama. It's just what we do."

"Nah. *We* worked hard so that *you* wouldn't have to, Savvy. Your mama pushes you because she thinks you have to climb the corporate ladder to stay on it." He wagged a finger at her.

She groaned, rolling her eyes. "Well, I am my mother's daughter, and I feel most secure knowing that if either of you need me, I am in a position to help."

Mama carried two, sometimes three jobs when Savvy and her brothers were little to make sure they were fed, that their shoes fit, and that they could participate in sports or other activities. Their dad had a wandering eye and left to be with another woman, leaving Mama to be Wonder Woman for the family. Savvy missed one first-grade field trip due to a lack of funds, and Mama worked herself ragged to avoid that ever happening again. Pops never really got his shit together, losing touch with Savvy when he started his third family.

"The roof money is from a rainy-day fund, and if you think about it, those rainy days are exactly what we need to keep out of this house. I can do my renovations anytime." She offered Uncle a crooked smile.

He shook his head, annoyed at her humor. "I know you're itchin' to redo that kitchen."

She stood, ready to leave before he could march into an assessment of her current setup. An updated kitchen was at the very top of her bucket list. "I am. But you always came through for me. Let me do that for you."

He pursed his lips, offered his cheek, and she leaned in to kiss it.

"You'll be back on your feet in no time. In the meantime, call me whenever you need. Got that?"

"Mmm-hmm. Love you, Baby Girl."

"I love you more, Uncle." Savvy winked at him and turned to leave. "Let me know when you and Miss Mabel go out on your hot date!"

2

On a Sunday afternoon, the lobby lacked its typical fluorescence, lit only by the sunshine streaming in through tinted windows. After walking down the hall, past the staff lounge, Savvy stopped at a large white board where the team tracked monthly goals, upcoming deadlines, and bar charts reflecting the production numbers of each team member. So far, her monthly numbers were far ahead of the rest of the other underwriters, but she had several big deadlines coming up that would catapult her further ahead. If she could stay consistent in her output, Mama believed the boss would have no choice but to recognize that hard work with a promotion.

The space was quiet except for the hum of the copy machine. Savvy unlocked her office, surveying the room. The L-shaped desk had an in-box overflowing with file folders. Degrees hung on the wall, and a desk calendar of highlighted deadlines lay flat on top of a short bookcase with her bamboo plant. She switched her cell phone to a Do Not Disturb setting, as she did every workday. *Just for a couple of hours.*

After stretching her fingers, she connected her laptop to its docking station, and two oversized monitors flashed awake. She answered the most urgent emails: *Savvy, can you explain the product details to this client? Can you prep our help desk team to answer questions about insurability?* She received a response from her boss, Warren, thanking her for the millennial data points she'd emailed that morning—they were exactly what he needed. Relieved, she logged into the client database system, reaching for the first file in her in-box.

Mama would have been all too happy for Savvy to become a doctor, but she was too squeamish to look at injuries and illness firsthand, so she focused her studies in public health policy. She'd gotten a paid internship her senior year, and she'd found the work so intuitive that her boss made her a job offer before graduation. Nothing made Mama prouder. Ultimately, Savvy postponed work to go to grad school, but the job offer remained secure. Over the years, she gained the trust and respect of her team, climbing from junior underwriter to underwriter within the span of a few short years. In this role, Savvy reviewed applications for life insurance to determine insurability.

Work kept her busy enough to shrug off any outside drama and she liked it that way. She never felt pressure from the team to work harder or faster. Instead, it was her mother's voice ringing in her ear, continually nudging Savvy to set the bar higher.

She kept a framed photo of Mama on her desk, embracing Savvy at her high school graduation. Mama decided to quit her third job the same week that photo was taken, with Savvy going to college on a scholarship that included a partial living stipend, and her two brothers going into funded graduate and doctoral programs. Mama came home the night before graduation and found Savvy on the couch reading a book. "Savannah Joy, what have I told you about putting your feet up on this couch?"

She huffed in frustration, not wanting to pull herself from the world she read about. "Not to." Setting her book down, she unfolded her legs, letting her feet skim the floor. "How was work?"

Mama reached over and tucked hair behind Savvy's ear with spindly fingers. "No more night shifts," she said softly.

"Really? For good?" For as long as she could remember, Mama had worked a full-time nine-to-five at the bank, a weekend part-time job in retail, and a night shift a few days a week stocking shelves at a local market. She would come home with weary shoulders, pinched high from stress and worry.

Mama nodded, eyes crinkling at the corners the same way that Uncle's did. The only lines that ever broke through her smooth, coppery skin. "For good, Baby. You did good." She pointed at Savvy.

"But what about the weekend job?" Mama never got enough rest.

She batted away the thought with her hand. "Now, you know you still need books and things for your dorm room. And I'll get more rest now, so please stop worrying." She always read the minds of her children.

Savvy sighed. "I just don't want you to have to work so hard. I feel bad."

"Nope, we don't do pity parties." She squeezed her shoulder. "Listen to me, Savvy. It takes hard work to care for yourself and the people you love. Your Granny and Pop-Pop worked their fingers to the bone, but they were proud of what they were able to do for this family.

"Look at this house they bought us. This is going to be yours one day. Good things come from hard work, Baby. This is what we do," she'd said.

"This is what we do." Savvy's office phone rang, pulling her out of her reverie. No one but Mama and Uncle knew the direct line once she transitioned from a cubicle into an office. Jason lost his privileges after he chewed out the team's file clerk, who had been tasked with screening Savvy's calls. "Hello?"

"Baby Girl, you really put your foot in this food."

His voice brought a curve to her lips. "Hey, Uncle. I'm so glad you like it!"

"Is there anyone who hasn't liked your cooking? I'm telling you, you ought to cater. Or write a cookbook."

She laughed. "Maybe a cookbook one day. I don't think catering is all that appealing—I just like to cook for people I love."

"Hmm. That's what makes it so good. That's how your granny's food was too. Cooked with love."

"Yeah. And a whole lot of chili peppers." They laughed.

"You making progress?"

"I need about two hours to knock out some files, and then I'll head home. I promise."

"Two hours and not a second more. It's Sunday, young lady. Make sure you take some time to rest."

She reached for a framed photo of her uncle next to Mama's. "You're right. I'll try, Uncle."

"Mmm-hmm. I love you, niece."

"I love you more."

They hung up, and Savvy opened the file in front of her, grabbing a ballpoint pen for notations. Getting into a steady rhythm, she pulled new files from the in-box on her left and made a pile of completed files on her right. When her fingertips found the bottom of her in-box, she looked up to make sure she'd reached the end, and her eyes caught the clock. Three hours had flown by. Cringing, she turned over her phone and saw a missed text from Jason. Headed back to your place. See you soon. *Shit.*

When Savvy pulled into her driveway, Jason's black Explorer sat parked on the street as if keeping watch. *Maybe he won't make it a big deal this time.* She glanced at herself in the rearview, fluffed her hair, and pressed her lips together, making sure her lip gloss was evenly applied. She stepped out of the car and grabbed her purse.

"Nice evening for a stroll."

Savvy's spine snapped straight at the deep, unfamiliar voice behind her, and she turned in its direction slowly. That same, dusty guy from the morning walked past with his chocolate Lab. The man had smooth brown skin and a bright smile. His jeans were torn at the knees and covered in dirt; a gaping hole in the seam of his white T-shirt exposed rippled flesh beneath. He stood there in those dirty work boots, back straight, arms hanging at his sides. Her mind raced to process what was happening. *Is he homeless?* He definitely didn't live in this neighborhood, but now she'd seen him outside her house twice in one day.

He smiled again, curving lips framed by deep dimples. "I'm sorry, I didn't mean to scare you. I just figured I'd say hi."

Tightening the grip on her purse, she gave him a tight smile. "Hi, how you doin'?" *Damn my mother and these manners!* She waited for the response, expecting him to ask for cash.

He cocked his head to one side. "I'm good, thanks. You?"

She hesitated, watching his chest rise and broaden as he inhaled. "Uh, good. You have a good evening."

He smiled once more, shaking his head as he led his dog farther down the street.

Savvy rushed up to the front door, which was unlocked. "Hello?" she called, as she locked the door behind her, kicking off her shoes.

"I'm in here," Jason called.

She passed the kitchen and dining room, and stepped into the living room, full of warm light, noticing that the edges of pale blue paper on the accent wall were beginning to lift. Jason sat in the middle of a worn chenille love seat, legs spread wide enough to leave no space for her to sit comfortably. A Clippers game played on the flat-screen TV.

She leaned over the arm of the love seat, kissing his thick lips. He smelled of fresh soap and cocoa butter. He'd stopped wearing her favorite cologne a while ago. "Hey, Babe. How was your day?"

He grunted, licking his lips, as she sank into the sofa against the wall. She folded her legs under herself, ignoring her mother's voice admonishing Savvy for having her feet on the couch.

"Where you been?" He averted his eyes from the television long enough to give her a sideways glance, his husky voice heavy with tension.

Her stomach turned, but she put on her best smile. "Remember? I had to go and see my uncle, and then I had to run errands." She pressed her lips together. *Liar.*

He stared at the TV screen. "Errands, huh."

She ignored the judgment in his tone. "Well, how was your day?"

He paused. When they first got together, he never held back what he thought. Back then, they told each other everything, and that level of openness refreshed them both—their previous relationships had ended due to poor communication. Savvy remembered sitting with him at Santa Monica Pier, talking for hours, never worried or self-conscious about sharing. Around the time that Savvy got her last promotion, they started avoiding certain subjects. "You've been acting different lately. You're always so busy, even on the weekends."

"I have a whole job, Jay—one I intend to keep. They have me working on extra client accounts to help team members, and I really want my boss to see me as reliable. He told me that there's going to be an opportunity for promotion, and I really want it."

"Is that why you decided to hide the fact that you went to work today?" Jason's tone dripped with judgment.

Savvy flinched. "I…"

He leaned forward, elbows resting on his knees. "Don't bother trying to deny it. Did you go shopping at all today? I don't see any bags." He eyed her, and guilt fell into the pit of her stomach.

"I was going to—I need some new slacks for work."

"You just bought some a couple months ago."

"Yeah, but the material between my thighs rubs and wears out. Then the seams fray and split, so they need to be replaced." She bit her lip, embarrassed by the admission.

"So, it sounds to me like you could be putting that work energy to better use in the gym. You're trying too hard to please your family."

Pump the brakes. "Let's not bring family into this. I may not have a lot of time for the gym, but I cooked us a healthy dinner last night. Remember?" Her voice took on a pleading tone that had become all too familiar; one that she never had before him. "And the salmon with roasted brussels sprouts that we're having tonight is unhealthy? I make an effort, Babe."

Her pleading tone calmed him slightly; he settled back into the love seat. "Fine, you know how to cook healthy food, but you still care more about a promotion than you do about anything else. You're becoming one of those women who puts their career before their men."

And that's bad? "Come on, Babe. I care about you. That job gives us some benefits too, though, right? Maui?" she asked in a soothing tone. Their trip was a full week of sunshine and beaches, with a drive to the summit of the volcano and a hike to some of the most beautiful waterfalls Savvy had ever seen. *I thought we'd never been happier.* "With a promotion, we could go somewhere farther. You've always wanted to spend time in Europe, right?"

He blew out a sharp breath, running his hands over his face. "Listen, I'm trying to be supportive, but you have to give me something worth supporting."

"You're right, Baby. I'm sorry, I'll make more of an effort." Not wanting to fight, she shoved it all down. Again. She blinked hard to hold back tears. "Listen, I'll go get dinner started."

He turned the game back on and grunted. She moved toward the kitchen, allowing the tears to fall silently once her back was turned.

"Babe, dinner's ready! I'm going to set it out in the dining room."

"Be there in a second."

Savvy basted the herb-roasted salmon with residual butter after placing four fillets on a platter with lemon wedges. In a ceramic dish, roasted brussels sprouts with caramelized edges received a drizzle of balsamic glaze. She carried the

dishes to the next room and set them on the round wooden
dining table her mother had left behind before returning to
the kitchen for the simple arugula salad with halved cherry
tomatoes and sliced shallots.

By the time she returned to the dining table, Jason was
seated, pouring himself a glass of wine. Savvy pushed an
empty glass toward him, hoping the sauvignon blanc would
dull the tension between them. She sat, placing the salad on
the table, as he handed her a glass. "Thank you."

He grunted, and she wrung her hands nervously.

"So my uncle asked about you, said to tell you hi," Savvy
lied to break the ice.

Jason shook his head. "You know your uncle doesn't even
like me. I'm sure if he asked about me, he had something
slick to say."

Savvy's shoulders tensed defensively. "He likes you just
fine. He's just protective. He helped raise me."

"Mmm-hmm. He reminds me every time I see him."
Jason licked his lips, eyeing the food. The last time Jason
came around the family, he'd gotten the third degree from
Uncle Joe. A real estate agent working for his family's
agency, Jason had yet to make a sale on a home, but he'd
sold two parking spots in a condo building and a boat slip
in the marina. It took him four years to make his first sale,
thanks to the coddling of his doting mother.

In college, he had been all ambition and potential, but
then they'd graduated college after the subprime crash hit
the housing market hard. Frustrated by the turned economy
that delayed his dreams to sell million-dollar estates, all of
Jason's ambition had recessed with the market. Thanks to his
mom's success and drive, the business had stayed afloat, but
any nudge Jason received to get his head back in the game
was ignored or met with resistance. Uncle had told him in

no uncertain terms that if he was going to be with Savvy, he needed to be about his business. It hadn't gone over well, and it had been hanging over them ever since.

They made their plates in silence, squeezing lemon over the salmon and the salad, taking their first bites without looking at each other. As Savvy sampled the fish, she closed her eyes, tasting the unctuous texture that melted into the smoothness of the butter, the mélange of fresh herbs crisped by the oven, the brightness of the lemon. She opened her eyes to Jason staring at her. Covering her mouth as she chewed, she asked, "Everything okay? Do you need me to grab something from the kitchen?"

He shook his head. "The food's great." He took a big gulp of wine and leaned toward her. "Listen, Sav, I have a lot of love for you, but I don't really see this working out." He took another bite gingerly, averting his eyes.

Savvy stared at him in disbelief. *Was this really happening?* "Say what now? You don't see what working out, Jay?" She bit her lip, wondering if she really wanted the answer.

"I think we should just chalk it up to incompatibility. Look, let's just finish the meal, okay?" He refused to look at her as he stabbed a brussels sprout with his fork.

"Jason, we've been together for six years. You don't think I deserve more of an explanation than 'incompatibility'?! Please just say it, whatever 'it' is."

Was he cheating? Savvy chided herself. She *had* been working too hard and given him time to find someone else. *How long had he been seeing her?*

He leaned back in his chair, holding out a hand to calm her. "Just remember, you asked." His shoulders relaxed, as if a burden had been lifted. "Now don't take this the wrong way, but I think it's time I start looking for an upgrade."

An upgrade? "What is that supposed to mean, Jay? Upgrade

what?" Filled with disbelief, she could only stare at his fingers fidgeting with the stem of his wineglass.

"Let's face it, Savs. You let yourself go, and you know it. That's why you cringe when I touch your stomach, and you got all red talking about needing pants." Eyes focused on the ceiling; he refused to speak his mind while looking her in the eye. "I haven't seen you work out in months. You stay home on weekends to work more hours, and the only thing that's changed these last few years is your weight going in the wrong direction. I'm about forward progress, and you no longer fit my plan. Literally." He sucked his teeth, dipping his head to take another bite.

She gasped, his words slapping her across the face. Her cheeks grew hot, and though anger boiled inside of her, her eyes welled with tears. *Nothing is ever good enough.*

He continued, mouth full. "You haven't bothered to update anything about yourself. I mean, cut your hair, or get a makeover! You're probably the only girl in the world who could stand to be a little *more* high-maintenance. I have new clients lined up at work, and my career is about to take off—I can feel it. I need someone who has time to support me and you ain't got time unless it's about your promotion."

Savvy watched his face, waiting for him to fire off more ammunition, but it never came. He had nothing left to say.

"So I should put you and your career before me and mine?" Savvy tried to hold on to her calm, but her voice trembled with incredulity.

"I'm not going to bother asking you, Savvy. You can't do it. You already put your career before yourself. Just look in the mirror." He looked at her in the eye for the first time, venom in his eyes.

"Get the fuck out of my house." Her voice shook, the words spilling out haltingly. *How did I not see this coming?*

He stood, wiping his mouth with the back of his hand, mumbling a thanks for dinner. He grabbed his keys from a table by the front door, twisted them around to remove his key to her house, and walked outside. Savvy stared after him, jumping as the front door slammed shut.

Swearing to herself, she rushed to follow him, immediately regretting what she'd said, trying to figure out a way to fix all of this, but he moved too quickly. He rounded the back of his truck and unlocked the driver's-side door with his key fob. He didn't even look back.

Her mouth gaped as he revved the engine and pulled away from the sidewalk. "Jason! Wait!"

Jason sped down the block, leaving Savvy hugging herself, alone on the sidewalk. Feeling the buzz of her phone in her pocket, her stomach turned as his name appeared across the screen.

I'm done, was all the message said.

She stood there, arms hanging at her sides, gulping for air. Her face grew hotter as the first tears fell. She almost jumped out of her skin when a voice behind her cut through the quiet.

"Hey, are you alright?"

She jumped. There he was again. The homeless guy with his chocolate Lab was walking back in the opposite direction. Concern creased between his furrowed brows, and he ran a hand over the day's stubble sprouting from his chin.

"Jesus, you are everywhere!" Embarrassed, Savvy wiped tears from her cheeks. "I'm sorry, but now isn't a good time, sir." She started back toward the house, but turned to yell at him, pointing her phone in his direction. "And I don't carry any cash on me!" She looked back and saw his puzzled expression, his eyes wide as she slammed the front door closed.

3

"What did that moron say to you? *An upgrade?*" Joan bounded into the living room to find Savvy nursing a glass of bourbon on the floor, her back against the sofa. "Let me have a sip of that," she drawled. Joanie's Southern accent was always more pronounced when she was angry. Or drunk. She sat on the floor next to Savvy—her muscular thighs flexing in biker shorts under her favorite Braves jersey. She twisted the bill of her baseball cap from the side of her head to the back so that she could pull Savvy close.

"*Moron?* That fool is one stupid muthafucker!" Maggie called, striding in behind Joan. Her tall hourglass build housed the biggest voice box in Los Angeles. Thick thighs and ass, big boobs, perfect brows, volume set to loud even in the library. Maggie never cared to use her inside voice—everything about her was loud and proud. She wore hot-pink and lime-green sneakers with tight blue jeans and a black cropped T-shirt featuring the silhouette of a Black woman sporting her natural hair. She couldn't care less if a bit of her belly poked out over her jeans—her motto was "let them look." She perched on the arm of the love seat and gestured toward Savvy. "Spill it."

Savvy recounted the dinner to her friends between sips of bourbon, gulping down the rest of her glass when she finished. "So, to sum up, I've taken a downward trajectory in the girlfriend viability category. A strong work ethic and some extra weight was enough to send him running. Somehow I found a man literally triggered by my drive for success."

"He's lucky I don't have his address," Maggie quipped, drinking bourbon straight from the bottle after refilling Savvy's glass.

We're all lucky.

Two hours later, Joan was treating them to her best impersonation of Beyoncé singing "Upgrade U" and dancing wildly around the living room until Savvy erupted in fits of laughter. She could not have asked for better friends.

The next day, Savvy sat at her desk and shut her eyes, cursing her friends as she felt the familiar throb that came after consuming too much liquor.

I need more coffee.

The break room buzzed with Monday-morning energy. She grabbed one of her oversized mugs from a cupboard above the sink, shoving it under the spout of the Keurig machine. She turned and offered quick smiles to her coworkers hovering over a big box of warm Krispy Kreme donuts as she dropped in a K-Cup. She bit her lip, eyeing a chocolate glazed donut. *Have some willpower, Savs. Jason said to look in the mirror.*

She let her office door close softly behind her as she nursed the hot mug of cinnamon-flavored coffee. Files covered most flat surfaces in her office. Sitting at her desk, she immediately shoved a framed photo of her and Jason in Hawaii into a drawer.

Instead of attacking the mountain of files on her desk, Savvy stared down at the park outside. Though technically still winter, Southern California in early March offered warm sunshine without a cloud in sight. Sunlight danced on the green leaves of gently swaying trees. Her office phone rang, and she reached for the receiver before it rang a second time.

"Savannah Sheldon."

"Savs. Kotter here. Just checking in on you. You sound so professional, girl!" Joan's upbeat, good-natured twang offered a welcomed excuse to continue procrastinating. Named after her Big Mama in Georgia, Joan embodied the nurturing spirit and jovial temperament of her family's matriarch. She playfully mimicked Savvy's greeting in a high-pitched voice. "Savannah Sheldon."

"Joanie." Savvy eased back in her chair. "What are you up to, aside from keeping me off the ledge?"

"You know, girl, the usual. Working on an ad campaign for this new tequila brand that's supposed to replace the need for light margaritas. All you need are a couple of limes, and a salted rim." Exasperation weighed heavily in her voice, and Savvy pictured her sitting on the edge of her desk staring at a bottle of this new tequila. "I always thought if you were going to drink your lunch, you wouldn't really worry so much about calories."

"For real, some margaritas have more calories than the meal. I do love good tequila, though. Any good lines for the ad yet?"

"Nope, I'm at a standstill. The ones I've got so far are complete shit. Figured it was the perfect time to give you a call. How's the office?"

Savvy surveyed the mountains around her desk and rolled

her shoulders back away from her ears. "I'm swamped. I haven't read a single file or email yet. Barely got a cup of coffee and just started staring out the window."

Kotter didn't say anything. Just listened, waiting for more. Savvy loved that she knew when to do that.

"How about Korean BBQ tonight? I'll be here until at least seven, but that means we should miss the crowd. Honey Pig?"

"You do know my weakness, Savs." Joanie's voice held her smile, her accent drawing out her words, even though she tried to hide it. "Sounds good, let's meet at 7:30? Here, tell me what you think: Perfect 10 Tequila—Atkins approved."

Savvy scrunched her nose. "It's already rivaling light margaritas, can't you at least try to make it seem appetizing? No one will want it if it tastes like a diet in a glass. Bring in some sexy people with great abs and make a signature cocktail. Then I might actually try it." *Even though it sounds terrible.*

She laughed. "Fair enough. I'll bring you a bottle tonight with a bag of limes. Not a bad idea to bring in the guy, though. Perfect 10 Tequila cocktails are like hot guys in a bottle. They may be lean, but they'll still get you into plenty of trouble."

"See, go with that! I'm into it. If I'm drinking tequila, I'm definitely looking for trouble. You remember what happened last time."

"Who could forget?" she joked.

Savvy laughed. Memories flooded back of their drunken girls' night in San Diego. Something about a bartender licking salt from the palm of her hand made her shiver. "Okay, love, I've got to hit these files. I'll see you at the restaurant."

"Bet. Kotter out!"

Joanie's dad, a retired Atlanta cop, had left his mark. She was forever using police jargon when she called, and she

was not the friend to watch a *Law & Order* marathon with—
she'd ruin the suspense by telling you everything procedur-
ally wrong with the arrests.

The line disconnected, and Savvy poked her head out the
door to see Lina, the file coordinator she shared with two
other underwriters. A petite Chicana with a mane of thick
brown hair, Lina ran circles around other coordinators with
her keen attention to detail. "Good morning!" she answered
brightly. "I saw you walk by earlier, and wow, your makeup
looks great today!"

"Long story," Savvy grumbled, tapping fingertips against
the dark circles and puffiness below her eyes that she'd carefully covered with concealer. "Listen, which files have the
Friday deadline? I know I still have a bunch out there in
my file bin, but I have to plow through what I have in here
first."

Lina took a bite of her morning pastry as she answered,
"Red ones first. I'll weed out any in your in-box. Finish
what you've got in there, and I'll give you any remaining
ones tomorrow. You can catch up on the rest Friday. No
worries!"

Savvy sipped her coffee, looking around the L-shaped
desk at four full file organizers that Lina had brought in that
morning, along with an extra pile centered on the round
conference table. Easily two hundred files, nearly half of
them red. She felt sick as she thought about the paper waste.
Though parts of the system were digital, the senior team
could not agree on a plan for moving forward with a completely paperless process, so Lina kept massive file bins behind her cubicle, and Savvy purposefully avoided looking
at its constant state of overflow. "Okay, sounds good. Can
you handle my calls?"

"No problem, Savvy. Let me know if you need anything.

I'll make sure you're not disturbed, and I'll check in with you later to see about a lunch order."

"Thanks, Lina, I appreciate it."

Returning to the open file on her desk, she flipped through the insurance application, reading about the applicant's medical history, then logged into the company's database. She accessed an electronic version of the applicant's medical records file, along with an in-person assessment report. This particular applicant was young, healthy, and in great shape. She signed off on a plus rating and tossed the file in an "outgoing" bin for Lina to pick up later.

Savvy turned back to stare out the window at the sunny day continuing without her. Impulsively, she opened the bottom drawer of her desk and looked down at the happy faces smiling up at her from Maui. Their tans made them darker than their typical matching golden brown, an aura of light surrounding them, her arms around Jason's waist.

Look in the mirror.

Savvy's bouncy curls were lighter in the sunlight, which reflected off her wire-rimmed glasses. The halter strap of her one-piece bathing suit showed above the neckline of a baggy Bruins T-shirt, which hung over a long sarong tied around her waist. One dimpled thigh protruded through a slit in the material. Because she'd turned and held on to Jason for the photo, her face was angled to show her profile, emphasizing her round double chin.

Jason stood proudly in board shorts. His strong arms and flat stomach reddened from his attempt at surfing the day before. Deep dimples and a sprinkling of dark brown freckles across the bridge of his nose accented his full lips.

Savvy's fingers itched to reach for her phone, but she closed the desk drawer and looked back out the office window. Women pushed strollers, a couple of people walked their dogs, and a handful of joggers made their way around the park. She imagined herself down there jogging with them, pictured her face beet red, sweaty, and gasping for air. *A trainer wouldn't be a terrible idea...*

While Jason surfed in Maui, she'd sat on the beach watching. She refused to take off her sarong, wading only a couple of feet into the water before retreating to her towel. Eventually, she took off the T-shirt, but she was too self-conscious about her belly, her breasts spilling over the top of her halter. If she'd had her college figure, solid and smooth, she still would have been nervous to show it off, but the threat of a little extra jiggle wouldn't have stopped her from surfing and snorkeling. *Maybe Jason was right.* Her shyness about her body had turned into ignoring it completely until she was forced to buy new clothes.

Savvy picked up the office line, tempted to call him, but she heard Mags and Kotter screaming at her to stop. Setting down the receiver, she reached for another red file.

The sunshine outside the window faded, turning fluffy clouds vivid shades of orange and pink. Her nose buried in another file, Savvy jumped when the phone rang. Without thinking or checking the caller ID, she picked up the phone, still concentrating on the medical records in front of her.

"Savannah Sheldon."

"Good, you're at work. You can't have your employer thinking that you don't value the opportunity that you have. And sit up straight, you know I hate it when you slouch over your desk."

Savvy's back snapped straight on cue, her chin lifted, and she started to roll her eyes, but Mama always knew. She didn't dare sigh, still believing that her mother could pop her through the telephone. "Hey, Ma. Yes, I'm at work. Thank you for calling to check on me."

"Savannah Joy, you know damn well I called to do more than check on you."

"You talked to Uncle." She groaned internally.

"Yes, I spoke with Joseph. You cannot keep wasting your savings on that house! Yes, your grandparents lived there. Yes, you have memories. And where are your memories now?" Her accent grew stronger when she raised her voice. Born in Bangkok and raised in South Central, Mama had a powerful demeanor that made up for her small stature. Her no-nonsense approach and incessant rule following at the bank made her the regional manager's favorite—she was offered the branch manager role several times, but she preferred to remain assistant manager to work more closely with the tellers. Patrons all over South LA were terrified of Savvy's five-foot-nothing mother. "Savannah Joy?"

Damn. She's middle-naming me. "In my head," she muttered.

"That's right. So if memories are in your head, why the hell do you keep dumping money into that rickety old house?"

She leaned forward, elbows propped on the desk, holding her chin in her hand. "Come on, you know that Granny and PopPop's house means a lot to me. It means something to Uncle too."

"Yes, well if Joseph hadn't spent his savings on those silly instruments, he could be repairing the house. It's his house to do with as he pleases. You should be saving that money to renovate your house." Her stern voice took Savvy back to all the times she got in trouble as a kid. "And I thought I told you to sit up," Mama snapped.

She leaned back, straightening each vertebra one at a time. "Okay, Ma. I'm sitting up."

"Maggie told me that you and Jason broke up. Good. Now where are you on that promotion?" Savvy had been best friends with Maggie and Joanie since sixth grade. They met at a tennis summer camp and had been thick as thieves ever since. Mama had become a second mother to both of them, and she started checking in on Maggie regularly after her mom died two years ago.

She always hated Jason. "Mom, it's not that easy. More than half of the team are vying for that spot, and I'm one of the most junior people on the underwriting staff."

"So? Don't you work hard the way I taught you? We're talking about your security here, Savannah."

She exhaled softly. Since she was six years old, her mom had lectured on how she needed to be financially independent and never have to depend on a man. And, of course, it stemmed from Savvy's dad leaving. The boy Mama met from around the way when she was fifteen.

Being the youngest child, and only daughter, Savvy was always in awe of her mom. She saw how tired she was working three jobs to make ends meet; her brothers were always too busy with sports or their friends to notice. "My savings are doing fine, Ma. All of my bills are paid, my car is paid off, and I increased my retirement withholdings. You taught me well."

She harrumphed and continued. "How much money did you give Joseph?"

"Mom…"

"I asked you a question, Savannah Joy."

Shit. "Yes, ma'am. I gave him $900. That's not a terrible amount of money for a roof repair."

"Okay, first, it is a lot of money. Second, where do you think this ends? You already helped repair the front steps. Next is the porch, or the water heater, or another hole in the roof. That house needs a complete overhaul. Better to tear it down and start over."

The house that Granny and PopPop purchased when they immigrated to the US in 1967 was their prized possession as they chased the American dream. They had no idea that their house was in the hood, but they were immediately em-

braced when the neighborhood realized that Granny could
burn in the kitchen. Any hungry kid in the neighborhood
could come see her for some spicy guay tiew reua, her pla
rad prik, or her pad kra pao gai. On Sundays, she'd make
a huge pot of Massaman curry, Kaeng Massaman, and the
whole block would come through to have a bowl. She'd have
three rice cookers going to make sure everyone had enough.
Savvy's first memories of the kitchen were with her grandmother. Her love of cooking grew because Granny taught
her everything she knew before she passed. Mama was always too busy working to learn.

"But building a new home is far more expensive than
these minor repairs. And what if I want to buy the house
from Uncle? Maybe I want to keep it in the family to pass
down to my kids." Savvy inherited her stubbornness from
her mom. *Karma's a bitch*.

"You need to focus, Savannah. You could win this promotion. And then you're one step closer to the senior team.
And then VP. You'll be able to graduate from your house to
a bigger home and put money toward college tuition when
you have kids. You won't have to struggle like we did, and
you certainly don't need to hang on to that property—it's a
drain on your finances." Her voice stiffened slightly.

Mama always worried about whether she did right by
Savvy and her brothers. Savvy's brothers were more im-
pressionable; she'd convinced one to go to med school and
the other to practice law. Mama's boys, literally and figu-
ratively. Savvy was the hardheaded one. "Thanks to you, I
already have a home, Mama," she said gently. "You raised
three strong kids, you know. Each of us found our way."

"Yes, but your brothers have more saved and make more
money than you do. Women in business are always dis-

counted, so I need you to focus, Savannah. Don't go through what I went through."

Savvy's face softened, always knowing where her mom's heart was. "I'm working hard, Mama. I promise. Why don't you let me get back to it?"

"Okay, Savvy. Listen, about the boyfriend, I know things may sting a bit now, but you're better off. He never had his shit together. Reminded me of your damn daddy."

Savvy chuckled. "Yeah, well. I'm not sure that he's completely out of my life yet, but it's always good to know where you're at on the subject of my love life."

"Well, moving on, make sure you go over to Mrs. Walker's house. She just had her entire first floor redone, and she said you're welcome to come and see the contractor's work. I gave you his info a month ago, but I'm assuming you didn't call him."

Savvy let out an exasperated breath. "No, Mama. I haven't had time to call him. Work has been too busy."

Her mom grunted approval; a compliment to anyone who knew her. "Well, she's expecting you to come by sometime this week. Just make sure you go and see it. Once you do some renovations, you'll be more settled. It's a good starter home until you need to expand, and doing renovations now will make it more valuable when it's time to sell."

"Yes, Mama. I'll go see Mrs. Walker this week. But I've really gotta go. I'm taking on an extra deadline this week."

"Good. Okay, I love you, honey."

"I love you too, Mama. Give Max a kiss for me." Mama hadn't allowed herself to date again until Savvy went to college. When she did, Max swooped in with a quickness; a smart man who'd sold a startup for big money. They retired soon after they got together and moved up to the Bay Area, where his family and both of Savvy's brothers were already settled.

"Max sends his love too. Now, back to work!"

"Bye, Mom." Savvy turned to look outside, just as pink clouds turned to purple, and orange mixed with a dusky blue.

"Hey, girl!" Joanie's drawl made Savvy smile. Her twist out curls were wrapped in a colorful print scarf, and big hoop earrings accentuated her long regal neck. Her dark blazer and jeans were matched with a worn pair of Chucks—pretty much her work uniform. She stood to pull Savvy into a giant bear hug, releasing the tension Savvy'd held captive all day.

"Hello, my love." Savvy laughed into Joanie's shoulder. "Thank you for being free again tonight."

Joan released her, then sat on one side of the booth. "Come on, Savs. Even if I had plans, they would have been rescheduled for you. You'd do the same for me in a heartbeat."

True. Savvy slid onto the bench on her side of the booth, pushing the table a little closer to Joanie to make room for her tummy. They opted for light Korean beer, perusing the menu of meat and seafood options for grilling. "Ugh, maybe this wasn't a good idea. I probably shouldn't be eating this stuff. And I can tell you now that I want everything."

Joanie rolled her eyes so hard that her neck followed. "And what are you supposed to eat instead? We're grilling meat. You have healthy options—you can wrap it in the rice wraps, the sliced radish, or the lettuce. If you don't want the fried rice at the end, we don't have to get it, but I really think that we should." This was, of course, one of their favorite parts of the meal. After all of the meat had been grilled, the server brought kimchi and rice, which captured some of the drippings from the meat. *Divine.*

"I know you're right. I just can't get what Jason said out of my head."

"That, my friend, is what we call a 'dick move,'" Joanie said as the server dropped off two bottles of beer, chilled glasses, and cups of cold water. He hid a smile and walked away. Joanie picked up her bottle and took a swig, ignoring her chilled glass. Savvy did the same. "What kind of thing is that to say to someone you love? He's an ass who didn't deserve you in the first place. Plain and simple."

Savvy tilted her head, raising her eyebrows in response. "Do you think that he thought all of those things all along? I can't believe that he let this fester into...into—"

"Resentment?" Joanie finished. "Honestly, girl, the size thing is a surprise. He has always had an issue with you being successful at your job. I would have thought his insecurity would be the thing that did you two in."

Tears filled Savvy's eyes. "I just didn't see this coming. I thought we were in a good place."

"But see—" Joanie leaned forward "—that's what makes this a dick move. We have no idea how long he felt the way that he did, because he never communicated it to you. At least, not in this way, right?" She reached her hand across the table.

Savvy's cheeks burned, and she looked down at Joanie's hand on hers. "Not in so many words, I guess."

Joanie's eyes widened and her eyebrows lifted. "You're leaving something out, Savs. Spill."

"Well, I always thought they were cute little nicknames..." Savvy trailed off. A tear escaped her lashes. "But I'm getting more and more annoyed with myself, because I just realized he's been putting me down for a long time."

"What kind of nicknames?" Joanie eyed her suspiciously. "What did he call you?"

A pit in Savvy's stomach, she thought back to the first time that Jason playfully gave her a nickname. "He called me Sway, which referred to my ass and the movement of my hips when I walk. He had a bunch of nicknames, but he always assured me that Sway and SavvyBear were terms of endearment. Now, I'm not so sure." Her voice trailed off at the end. *But why did he stay with me?*

Thankfully, the server returned. She smiled at him weakly as he shared special cuts that they had for the day.

Savvy ordered for the table, choosing the seafood pancake, the special seasoned pork belly, the marinated beef short ribs, the calamari, and the kimchi fried rice. When she finished, Joanie nodded. "I love a woman who can take charge." Turning to the server: "Could we have extra rice sheets and lettuce?"

"Oh, and extra soybean paste and that sesame oil sauce for dipping?"

"Good choices." He smiled at Savvy.

As he turned to leave, Joanie took a sip of beer and raised her eyebrows at her friend, signaling for her to continue, but she couldn't. "You know, the more I think back on this entire relationship, the more pissed off I get. I'm still unpacking what he said and why he didn't sit me down sooner if how I looked was such a problem to him."

Joanie nodded slowly. "You're right. You do need time to process it all. Just remember that we're all here for you. I just want to make sure that you're okay and that you know Jason's asinine words don't reflect how you're seen by others."

"But I do think that some people see me the way he does—too big, not taking care of myself." She took another sip of beer. "A lot of people are bold in telling me what they think I should or shouldn't do with my body."

"Give me a for instance." Joanie tapped her finger on the neck of the beer bottle.

She shrugged. "People eye me all the time, judging me.

SAVVY SHELDON FEELS GOOD AS HELL 45

Or they'll make little snide comments that are supposedly meant to be supportive but make me feel like a complete failure. I started to soak all of that up and accepted it as truth, because it wasn't just Jason. Like my coworkers, we'll be planning lunch and someone changes the conversation to boot camp workout plans or Whole30. Grocery store clerks will ask me what diet I'm on just because I buy fresh produce. It happens all the time, and I swear it's not just in my head."

Savvy knew that she'd gained some weight over the years, but it never bothered her until she started to notice the looks people shot at her while she ate. People judged her without explicitly saying it. She would pick at her food in front of them, preferring to eat in private once she got home.

Joanie listened, grimacing. "I sincerely hope that we never fed into that."

"Oh, no," Savvy assured her. "You guys were really the only ones who didn't hint in some way. Even my mom hints at healthy habits, and I know what she means. She'll cook meals without carbs, or nudge me to choose a salad as a meal when we go out to dinner. With her, it comes from a place of love, and I get that. She knows that I'm not completely happy with myself, and I can see that she is trying to help me feel like I'm getting 'back on track.'"

"I guess I see that." She shook her head thoughtfully. "This is a whole lot, Savvy. I'm so sorry that you had to go through this."

"I'm still going through it. But now that I'm finally seeing what a fucking asshole he is, I want revenge. I want to make him eat his words." A fire began to build in her chest. "I want him to see everything he can no longer have. Let Project Upgrade begin."

"Damn, girl. I'm low-key impressed. But why even bother focusing this on him?" She looked at her friend. "None of us has confidence one hundred percent of the time, Savs. Sometimes, you just have to fake it till you make it."

Savvy's eyes started to fill with tears, but she caught herself before they could fall. "Maybe I'm just not good at faking it anymore. I want him to *see me*. I didn't let myself go—priorities just changed. I worked hard FOR HIM. For us. I stayed in that relationship for far too long feeling unseen, but yes, girl. He gon' see me now."

Joanie's eyes widened. "Okay. Well, damn."

They clinked their beers together and sat silently until they both burst into laughter. Joanie laughed until she had tears in her eyes. "You know you sound like you're ready to choose violence, right?"

"I sound like a woman scorned. Auntie Maxine was reclaiming her time. Well, I'm reclaiming my sexy. Fuck him. Ole insecure, needing-external-validation-with-a-trophy-girl head ass." Savvy picked up her beer bottle and took a long slug.

"Shieeeeet."

They both laughed.

The server arrived with their seafood pancake and another round. Using tongs, he put the first few pieces of protein on the grill for them, dropping off extra plates and dipping sauces. They nodded their thanks and started pulling pieces from the pancake with their metal chopsticks, nibbling quietly.

"Savvy," Joanie started while still chewing, "you don't ever have to fake it with us. Maggie and I are here for you. You're our best friend. You're *my* best friend. Both of us would do anything for you, including—" she lowered her voice "—hiding a body if necessary." She looked over her shoulder slyly, and Savvy cracked up.

"I know you would." She used her chopsticks to flip the

squid on the grill, letting the ribs and the pork cook a little
longer on the first side. "You two are more than I deserve
sometimes. Real talk."

"You never think you deserve good things, and that's a
part of the problem. We're all a work in progress, Sis. We're
going to get there."

"I sure hope you're right."

"Oh, I'm right. He's going to be so sorry that he didn't
see you for who you are."

"Well, in the meantime, I need you to help me figure out
a way to apologize to this homeless guy in my neighborhood. He saw me chasing after Jason when he left and was
trying to be a nice guy, and I yelled at him."

"You yelled at a homeless man that was trying to help?"
Joanie busted up with laughter, cackling loud enough to
disturb other tables.

Flustered, Savvy lowered her head. "Every time I see this
guy, I get so squirrelly, but he's just so nice. And he has the
cutest chocolate Lab."

Joanie took a big swig of her beer, her eyebrows meeting
her hairline. "Hold on! You've got the hots for the neighborhood homeless guy? Seriously, this is the best thing I've
ever heard." She rested her chin in her hand, waiting to
hear more.

Savvy flipped her the bird. "Anyway, maybe I should
make him a care package or something."

"He best not be living on your couch when I come over
this weekend, Savs. Jason was already a charity case. No
more."

Savvy chewed through a plump oyster. "Noted."

4

The following week, Savvy pulled up outside of the SLS Hotel in Beverly Hills. She eyed the brightly lit building, self-consciously adjusting the shapewear that cut off the circulation to her thighs. Joanie's successful pitch to her tequila client warranted a celebratory girls' night. Savvy adjusted her gauzy white skirt and pink camisole, sucking in her stomach as the valet opened the car door and offered her his hand. "Thank you." She blushed.

"Hey, girrrl!" Joanie bellowed at the top of her lungs, her Southern twang strengthening after good liquor. Wrapped in tight skinny jeans, ankle boots, and a button-up blouse covered in embroidered foxes with a fitted blazer, Joanie beamed. Her golden-brown twist out glowed under the setting sun. Joanie gestured toward the door after a big hug. "Mags is inside—they already took us to our table."

"Sounds great."

They entered a dark room glowing red with recessed

lighting and shaded chandeliers hanging from a coffered ceiling. Display cases on the far side glowed with an array of chocolate truffles. Some tables glowed from lighted patterns on their surfaces, with ornate chairs and stools staged for seating. Feeling a rush of excitement at the prospect of new cuisine and cocktails with her two best friends, Savvy nodded along with rhythmic music playing. Making their way through the restaurant to a candlelit booth, her mouth watered as various dishes and cocktails were carried by. At the sight of foie gras wrapped in cotton candy, which she'd seen featured on a recent TV show, she forgot she ever had a boyfriend in the first place.

Maggie stood and wrapped her arms around Savvy, grabbing at her purse. "Tory Burch? Savvy, when are you going to let me raid your bag collection?"

Cracking a smile, she gazed fondly at the camel-colored tote. "Maybe sometime soon. I could use some retail therapy, so why don't you come by and peruse my Kate Spade collection?" Accessories were one of her guilty pleasures when she allowed herself to splurge, but lately she'd focused on saving for her renovations.

Maggie's eyes lit up like it was Christmas Day. "Seriously?" she exclaimed. "You love your Kate Spade bags!"

"Yes, because you're saving for that condo down payment. Seriously, with everything you've been doing for me, come take one." Joanie watched the exchange, rolling her eyes. She had to be convinced to buy a crossbody purse as an alternative to keeping her wallet in her back pocket during her last trip to Europe. "That's okay, Joanie, I've got something for you too. Congratulations on your new Perfect 10 Tequila ad!"

Savvy pulled out a small case, and Joanie's eyes grew as big as saucers. "When did you even find time to get me something?!" she exclaimed. Her eyes brightened as she recognized the brand name on the box—the new noise-cancelling earbuds she wanted for work travel. Plopping a kiss on Savvy's cheek, she said, "Girl, you are the queen of accessories! Thank you, I love them."

"I'm just glad you gave us a reason to celebrate. I can't believe it's taken us so long to finally come to this restaurant!"

The server arrived then, took their drink orders, told them about the specials, and gave her recommendations. As she walked away, Joanie tilted her head to get a better view. "She's kinda cute. Excellent assets."

"Nope, no hitting on our server tonight," Savvy laughed.

They decided to indulge in the tasting menu, sharing everything and basking in the ignition of their taste buds. Starting with the foie gras wrapped in cotton candy, each course added a layer of decadence that made them close their eyes and savor. Near the end of the meal, they sampled sweets and cappuccinos, groaning happily with stuffed satisfaction.

Maggie giggled, having had one too many St-Germain cocktails. "That was sinful. I have a very happy food baby." She rubbed her tummy, but the expression on her face changed from satiated to hot fury so fast that Joan and Savvy whipped around to see what caught her attention.

Jason stood at the bar in jeans and a blazer. Savvy could tell he had been to the barber for a fresh cut. He looked good. Her breath caught in her throat; he wasn't alone. He faced a pretty girl who could have been RiRi's cousin. Her red lips pouted playfully at whatever he was saying to her, long lashes fluttering over light eyes, and his smile grew until he glanced up.

"I take back what I said about the server," Joanie muttered. "*That* chick is sexy as hell. The fuck she doin' here with him?"

Jason froze when his eyes met Savvy's. The girl at his side didn't notice his reaction, still chatting away. She reached toward Jason, grabbing his hand. He hesitated, but his fingers slowly wrapped around hers. Savvy turned back toward the table. She'd seen enough. As much as she willed it not to hurt, an ache throbbed beneath her sternum and her breath shallowed. She'd talked a big game about wanting revenge, about what a jackass he was, but she'd still held out hope that he might come crawling back. Well, the window of opportunity for a comeback had just snapped closed thanks to the hand clutching her ex's. She couldn't breathe.

"Would you look at this muthafucker!" Patrons at another table turned. Maggie had steam coming out of her ears. She pulled off her watch and earrings, dumping them into her clutch before smoothing her mane of curls back into a bun.

Spotting their friendly server, Joan flagged her down and asked for the check. "Listen." She lowered her voice, making meaningful eye contact. Woman to woman. "My friend's ex just walked in here with a date. We've got about two minutes before my girl gets out her Vaseline." Joanie gestured to Maggie, who removed the rings from her fingers and cracked her knuckles.

"I got you!" The server rushed away and had our check on the table a minute later. Joanie whipped out her card before she could walk away, putting a hand on Savvy's before she could protest.

"This one's on me, Savs. It's cool. This fool shows up with Rihanna's busted stunt double means you don't pay for shit."

Savvy's mouth opened to object, but her body went rigid as a familiar touch grazed her shoulder.

"Savvy." He glared at her, annoyance in his eyes, a stab piercing her stomach. "I didn't expect to see you here."

Any second, Maggie's head would explode. Her eyes flashed as she spoke for Savvy. "We didn't expect to see you here either, Jason. On a date, no less."

He sighed. "She's a friend. We're just two people having a drink after work." He gestured with his hands that he was finished.

"Holding hands," Savvy whispered, willing the air to return to her lungs. "You don't hold hands with other friends I've met."

Jason opened his mouth, but the server returned with the receipt. Joanie signed the bill quickly and thanked their server for a great meal as she got ready to herd them all out of there. Savvy gave the server a weak smile, and the woman squeezed Savvy's arm in response as she turned to greet another table of guests. Savvy started to walk away, ready to leave this moment behind her.

"Savs." His arms dropped to his sides. "I just wanted to come over and say hi. Maybe we can be friends?"

"You said it best yourself, Jason." She straightened, lifting her chin to look him in the eye. "Time for an upgrade."

Joan sucked her teeth at him, leading Savvy toward the door. Mags stayed behind, snorting in angry astonishment. She grabbed a full glass of ice water off a neighboring table and hurled the liquid at Jason's chest, collective gasps echoing around the restaurant.

"Yeah, friend…" Maggie turned, rolling her eyes. "You're done. Remember?"

Savvy glanced sideways at mini-Rihanna, whose gaze ran back and forth between Jason and Maggie, confusion furrowing her brows. Maggie joined her friends by the door, and they left the silenced restaurant arm in arm.

★ ★ ★

The next morning, Savvy turned on her shower, undressed slowly and evaluated her features in a full-length mirror. The product of a Thai mother and Black father, she had smooth, bronzed skin and narrow brown eyes. She removed her glasses. A sprinkling of freckles ran over the bridge of her nose, and a deep dimple pierced her right cheek. With full lashes and high cheekbones, she opted out of wearing a full face of makeup most days. Her head of big dark curls would tighten up at any sign of humidity, but the dryness of LA allowed her to maintain a fresh blow-out.

Her confidence shook as she lowered her gaze. A tiny hint of a collarbone peeked through the flesh just below her neck. Faded stretch marks ran like spider legs under her arms, over her breasts, across her stomach, and around her hips. Full, heavy breasts sagged more than they used to and led to a flabby stomach with a pronounced muffin top and pooch. Her rounded hips spread around to an ample backside. Never got any complaints about the backside, but that didn't stop Savvy from worrying about its growth. Thick thighs with zero space between them led to wide calves, slender ankles that swelled up with too much sodium, and relatively small feet for a five-foot-nine-inch frame.

She poked at her stomach and grabbed at her love handles, exhaling deeply as she turned for a profile view. The girth of her belly protruded out farther than her breasts, flesh rolled on her back, and cellulite dimpled her butt and the backs of her thighs. Her hair hung to the middle of her back in long layers, partially hiding her excess. She sucked in a breath and lifted her pooch, thinking back to when she had the body of an athlete; when she could run miles without having to be chased by a mass murderer for motivation.

Watching herself in the mirror, Savvy resolved to get back

into the sports she loved and ultimately make Jason eat his words. She wanted him to suffer. Grabbing a lipstick, she started a list on the mirror:

Project Upgrade:
1.Revenge body—get back to tennis.
2.New look—hair, clothes.
3.Meal prep.
4.Find balance.

She stepped into the shower, letting the force of the water knead her shoulders and the back of her neck, and lathered a grapefruit-scented soap over her face, taking in the citrusy smell. She turned, letting water hit her as she grabbed a loofah and creamy body wash, fragrances of lavender and almond oils rising in the steam. As she scrubbed her body, she thought about her list, planning her method of attack. The soap rinsed away along with all of her worries. Savvy stepped out of the shower, got dressed, and grabbed a banana before walking out of her apartment. Time for something new. *Step 2 of Project Upgrade: New Look.*

"Heyyy, Savvy!" A chorus of voices met her as she pushed in the glass door.

"What up, ladies?" Savvy grinned at the faces of women she'd known since her teen years.

"You doing okay, girl? You know I heard what happened." Nikki, her hairstylist, stopped fluffing the curls of a woman in her chair to put her hand on Savvy's shoulder.

"Mmm-hmm, we all did," Angelique chimed in, sitting on a plush couch in the front of the salon. The shop owner for over twenty years, no one ever saw Angelique touch a head of hair that wasn't her own. "Heard your homegirl threw a drink at him."

A few patrons clucked with amusement, heads tilted under the salon dryers so they could catch the tea as it spilled.

Savvy waved it all away, perching on the arm of a velvet upholstered chair. "Come on now, it was only water. He'll live."

Nikki cackled. "I know that's right!" She slapped Savvy five. "But what happened between you two? I thought y'all were gonna go all the way."

She shrugged. "Yeah, me too. But apparently I work too much, and I'm too fat."

Angelique raised a church finger. "Excuse me, say what?"

She pursed her lips, nodding. "You heard right."

Angelique tossed three bundles of Brazilian weave over her shoulder and popped her tongue. "I know this muthafucka didn't. I KNOW he didn't." She pulled herself up off the couch, her generous curves jutting out in all the right places. "Where he stay at? I just wanna talk to him." She flexed her fingers, the jewels on her sharp stiletto nails sparkling.

Nikki slumped into Savvy's armchair. "Now, Angie, calm down. A visit from you is never just a conversation." She rested a hand on Savvy's back. "I'm so sorry."

She offered a weak smile in response. "Wasn't meant to be. He's already moved on anyway."

"Say WHAT NOW? Where this ho at? I just wanna talk to her." Angelique's voice rose an octave. She clapped her hands together with each syllable to show her intensity.

"Will you calm down?" Nikki scowled.

"Well, I'm sorry, but I'm mad as hell. Savvy over here tryin' to be all mature about this shit. I'm prepared to be ignorant enough for the both of us, girl."

Savvy reached out and squeezed Angie's hand. "And I appreciate you for it, girl. But I promise you, I'm not that mature."

Angie caught the sparkle in her eye. "Okay, you little deviant. What you got brewing, then?"

Nikki leaned in. "What are you thinking, Savs?"

The woman in Nikki's chair leaned forward, as did the patrons under the dryers. Savvy looked each one of them in the eye conspiratorially. "I'm thinking big chop."

The ladies gasped.

"Heavy swoop."

One of the patrons fanned herself.

"Give me some color."

Angelique nodded.

"Give me some edge."

Nikki's eyes grew wide.

"Long as I can get it into a ponytail, take the rest."

Angelique whooped. "That's what I'm talkin' 'bout, girrrrrl." She clasped hands with Savvy. "I know that's right!"

The curly girl in Nikki's chair got up and reached toward Savvy's hair. "Girl, you sure you want to get rid of all this length? This takes years, and yours is so healthy."

She looked at the ceiling, trying to find the words without showing they broke her, but her voice cracked. "He said he wanted an upgrade."

Five mouths sucked in a breath at the same time.

Angie shut her eyes, taking a deep breath to compose herself. "I just want to talk to him," she whispered through clenched teeth.

Savvy straightened her shoulders, set her jaw. "So let's show him that he was never on my level to begin with."

"Ooooh, chile. I'm scared of you." Angelique ran her fingers over Savvy's tresses. "Come on, let's get you washed so that Nikki can work her magic."

Three hours later, Savvy stared at herself in the mirror. Her dark brown hair was chopped more than ten inches shorter—enough to make a donation to Wigs for Kids. Her long layers had morphed into a chunky cinnamon bob, a heavy swoop bang framing the top of her glasses. It was just long enough to squeeze into a ponytail, per her instructions.

"Wow," she breathed, running fingers through her hair. "This is incredible."

Under the bright lights, facets of color with subtle highs and lows shimmered with a sun-kissed glow. She hugged Nikki, who smiled in smug satisfaction, running her fingers over her masterpiece one last time. "He won't know what hit him, Sis." She begged Savvy to keep her posted on all things Jason.

After leaving a generous tip, she guided her car toward the mall. She bought new workout clothes and a fitness watch to track her exercise progress. She found some cute cloth headbands and clips to keep her bangs out of her face, and she felt ready to get started.

Feeling accomplished, she put on her new shoes and walked the entire length of the mall twice. She was invincible. Until she realized that her car was parked just outside the food court. Hanging her head, she walked to the car carrying bags of workout clothes, hair accessories, and a large order of waffle fries sprinkled with black pepper.

5

"I can't believe you did it!" Mags gushed as Savvy opened the front door to let her in. "You look amazing!"

She scrunched up her face. "Come on, only the hair changed. The rest of me is still here in all of my glory."

"Savs, you are being way too hard on yourself." Joanie reached out to touch her hair, looking at her with big brown eyes. "You don't have to make fun of yourself with us. We love you for who you are inside, but we're not lying when we tell you that you're beautiful on the outside."

Savvy looked down, her go-to move whenever her eyes welled with tears. "It hurts less when I get to the punch line first." She led her friends down the hall into the living room and gestured to the sofa.

Maggie looked at her with tears in her eyes. "Savs—"

"No. I hate going to the mall to buy clothes, because then I have to look at myself in the mirror. Department stores make you feel like crap because their plus-sized clothes are all frumpy and hidden away in some tiny corner where no one else ever goes. It's not fair. And when was the last time either of you placed an order at a restaurant and had the server ask you if you were sure you didn't want to look at the low-calorie selections?"

Kotter gasped, shock in her eyes. "That really happened?"

Savvy nodded, looking down once again, reliving the humiliation. "More than once, actually. Really, I blame the fact that we're in LA. This breakup has been eye-opening in a lot of ways, and as much as I've been talking about a revenge look—" she eyed them "—am I just being child-ish? I mean, Jason's got me fucked up, y'all." She burst into ugly tears so quickly that her friends froze.

Joan's mouth dropped open, eyes growing wide, as her brows furrowed into a pained cloud across her forehead. "Savs, listen. No one deserves to be treated that way. No one has the right to judge you. I could kill Jason for what he said to you."

She tried to laugh it off, but she wasn't convincing any-one, least of all herself. "But I'm not sure that he's wrong. I look in the mirror and I don't recognize this person. I still think of myself as that tennis player with the college schol-arship. I wanted to be the next Serena. And then I got hurt, and had to make a new plan, so I threw every ounce of en-ergy I had into my work. And I changed.

"So maybe Jason was right. He did take a back seat to my career, so his feelings of neglect are valid. Maybe I want him back, maybe I don't. I probably shouldn't go back to him. But a haircut isn't enough for me to cement the fact that we're done." She used her fingers to accentuate that last word, wiping away tears with the back of her hand.

Maggie and Joan exchanged a look, but said nothing. They came closer and wrapped their arms around her, enveloping her raw nerves. Savvy's breath caught, fighting to control her tears, and she smiled with gratitude even though her lips trembled. "What would I do without you two?" she whispered.

Maggie, always their strength, shook a finger at her. "Okay, Savs, no more tears," she warned. "You asked us over here for a reason, so let's press Pause on this Oprah moment for a little while. Put us to work." She gestured toward the kitchen.

Maggie's blunt nature was one of Savvy's favorite features. That, and her unruly curls. Her last donation to Wigs for Kids had been enough hair for three people. Her smooth brown skin and full lips turned plenty of heads, and she exuded confidence with every step.

"Okay," Savvy gulped. "I asked you both over to help me clean out my pantry and refrigerator. I want to make a real effort here, so I'm going to try clean eating for a while, see if I can feel a difference."

"What the hell is that?" Joanie asked. "Is that some weird fad diet?"

"No, Sis," she laughed. "It's just focusing on fresh produce and lean proteins."

"Does that mean no alcohol?" Joanie protested. "You'd have to give up margarita nights! Sometimes all these rules just make it harder to make healthy choices when, in the back of your mind, you really just want chili cheese fries, a hot dog, and a beer."

Maggie nodded. "I've heard of clean eating before. Don't you also have to give up cheese? And sugar? And bacon?"

"Are you two really trying to talk me out of this? It's just about avoiding processed foods. I can have cheese and turkey bacon."

"No, of course not." Maggie held up her hands in protest. "But what about everything in moderation, and we all start with being more active?"

Savvy shrugged. "That's not unreasonable. This may sound extreme to start, but it'll transition into moderation. I just need a clean start." Joanie still looked doubtful. "How about I have a moderation day once a week? Then we can have a cocktail, or something decadent, without completely undoing all of the efforts of the week."

She could see Maggie mulling it over, and she waited for her to craft a rebuttal. Instead, Maggie nodded. "Okay, I'll do it with you."

Savvy eyed her suspiciously. Mags had the perfect shape already, and she was a cupcake fanatic. "Really? Are you sure?"

Maggie's brow pinched. "Ma'am. Don't look at me like that. I hear that people feel really good when they get rid of processed food. It's supposed to help you sleep better too." She patted her hips and outer thighs.

Savvy eyed Maggie's strong arms framing her hourglass figure, and Maggie looked back at her inquisitively.

She shrugged. "I'm sorry, I know I shouldn't judge. I just can't wrap my head around you wanting to lose any weight. To me, you're perfect."

Maggie smiled and hugged her around her middle. "The feeling is mutual, chick. But I'm plus-sized just like you—you're just used to me being this size since I haven't changed much since high school. And I have good days and bad days, but mindset is everything."

Savvy leaned against the counter. "So what should I be focusing on?"

"Let's not be concerned with the scale at all. We're not worried about weight. Let's think in terms of strength. I want to get stronger. Tighter."

"I like that. I want to get stronger. I want to get active again. I want to purge my kitchen and start fresh."

"Well, we've got you. Don't we, Kotter?" Maggie tilted her head, cutting her eyes at their friend.

Nothing like a little peer pressure to motivate. Joanie sighed. "Alright, well then, count me in. I could use more quality sleep, and I could definitely be drinking more water and a little less liquor."

Mags clapped her hands together. "Okay, then let's attack this pantry, because we now have two more kitchens to scour after Savvy's."

Savvy watched her friends set to work, pulling processed foods and sweets from the shelves. A fresh pint of Cherry Garcia went into the waste bin. She even let them find her cookie butter stash.

Early Monday morning, Savvy stood in line at her neighborhood coffee shop, notorious for making pretty designs in the froth of their espresso drinks. One week into the clean-eating challenge with Joanie and Mags, and she was staying true to her motivation.

Rather than drive, she'd taken a brisk three-mile walk before heading to the coffee shop on her way home. While waiting for her unsweetened almond milk latte, she observed others walking by. The early spring weather offered a warm sunny day. A light sheen of sweat dusted her forehead, and she whisked it away with her forearm, pulling the band off her ponytail to rake her fingers through damp hair.

"Wow, you look great."

Savvy turned to get a peek at whatever extraskinny vanilla latte was the beneficiary of this compliment, but only a man stood behind her. A man in dusty torn jeans covered in flecks of white paint. She eyed the layer of dust on his

Timbs and his thick muscular arms covered in black tattoos. Her hot homeless guy. He looked right at her, waiting for a response. Savvy's eyes widened. "Me?"

He smiled, dimples piercing smooth brown skin. "Of course. You cut your hair, right? I've only ever seen you with long hair. It's beautiful both ways, but now I can see more of your face."

A flurry of butterflies took flight in her stomach. She stared at him and caught herself. "Um, thank you!" *He can't mean that.*

He laughed, running his hand over short curly hair. "I know I've never had a chance to introduce myself before, but our paths have been crossing so frequently." He extended his hand. "I'm Spencer Morgan."

Savvy eyed his calloused hand and then shook it, becoming increasingly aware that others watched their exchange. A couple of women at a nearby table whispered and glanced in her direction. "Savannah. Nice to meet you, Spencer." At a loss, she had no idea what to say to this man. He was so handsome when he smiled. She assumed that the shoulder bag he carried held his most important property. *Maybe he's just newly homeless—could have gotten laid off or something.* "So, you're a big fan of the coffee here?"

So not cool. Savvy's cheeks flushed, and she prayed that he didn't notice, but Spencer's smile broadened. "I use this coffee shop as my office most days. Plus, my dog, Teddy, likes the attention." He gestured out the window to a chocolate Lab being scratched behind the ears by one of the baristas who had just gone on break.

"Office," she said with finger quotes. "Right, that makes sense. Plus, the bathrooms here are so clean in case you need to wash up."

Spencer's eyebrows furrowed. "Uh, what?"

She immediately recognized the dog. "Teddy must be such great company for you. I'm sure that it gets lonely sometimes on the street."

Spencer stared at her. A crease formed across his forehead as some realization dawned on him. "It all makes sense now." His deep voice slowed as if stunned.

"What does?"

"You yelling about cash. And now washing up in the coffee shop bathroom?"

Savvy grimaced. "Yeah, listen, I'm really sorry about the yelling. You caught me in a really bad moment, and I shouldn't have treated you that way."

His eyes narrowed, and he leaned closer, lowering his voice. He smelled clean and citrusy. "Savannah, are you under the impression that I'm homeless?"

Savvy blinked slowly, panic swirling in her chest as she froze in place. "I'm sorry, is that an offensive term? I've heard people refer to homelessness as housing insecurity before…"

"I'm not homeless." A flicker of amusement sparkled in his eyes, though he took a slight step back.

"But… I don't understand," she stammered. Her face grew hot, sweat building above her upper lip. On one hand, she didn't want him to see her sweat and turn bright red. On the other hand, she wanted him to step closer. *He smells so damn good.*

"You don't understand why I'm not homeless?" His eyebrow rose.

"I just… You're always so dirty." She gestured to his clothing, immediately regretting the word choice as it left her mouth. But she couldn't stop. "Always wandering around my neighborhood with your dog, and I know you don't live there—I know all of my neighbors."

"Dirty," he repeated. "I've been working in your neighborhood. And I bring Teddy, who can't walk himself." He raised an eyebrow, and Savvy zeroed in on the thick curly lashes framing deep brown eyes. His full lips set in a straight line as a muscle in his jaw twitched.

Silence hung in the air as Savvy tried to process what was happening. She jumped when she heard her name.

"Savvy? Here's your almond milk latte." Jessica, one of the baristas, handed her the cup. "Love your hair, by the way!"

She touched her hair. "Thanks, Jessica." Savvy turned to Spencer and saw a leggy woman saunter closer, clearly looking to start a conversation with him. Spencer noticed her approach too, giving a quick glance in Savvy's direction. She gave a tight smile and raised her cup in farewell, walking out of the shop past Teddy, who napped in the sunlight.

Spencer. Savvy wondered why he even took the time to speak with her after she'd yelled at him on the street. *I actually thought he was homeless.* Heat crept up her neck, her cheeks, and colored her ears. *So, this is rock bottom.*

Savvy looked around her office, remembering the richness of his voice and how good he smelled. *He said I looked great. But then he mentioned my hair. Did he mean only my hair? What did he think about the rest of me? He did say he could see more of my face... But OH MY GOD, I can't believe I suggested he bathed in the coffee shop sink. Classic, Savvy.*

A knock at her office door yanked Savvy out of her thoughts. "Savs? Do you have a minute?" Lina fidgeted in the doorway.

Savvy eyed her suspiciously. "Uh-oh, I know that face. Who fell behind?"

Lina exhaled deeply. She turned around and pulled a file cart into the office. "Sam had to take maternity leave early, and she had a big closeout deadline coming up on Wednesday."

"Oh, no! Is she ok?" She leaned forward, her brow creased with concern.

"Early labor, but she's doing fine."

"Whatever I can do to help." Savvy eyed the file cart—a double-decker bus full of yellow files. She groaned. "Day after tomorrow, Wednesday? We're talking end of day, right?"

Lina offered a pained smile. "I need them all signed and ready to go by 10:00 a.m. I'm sorry, Savvy, I know this is going to mess up the beginning of your week, and you have a Friday deadline for your blue files."

Savvy surveyed her office, buried in a wave of blue files. "Wow, I can see that this week is not going to be easy. I'm going to work remotely to avoid distractions. Can you send me the file lists, and I'll send you electronic signatures on these files in batches? We should meet both of these deadlines."

Relief crossed Lina's face. "No problem. Just remember to complete Sam's first. I'll send her file lists to you."

Savvy thanked her. "I'll call you this afternoon with progress."

She nodded. "No one works harder than you, Savvy."

"Never let them forget it, Lina."

6

Spencer wasn't at the coffee shop when Savvy returned for an afternoon latte, arriving near the end of Jessica's shift. She smiled brightly. "You're back!"

Savvy smiled back at her. "I am! Could I bother you for another almond milk latte?"

"Sure thing! Anything to eat?"

"No thanks, I'm all set. I need to get some work done at home, but your coffee's better."

"You're right about that." Jessica nodded and rang her up, stepping toward the espresso machine.

Savvy looked around, seeing people on their laptops settled in at tables with comfortable chairs and built-in lamps. The coffee shop as a home office made a lot of sense. She thought of the incredulity on Spencer's face. *No wonder he left. Sweaty woman assumes he's homeless. That'll do it.*

"Here you go, Savvy!" Jessica slid a latte toward her, little hearts leading to a big heart in the foam.

"Thanks, girl." She snapped a lid onto the cup and headed home.

The second bedroom in Savvy's house served as a guest room and an office. Bright windows with whisper-thin curtains faced the tomato and herb garden out back. As a child, Savvy shared this room with her brothers until they were too cool and too smelly to share a room with their preteen sister. They moved her twin bed into Mama's room, which she shared until they both left for college. Now, a daybed covered in a thick comforter and fluffy pillows sat beneath the windows adjacent to built-in bookcases stacked with women's fiction, cozy mysteries, and framed photos. A standing desk faced the wall opposite the daybed with a large monitor and docking station for her laptop.

She settled in at the standing desk, turning on a floor lamp that spread warm light into the room. She opened Sam's file list, noting that over three hundred files required completion by Wednesday morning, and blew out a fortifying breath.

As she evaluated the hundredth file, Savvy's vision blurred from deciphering the doctor's script in the medical records. She scribbled together a grocery list for a dinner with the girls that she wanted to host later in the week. She was just getting up to grab her purse when the doorbell rang.

Looking through the peephole, Savvy groaned inwardly.

"I know you're home, dear—your car is in the driveway," her neighbor's sing-songy voice called through the door.

Savvy put on her friendliest smile and opened the door. "Mrs. Walker! What a surprise!"

"Is it, dear? Your mom told me that she'd spoken to you. I thought now might be as good a time as any for you to come over and see the renovation." One of Mama's oldest friends, Mrs. Walker had known Savvy her entire life. There was no excuse that Savvy could give that wouldn't make it back to her mother.

"I was just getting ready to head out to the store, but sure, I can stop by for a few minutes." Savvy stepped out onto the porch, brandishing her purse and grocery list.

Mrs. Walker nodded her approval. "I was surprised to see you home during the day." She led the way back to her house two doors down.

"Oh, yes. I have a couple of huge deadlines this week. It's best for me to work from home so I can concentrate."

"Such a hard worker. Your mother is very proud of you, dear."

The corners of Savvy's lips curled slightly as she attempted to keep her voice light and upbeat. "Well, I learned it from her."

"She mentioned that you're recently single?"

Savvy rolled her eyes. "Very recently, yes."

"I see." Mrs. Walker pursed her lips into a small smile as she opened her glass-paned front door. "Well, I'm sure you'll bounce back soon, dear. Anyway, my contractor did an excellent job updating the entire first floor. Feel free to walk around."

"Wow." A small, formal sitting room opened to a dining area, a massive kitchen, and a cozy family room. Worn carpet had been stripped out and replaced with dark hardwood floors covered in rich patterned rugs. Mrs. Walker's old plastic-covered couch was replaced with a modern L-shaped sofa. But the kitchen...

Passing the sturdy farmer's-style dining table, Savvy's eyes grew wide at the oversized island with a built-in sink and quartz counters. Light gray shaker cabinets framed a double-door refrigerator, a new stainless steel dishwasher, and a deep farmhouse sink. The island held a wine fridge and shelving for some small appliances. A coffee nook was built into one corner of the room with plenty of space for all of Mrs. Walker's cookbooks. "Mrs. Walker, this is phenomenal."

Savvy ran her fingers over the countertops, admiring how the specks of white and gray tied together the counters and cabinets. Slab tiles shone on the floor, and small glass tiles with hints of blue and green made up the backsplash.

"I'm glad you think so," a familiar voice responded.

Savvy jumped, and Mrs. Walker raised an eyebrow. "You okay, dear?"

"Oh, yes, I'm sorry. I just didn't realize anyone else was here." She fanned herself as her nose picked up a familiar scent.

"Spencer came by to check on me, so I thought I'd introduce you. Your mother tells me you've been wanting to renovate for some time now."

"Recently single, huh?" He smiled smugly. "Now that's unfortunate."

Savvy's eyes narrowed. "You don't mean that."

Spencer chuckled. "Not one bit. You probably dodged a bullet." His mouth curved into a smile as he came closer.

Savvy sucked in a breath; his brown eyes burning into her skin. She ran her fingers through her hair. "Well, thank you for that. I—I'm still processing."

He nodded slowly. "Don't hesitate to give me a call when you're open to it."

"A call?" She looked up at him questioning his offer.

"I hear you're looking to renovate." He raised his brows, clearly enjoying this exchange.

"Right." She nodded quickly. She gestured around the room with a nervous laugh. "Your work is beautiful." Clutching her purse, she turned to Mrs. Walker. "Thank you so much for letting me come over. This renovation is everything. I should really get to the store, though."

"Thank you, dear. I thought you might enjoy it. Your mother mentioned that you already have Spencer's information?"

He raised an eyebrow.

"Y-yes," Savvy stammered. "I have it."

"Good. I suggest you have him over soon for a walk-through."

Savvy nodded, inching toward the door. "Work is a little hectic, but yes, I'd like that. I'll be in touch." She pulled her hair behind her ear, giving a quick smile and a wave before ducking out.

It took all of Tuesday for Savvy to finish Sam's files. On Wednesday morning, before starting on her own Friday deadline files, Savvy walked a half mile from her Los Feliz house to Griffith Park. Lush and green, the park housed hiking trails, bicycle paths, tennis courts, picnic grounds, caves, and the Griffith Observatory—and Savvy had hardly made use of it in the last few years. She picked up her pace as she passed a boot camp underway, avoiding eye contact. Weary faces of the participants strained as their instructor demanded one more round of burpees. *That SUCKS.*

Reaching the trail directory, she searched the walking paths and hiking trails for something challenging but manageable. She chose Glendale Peak, a less-traveled, moderately difficult hike just over three miles. *Now that, I can do.*

The trail started near the Greek Theater, and several people walked toward the Mount Hollywood trail on the opposite side. Almost immediately, the trail steepened. Savvy huffed and puffed, forcing herself forward until it leveled out and she gained a comfortable stride. The heat from the sun warmed the air, so she took off her track jacket and tied it around her waist.

The trail wound around a bit, but the remaining incline

was manageable. Motivated by one of the best views of Los Angeles, Savvy trudged on, watching birds fly overhead. Sunlight broke through a canopy in the treetops, and she stopped to take a picture of sun rays crisscrossing the path ahead. When she reached the peak, sweat streaked down her temples and her heart raced, but the view took her breath away.

The skyscrapers of Downtown Los Angeles spread out below, and the sky was so clear that she could see all the way to the Pacific Ocean. Taking deep breaths, she took out her phone to take more photos, including a selfie with Downtown in the background. She put on a big smile for the photo, memorializing her first solo hike, feeling amazing, unbothered by her red cheeks, the glisten across her forehead, and the lack of eye makeup. Though open and vast, the secluded peak was the perfect spot for solace and reverie. When she had soaked up her fill of tranquil sunshine, she sent the selfie to Mags and Joanie.

Walking back down felt easier, but the heat rose. Perspiration ran down her neck and collected in her V-neck T-shirt. Savvy's lower back felt damp, and she probably looked a mess, but she basked in the accomplishment.

Reaching the clearing where the boot campers had been, she smiled to herself, satisfied. *I will do this again. Soon. Joan would love this trail.*

"Hey," a familiar voice called.

Inwardly rolling her eyes as she turned around, Savvy squinted in the sunlight. "I'm trying to remember a time when I didn't see you."

In a University of Kentucky sweatshirt and basketball shorts, Spencer stood haloed by sun rays streaming through the treetops. Deep dimples dug into his cheeks as his lips curved into a smile. "It'll grow on you." Not a speck of dust on him this time. His shoulders back, he peered down at her with amusement.

"We'll see." Savvy picked up hints of his citrusy cologne in the breeze and tried not to fervently draw in the scent.

"Do you hike here often?" he ventured.

"Is that a pickup line?" She smirked.

"Do you always answer a question with a question? More importantly, do you want it to be a pickup line?" He tilted his head, watching her.

She shifted from one foot to the other, trying to ignore the intensity of his gaze. "Are you going to answer my question?"

He exhaled slowly, meeting her eyes as he took a sip of water from his aluminum water bottle. "You're trouble."

She dropped to a squat to be face-to-face with Teddy, who nudged her hands with his nose. "I guess we'll see."

Spencer ran his hand over his hair, still smiling. "I don't mind a challenge. And, no, that wasn't a pickup line." He squatted down next to Teddy, patting him on the back. "I like to make my intentions clear."

Savvy opened her mouth to respond, but no words came out. She closed her mouth and nodded, inching her fingers behind Teddy's ears.

"You headed home?"

She nodded again.

"What do you think about me coming over this weekend to see your kitchen? Your mom and your neighbor both told me you like to cook, and that the space isn't what you need it to be. No pressure. Just to get a feel for what changes you are thinking about, and maybe start a quote for you."

"I—I'm not sure I'm ready." She scratched Teddy's chin, and he panted, his tongue hanging out the side of his mouth.

Spencer's head tilted slightly as he watched her. "You don't

have to act on it right away, and I would completely understand if you wanted to get additional quotes. I just figured
if your mom has called me three times, she's probably calling you even more."

Her face went red. "God, she's been hounding you? I'm
so sorry!"

He waved her off. "She's just determined. Your mom
is funny. I can tell she really wants you to make the house
your own."

"Well, yeah, we should probably go ahead and have you
come by this weekend. Maybe then she'll leave you alone."
She thought better of it, shaking her head. "On second
thought, you should expect that the moment I have a quote,
she'll be calling you with all kinds of questions and trying
to haggle the price. I apologize in advance."

"No need to apologize. She wants you to get a good deal."
Spencer stood, giving her a crooked smile.

They started walking across the park in the direction of
Savvy's house when a golden retriever bounded toward her
without a leash, barking loudly. Savvy froze, not out of fear
for the dog, but because she recognized her. *Oh, God.*

"Ginger?" She reached Savvy, whimpering with excitement and wagging her tail so hard that her entire backside
wiggled from side to side. Savvy stroked her ears, looking around until she spotted him, but he wasn't alone.
"Dammit." Ginger looked at Savvy with pleading eyes,
guilt-tripping her for her absence. Savvy squatted down,
continuing to scratch behind her ears, Ginger busy covering her with kisses until she spotted Teddy. Ginger moved
toward him so that they could sniff at each other.

Jason strolled toward them with a petite smiling brunette.
A different girl than the one at the bar at the SLS. Though
he laughed at whatever the brunette was saying, pure irrita-

tion crossed his face. Savvy stood, willing herself not to react to Jason's annoyance. She had every right to be there, and if anyone was in the wrong, it was him. Ginger sat at her feet.

"Savs," he said.

"Hey, Jason." Nerves crackled in her stomach. "How've you been?"

"Fine, thanks." His tone cut like sharpened steel. "This is Cheyenne. We were just taking Ginger for a walk."

The brunette smiled and raised a hand in greeting, but slowed when she met Savvy's eye. Savvy nodded and waved at Cheyenne, bringing hands to her hips. "I'm Savannah. Nice to meet you. This is Spencer. He's been working on Mrs. Walker's renovation."

Spencer stepped forward, reaching out to shake hands. Cheyenne obliged, Jason didn't.

Ignoring Spencer, Jason looked confused and uncomfortable. "What are you doing here?"

Savvy shrugged, irritated by his coarseness. "I live right down the street, as I'm sure you recall. I hiked one of the trails."

He snorted. "You hiked a trail? And what the hell did you do to your hair?" Savvy watched Cheyenne's smile fade. She was sure the girl had no interest in joining this conversation, though Savvy appreciated that her reaction showed a dislike for Jason's attitude. They weren't going to be besties, but at least this girl seemed to have a backbone.

If he were less of a jerk, he'd have been easy to miss. "I've been trying some new things lately."

He shrugged. "Your hair is shorter, and you look sweaty. That's it."

Savvy swallowed a rush of anger and sadness. *How could she ever have loved this man?* "Okay," she said, finality in her tone. "You two have a nice walk." She gave Ginger one final pat goodbye. Ginger looked up at her, whimpering.

Cheyenne gestured like she wanted to say goodbye, caught in the awkward exchange, but Savvy was too far into her feelings to respond. She stood there for a minute as they walked away, staring into a void until Teddy nudged her hand. She leaned down to kiss his nose. "Hey, Spencer. I think I'm going to hike a little longer." Defeat sounded in her voice.

Spencer frowned. "Do you want some company? Teddy and I could…"

"Thanks, but no. I just need to shake it off." Savvy's body was flushed with humiliation, her heart pounding with a mix of sadness and rage. Though she didn't want to be alone, it would be unfair to subject Spencer to the mess Jason left behind.

"You sure? That seemed a little intense." Concern creased his brows.

Savvy tightened her ponytail. "I'm not really sure of anything, honestly."

Spencer turned in the direction Savvy was heading. "Come on, we'll tag along for a little while. Teddy's not ready to say goodbye to you anyway."

"Thanks." She shook her head, still mortified by what just transpired. "I can't believe that just happened. I'm sorry you had to witness it."

They walked past the boot campers, who spread out on the grass to stretch. One woman lay sprawled on her back, taking in gulps of fresh air. Past her, the mouth of a trail curved behind the trees.

Spencer placed a hand lightly on Savvy's arm. "There's no need to apologize."

The lightness of his touch grazed her damp skin, and she

sucked in a breath. A tingle traveled up her shoulder toward her neck, coloring her cheeks, though she was certain he was just being nice. She blew out a breath. "I am really embarrassed."

"Want to talk about it?"

"Maybe we should stick to subjects that don't run the risk of making me cry?" *I'm already a sweaty mess.*

"Deal." He eyed her carefully, keeping her pace. Teddy walked between them, nudging his nose into Savvy's hand every few steps. "So, tell me about your house. Mrs. Walker said it was your family home?"

She nodded. "My grandparents bought that house for my mom when my brothers and I were little. My mom remarried while I was in college, and she relocated up to the Bay Area. Her husband is a tech guy. My brothers and their wives are up there now too, so my mom left me the house."

"What a blessing."

"Yeah." Her voice was quiet. "I've never had to pay rent anywhere, and I've known my neighbors my whole life. It's just time for updates to make it more me, you know?"

He bobbed his head. "I do know."

"Are you from Los Angeles?"

"Pasadena. My parents are still there, but now I live in Silverlake."

Savvy glanced up at Spencer. "You went to Kentucky?"

"I wanted to—I've always been a fan of their basketball team—but we couldn't afford for me to go out of state. I went to PCC and then transferred to UCLA."

She turned. "What you know about that Bruin life?"

Spencer stopped short. "Wait, you went there too? When did you graduate?"

"Well, I could never go to the University of Spoiled

Children. Class of 2013." She grinned, slapping her hand against his.

"I was the year before. I wonder why I never saw you on campus." He smiled wide, shaking his head. "Small world."

"I was a Powell Ranger. I was on the tennis team until I suffered an injury. After that, I only left the library to eat, sleep, or shower."

"It was always too cold in there for me," Spencer laughed. "Well, you know that means if I do your renovations, I'll have to give you the Bruin discount."

"I guess this means your quote is going to be given a little more deference now."

They eased into a comfortable silence, and Savvy couldn't remember the last time she'd had one of those with Jason. Over the years, their silences had become loaded; Savvy always worried she'd do or say the wrong thing. This was nice. The trail opened to a clearing with benches and the sound of water moving through a small creek. A couple of butterflies darted around the clearing, dipping toward the poppies that lined the trail.

Savvy sat on a bench and Teddy immediately rested his chin in her lap. "It's beautiful back here."

"Teddy and I come here to think sometimes."

Sunlight snuck through the trees overhead, but the warmth felt like it was emanating from Spencer's proximity. He propped his arm up along the back of the bench, his forearm millimeters from her shoulder. His cologne smelled of citrus, cedar, and spice. She was tempted to lean in, but instead she turned to face him, taking in more of his woodsy smell. "Seems like a good place for someone who has a lot on their mind." *I wonder who else he's brought here.*

He nodded, and they sat back in that serene silence for a moment. The sounds of water bubbling down the creek

and birds calling overhead filled the space with a comfortable tranquility.

"How long have you been a contractor?"

A hint of a smile played at the corner of Spencer's lips.
"That's a loaded question." He ran his hand over his hair.
"Technically, I've been doing this work since high school—
family business. I took time away from it, though, for college and to try work in the corporate sphere."

She watched his jaw clench and release. "You decided it
wasn't for you?"

He turned to look at her. "Dad got sick. Couldn't run the
business anymore, so I took over about a year ago."

"I'm sorry to hear that. Is your dad okay?"

"Very happily retired." Spencer grinned. "Now he's at
home all day getting on my mom's last nerve with his projects around the house."

Savvy laughed. "I bet she secretly loves that he's home
more."

His head bobbed slowly. "I'd like to think so."

"Do you miss your corporate job?"

"I did at first, but the last few months have been better.
Mrs. Walker's house was a lot of fun to work on. She pretty
much gave me carte blanche to decide what worked best in
the space, as long as I met her list of must-haves."

"That means she really trusts you." Savvy glanced at her
phone for the time. "Listen, I've got to get back home. I
have a ton of work to get through, but I really want to thank
you for earlier. This was the perfect place to go to distract
me." She placed a hand on his forearm, which still rested
along the back of the bench. Feeling the muscle in his arm
tense, she pulled back. Savvy cursed herself for misread-
ing the moment. Here he was, pitching his business to her,

doing his job—the least she could do was respect that and keep her hands off him.

"Anytime, Savvy."

She gave Teddy a quick scratch behind the ears and waved to Spencer. "I'll see you around." She turned and walked briskly toward her street.

Once home, Savvy showered, grabbed her laptop, and drove to the coffee shop for a change of pace. She set up to work and ordered a full-fat latte with buttery caramel syrup drizzled over the top. Jason's cold words bolstered her resolve to have him eating his heart out the next time he laid eyes on her, but she'd earned this treat, savoring the caramel latte as if it were her last.

7

Friday evening, Joanie invited Savvy to a Bikram yoga class to de-stress after a week of tough deadlines and excruciating social encounters. As they walked into the studio, Joanie handed Savvy an envelope. They had a tradition of exchanging refrigerator magnets displaying motivational quotes or beautiful scenic views—souvenirs of the challenges they'd battled together and messages appreciating each other throughout the journey.

Savvy stopped to open the envelope as Joan checked them in for the yoga class and filled their water bottles. Inside was a rectangular magnet that said "Keep calm and yogi on," with a silhouette of a yogi meditating.

Savvy smiled. "This is really cute, Kotter! Thank you." She hugged her and grinned.

"You're so welcome! Are you ready for this?" Joanie looked at Savvy skeptically, and Savvy would be lying if she hadn't considered running the second that the heat from the studio touched her skin.

"I mean, yes and no," she laughed. "I really want to try this. Bikram yoga is supposed to be so good for you. And I really can sit down if I feel dizzy or nauseated, right?"

Joanie nodded. "I'm sure you'll be fine! Everyone goes through it their first time, but you leave feeling amazing. More than anything, the goal the first few times is simply to stay in the room. Sit when you need, and join back in when you can."

"Real talk, it's a little pungent in here, girl." Savvy's nose wrinkled, as they walked into the women's locker room to lock up their shoes and purses. Though clean, the room smelled of heavy sweat covered with lavender mist from several diffusers. Floral and musty.

Looking around, Savvy noticed the other girls wore far less than her cropped yoga pants with a thick, tight sports bra and a thin pink T-shirt with "Love" printed on the front. Joanie wore basketball shorts and a Red Sox tank top. *Typical.* She was a Southern girl to the bone, but she'd fallen in love with the Sox when she went to Boston for college.

Girls all around them had forgone shirts altogether, wearing just their sports bras with tight leggings or tiny shorts, all baring smoothly sculpted abs, colorful tattoos, and belly rings. Shirtless men walked into the studio wearing only shorts. Savvy gave Joan a wide-eyed look that asked, "Where am I?"

Joanie shrugged, smiling. "You'll see."

They carried mats, towels, and waters toward the heated studio. As she opened the door, a gust of humid air and perspiration hit Savvy. *Shit.* Joanie shoved her forward, leading her toward the other side of the room by the windows.

They spread colorful mats out, laying towels on top to soak up the sweat and prevent slipping.

Joanie moved onto her mat, immediately sitting down on her knees. Savvy copied her, wincing at the strain on her joints and rearranging herself into a cross-legged position. The warmth in the room clung to her skin, sweat beading on her forehead and across her upper lip. She tried not to focus on the sweaty heat invading her nostrils.

People filed in, arranging their mats and greeting each other in whispers. Several lithe ladies set up confidently in front of the mirrored wall, with an older couple setting up right next to them. Some people sat on their knees, some lay flat on the floor, and a few experienced yogis were in headstands or other poses testing the limits of flexibility, and seemingly designed to intimidate the uninitiated.

Joanie leaned over to whisper. "This is an all-levels class. Beginners and more seasoned yogis are all in the same room, but everyone is working on something when it comes to their practice. Just focus on your breath, on your reflection in the mirror, and what your body is telling you. If you feel like you can push yourself, go for it. If you feel like your body is saying no, be sensitive to that. This isn't a cakewalk for anyone."

Savvy nodded, anxiously surveying the room. A bell chimed outside the studio, and the instructor walked in, headed toward a small platform at the front of the room. She smiled as everyone stood. "Welcome to Friday evening, everyone! You made it." Her voice rang loud and clear, but it was also reassuringly calm. "This time will be just for you, to align your focus before you enter the weekend. Before we get started, do we have anyone new to the Bikram practice?"

Savvy raised her hand sheepishly, grateful that the girl

on the other side of her raised her hand too. She smiled at Savvy and then made a face showing she had nerves too.

Savvy smiled back.

"Welcome to our new yogis. I am Charlotte. Now if everyone will step toward the center of your mat, bringing your feet together, we can start with a breathing exercise." Charlotte stood atop a small, stage-like podium, which was just big enough for her own yoga mat. She smiled at Savvy, who was sure her own expression was like a deer in headlights.

Two minutes into class, every inch of her body was covered with a sheen of sweat. Her shoulders, knees, neck. The end of her ponytail curled from the moisture. The women in tiny yoga clothes glistened, while moisture poured from Savvy's forehead, burning her eyes, falling in fat drops onto her towel.

Savvy fought with her body, trying to contort it into several positions unsuccessfully. Thick thighs refused to be crossed; heavy arms couldn't hold for a full pose without dropping. Savvy tried modifying where she could.

The heat. The room grew so thick with humidity that she forgot all about the smell. Her heart raced, breath laboring, as she attempted poses that shouldn't have required any cardio. *Why am I breathing so hard?* In the mirror, her face shone bright red; her eyes bulged with strain. The thickness of the air tightened around her, and the room spun. Savvy sat down to steady herself and towel off, and a wave of guilt washed over her. *Look at that, the energy in the room shifted because the chubby girl in the back can't get it together.* Savvy pushed herself back to her feet too quickly, dizziness washing over her.

As they prepared to enter "standing head-to-knee pose," she took a deep breath. Bringing her palms together over her head, thumbs crossed, bending forward with the rest of the class, Savvy brought the tips of her fingers toward the floor.

Charlotte's voice was steady and supportive. "That's great, Savvy. Now try to touch your forehead to your knee. You're almost there. It's okay to bend your knee, if you need, so that you can achieve the goal of the pose."

Try as she might, her forehead refused to get any closer to her knee. Her stomach and breasts blocked the way, and the more Savvy pushed herself forward, the harder it was to breathe. Her breasts choked her, as gravity pulled her cleavage closer to her throat. Savvy heard her heartbeat in her ears, loud and strong.

"It's okay, Savvy, this is a difficult pose. Take a breath, and then as you exhale, try one more time to touch your forehead to your knee." Charlotte came closer to show support.

Everyone else in the room was in the pose, waiting for her to get there. Savvy could feel eyes on her, though it was a different experience since everyone was upside-down. Blushing, she inhaled sharply, unable to take a deep breath. She huffed and pushed herself farther forward, getting the tiniest bit closer to her knee, as little spots muddled her sight and Savvy gasped for another breath.

"Are you sure you're okay, Savs?" Worry etched Joanie's face.

Savvy blushed deeply, sipping on an Arnold Palmer. She couldn't believe she'd actually passed out, tumbling over onto her side. She woke to Joanie, the instructor, and the other newbie all kneeling over her. The instructor placed a chilled towel over her neck and put a bottle of Gatorade next to her, making sure that Savvy was okay before she continued the class.

Even when you faint—and apparently it wasn't all that

uncommon for beginners—the goal of the class was to remain in the room, so Savvy relaxed into the Savasana pose,
mindful of her breathing, aware of her limbs, focusing on a
fleck of paint on the ceiling above her.

When they got out of the class, Joanie and Savvy grabbed
their belongings and thanked the instructor. Her regular
coffee shop was only a block away, so they walked over for
a slightly sweetened reward. Savvy's sweat-drenched clothes
hugged her curves, but this wasn't an unusual sight at the
coffee shop; several other yogis had already trekked over.
They waved with empathetic smiles.

Sheepishly, she waved back and sighed. "That was really
embarrassing."

"Savvy, I promise that no one was laughing at you or poking fun. It's not that type of crowd." She knew Savvy would
never go back if she believed she was the running joke.

Savvy watched the other yogis, stretching their limbs in
leather chairs. No one looked at her funny or pointed in
her direction. "That was definitely an experience, Joanie. I
don't know, I guess I would try it again, now that I know
what to expect. Do you think Mags would come?"

Joanie shrugged. "Maybe. You know she loves a group
class."

"Yeah, but she hates sweating out her hair."

"Ah, touché."

The door to the coffee shop opened, and more yogis wandered in. Before Savvy could wave at Charlotte, she heard a
woof and felt two paws against her chest. The air knocked
out of her, Savvy pictured another awkward scene with
Ginger and Jason. But this pair of paws belonged to Teddy.
"Hello, Teddy! I'm so happy to see you too!" She hugged
the dog as he jumped up and licked her face.

Joanie exclaimed and laughed in surprise, reaching in

to pet this sweet pup. He lay his head in Savvy's lap as she stroked his ears. He looked up at her with his big soulful eyes.

"Wow, Teddy is clearly in love." Spencer joined them, smiling.

Her already-red cheeks blushed further. "The feeling is mutual," she laughed. "Hi, Spencer. How are you?" Joanie and Savvy continued to pet Teddy, Joanie's eyes sliding back and forth between her and Spencer. *Oh, Lord.*

"Not as great as Teddy, but I'm doing well. How are you?"

Savvy laughed. "I'm recovering from an attempt at Bikram yoga. We tried out the studio right down the street."

Spencer smiled, looking impressed. "Oh, really? I've been to that studio before. How did you fare?"

She winced. "I may or may not have passed out?"

Joanie nodded in confirmation, attempting to hide her smile.

Spencer's eyebrows shot up in surprise. He placed a hand on her damp shoulder, sending an electric shiver down her spine and leaving a warm imprint after he pulled it away. "Are you alright? How do you feel? It can be so hot in that studio!"

Savvy waved lightly, barely breathing. "I'm fine, really. I just pushed myself too hard on my first try. Thankfully I had a group of supporters ready to triage." Savvy nodded to Kotter. "This is my best friend, Joanie. Joanie, this is Spencer."

He turned to Joanie, who held his hand a little longer than necessary. "Call me Kotter. So how do you and Savvy know each other?" The suspicion in her friend's voice rang clear.

If any additional color could enhance her tomato-red exterior, Savvy was certain Spencer noticed. He smiled at Joanie, his deep dimples bookending a smile worthy of a toothpaste ad. "I officially met Savannah a few days ago, but I've been frequenting this coffee shop for over a year, and I see her here from time to time, though I think she only recognized me from walking down her street. Clearly, Teddy already claims her as his own."

Joanie released Spencer's hand and smiled. "Well, Teddy is a keeper. Why don't you join us?"

Spencer nodded and laughed, turning to her. "I suppose the jury is still out on me." He winked in Savvy's direction.

Joanie looked at her with raised eyebrows. Savvy covered her eyes with one hand as she continued to pet Teddy with the other. "Dear God…"

Spencer asked them if they needed anything else, and when they declined, went to the counter to order. One of the girls from the yoga class scurried over to them while his back was turned. "Girl, is that your man?"

"No," Savvy coughed, choking back a laugh.

"Well, is he single?"

Savvy sipped her tea. "I have no idea, but I can find out." She winked at her.

"Girl, let ME know. If you don't want him, my whole table is prepared to fight *Hunger Games*–style for him." She slapped Savvy five and hurried off to the ladies' room.

"Spencer…wait, that's not the hot homeless guy that you yelled at, is it?" Joanie half whispered. "Are you kidding?!"

Savvy shushed her. They looked up slowly to see Spencer standing at the bar smiling. They covered their mouths, laughing as Teddy nudged her to continue his ear massage. Savvy leaned forward to kiss his nose, holding his face in her hands. He affectionately licked her chin.

Spencer took the open seat at their table, conveniently next to her, and placed a water dish on the floor for Teddy. "Y'all are having too much fun over here. Teddy has all but disowned me."

Teddy glanced in Spencer's direction at the mention of his name, but he didn't move an inch. His head lay comfortably on Savvy's lap, his tongue partially hanging out of his mouth as she rubbed behind his left ear.

"And just to reiterate, I'm not homeless." Spencer gave Savvy a side-eye, sipping his coffee thoughtfully. "You thought I was hot?"

"Oops." Sinking lower into her chair, Savvy focused her attention on Teddy. If she melted into the furniture, maybe she wouldn't have to respond.

"Awkward," Joanie whispered.

"I'm going to Savvy's place this weekend to evaluate her kitchen."

"Uhhh." Joan turned to stare suspiciously at Savvy. "Is that right?"

"My actual cooking kitchen, Kotter. Sweet baby Jesus." Savvy needed to go home. She didn't think her heart could handle any more today.

8

Savvy paced back and forth, checking her hair in a full-length mirror, which hung on the inside of the closet door. She wore black cigarette pants and a sleeveless V-neck top with a bright fuchsia cardigan. Turning from side to side, she admired her new outfit, wondering if Spencer would admire her curves. "Oh, what am I doing? He's not here to evaluate *me*." Leaning forward to make sure there wasn't lip gloss on her teeth, Savvy shook her head at her reflection. "Really, Savvy? Pathetic." She slammed the closet door shut.

The doorbell rang, and she rushed down the hall, shaking out her hair and adjusting her glasses. Opening the door, her breath caught at the sight of Spencer in freshly creased slacks and a polo bearing his company's insignia. *No one should look that good in a polo.* "Hi," Savvy squeaked.

Spencer smiled. "I really do like your new hairstyle."

"Thank you. I like your look too." She gestured toward

his polo, which fit snugly across his muscular chest. His strong, sculpted arms were wrapped in black ink.

"I was shooting for 'not homeless.'" His eyes cut toward her, and she coughed.

"Mission accomplished." She stood admiring him, still blocking the doorway.

"Great. So can I come in?" He pointed inside.

"Of course! Sorry." She mentally cursed at herself as he stepped through the doorway. "Kitchen's the first door on your left."

"Thanks." He walked ahead of her, taking in the space, touching the toe of his shoe to a loose tile. "This can be dangerous. You should be careful."

Savvy crossed her arms over her chest. "I've been meaning to get that fixed." Color rose to her cheeks as she wondered what else he would find in disrepair.

"No judgment, Savvy. And I wouldn't say anything except I broke a toe on a loose tile once. Not fun."

Grimacing, Savvy ran her fingers through her hair. "Ouch. So anyway, this is the kitchen. It's pretty tight, and I'm fairly certain everything in this house is as it was when it was built."

He nodded, looking around, touching cabinets. "Are you wedded to any of this stuff?"

"No. The contents of the cabinets, yes. The cabinets themselves, no."

He fingered the cabinet door that her brother broke. "Lived in."

"Yes."

His face inscrutable, Savvy watched and waited. "Do you like certain colors for kitchens? You mentioned watching HGTV. Anything stand out to you?"

"Actually, I have a whole kitchen board on Pinterest.

Things that caught my eye, most of which I doubt would fit in this small space."

"Great—I can connect with you on there to get a sense of your style. Do you mind if I see the rest of the house? The living and dining rooms." He gestured his thumb toward the back of the house.

Thinking of clutter, Savvy balked. "Is that necessary?"

"Would I have asked if it wasn't?" He raised an eyebrow playfully. "Well, it's not like this would be the first time you've had the wrong idea about me."

Savvy rolled her eyes. "Fine." She led him down the hall, where the next doorway opened into a small dining room with a stack of cookbooks that almost reached from the floor to the ceiling. Then they continued to the living room.

"Good size." He nodded. He examined the wall between the living room and dining room. "This doesn't appear to be a load-bearing wall."

"Meaning?"

"I thought you said you watched a lot of HGTV?" He winked at her, and her cheeks flushed.

"Pretend I exaggerated." She fought back a smile.

He grinned, turning toward the wall with his hands framing his view. "Well, what if you were to open this entire side of the house? Since the walls are not load-bearing, I could knock these down. Have an open floor plan for the living space. Then the only enclosed spaces are the bedrooms and bathrooms. Makes for great entertaining, if you're really a cook the way Mrs. Walker described."

Savvy pictured the kitchen and dining spaces opening to the living room, imagining being able to talk to dinner guests as she set out the food. "I love that. You could really do that here?"

He nodded. "I've got some ideas. What if I come back

tomorrow with a few digital mock-ups? That way, you can get a sense of what could be, and I'll be able to give you some cost estimates."

"I'm nervous about the cost," Savvy admitted. "But questioning Mrs. Walker's descriptions of my food sounds like a challenge."

He raised his hands in the air. "Hey, if you feel like proving yourself, I'm never one to turn down an opportunity for good home cooking. Mrs. Walker practically drooled talking about your desserts."

"Well, since you're coming back tomorrow, and I planned to have my friends over for dinner anyway, why don't you join us? Though it means I'll be cooking while you show me your mock-ups."

"That's actually a good thing. I can see how you move around in the space." His brown eyes fixated on hers.

The thought of him watching her move sent butterflies flitting to her stomach, and she had to remind herself he was purely professional. "Wow, okay. Is there anything you need from me?"

"Just a couple of questions about colors and materials, I need to take measurements of the space, and I'll be on my way. The renderings won't be final. We can make changes as I learn what you like."

Sunday morning, Savvy met Joanie for yoga again, glad for the opportunity to try and center herself before Spencer returned to her home. For ninety minutes, Savvy focused on the woman staring back at her in the mirror; not work, not Spencer, not Jason. She couldn't do all of the poses, and the room still smelled like a high school locker room, but the end of the class felt different. Savvy left the studio with a calm that quieted her anxieties.

At home, Savvy cleared cookbooks off the dining table, replacing them with a red table runner down the center of the walnut slab. She pulled rattan chargers and white bone china plates from a server cabinet. She set the table for four and manipulated white cloth napkins with red stripes into rose centerpieces for each plate. Silverware and wineglasses with flared bowls completed the aesthetic.

While she set the table, a package of thick oxtails came to room temperature on a butcher block slab. With a ruffled apron tied around her waist and her hair pulled back, Savvy rolled her shoulders then opened the paper package. She laid each oxtail flat, grabbing her special spice rub and a container of flour. Turning the heat high under a Dutch oven pot, Savvy drizzled in a generous helping of oil and hummed to herself as she seasoned the meat. Just as the oil reached its smoking point, she used tongs to place the oxtails seasoning side down into the hot oil. Savvy lived for that first sizzle. Once all of the oxtails were in the pot, she seasoned the other side, turning them one by one. Cursing to herself, Savvy clicked on the vent hood above the stove, waving a baking sheet at the fire alarm just before it sounded.

Seared on both sides, the tails came out of the pot, and she drizzled in more olive oil, then tossed in julienned onions. After they sweated out their moisture, garlic went in, and as soon as the fragrance reached her nose, the oxtails went back in with red wine and tomato paste. One of granny's old recipes, oxtail stew was a one-pot meal of layered flavors and ultimate comfort. The alcohol cooked off the wine, and then beef stock was poured in with a bay leaf and more pepper. After covering the pot with a heavy lid, Savvy moved on to start a crust for her apple tart. *Good thing today's a cheat day.*

Crumbling butter into her flour and dry ingredients, she

set out to make a dough, kneading it lightly to avoid over-working it. She wrapped it in plastic wrap and put it in the fridge to let it rest. Before moving on to the rest of her prep work, she wiped down her counters, washed the used dishes, and placed them on a drying rack.

Music thumped through a Bluetooth speaker at the end of the counter. Singing along with Erykah Badu, Savvy swayed her hips along with the beat. She started to peel a Granny Smith apple, its green peel curling on the other side of her paring knife's blade, when the doorbell rang. Rushing toward the sound, Savvy yelped when pain shot from her bare toe, stubbed hard against the loose kitchen tile. "Son of a muthafucking BITCH!"

Limping toward the door, apple and knife still in hand, Savvy opened it to Spencer covering a laugh with his hand. "Hey, did I catch you at a bad time?"

Remembering that the windows were open, Savvy cringed with embarrassment. "Sorry, my floor attacked me."

He chuckled. "All good. Besides, I would never say anything against a woman with a knife in her hand."

"I'm not dangerous at the moment." Gesturing him in, Savvy led the way back to the kitchen, still walking gingerly.

"Need me to take a look?" he asked as he took in her limp.

Heat crept from her stomach to her chest, spreading up her neck to rest in her cheeks. "I'm sure it's fine. Let me find some slippers. You're welcome to take your shoes off if you want. I'm not as strict as my mother, and she'd kill me for making it optional, but—"

"Do you take off your shoes right when you come in the house?"

Savvy nodded. "There's a little shoe rack below the console table where I put my keys."

"Well then, I will too. Though if we agree to move forward with renovations, you'll understand the need for an exception." He grinned at her, and she thought he might wink as he turned toward the front door to take off his shoes. Returning, he surveyed the kitchen. "Wow, something smells amazing."

On cue, Savvy lifted the lid to the oxtails, setting it aside. She added in carrots, potatoes, and a little more broth, stirring the liquid as the hearty smells of beef, wine, spice, and garlic wafted upward. Spencer leaned over her shoulder to peer into the pot, his chest lightly touching her arm. "Mrs. Walker wasn't lying. That looks really good."

His proximity and the scent of his woodsy cologne sent a shiver up her spine. "Thank you." She cleared her throat. "I hope you brought your appetite."

He stayed where he was, turning his face slightly to look down at her. "You never have to worry about that. So, what's next?" His voice lowered to a gentle quiet.

His breath tickled her ear, and Savvy shuddered. Looking up at him, his smooth lips parting slightly, she stammered, "Uh, I have to finish the tart. The girls will be here soon."

He surveyed her face slowly, backing away. "Okay. Do you mind if I watch?"

"Not at all." Gesturing to a stool, Savvy set about peeling the rest of the apples, removing their cores, and slicing them thinly. Savvy macerated the apples in lemon juice, brown sugar, and spices while she made the dough for the crust. Spencer watched as she rolled out the dough and pressed it into the tart pan, trimming the edges for a smooth finish after a blind bake. Aware of his eyes, Savvy wondered whether he ever cooked for his significant other; if he had learned any family recipes from his relatives. She took her time with the apple slices, curving them into a round cascade. "So, do you cook?"

"I can grill well, but I've never done anything like what you're doing right now." He watched her curve one slice into the cascade at a time, placing them with meticulous care.

She didn't look up. "Did you learn from relatives?"

"More out of necessity, really. I did learn how to make omelets from a significant other," he offered.

Savvy looked up at his admission. "You must be a pro at making breakfast in bed now." She curled in the last few slices of apple—the final masterpiece resembled a giant rose.

"It's been a while since I've had someone to do that for." Their eyes met for a slow second, but Savvy looked away first, returning her attention to the tart. He cleared his throat. "Wow, I can't believe I just watched you do that. And to think, I brought artwork for you to look at for your kitchen. I don't know if it can stand up to this." He reached into his shoulder bag for a large tablet.

"Yes! Show me!" Savvy wiped her fingers on her apron and clapped in anticipation.

With their shoulders touching, he walked her through three different digital renderings of her living space, which were so different from her current setup that Savvy didn't recognize the place. Each one had parts that she liked and parts that she didn't. He emailed her the mockups to look over again, and Savvy promised to email him some thoughts that could get her to yes. The quotes he proposed were more reasonable than Savvy expected, and his confidence that he could get the work done in less than six weeks impressed her since she anticipated needing to work from home more.

"I can't believe you did all of this overnight," she gushed, manipulating the screen to make the rooms bigger.

Eventually she pulled herself away from the tablet and brushed a glaze of apricot jam over the top of the tart, putting it into the oven as the doorbell rang.

Spencer rose and held up a hand. "I'll get it."

They looked at each other for a long moment, her heart dropping into her stomach as he licked his lips. "Thanks," Savvy whispered, watching his mouth. He watched her, watching him, until the doorbell rang again. Savvy blew out a deep breath after he turned to get the door. *What the hell was that?!*

She heard their voices climb an octave as Spencer opened the door. Kotter and Mags, the exact opposite of subtle. "How are you, Spencer?" Mags crooned. "I'm Maggie—I've heard so much about you! Look at you opening the door. So helpful." *God, she was laying it on thick.*

Savvy's eyes finished a full rotation as the girls entered the kitchen. "Yes, but you love us." Joanie smirked as she hugged her.

"Sometimes, I wonder why," Savvy muttered.

"I'm starving," Mags whined. "How long until the food is ready?"

Joanie spied Spencer's look of amusement. "Trust me, you've never had her cooking. We starve ourselves in anticipation of meals here."

"We're about thirty minutes away. I just need to thicken the gravy. Do y'all want double servings with rice?"

Spencer looked at the girls, who both nodded, so he followed suit.

"Okay, y'all get washed up, pour some wine, and I'll meet you in the dining room. Spencer can show you the mock-ups he made in the meantime."

"You sure you don't need any help?" Spencer offered.

The corner of her mouth curved with confidence as she looked up at him. "I got this."

Joanie looked between the two of them. "Sho' does."

She and Mags slapped each other five and waved for Spencer to follow them.

Savvy poured a slurry of cornstarch and water into the stew gravy, then stirred in frozen peas. Once the gravy had the right consistency and the peas were cooked, she garnished the top with scallions. Lifting the lid off another pot on the stove, steam poured out, exposing fluffy white rice. Savvy filled decorative bowls with rice and tender oxtails, ladling on the thick gravy and vegetables. After sprinkling more green onions on top, Savvy carried the first two heaping bowls to the dining room, placing one in front of each of her girls. "Be right back."

Returning with bowls for Spencer and herself, Savvy sat next to Joanie, across the table from Spencer. Mags's cheeks were already full of food as Savvy closed her eyes to pray. "Father, thank You for the food we are about to receive." Savvy opened one eye to glare at Mags, who swore and rushed to chew her mouthful as Savvy continued. "Bless this meal, Lord. Let it be nourishment for our bodies. Let no harm or foul become of it. In Jesus's name, we pray. Amen."

"Amen," Spencer and Joanie repeated.

A loud hiccup sounded from across the table. "Amen. Excuse me." Mags covered her mouth. "Ow! That hurt, Kotter!"

Joanie leaned forward, having kicked Mags under the table. She smiled through gritted teeth. "We have company, ho."

Spencer watched in amusement, and Savvy gestured toward his bowl. "Please, eat. Ignore my silly friends—" Savvy turned to them with widened eyes "—who are embarrassing me."

"Oh, don't worry, I think they're hilarious." He took a piece of meat, which had fallen off the bone, with the rice and gravy to his lips. "Everything looks amazing." He took a bite and immediately his eyes closed. "Wow."

Joanie and Mags nodded. "We know," they said in unison.

"Hive mentality." Savvy shrugged when Spencer looked at them both in surprise.

They all dug in, and for a long moment, no one talked. Joanie hummed happily as she ate, and Mags swayed from side to side. Spencer closed his eyes and savored each bite. The scent of spiced apples and a buttery crust hit Savvy's nose. "Tart's ready! I'll be right back."

"Wait, how can you tell? I didn't hear a timer," Spencer observed.

"She's a complete freak," Mags said with food in her mouth. "She knows by the smell."

Savvy tapped her nose. "I always know."

Back in the kitchen, the scents of fruit and sugar wafted up as Savvy opened the oven. With lobster claw oven mitts, she pulled the tart out, setting it on top of a jar to remove the outer rim of the pan. Savvy slid the tart onto a decorative plate and grabbed fresh whipped cream from the fridge.

"Ta-da!" Savvy sang.

She set the plate in the center of the table, along with the whipped cream and a chef's knife. The tart's golden crust hugged the sliced apple rose tightly, the apples having softened and browned; the glaze spread a sheen across the top. Everyone's eyes lit up, though their mouths were still full.

Mags began sucking on one of the oxtail bones to find the marrow; egregious slurping likely to impress any man in earshot. Savvy took a sip of wine, and glanced at Joanie, whose mouth fell wide-open as she watched Mags work. Mags finally looked up, surprised to find three pairs of eyes on her. "What did I do now?" The bone still at her lips.

"You're, uh, really goin' to town there." Joanie nodded her chin toward Mags's oxtail.

"What? The marrow is the best part!"

"It is, and you're winning all kinds of awards right now for how you're slobbing down that bone."

"I'm not—"

Joanie brought a bone to her lips and imitated Mags, down to the shoulder sway she was doing. Mags put the bone down, and Spencer laughed so hard tears formed in his eyes.

"I'm so sorry," Savvy laughed. "I'm completely mortified. My girls are in rare form this evening."

"Girl, we all do this. Don't front," Mags warned, finishing off her bowl.

"Maggie, I have to tell you, I'm proud of the work you put in," Joanie said, grinning. "You're going to make some man really, REALLY happy."

Spencer bounced his eyebrows in agreement. "It was impressive."

"So what's your deal, Spencer? Do you have a special someone who puts in work like that for you?" Joanie rested her chin in her hands, eyeing him curiously.

Jesus. Savvy coughed, glass of wine suspended midair.

He cleared his throat. "Nope, I'm single. Looking for that special someone, but work takes up a lot of my time."

"I know that's right," Savvy muttered into her wine. Their eyes met over her wineglass, and Savvy jumped when Joanie poked her thigh under the table. "Right. Let me serve dessert." She sliced into the tart and spooned fresh whipped cream onto four dessert plates.

Mags dove in immediately, and Spencer snapped his fingers. "I should have taken a picture of that. It was so pretty."

Savvy shrugged. "I can always make another."

"You really do love to cook, don't you?"

She nodded slowly. "I get it from my grandmother. It was in her spirit to feed people, and it's in mine too. It makes me happy to prepare a meal for people that I care about. And to me, baking is like therapy. I always feel better when I'm done."

"And we are always happy to make her happy," Mags said, her face slowly darkening. "We ride hard for our girl, though. You'll be on your best behavior around Savvy, won't you?"

Spencer swallowed the piece of tart he'd been chewing, looking at her before he met Mags's gaze. "You have my word."

Savvy tried to laugh it off. "Come on, guys, we're about to go into business together. He's been a perfect gentleman."

"Mmm-hmm," they said in unison.

"We'll see," Mags said, giving Spencer a side-eye.

He looked at Savvy, unsure what to say.

"Again, I'm sorry." Savvy sighed.

9

Thunk. Slap. Thunk. SLAP.

"That's great, Savvy. Make sure that you follow through with your racket."

Savvy nodded, trying to keep her feet moving, beads of sweat accumulating across her forehead. She hid the fact that her lungs screamed for air. For the life of her, she didn't understand how runners could breathe through their noses.

The last Saturday of March marked her second tennis lesson with Beth, a personal trainer who'd previously coached women's tennis. Savvy'd found a listing that she'd posted on the community board in Savvy's office building and hoped that Beth wouldn't be too much of a hard-ass.

Thunk. Slap! The machine spat a tennis ball in her direction. Savvy held out her left hand in front of her to help gauge where she wanted the racket in her right to connect with the ball, making sure that she continued her swing after she connected.

"That's good, Savvy. Much better." Beth nodded. "Keep those feet moving." Her encouragement gave Savvy the boost she needed to straighten her shoulders and focus harder at the ball machine, anticipating its trajectory. Savvy needed to make her proud, needed another cheerleader.

Her knees bent slightly, Savvy was light on her feet as she stutter-stepped to the ball, shoes squeaking against the hardcourt surface. Ambling all over the court, she connected with the ball, employing techniques Beth taught her, and refreshing the skills she'd honed in college.

"Yes, Savvy. Pick up your feet. Let's go!" Beth clapped, emphasizing her words.

Savvy reached the ball just in time to send it sailing back over the net, but it landed just wide of the line. Jogging back to the center of the court, she tried to shake it off and reset. Sensing her frustration, Beth grabbed the wireless remote and shut off the machine.

"Hey, Savs. Let's take a quick break. Come grab some water." She waved her over to the bench.

Savvy knew why they stopped. "Hey, Beth, I'm sorry. I got down on myself there, but I can shake it off."

She smiled. "Don't worry, I know you will." She tossed Savvy a bottle of cold water. She stood with one foot up on the bench; her track jacket slung over her gym bag. She wore a baseball cap to cover her short hair. Beth could be Ruby Rose's Black sister. Tall, brooding, androgynous, and solid. Her throaty voice and tattoos were ultrasexy, and her empathetic nature was immediately apparent.

Savvy twisted off the cap and took a sip, perching at the edge of the bench. "Getting back into shape has been hard. I am trying not to feel discouraged, but I have a lot of doubt that I'll really be able to do this."

Beth took a big gulp of water before she responded.

"Listen, Savvy, nothing happens overnight. We don't gain weight overnight, we don't get in shape overnight. Either direction takes some level of effort, right? This is going to be a work in progress. You'll start to see changes in no time, but you have to be patient with yourself."

We'll see. "You really think that I can meet my goals?"

Beth sat down next to her, nudging her with her elbow. "Come on, you're already moving better than you were a week ago. How was yoga this week?"

"I went twice. It was actually pretty good. I only sat down once when the heat was too much, and I attempted each of the poses, though most of them I can't quite do yet."

She tilted her head. "I like that you said 'yet.' You'll get there. Everyone knows Bikram isn't easy. I've been practicing for almost a decade. There are days that my body just doesn't want to do certain poses. But you work with where you are on any given day."

"Makes sense." Savvy tried not to picture Beth half-naked and sweating through a yoga class. Another beautiful girl who belonged in that room.

"So then you'll approach this revenge body in the same way. Each day, you'll work with where you are."

"You're right." Savvy smiled, reassured. "So what's next, Coach?"

"Don't smile just yet, Savs. It's time for some drills." Beth grinned, and inwardly Savvy questioned her own sexuality. *Why is this woman so fine? Wait till Kotter gets here.*

The dreaded drills. Last week, Beth ran her through W-sprints, high knees, volley challenges, planks, push-ups, and lunge squats. Taking one last sip of water, Savvy nodded. "Let's get it." Beth nodded in approval.

After drills, Beth put numbered cones out in different quadrants of the court for her to hit balls toward. She set the ball machine to shoot at opposite corners, so that Savvy could run back and forth across the court. Once Savvy reached the ball, she'd yell a number, and Savvy was to aim her return at the corresponding cone.

"Yes, Savvy! I know you're tired. Push through it. Just a few more."

Savvy huffed, feeling herself slowing down. She hopped a few times, trying to stay light on her feet. After hitting a ball down the right-hand line and knocking over cone number four, Beth turned off the machine and let out a big whoop. "That was a great shot!"

Savvy hunched over with her hands on her knees to catch her breath. Panting, she looked up at Beth. "You're not just saying that?" Her heart pounded away, and she pictured herself laid out on the court.

"Savvy." Beth grinned at her. "As you get to know me, you'll understand that I don't pay empty compliments. Trust me, that was a tough shot."

Savvy stood up straight and put her hands on her hips. "This actually felt good today."

Beth nodded. "Good. So now do three laps around the courts, and we'll finish with one last plank."

Savvy groaned, shaking her head in exasperation. "Spoke too soon."

After they finished, they sat across from each other on their mats, planning out their workouts for the month of April. Savvy increased their sessions to twice per week, which would supplement two yoga sessions per week. For a fifth workout, Savvy would do any activity of her choosing. Beth assured her that during their workouts, Savvy would get in plenty of conditioning. As they stood, she gave her a high five and a hug.

"Keep it up, Savvy. You can do this."

"I really appreciate all of your help, Beth. Thank you so much."

"Hey, girl!" Joanie held on to the end of each word in a long drawl as she walked up to them in leggings and a long-sleeved pullover. "How was practice?"

"You say that like I'm on a competitive team."

"Aren't you?" Joanie joked. She nodded at Beth and extended a hand. "How's it going?"

"Beth, this is Joan, but she prefers that we call her Kotter." Savvy gestured to her friend, who was attempting to smooth her mane, which was flying in every direction from the breeze.

"Kotter, nice to meet you." Beth smiled. "Where are you coming from?"

"Oh, just SoulCycle today." Kotter shrugged.

"Just SoulCycle?" Beth raised an eyebrow.

"She hikes and does all kinds of group classes. She's actually the person who talked me into trying Bikram." Savvy smiled at her friend, and Beth looked impressed.

Joanie nodded and turned to her, giving her a fist bump. She seemed flustered and tried to change the subject. "So how was it, Savs? Did you feel tortured this time?"

Beth tilted her head, her hands on her hips, glaring at her playfully. "You told her I tortured you?"

Completely put on the spot, Savvy pulled at the collar of her T-shirt. "I tend to be a little dramatic at times. I mean, I am trying for a revenge body right now."

Beth looked at Joanie for confirmation, but she just shrugged and laughed. "She's not exaggerating on that point, but I think she's going to love this in the end. Tennis was her thing even when we were in middle school. Besides, she won't need a revenge body when she hooks her homeless guy!"

Savvy sighed, looking at Beth. "He's not homeless."

"Well then, maybe you should join Savvy for the next session. Keep her honest." Beth gave Joanie a smoldering look that made Savvy blush.

Joanie side-eyed Beth, but she never backed down from a challenge. "Maybe I will. I could use some practice."

Beth threw Savvy another bottle of water. "Stay hydrated, Savvy. I'll see you on Wednesday." She turned to smile at Joanie before walking away. "I guess I'll see you then too."

Savvy nodded, calling after her. "Thank you, Beth!"

Joanie watched her departure. "That girl is sexy." She shook her head, taking a sip of her water. "What time do we need to be here on Wednesday?"

"You're back to playing tennis?" Maggie asked incredulously.

"Why are you so surprised?" Savvy dragged a carrot stick through white bean hummus.

Maggie eyed her. "Because you hated tennis in high school, and you always shied away from the idea of playing after your injury in college."

"I never hated tennis," Savvy balked. "I remember feeling inadequate when I made varsity. I wasn't chosen to play singles, and I had that hard-core doubles partner who yelled like Maria Sharapova in prescription goggles."

Mags snorted, almost spitting out her cucumber lemonade. "Oh my God, I almost forgot about the goggles! Why didn't she just put a strap on the back of her glasses?"

Savvy shrugged, eating another carrot. "Goggles made her hard-core. Anyone willing to wear those in high school is braver than me by far."

Joanie shook her head as her sweet chili wings were delivered. On her designated cheat day, she always chose wings. "Now this is what I'm talking 'bout."

Maggie turned to Joanie. "Don't think for a second that Savvy forgot to tell me about that little moment you had with her tennis coach."

Joanie's mouth was stuffed with chicken, sweet Thai chili sauce at the corners of her mouth. "Who, me?" she gestured toward herself with her half-eaten wing.

"Yes, you!" Savvy laughed, turning to Mags. "Joanie looked at her like she was a full course meal!"

Kotter brought her hand to her chest, feigning surprise. "I have no idea what you're talking about, Savvy. Maybe you were dehydrated."

Maggie rolled her eyes. "I low-key want to come and watch your session on Wednesday. If this woman is half as fine as Savvy described, you better not slow play this one, Kotter. Don't play hard to get and then regret missing out on a great girl."

Joanie picked apart another wing. "Seriously, I just met her. And though she is a grown woman—tall, sexy, and special dark chocolate—I'm not jumping at a woman that I barely know. We'll see how Wednesday goes."

"Joanie." Savvy laughed, picking at her grilled chicken and avocado salad. "On first meeting, you agreed to let this chick make you sweat and shoot balls at you. I'd say you jumped."

Mags threw her head back and laughed while Kotter grinned mischievously. "Right off a cliff."

Mags pointed a carrot in her direction. "So what about you?"

Savvy snagged one of Joanie's wings. *One couldn't hurt.* "What about me?"

"Tell me you're jumping toward that sexy contractor!"

"Girl, that's not appropriate!" Savvy shielded her full mouth with her hand. "We just signed a contract for my renovations. I can't be chasing after that man." Savvy put her wing down. "He's probably not even interested in me. Besides, I'm still getting myself together after Jason."

"What's left to deal with? Jason ain't shit." Joanie licked her fingers. "Spencer seems like a good guy. Though the jury's still out on whether he's homeless."

Savvy cackled. "Shut up—the man is not homeless. Clearly, I misjudged him." She thought about his lips curving into a smile. How his eyes crinkled at the corners when he laughed. "I mean, he does seem like a good guy, but the timing isn't right. I'm not ready to be jumping into another relationship."

Maggie raised her eyebrows suggestively. "It doesn't have to be a relationship, and we aren't imagining things, Savvy. We saw the way he was looking at you the other night. Fine as he is, he could pitch a tent in your backyard, and I wouldn't be mad."

Savvy stared at her friend. "I have no idea what you're talking about! Either way, I'm not sleeping with him while he has access to my house for the next six weeks."

"Okay, damn, good point." Maggie reached for the hummus.

"Listen, I've got two priorities right now. Promotion and revenge body. Everything else important is on the back burner, and dating isn't even on the stove."

Joanie leaned back and pretended to drop the mic. "Fine, but we're going to revisit this six weeks from now. Homeless hottie is into you, Savvy."

"I need another cocktail."

10

The following Sunday afternoon, Joanie and Savvy chilled, sipping cold brewed iced coffee, still wearing their workout clothes. They'd met earlier for yoga and then grabbed seafood cobb salads for brunch.

Maggie strolled in wearing sunglasses, waving sleepily at them as she joined the line to order her coffee. She ordered her usual, a large cinnamon cappuccino and a streusel-topped blueberry muffin, and slid into the empty leather armchair next to Joanie, grunting her greeting.

"Wow, what did you get into last night?" Savvy eyed Mags suspiciously. "I'm not going to lie, Sis, you look a little rough."

Maggie lifted her sunglasses long enough for them to see the dark circles underneath and had them rolling before Joanie could describe what she'd done.

Joanie eyed her sheepishly. "Well, I thought it might be fun to bring Mags to an industry party. One of the premium liquor companies that I represent was hosting an event to showcase their new bourbon release."

"So what's wrong with that?" Savvy scrunched her nose, turning to Joanie. "Mags loves bourbon. And you were up early enough to work out with me this morning. Why does she look like hell paid her a visit?"

Jessica brought over Maggie's cappuccino and muffin. Mags nodded her thanks, finally peeling off her sunglasses. She took a sip of her cappuccino carefully, trying to avoid getting foam on her face.

Joanie pulled an end piece off her croissant and took a bite. "One of the executives tried to bring Mags something lighter because he felt the bourbon would be too strong for her."

Savvy scrunched her nose. "Why would he think that?"

Mags peeled down a portion of parchment paper and took a huge bite of her muffin. "Because ladies prefer wine," she mimicked. "Tuh!"

"Oh, no," Savvy groaned. "You didn't."

Maggie shook her head, taking another sip of her cappuccino. "He shouldn't have."

Joanie sighed. "Never tell Maggie what she wants or how she feels. She will immediately double down to smash whatever doubts or limitations she thinks someone placed upon her."

"I think you might be exaggerating a bit, Joanie," Mags muttered as she pulled her sunglasses back on, pushing them to the bridge of her nose. "I'm not that fucking competitive."

"Uh, try again," Savvy mused. "Is the light hurting your eyes there, Dracula?"

Maggie grunted, slouching down farther in her chair and flipping her off in the process. Joanie bit her lip to stifle a laugh.

"So how much did you drink, Mags?" Savvy prodded. "I've never seen you fold to bourbon before."

Maggie took another big bite of her muffin. As she chewed, she gestured broadly. "All of it. I drank all the bourbon." Little crumbs of muffin flew from her lips.

Savvy's eyes widened as she glared at Joanie. "You let her drink *all* of it, Kotter?!"

"Have you ever tried to stop Maggie from doing something that she was determined to do?" Joanie countered.

"Okay, fine. Maggie, don't you think that you could have proven yourself without drinking *all* of the bourbon?"

Maggie lifted her sunglasses just high enough to make squinting eye contact with her, her voice dulled to avoid aggravating her headache. "Well, in retrospect…yes."

As Joanie and Savvy burst out laughing, Maggie put her fingers up to her temples. In the reflection of her sunglasses, Savvy saw a moving object getting bigger, and Maggie shrank back as the figure drew closer.

"Teddy!" She heard the heavy thumping of paws and braced herself for impact. Joanie grabbed her iced coffee, avoiding potential spillage.

Teddy jumped up and put his front paws on the arm of her chair, pushing his wet nose against Savvy's cheek, whining with happiness, placing slobbery kisses all over her hands and chin. She brought her hands to either side of Teddy's face, rubbing behind his ears as he continued to give her love. "Hello. Oh, I love you," she whispered.

"If only it were that simple," Spencer said behind her.

Even Maggie broke into a smile. "Hey, Spencer. How are you doing today?"

Joanie waved in Spencer's direction, all smiles. Savvy rolled her eyes, trying hard not to crack a smile. Joanie found her voice first. "Pull up a chair!"

Savvy opened her mouth to speak and then thought better of it, refocusing her attention on Teddy, who had laid his head in her lap and was peering up at her lovingly. She puckered her lips as if to kiss his nose. He lifted his head to let her scratch under his chin.

Spencer walked around to the other side of the table and pulled a free chair between Joanie and Mags, who were only too eager to make space. "I guess I can join you ladies for a few minutes. I actually came here to get some work done." He and Savvy finally made eye contact. "How are you, Savannah? I haven't seen you in a few days."

Maggie and Joanie turned their attention to her. Maggie raised her eyebrows and folded her hands in her lap. Savvy looked down at Teddy to regroup. "I've been good. This past week has been busier than normal. How about you? What's new?"

Spencer was watching Teddy, whose eyes moved between the two of them. Smiling, he ran his hand over his hair. "Everything's been really good. I just picked up a new client. That's why I'm here to work on a Sunday."

"Oh, congratulations!" Maggie and Kotter exclaimed in unison.

"You already know this, y'all. I'm the new client."

Mags leaned back in her chair. "Oh, right. Well damn, Savs, you've already got the man working on Sundays. Stop being such a hard-ass."

Spencer waved his hand. "I actually like it—helps me plan for the week ahead. We're starting demolition this week, and we're going to start ordering materials and appliances. For now, we'll move Savvy's fridge to her back patio near the grill."

"Yeah, I'm going to stay with Kotter for a week or two, until the dust settles," she told Mags.

She nodded. "Yep, your room's all ready. Just don't drink all of the tequila."

They looked at Mags, who was groaning softly. "Yeah, I don't think that will be a problem," Savvy deadpanned.

"So how did you get into contract work, Spencer?" Kotter chewed on a piece of croissant.

"It was my dad's business originally, which he owned with his brothers. They've now all retired, and the business moved to me. All of my uncles had girls who don't like getting dirty, so I'm the only one left to run the business, though one of my cousins is my bookkeeper. I've been working for the business on and off since high school."

"That's really cool," Savvy said, sipping on her iced coffee thoughtfully. "I'd love to work for myself someday."

"What would you do?" he asked, leaning forward.

Maggie jumped in. "I don't know if you recall, but Savvy is an amazing cook. We've tried getting her to become a caterer or consider opening her own spot. A true renaissance woman."

"It's true!" Joanie joined in, and Savvy fought the urge to roll her eyes again. "I work in advertising, and I am always asking her for advice when I'm preparing a pitch for a new client."

"So you want to be a full-time chef?"

She shrugged. "I love it, but I'm not convinced that I could afford to do that here."

"Oh, well, we can't have you leaving the area anytime soon. I'm finally getting the chance to get to know you." Spencer smiled brightly, and she felt color rush to her cheeks. If he weren't so damned polite, she'd have thought he was flirting with her.

"I'm sure I'll be here for a while. I'd love to do a cookbook first," she said shyly. She couldn't think of what to say next, looking to Teddy for any kind of hint. His soulful gaze offered no answers.

"So, Spencer, what did you do before you took over the family business?" Kotter changed the subject, giving Savvy time to collect her thoughts.

"Oh, I used to do strategic communications and diversity outreach."

"Wow, that sounds awesome," Joanie gushed. "I've been looking to branch out on my own doing something similar."

Spencer nodded. "If you're thinking about it, I'd highly recommend being certified as a diversity trainer."

"Wow, thank you—that's really helpful. I'm thinking about making moves within the next year or two."

"I say go for it. Working for myself has been such a relief—even as I transitioned back into contracting." Spencer's eyes lit up as he spoke. His passion for his work had Joanie sold.

Spencer reached into his work bag and produced a business card. "Here, take my card. When you get to a place where you want to map things out and make a plan, give me a call. I can talk you through it."

Floored, Joan sat back in her chair. "Really? You mean that?"

Spencer smiled easily. "Absolutely. Any friend of Savannah's is a friend of mine."

Kotter turned to look at Savvy, the expression on her face was crystal clear: *I like this one.*

"That's really amazing. Thank you so much, Spencer." Savvy gazed at him gratefully. As their eyes met, his lips parted slightly, and she had the urge to bite into the thickness of his lower lip.

He studied her face for a moment, averting his eyes upon the realization that he had two other pairs of eyes watching him too. "You know, I'd better get to work. Hopefully I won't have to put in more than a couple of hours today." As he stood, he turned to her friends and smiled. "Thank you, ladies, for letting me sit with you. Hopefully I'll see you all again soon. I'll take him off your hands." He moved to reach for Teddy's leash.

"Oh, he's never a bother." She leaned forward toward Teddy, who turned and licked her nose. "He is the sweetest thing."

"He's sweet on you." Spencer's mouth curved into an easy smile. "I'll reach out to you tomorrow once we get started. Come on, Teddy, let's get you some water."

Teddy stood and walked toward Spencer, though he turned to send a longing glance in her direction. Spencer waved to all of them and walked toward the coffee line.

Her friends leaned toward her. "Savs, you know Teddy is not the only one who's sweet on you," Maggie whispered.

"I promise you that I am not seeing what you're seeing. He's just being nice! And even if he was interested, timing isn't right. He's sweet, and gorgeous, but I'm just not ready to jump into something yet. I haven't been single for years, and Spencer doesn't seem like the type to casually date."

Kotter nodded. "That's true. Can't having you jumping in the deep end when you've forgotten how to swim. You haven't dated since college, and it's not as easy as it used to be. Trust me."

Maggie raised a finger in triumph. "I've already got something in mind." She pulled her MacBook out of her bag. Maggie was the MacGyver of their group. In her bag, she was known to have Band-Aids, a miniature pharmacy, a paperback book, a day planner, a set of colorful Sharpie pens, a makeup bag, and often a flask of bourbon. "Savvy, I think you need to add something to your Project Upgrade list. You need to figure out what your likes and dislikes are when it comes to dating. To that end, Joanie and I have been putting together a Tinder account for you."

"Excuse me? As in, this has been happening behind my back and you're just telling me now?" Savvy frowned. "Am I happy about this?"

Mags and Joanie exchanged a glance. "Medium happy? You can get to know some people in a completely casual environment. More than anything, it will give you an idea of what your preferences really are," Joanie explained.

"I don't know," Savvy said. "Doesn't that just lead to a lot of rejection? I'm not sure that I could handle that right now. The last thing I need is to find a bunch of Jasons online who want nothing more than to tell me what's wrong with my body."

"But I think this works because of the way the app is set up. You never hear anything about those who swipe left, you only focus on the ones who saw your profile and photos who then expressed interest."

Savvy didn't have much of a choice. "I guess I'll give it a try," she said slowly. "I don't even know that I want to find anything, but maybe you're right. Maybe I will learn more about what I want."

"Excellent." Maggie smiled. "Let her show you what we've put together so far." She turned her MacBook in Savvy's direction while Joanie grabbed her phone. "Kotter's going to download the app for you, and we'll get you all squared away."

"Uncle! Where are you?" Savvy called into the house as she made her way to the kitchen.

"Hey, Baby Girl! Wow, look at you!" Hobbling in from the backyard, Unc smiled big as Savvy kissed him on the cheek. He admired Savvy's new haircut, playfully tugging at her bangs. "Was enjoying the sunshine out back." The spring weather painted a picture of perfection. With only a thin sprinkling of clouds, and a gentle breeze coming in off the coast, it had been the perfect afternoon to sit outside with a glass of lemonade and a good book. Now that dusk approached, the gentle clouds were set ablaze, and the bright white sun burned a deep orange.

"Why are you hopping around without your crutches, Unc?"

He huffed, looking annoyed. "Those things hurt! It wasn't far to my chair, and I wanted a break from feeling like such an invalid."

"Uncle…" They sat down at the kitchen table. "Are you already back to work?"

"Not full-time yet, but back as of last week. And I don't want to hear no nagging from you. I'm getting enough already."

Savvy gave him a side-eye. "Ms. Mabel giving you a hard time?"

He smiled boyishly. "Nah, she's great. But she is so active. I just need to keep up."

"Mmm-hmm."

"Mind yo' business, young lady." He winked at her.

Savvy threw her hands up, grinning. Uncle hadn't dated in over a decade. He was practically blushing. *So cute.* "Yes, sir."

He looked at the bag she placed on the counter, eyes shining. "So, what you bring me?"

Savvy grinned at him. "Look at you, changing the subject." Chuckling, she grabbed the bag and brought it back over to the table. Savvy reached inside for the containers of food, one by one. "Let's see. This is garlic and rosemary roasted potatoes. You have sautéed string beans here, or haricots verts if you're fancy." He laughed. "I made a rack of lamb. And because I love you, I made your favorite cake just like Granny used to make."

"You made Mama's apricot lemon pound cake?!" he exclaimed. "Aw, come here, Baby Girl. You know Uncle loves you." He pulled her into a hug, kissing the side of her jaw. He loved when Savvy brought back Granny's recipes.

"I love you too, Uncle. Here, let me put on some coffee. I'll put the other food in the fridge, and we can have a piece of cake." Savvy walked over to the counter to plug in the coffeepot. As she pushed the plug into the nearest outlet, a quick current zapped her fingers. "Arghh!"

"Oh, Baby Girl, I don't use that outlet. You got to use this one over here." He pointed.

"What is going on over there?" Savvy wiggled her fingers, still tingling from the electricity. "Isn't that dangerous?"

Unc waved her concerns away. "Just some faulty wiring. I'll take care of it soon. Did you see that they patched up the roof? Looks good up there!"

Savvy plugged in the coffeepot, thinking of her phone call with Mama. "No, I didn't notice, but I'm glad it's done. Uncle, how much do you think it's going to cost to do all of this wiring?"

"Naw, I don't want you worrying about that, Baby Girl. You've done more than enough. Let me take it the rest of the way."

"Uh-huh. That means Mama is on your back."

They exchanged a knowing glance, and Uncle Joe sucked his teeth. "You know your mama, Savvy. She'd rather we sell this place."

"I know." Savvy looked around the kitchen, remembering Granny singing church hymns while she prepared their Sunday dinners. "I just can't imagine parting with it."

"Me neither."

The coffee maker began to percolate, and Savvy pulled the Bundt cake out of the bag. After cutting one thick slice and one thin, she plated the cake and poured her uncle a cup of black coffee. She brought the food and mugs to the table, and then sat back down with a weak smile.

Unc patted her hand. "I see it on your face, Baby Girl. You ain't gotta worry about me."

Savvy grabbed his hand, leaning toward him. "But I do, Uncle. What if Mama's right? Do we have what it takes to keep this house up?"

"I know it feels like a lot, but the house is almost there. I'm not looking to make renovations. I like the house just fine. Once the wiring's done, we'll be all set, I promise."

Savvy sipped her coffee slowly, watching as her uncle took his first bite of cake. He closed his eyes, shaking his head. Savvy took a bite too, remembering her grandmother singing as she poured all of her love into a buttered Bundt pan. Uncle had a faraway look in his eyes, and Savvy guessed he thought of the same moments. "Bless the Lord, oh my soul, and all that is within me..." Savvy sang.

Her Uncle looked up, a smile beaming from ear to ear. "Bless his ho-ly-y-yyyy, name," he sang back. A tear fell from his eye, and he wiped it away with the back of his hand. "I sure miss your Granny and PopPop. Your cake tastes just like Mama's. She always said she put something special in there. What was it?"

Savvy leaned close to whisper to him, her eyes wide. "Butter."

They laughed hard, enjoying the last of their cake. Savvy

cleaned up the dishes and put the food away, singing more of Granny's favorite hymns, as her uncle sat and listened.

"Okay, Unc. I need to get going." Savvy leaned over him to kiss his cheek. "I'm going to check in on you to see how the doctor's appointment goes, okay?"

"Okay, Baby Girl. Don't you work too hard this week."

Savvy grinned at him over her shoulder as she walked toward the door. "If only!"

"What do you think about this color?" Spencer held out a small square of marble stone.

In the drafty warehouse, Savvy squeezed past giant slabs of wood, marble, granite, soapstone, and quartz to follow Spencer. She'd told Maggie and Joanie she wasn't ready to jump into anything with him, but his snug T-shirt and the fit of his jeans left her questioning her own judgment.

"Oh, that's pretty." Holding out her hand, Spencer placed the heavy square in her palm. The warmth of his hand emanated from the smooth marble, and she wondered whether his hands were rough with callouses. "It's a little too brown for me, though."

He puckered his lips, nodding. "Okay." He pulled another piece from a bin. "This one?"

She scrunched her nose at the gray stone marbled with blue swirls. "Far too busy for me. I like clean."

Spencer leaned against a bookcase filled with inventory binders and descriptions of different materials, watching her run her fingers over the edge of a Carrara marble slab. Speckled gray veins streaked through the white rock. "Do you like that?"

Savvy tilted her head, studying it. "I do…" She wondered if he asked that in more intimate settings. *Get your head out of the gutter, girl. This man is trying to do business.*

"Let's try this another way." The corners of his mouth curved into a smile. Standing up straight, he closed the space between them in two strides. "I want you to think about your dream kitchen. No budget, no unattainable items, just dream. What does that kitchen look like?"

She closed her eyes, but her thoughts were obscured by the image of his face nearing hers. He was close enough for her to smell his cologne, cedar and citrus, filling her nostrils. *Pull it together, Savvy.* "Hmmm. I'm sorry, I can smell your cologne. It's distracting me." She opened her eyes and caught him watching her intently. *You are distracting me.*

Spencer's eyes blinked wide. "My bad. I'll fall back."

"No, it's okay. It's nice cologne. I just—" Her voice trailed off as he licked his lips, the smile returning to his face. Shielding her eyes with her hand, she turned away. "I'm just going to look over here, okay?"

His voice was so close to her ear that she jumped at the sound. "You don't really have to do that, do you?"

"Um…" Strong hands wrapped around the fleshy part of her arms, pulling her back in Spencer's direction. She laughed nervously, wondering whether he noticed the softness of her frame. Whether he was repulsed by it the way Jason apparently was. "You think this is funny, don't you?"

"It's cute." He grinned. "I didn't think you were shy."

"I'm not!" She blushed. *Did he just call me cute?* "I don't know what's wrong with me today."

His brow furrowed. "Is there something wrong?"

"No! I just…this is a business outing. I need to be more professional."

"I don't know, I thought maybe we were having a moment." Spencer's eyes bore into Savvy's, and she wanted nothing more than to stand on tiptoe and kiss him. As if he heard her thoughts, he leaned forward to her eye level. "I think you did too."

Holy shit, he's serious. Was Joanie right all along? Her mouth dropped open slightly, and his eyes fixated on her bottom lip. "I—um… Okay, maybe there was a moment." She took a step back. "I'm just not sure I'm ready to explore that just yet."

Spencer's back straightened. "Too soon?" he asked gently. She grimaced. "I think so?"

"That's okay. I'm a patient man, and I'm not going anywhere anytime soon." He led her toward several slabs of quartz. "Back to our original exercise! Dream kitchen—what does yours look like?"

Savvy eyed the quartz arrayed before her. The speckled, white slab stood out. Touching the cool stone, she murmured, "I've always wanted an all-white kitchen." She closed her eyes to visualize it and was surprised to find she knew exactly what she really wanted. "Herringbone design in the backsplash, brushed nickel fixtures, shaker style cabinets."

"Go on," he encouraged.

"Lots of counter space for food prep. A big island. Wine fridge. Slate tile flooring. Six-burner stove top and double ovens."

"That sounds beautiful. Here, there's more white quartz this way." He led her farther into the store.

"Ooo, yes, this one." Savvy gestured to a speckled white slab. "I love this."

Spencer nodded. "Now we're getting somewhere."

Savvy smiled. They really were. But then she remembered the stacks of files at home waiting for her, the looming deadlines. "I'm so excited, but is it okay if we get going? I have to get back to work."

"You sure work a lot."

"Yeah, I get that a lot," she joked. "I'm being considered for a promotion, so I'm trying to show my boss that there isn't a better candidate than me."

"I see you. Alright, well, thank you for joining me on this little date."

"Date?" She laughed. "Boy, you play too much."

"Alright, fine. We haven't been on a date. Yet."

Avoiding his eyes, Savvy grabbed his arm where he'd touched hers earlier and led him out of the warehouse. "You know you're being fresh, right?"

He chuckled, folding his hands behind his back as he licked his lips. "Yes, Ms. Sheldon."

11

Over the course of the next week, Savvy logged three hours of yoga, four hours of tennis, and a two-hour hike. Joanie came to both tennis sessions, and Beth took the opportunity to pit them against each other. Their competitive spirits ignited, as Joanie tried to impress Beth. The level of trash talking was in such rare form that Maggie came on Saturday to observe the second session.

After ninety minutes of grueling drills, serves, and rallying, Joanie and Savvy stretched out on the ground while Mags sat on the bench teasing them. Maggie had come straight from work and had grabbed a giant bacon-wrapped hot dog from one of the street carts outside the complex. The smell of bacon and caramelized onions carried in the breeze, regularly tempting everyone on the courts.

Maggie had given up on the whole clean eating thing in favor of moderation about a week in. With it being her busy season as a tax attorney, she didn't want to feel so constrained when she didn't have time to meal prep. Beth gave her a side-eye for bringing snacks, but Mags couldn't care less. She took a big bite. "Savs, I can't believe you hit Kotter in the face. I think she's going to have a shiner," she said, her cheeks full of food.

"Well, if Kotter was paying attention, rather than flirting with Beth, she wouldn't have gotten hit in the face." Savvy grinned, leaning forward to stretch out her hamstrings.

Maggie giggled, watching color rush up Joanie's neck and brighten her cheeks. "I don't know what you're talking about," she muttered.

"Ah!" Mags cackled. "There is absolutely no way that statement is true. She started to take off her track jacket, and you took one to the face." Maggie struggled through a mouthful of hot dog. She took a big gulp of Gatorade. "You were hoping she was going to continue removing her clothes."

Joanie rolled her eyes. "Well, weren't you? I mean, have you seen that woman?"

"Uh, ladies? You know that I'm still here, right?" Beth was standing directly behind the benches. "I just went to take a call."

Maggie's eyes widened as she took another bite. Savvy shook her head slowly, switching legs and leaning forward toward her shin.

Joanie blew out a deep breath, hands on her hips. "Yeah, that was… I don't even know what that was. Just girl talk, you know?"

Beth smiled, coming around to the front of the bench where Maggie sat. Mags scooted over so that she could sit down. She reached toward Joanie to hand her a bag of ice. "I do. I thought you might need this."

Kotter's face was beet red. "Ehm, thanks." She placed the

ice pack on her left cheekbone, where the start of a bruise was beginning to show. The ice helped Joanie avoid looking directly at Beth.

Beth leaned back to rest her elbows along the back of the bench. "So," she started slowly, a sly smile creeping across her face. "You were picturing me without my clothes? That's why you lost your focus?" She tilted her head, eyeing Joanie playfully.

"I mean, I'm not a creep, if that's what you're thinking. Maggie is just exaggerating." She waved a hand at Mags, dismissing what she'd said.

"So then you didn't want me to take off my clothes?" Her eyebrow rose.

In the midst of a butterfly stretch, Savvy watched Beth and Joanie volley. Her face read somewhere between sweaty exhaustion and complete amusement. Beth had the upper hand at the moment, but her girl never failed to rally for a comeback.

Joanie fumbled over her words for a second, running her fingers over her damp hair. She lowered her ice pack, half smiled, and gave Beth a slow shrug. "You're grown. If you want to be out of your clothes, who am I to stop you?"

Maggie looked at her, her eyes wide, snapping hard a few times to show her respect. Savvy gave Joanie a slow nod of approval, reaching out an arm to bump fists with her. "That's my girl," Savvy said proudly.

Beth's smile widened, and she bit her lip. She looked up to whatever challenge Joanie threw down. "I see."

Savvy got up to check her phone, giving Mags a high five in the process. Mags made room for her on the bench, and Savvy scrolled through her phone for notifications. The heat was turning up between Joanie and Beth, and Savvy wanted to give them a minute to gather themselves.

"Have you talked to anyone interesting on Tinder this week?" Mags asked.

Savvy made a face that expressed her lack of enthusiasm, but Beth was first to speak. "You've gotten yourself on Tinder already?"

"You sound surprised."

"I didn't think you'd be ready to put yourself out there just yet. Seemed like you took that breakup pretty hard." She held zero judgment in her tone.

"I'm not actually sure that I'm ready to be on Tinder either," Savvy admitted. "My girls here seem to think that meeting other people will help give me some perspective on what I really want."

"Any luck yet?"

Savvy shrugged. "I was with Jason for so long, I'm not sure that I know how to be without him. I'm not even sure I know who I am without him."

Beth pondered that for a moment. "Well then, I think your friends nudged you in the right direction."

Her brow furrowed in confusion. "You do?"

"Yeah. If you're not sure who you are, these dating apps are great for helping you figure out your preferences. You'll talk to all kinds. Some may be a little awkward or maybe they'll misjudge boundaries, but if nothing else, you'll at least learn some of the things that you count as red flags."

Savvy's slight frown turned to a full scowl. "So it's good to meet a bunch of guys that I don't want?"

"Exactly." Standing, she clapped her on the back. "Don't take it too seriously." She turned to Joanie. "Can I talk to you for a minute?"

Savvy and Mags catcalled after Kotter obnoxiously as she followed Beth toward the other side of the courts and turned to give them a death stare and crossing her index finger over

her throat. Cackling, they blew kisses and made other ob-
scene gestures until Kotter turned her attention back to Beth.

Maggie snatched her phone. "I want to pick a few guys for
you." She opened the Tinder app and began swiping away.

Her level of excitement was concerning. "Please don't
choose anyone weird. I don't have the energy for something
that we both know I would consider a red flag."

"Whoa." Maggie brought her phone closer to her face to
confirm whatever she thought she saw.

"What is it?" Savvy eyed her cautiously, worried some
weirdo had popped up on the screen.

"It's not what, it's who." Stunned, she looked up at Savvy.

"Well, who is it?"

"It's Spencer," Maggie said.

"Oh." Savvy reached for her phone to check out his profile, and there he was, smiling up at her.

"You realize that you just made a little sound, right?"
Mags grinned at her. "I mean, I would have that sort of reaction too. That man is gorgeous."

Savvy giggled. "Well, I can't swipe right, the man is in
my house right now. We talked about this!"

"Now that is a little awkward, I admit, but this renovation will be done before you know it. I say lock Spencer
down before he gets away."

"God, yes," Joanie chimed in, returning to the benches.

"Who is Spencer? Would I approve?" Beth asked, trailing behind her.

Joanie smiled at Beth. She won big points. "It's like you've
already adopted Savvy into your family," she observed.
"That's cute."

Beth shot a look at Joanie. "It's more like Savvy will be
adopting me into her family once you finally agree to go
out with me."

Maggie's mouth formed a perfect O as she turned to look up at the sky, fanning herself. Savvy tittered like a schoolgirl.

Joanie turned bright red, stammering, "I—I thought we talked about this over there."

"We did. I want a definitive answer." Beth waited.

Maggie raised a finger. "Excuse me," she said. She looked at Beth and then used her hand to create a barrier, like her hand blocked the sound of her voice. "Kotter, what exactly is there to think about?"

Joanie looked mortified. "Seriously," she whispered. "She can hear you!"

"Uh, Kotter?" Savvy piped up. "You know, she can hear you too."

Joanie turned to her. "Savs, help me out here!" She threw up her hands.

"Now, I don't mean to objectify you at this moment, okay?" Beth nodded as Savvy gestured in her direction. "Joanie, do you see this woman? I mean, look at her."

Joanie rolled her eyes. "Looks aren't everything," she muttered.

"Looks aren't everything, but they're not nothing. You're fighting a battle that no one should fight," Maggie reasoned. "She's hot, has a great job, stays active, seems like she has a good head on her shoulders, and she has the approval of your two best friends. Let her take you to dinner."

Savvy made a face and started packing up her rackets. "Well, kids, this has been fun, but I want a poached pear salad with salmon." She stretched her arms behind her back. "Even my food cravings are getting healthier."

Maggie scrunched up her face. "Seriously. Who craves salad?"

"Do you know how hard it is to play tennis while Maggie is shoving down hot dogs? One of those would kill my goals for the day." Joanie glared at her friend.

"Oh, are you eating clean with Savvy?" Beth asked. "It's good that you are supporting each other."

Savvy nodded. "I don't know if I could hold myself as accountable without Kotter being there with me. As you can see, Maggie already fell off the wagon."

Maggie flipped her off. "Listen, I didn't have lunch, and I came straight from work. You wouldn't want me here hangry."

Savvy pictured Mags breaking tennis rackets in half. "True."

"You're doing great work, Savs," Beth chimed in.

"Thanks, but it would be really great if I could just wake up and be some fit sex goddess." All three women raised their eyebrows in unison. "I mean, I can put it down in the bedroom, so really I guess I just want to wake up and be fit," Savvy clarified.

"That sounds completely reasonable." Maggie held a deadpan expression and nodded. "That's like doing one squats workout and then wondering why your ass didn't transform."

"Well, either way, you are making huge progress toward your goals," Beth assured her. "You can do this."

"Are you increasing the number of sessions you're doing?" Maggie asked, shoving the last of her hot dog into her mouth. She struggled to chew while speaking. "I would think that you couldn't take on too much with your work being so busy all the time."

Beth grimaced at their friend's eating habits, while Joanie and Savvy fell out laughing. "You'll get used to it."

She ran her hand over her hair and laughed. "I don't know that I will."

Savvy groaned. "Savs. Hungry. Must. Have. Salad."

Mags looked between Joanie and Beth. "Will you two just agree to a date, already?"

Beth smiled and looked at Joan expectantly. "Well?"

Joan threw up her hands. "Fine. But don't think that now you can always wear me down."

Savvy clapped Beth on the back. "Beth'll be on her best behavior, Kotter. Otherwise, I'll tie her up and aim the ball machine at her ovaries." Joanie clapped a hand over her mouth, while Maggie winced in reaction to Beth's fate. "Don't try me, Beth. You don't want these problems."

Beth looked at her solemnly. "Message received, Savs."

Winking at her, Savvy headed toward the car. "Glad we've reached an understanding. See you Tuesday."

12

After poached pear salads, Kotter agreed to meet Savvy the next morning for a Sunday yoga session. Fueled by subtle changes in her endurance and friends agreeing to go with her, Savvy had begun to crave the next workout. The Sunday morning air blew warm and breezy as she strolled into the yoga studio.

"Good morning, Savvy, I'm so glad that you could make it today!" Charlotte exclaimed, welcoming her with a big hug.

"Girl, I made it!" Kotter bounced in after her, all smiles.

"Well, hello, lady," Savvy murmured. "I am so ready for this class!" She turned to Kotter as she began putting her jacket and shoes into a cubby. "Work has been kicking my ass. Every time I turn around, we're approaching another big deadline."

"Does your boss know how hard you've been working?"

Savvy grinned. "I let him know every chance I get. He actually thanked me in our most recent staff meeting."

Joanie's eyebrows rose. "That promotion is coming, girl!"

"What a surprise! I didn't expect to see you ladies in here today." Beth sauntered up with a big grin on her face.

Savvy's mouth dropped open in surprise, sensing that Joanie was equally stunned. Now in a cropped tank top and Capri-style yoga pants, she crossed her arms and sputtered. "What are you doing here?"

Beth smiled and then feigned confusion. "Wait, you didn't invite me to join y'all?"

"You told her we were coming here?" Savvy asked warily. "I'm already self-conscious in these classes. The last thing I need in here is my trainer."

Beth wrapped her arm around Savvy's shoulders. "Come on, Savs. I promise I won't disrupt your class." She and Joanie eyed each other for a few seconds, and she began unzipping her track jacket. Joanie blinked and turned away, attempting to pull her hair back into a tight bun. Beth removed her shoes and socks, putting them into a cubicle with her track jacket. Her arms, shoulders, and back were covered in tattoos. Her right arm held the silhouette of a woman whose gown stretched into the body of a rattlesnake, which wound its tail around her forearm. The detailed head of a dragon stretched from her left shoulder across her back. She wore a pair of yoga shorts, a sports bra, ink, and a smile.

Savvy turned to sneak a glimpse of Joanie, who had yet to blink. She licked her lips slowly before sensing Savvy's gaze. Once they locked eyes, hers widened to relay her reaction to everything that they had seen. Savvy turned to Charlotte, who offered the same wowed glance. Savvy shook her head in amusement, grabbing her water bottle to fill at the hydration station.

As they traipsed toward the studio door, Beth sidled up next to Joanie. The heat and humidity in the room imme-

diately calmed them as they walked in, and Joanie moved
forward to claim her favorite space in the room at the far
end, in front of the mirror, right next to the brightly lit windows. Beth chose a spot behind her, undoubtedly to keep
Joanie in her sights.

Savvy picked a spot in the center of the back row, facing
Charlotte. They laid out their mats and yoga towels. She
sat down cross-legged and closed her eyes. Others filed into
the room, claiming spaces all around. Everyone took deep
breaths to prepare themselves mentally for the next ninety
minutes. A bell chimed, and Charlotte turned on the lights
as she entered.

"Good morning, Los Feliz! I'm so glad that you chose
to come to class on this beautiful Sunday. Welcome to our
newcomers, Sydney and Rachel. Know that every class is a
beginner's class. Everyone is working on something new, and
all I ask is that you listen to your body. If you need to take
a seat for a moment, that's perfectly fine, just please stay in
the room to receive all of the benefits of the class. Today, we
will cover twenty-six postures and two breathing exercises.

"Now, let's get started. First is the breathing exercise,
Pranayama Breathing, deep breathing. Place your feet together nicely, toes and heels touching each other, all ten fingers interlocked under the chin, your hands tucked tightly
under your chin, always touching..."

Charlotte led them through ninety minutes of poses,
pushing them to go back, fall back, way back. Savvy kept
her eyes forward, staring hard at her own reflection, but
her eyes wandered to people in the front row; their years
of practice demonstrated in the surety of their forms. She
tried not to compare herself, knowing that her own practice had barely begun.

As if reading Savvy's mind, Charlotte appeared at her side

and whispered, "Be patient with yourself, Savvy. You're doing great."

Reassured, she settled back into her pose. As they moved into the postures on the floor, she savored the changes from poses into Savasana, where they lay on their backs, their arms at their sides, palms facing up. They each focused on a spot above them on the ceiling, completely aware of their own bodies, controlling their breath.

Class ended with a final, longer Savasana. As they lay on their backs, Charlotte spoke softly. "Now take a moment to honor yourselves and this step forward in your practice. Let go of what didn't work, where you struggled, where you weren't perfect. Honor yourself, thank yourself, accept yourself where you are right now." That last line struck a chord deep inside, and Savvy's eyes welled with tears.

"You could have stayed home today, but instead, you came to yoga this morning, you put in the work, and you worked *hard*. Forgive yourself for whatever you believe went wrong. Accept yourself in this moment. Be generous to yourself today."

Tears fell freely from the corners of Savvy's eyes. Joanie had told her that there were moments where emotions boiled over in class, but she hadn't expected this. Charlotte's words echoed in her mind. *Accept yourself in this moment.*

As she lay on her back with her hands and feet splayed out, she basked in a wave of calm, pleased with her practice. She got up quietly, grabbed her stuff, and made her way into the lobby. Charlotte handed out chilled towels scented with lavender and eucalyptus oils. Savvy gave her a sweaty hug and wrapped the cold towel around her neck. Plopping down on a bench, she leaned back against the wall enjoying the cool air, letting the essential oils permeate her senses.

Joanie and Beth filed out of the studio. Everyone held

relaxed, blissful expressions on their faces. Beth sat next to her, holding the cold towel against her face before wrapping it around her neck. "That was a great class," she observed.

Savvy nodded, too tired to speak. Joanie gave her a lethargic high five. Charlotte came over, all smiles. "You guys are rock stars! Savvy, was that your third class this week?"

"It was." She smiled, slow to find her voice. "This is the most I've worked out since high school, I think."

Beth eyed her. "How do you feel?"

"A little tired, but actually really good." She looked at Joanie. "I definitely earned brunch this week. Charlotte, thank you so much—class was amazing."

Her friends echoed similar sentiments, and they all began to grab their shoes and jackets. They waved to Charlotte, thanking her again, and they headed outside. The day grew warmer, the sun bright overhead. Savvy turned to Beth. "Did you have plans?"

"Why, are you actually inviting me to brunch with y'all?" Beth's smile held a mixture of surprise and mischief.

Savvy made quick eye contact with Joanie, who blinked once to show her approval. "Yeah, you earned it today. We all did."

"Now, just because you've been invited, don't get all judgy on the food choices, Miss Trainer," Kotter warned. "When ladies brunch, they may have salad, or they may have cream cheese–stuffed french toast with six mimosas. Either way, you're going to let it happen."

Beth chuckled. "Do I give off the vibe that I don't appreciate a woman who can eat? I love a woman with a good appetite." She eyed Joanie playfully. "Where are we eating?"

"Ever been to Harry's in Los Feliz? It's one of our favorite spots," Joanie said. "Their red velvet pancakes are my favorite."

"I haven't been there, but that sounds great. Do they have chicken and waffles?"

"And then some." Savvy headed toward the parking lot.

"I'm in. Can you text me the address?" she called to her.

"I'm sure that Kotter can handle that. She gave you our location for this morning, after all." Savvy threw up a peace sign.

"Very funny." Joanie flipped her off. Savvy grinned at her as Joanie pulled out her phone to text Beth.

"See y'all there. I'll call Brenda to get our name on the list." They waved at her, and Savvy climbed into her car.

The drive over took less than ten minutes. As Savvy walked in, she gave a hug to Brenda, the lead hostess for their Sunday brunch. They'd been regulars here for years. "Hey, girl! How have you been?"

"No complaints. How are you, Savvy? You look amazing!"

Savvy blushed. "Thank you. We just finished a yoga class, and we are starving."

"Well, it looks good on you, girl." She nodded her approval. "We'll have a table on the patio ready by the time the rest of the gang gets here. Just give me a nod once they've arrived."

"Thanks, girl, I appreciate you!" Savvy stepped aside so Brenda could attend to a couple who walked in behind her. Her smile froze when she realized that she knew half of the pair. Jason. *I really regret introducing him to all of my favorite restaurants.*

Jason didn't recognize Savvy until she turned around. He had been laughing away with a girl on his arm. She was a pretty Latina with hazel eyes and a colorful sundress. Savvy felt exposed in her tank top and yoga pants. She'd let her hair down on the drive over, but it was still damp from class.

"Savvy?" Jason asked.

She offered a quick wave and a tight smile, crossing her arms over her chest. "Hi, Jason. How are you?" she blurted out.

"I'm great. This is Chloe." He gestured to his date, wrapping his arm around her waist confidently as she stepped forward to shake Savvy's hand.

"Hi, it's nice to meet you." She smiled.

The corners of Savvy's lips turned upward slightly, as she silently thanked the universe for the calming aftereffects of yoga. *Woosah, bitch, woosah.* "You as well."

"We made it!" Joanie exclaimed, as she strolled in with Beth. "Hey, Brenda, how are you? We just need one more seat for Mags, she's parking now—" Joanie's voice trailed off when she laid eyes on Jason. The smile on her face morphed into a grimace.

Jason grew increasingly antsy, shifting his weight from one foot to another. Though he knew that Joanie was unlikely to make a scene, hearing that Maggie would be walking in at any moment seemed to unnerve him.

"Hey! Wow, you are brave to join them!" Maggie exclaimed as she sashayed in wearing a tank dress that hugged every curve of her body, giving Beth a big hug. "Brenda, how are you? Wait, what the—" Her eyes rested on Jason, who looked down to his feet quickly. *No, you're not invisible.*

Joanie was on Savvy's left, and Mags stepped forward to flank her other side. Beth stood behind them quietly, ready for anything. "Jason," Maggie acknowledged slowly.

"Hey, Maggie, how's it going?" Jason asked uncomfortably, still looking at the floor.

Maggie, on the other hand, stepped closer, forcing him to look her in the eye. "You tell me. Who's your friend?"

Chloe took a step back, observing the tense expressions of four strangers. "Jason?"

"This is Chloe." Jason gestured.

"Uh-huh. Why is it that we see you with another woman every time we run into you?" Maggie stood tall, hands perching on either hip. Chloe turned to look up at him.

Jason ran his hand over his fade and rubbed the back of his neck. "Ah…"

"Savvy? Your table's ready," Brenda cut in. She'd had the busboys rush the turnover of the table on the patio the moment she saw Jason.

Savvy smiled at her weakly, and Brenda started to lead the way to the table, placing an arm around her waist. Beth stepped toward them, pausing because Joanie and Mags stayed behind. Maggie looked at Jason contemptuously, completely ignoring Chloe. "You never deserved her."

Savvy turned, hearing Maggie's voice.

Jason scoffed. "Okay, Maggie. If you say so." He laughed to himself, as if things couldn't be further from the truth. Joanie was beside herself with rage.

Beth inched closer to her friends, as Joanie stepped forward, inches away from Jason's face. "What's funny, Jay? Let me tell you something that you've missed all of these years. Savvy is everything. She is beautiful, and she has so much more to offer than any trophy you could ever hope to find. You're going to recognize that one day. This is your loss."

Joanie turned toward Beth, who put her arm around her shoulder in support. As Maggie turned to follow, she gave one last sideways glance in Jason's direction. "Asshole." Turning to Chloe, Mags offered a warning look. "I hope you know what you're doing, Sis."

Brenda kept Savvy company, leading her to the table. Savvy tried to fight off the tears threatening to fall, but a few escaped, and she brushed them away quickly with her fingertips. She refused to let him take away everything she'd gained since he walked out on her. Brenda placed a hand on her shoulder. "I know it's hard to imagine now, but it's all going to work out, Savvy. You deserve so much better."

Savvy nodded, feigning a smile. "Thank you so much, Brenda. I really appreciate that."

As her friends sat, Savvy ran her fingers through her hair and put her sunglasses back on. Beth and Joanie sat across from her, and Maggie sat by her side, putting her arm around her shoulders. "Are you okay, Savvy?"

"I will be."

Maggie turned to her, grabbing her hand. "You will be."

13

On Monday, Savvy attended a morning staff meeting, where they discussed upcoming deadlines and client updates. Her boss, Warren, shared that senior management planned to pay close attention to performance, given some upcoming staff changes. Returning to her office, Savvy surveyed her workload, eager to show Warren that she could handle greater responsibility. All of the hard work she'd put into her workouts gave her more energy to throw into her work during the day, and people were noticing all the gaps she filled to help the team meet their goals.

Staying at Joanie's place for the past week had been an easy transition—they worked the same hours and often met after work to work out or grab dinner. Joanie was not into cooking and never bothered to invest in quality cooking supplies. Savvy hadn't seen Spencer since they went to look at slabs for the kitchen counter, but he'd texted her regular updates. Demolition was finished, and he was in the process of having all of the materials cleared to make way for the new flooring. Savvy pictured Spencer wielding a sledgehammer and shivered at the thought. *Why does he have to be so fine?*

She exhaled deeply, leaning over a mug of fresh coffee. Lina appeared in her doorway, a grimace on her face. "Savvy, I hate to ask, especially because you've already backed up three others on their deadlines, but Margot has a family emergency. She had to fly out of town today to get home to her parents."

"Oh, wow, is everything okay?" Her thoughts immediately went to Margot's mother, who had been in remission for the last two years.

Lina shook her head slowly. "Her mom's cancer is back. Margot went home to be with her parents when they talk to the doctor about next steps. It doesn't look good."

Damn. Savvy shook her head. "That's terrible. I am more than happy to take on Margot's load while she's gone. I could use the distraction—I've been obsessing over potential renovation projects."

Lina cracked a relieved smile. "The other distractions you've taken on aren't enough? You're already our fastest underwriter, and now you're tackling yoga and tennis. You look great, by the way."

"Thank you." She blushed. Savvy wore a pair of cropped navy slacks with her favorite block-heeled sandals. Her sleeveless silk blouse was a mustard yellow with a white-and-green pattern. She hadn't felt good in something so formfitting in a long time. "I've been working out a lot, yes, but it's feeling really good. Plus, it's a welcome distraction from the wreck that is my love life. So what does Margot have on her plate? Big deadline this week?"

"Three, actually." Lina half grimaced, half smiled. "She had fallen behind on a deadline that is due tomorrow by

COB, she has a deadline on Friday, and then next week she has her quarter close."

"You think she'll still be out next week?" Savvy stretched her arms above her head, clasping her hands and turning her palms outward to stretch her shoulders.

"I anticipate her being out this week for sure. Her family is all the way in Philadelphia, and I know she'll want to get her mom squared away before she returns." Lina looked at Savvy hopefully.

She nodded. "So we'll meet her first two deadlines, and get through what we can of the close so that she isn't inundated when she gets back? That seems reasonable." Taking a sip of her coffee, Savvy rolled her head from shoulder to shoulder.

Lina gave her a look that let her know she wasn't quite finished. "Well, there's one more thing."

Savvy groaned. "I am sensing impending doom, Lina."

"We received a priority request on a subset of your client's files. They've got a special going for new enrollees, which they failed to communicate to us until yesterday. They need applications with this rate processed by COB on Wednesday." Lina bit her lip, likely hoping Savvy wouldn't have a complete meltdown.

She waited a beat, knowing that several of the other underwriters were slower to process applications and threw complete fits when Lina had to communicate priority messages from the insurance carriers they administered policies for. They unfairly projected their frustrations onto Lina. "Shit," she breathed.

Lina's eyebrows rose. "That's it? You took that better than I anticipated."

Savvy laughed. "It's either the yoga, or I'm still in shock. Okay, so we have deadlines tomorrow, Wednesday, and Friday. Then we have to get Margot a cushion for her quarter close." She clicked her tongue as she thought through her game plan. "I'm assuming that you have all of these piles ready for me already?"

Lina nodded and ducked out of her door, wheeling in three double-decker file carts one by one. Two carts were completely full on both levels, while the third had files only on the top. Lina crossed her arms, expecting the worst.

Letting out a low whistle, Savvy pushed back in her chair to get up onto her feet. "Okay, so let's see what we've got here. What's what?"

Always one step ahead, Lina pointed her to a Post-it that she stuck to files to let her know where one deadline ended and another began. "This top row of yellow files is Margot's late batch, which have to be done by the close of business tomorrow. Below them, I put your red special client files that they need by COB on Wednesday. This entire cart—" she gestured to the second cart, which was filled on both levels with blue files "—are Margot's Friday deadline. The last cart of orange files will close out Margot for the quarter."

"Oh, my," Savvy murmured. "Do I have a quarter close next week too?"

Lina shook her head. "Yours is the following week. I try to stagger you guys to avoid major overlap. Your accounts shouldn't be heavier than usual next week, so it's really the three deadlines this week that will be the challenge. The files that you have in here already—" she pointed to the green files on her desk and in the bins on her conference table "—aren't due until your closeout, so you can see how ahead you are. If you wanted to get past Margot's Friday deadline and then alternate between your closeout and hers, I think that would be most efficient for you."

"That makes sense. I'm guessing the rest of the team is behind?"

Lina nodded. "Ed and Neil are both supposed to meet closeout deadlines this Friday, but they're each about a week behind. Madison has the same deadline as you, but she's out right now with the flu. Once she gets back to the office, she has a mountain of files to get through. Tessa was on schedule to close out next week, but she has two special deadlines that popped up for her this week, so she's behind now too."

"I can see why you asked me."

Lina tilted her head. "Well, you're the only one ahead, and if I'm being honest, you're the only one who could get this kind of volume done in a week. No one on the team gets through more product than you."

Savvy grinned at Lina. "Does Warren know that?" she asked playfully.

Lina nodded with a smile. "I tell him every chance I get."

Savvy exhaled deeply, mentally planning out her week. "Okay, so here's the game plan. I'll get through tomorrow's deadline before I leave for the day. Do me a favor and call Joanie, ask her if we can push dinner back an hour. She'll say yes." Lina nodded. "I'll try to complete my Wednesday deadline tomorrow from home. Wednesday morning, we'll get started on the Friday deadline."

Lina's face lit up with a relieved smile. "You got it, Savvy. You're a lifesaver."

Savvy grabbed the files occupying her desk and moved them onto her conference table, creating space for Margot's yellow files. "I want to help where I can. Margot needs it right now, and I know she would do it for me."

"She would. I'll let you know once I've confirmed your dinner plans with Joan."

"Thanks, Lina."

"No, thank you." Lina hurried out and closed her door behind her.

Opening the bottom drawer of her desk and grabbing a hair tie out of her purse, Savvy tied her hair into a pony-tail. She chugged her remaining coffee and walked toward the break room for a fresh cup.

"Hey, Savvy, I heard you are the office saint yet again," Ed teased, leaning against the counter.

"That might be a bit of an exaggeration, Ed." Savvy set the Keurig machine to brew a fresh cup of French roast coffee, then grabbed cinnamon-flavored creamer from the refrigerator and a couple of sweetener packets.

Ed watched her, his beady brown eyes tracking every movement as he sipped his coffee. Savvy poured creamer and put her filled mug into the microwave, then turned to put the creamer back in the refrigerator, preparing herself for whatever annoying comment Ed was fixing his mouth to say next.

"Ed, you're lurking again. We talked about this." Warren strode into the room, a half smile on his face. A handsome, fortysomething-year-old family man, he moved with confidence and a good sense of humor. Savvy told her girls that he was the "smooth brother that half of the women in the office would sleep with if he weren't happily married." She loved seeing a Black man on the senior team—he was a big proponent of recruiting a diverse staff for the company.

Warren nodded at her and spun the office K-Cup carousel around, grabbing a butter pecan–flavored coffee cup.

"Oh, sorry, boss. I was just telling Savannah that she is the office saint again." Ed gave her a thin-lipped, leering smile. "I am starting to think that she is trying to make the rest of us look bad."

Warren turned his back to the coffee machine. He leaned against the counter and crossed his arms, giving Ed a hard look. "Do you want to know what makes the difference between trying and achieving, Ed?"

Under the boss's gaze, Ed stood up straight, his expression serious. "What's that, sir?"

"Continued effort. Savannah isn't trying to be anything but good at her job and considerate of her colleagues," Warren said sternly. "How about you try to achieve your close-out deadline. If we have to ask Savvy to get you caught up yet again—" his tone sharpened "—you won't be here to thank her when she's finished."

Ed's face reddened, and he turned on his heel. "Yes, sir. I'll work through the night if I have to—"

Warren interjected coolly, "Yes, you will." His stare made Savvy nervous for Ed.

"Thank you, sir." Ed waved quickly and power walked back to his office.

Warren turned to her as she grabbed her coffee out of the microwave, holding the mug carefully. "Sorry about that, Savvy."

"Oh, it's fine, boss. I'm happy to help, especially given the circumstances." Savvy smiled at him. "Thank you for asking Ed not to lurk. It gets a little creepy sometimes."

"We need to know when the creep flag flies, Savvy. We can't address it if we don't know."

"I understand. Honestly, being called the 'office saint' bothers me more than his staring. I appreciate that he knows I help out the team, but I don't do it to kiss ass. Excuse my French."

Warren waved away her last statement. "Don't worry about it. Listen, you have been dependable for some really tight deadlines, many of which weren't yours, and you saved us from having to pay penalty fees to our clients. It's become too regular an occurrence to go unnoticed."

Savvy smiled. "Thank you, sir, it means a lot to have my work recognized."

Warren looked at her dubiously. "Savvy, your output is almost double that of anyone else on your team. We have been wanting to recognize you more formally for quite a while, but you were also one of our newest additions. We needed you to get a little bit more time under your belt before they could recognize you in the way that really makes the most sense."

Savvy frowned. "Thank you, but I'm not quite sure I know what you mean by that. How is it that you and the rest of senior management wanted to recognize me?"

Warren sipped his coffee, his dark eyes crinkling at the sides, and her blood pressure spiked as her anxiety got the better of her. "I really should have scheduled a meeting with you, but I know you're pressed for time, so I'll just tell you now and follow up formally in writing. We're promoting you to senior underwriter, Savannah. You've certainly earned it—twice over at this point. You should be proud of yourself."

He looked around the room, closing the break room door. "As you may have heard, Sheila has decided to take early retirement to move with her daughter and grandchildren to South America. Her daughter accepted a job in Costa Rica, and Sheila is planning to help with the kids until her son-in-law can join them."

Savvy nodded, still in shock. "Yes, Sheila's retirement party is on Friday. She helped train me when I first started here. I know that she is so excited to be at home with her granddaughters." Thoughts flew through her mind. "Sir—"

"Come on, Savvy. Call me Warren, we are colleagues."

"Warren," Savvy started slowly. "I can't thank you enough for this opportunity. When do we talk through the workload and other details?"

He gestured to one of the break tables, and they sat opposite each other, still cradling their coffees. "I know that you have several big deadlines this week, so I won't keep you long, but let's talk through a few of the details now just so that you know what to expect." She nodded, and he continued, "You officially start as senior underwriter on Monday, and you will be moving into Sheila's office, since she's going to be out of there on Friday. Lina has expressed an interest in rotating with Rosie, Sheila's executive assistant, so that she could be assigned directly to you if you are open to that change."

"There's nothing to think about there—I would kill to have Lina as my executive assistant. What else?"

"The workload you'll have this week is likely going to become your regular workload. You can still do remote work when you need to meet your deadlines. You'll take on managing Sheila's team, which usually has four underwriters and two junior underwriters. She's been understaffed for the last couple of months, so you will have to fill those vacancies. You'll now be reporting directly to me, and you'll be expected to attend senior staff meetings. Obviously, your salary does increase given the added responsibility. You were already due for performance evaluation, and you received perfect marks from your team leads in addition to really positive notes submitted by several of the people you bailed out by helping them with their deadlines."

She hung on to each word. *Karma also came back around to reward the good.*

"Now, part of your salary increase is an incentive to keep your output at the level where you currently produce, but we also intend to bring you in on some strategy meetings where we assess levels of risk for specific products. We're going to reassign you to some of our bigger clients that Sheila handled, plus we have a new client coming on board that I am assigning to you. You'll have a big presentation to prepare soon."

Her eyes widened. "That sounds fantastic. I'm ready. Thank you so much, I can't believe that this is happening," she gushed.

Warren stood, raising his coffee mug in her honor. "Believe it, Savvy. If you keep doing work at this same level, you're going to be in executive management with me before you know it."

She nodded numbly. *Mama will be so proud.*

He reached out to shake her hand. "Congratulations! You'll knock it out of the park."

Savvy gave him a big smile. "Thank you, Warren. Should I wait until Monday to say anything?"

He considered her question for a moment. "Let me talk to Lina and Rosie first, so that Rosie isn't blindsided by the rotation. Once they're filled in, I'll send out a company-wide announcement, and it will be officially out there. After that, you'll be free to shout it from the rooftops."

They shared a laugh. "That sounds like a plan."

"You and I will have weekly meetings, so let's plan to sit down on Monday at 10:00 a.m. Does that work for you?"

"Yes, of course. I'll be there."

Warren extended his hand to her once more, and Savvy shook it, making sure to meet his eye and give him her full hand. *No wimpy handshakes.* "Welcome to the team, Savannah. We are lucky to have you."

Savvy took a deep breath and smiled. "Thank you, Warren, I won't let you down."

"I have full confidence in you. See you Monday." He waved quickly and left.

14

"You guys, I am so sorry I'm late!" Savvy rushed toward the kitchen island at Joanie's place, where she and Mags sat enjoying a cocktail and a cheese tray. Joanie wrapped her arms around Savvy, who reached across the table and swiped a sip of Maggie's cocktail. "Mmm, what is that?"

"It's got a smoked Hawaiian sea salt rim and yuzu juice with Kotter's tequila." Maggie grinned. "Isn't it good?"

Savvy nodded, picking up a cube of cheese. "It's delicious. Really fresh, but then the smokiness adds a little something extra. I am starving. Sorry to keep y'all waiting." She shoved the cheese into her mouth and reached for more.

"Wow, you're getting started right away! You can take your time, girl, it's not going anywhere. Let me make you a drink." Joanie smiled and then tilted her head, eyeing Savvy. "What's goin' on with you? Something's different."

"I have some news." She took another sip of Maggie's drink.

"Well, it looks like good news, girl," Kotter drawled. "What's with all of the suspense? Tell us!"

"Seriously," Maggie chimed in suspiciously. "What's up?"

Savvy grinned, reaching for more cheese, relishing in the anticipation. "I need my drink first." Savvy smoothed some Taleggio and raw honey over a Croccantini cracker, savoring a bite as the saltiness of the cheese and sweetness of the honey combined on her tongue.

Joanie grunted, rolling her eyes as she mixed together a lemony cocktail. "Spill."

Savvy pulled a reusable grocery bag onto the table, unloading ribeye steaks, red potatoes, butter, cream, a head of garlic, and fresh spinach. "Okay, fine. Well, I hope y'all are in the mood to celebrate, because Sister Savvy got the promotion today." She beamed, taking a sip of her drink, doing a little shimmy.

Joanie wrapped her arms around her, squeezing so tightly that Savvy almost spilled her drink. "Let me get these paws around you, girl! I'm so proud of you!"

Maggie reached across the table to grab one of her hands, a big smile spreading across her. "That's my girl!"

"Tell us more!" Joanie exclaimed.

"So I'll be moving into a corner office on Monday, I'll be managing my own team, I get a generous raise, can still work from home when I need to, and the best part is that I get to steal Lina from my current team to be my executive assistant on the new team."

The girls cheered. Savvy curtsied, turning from the island to start prepping the steaks by preheating the oven and grabbing a stainless steel pan.

Joanie raised her glass for a toast. "To Savvy. You've had a tough start this year, but it's all about how you finish."

"Yasss!" Maggie exclaimed, shouting her favorite quote. "You is smart, you is kind, you is important!"

Savvy's cheeks burned, eyes filling with moisture. Maggie and Joanie beamed with pride, whooping and hollering with their glasses raised. "To Savvy," Joanie continued. "Senior underwriter, true ride or die, and tennis extraordinaire."

"To Savvy," Maggie echoed. They clinked their glasses together, laughing as the tequila warmed their bellies.

Savvy's phone lit up with a notification from Tinder, so she opened the app to see who might catch her eye. Instead, the app opened to a face she knew; a face flanked by dimples she'd recognize anywhere.

"Whoa." She looked at Maggie. "You're not going to believe this."

Her brow furrowed. "What is it? This isn't going to kill our vibe, is it?"

She smiled, puzzled. "I actually have a feeling that you are all going to get a big kick out of this." She handed her phone over to Maggie first, whose mouth immediately formed a giant O.

"He messaged?!" Maggie looked up at her. "You're kidding, right? Joanie, look," she whispered. They turned to eye her once Joanie recognized a familiar face.

"Spencer messaged you?" Joanie chuckled. "Oh, this is too good. Is he asking you out? Did you swipe right on him, Savs?"

"Uhhh, it's not good. I've been too busy to even go on the app. So who swiped right on Spencer?"

Maggie's eyes widened as she took a massive gulp of her drink. "So…"

"Mags! Remember when I said I didn't want to consider him while he's working in my house? He's on his way over here to show me samples. How awkward is that?"

"It's only awkward if you go all catatonic once he gets here."

"I don't plan on mentioning it. We can just pretend like we didn't see his message yet."

"Yeah, no." Joanie pressed something on her phone, and instantly Savvy felt her heart begin to race.

"Hey, what are you doing? I hadn't decided what I was going to do there." She reached for her phone, but Joan kept it out of reach.

Mags rolled her eyes at her. "You wouldn't really ignore a message from Spencer, would you?"

She shrugged, knowing her cheeks were red, but she tried to downplay her trepidation anyway. "I still don't believe he's serious. Just because he swiped right in some app, does that mean I should automatically go for him?"

Maggie's hand dropped to the table. "Savvy, who are you kidding? Yes, he's good-looking, but he also has a good job, is clearly interested, and doesn't run when he's surrounded by your entire inner circle. He liked you before you went on this whole journey to change your look—you just didn't know it yet."

"Well, maybe I need more than that the next time around? Besides, I thought that this whole Tinder excursion was supposed to be casual and not about actually dating someone. Isn't this counter to what we've been talking about this whole time?"

"So what?" Maggie said. "No one is saying you have to marry the guy, but why not at least see what is there? Half of the guys you're seeing on here aren't all that appealing, and the ones that are still have to be vetted. With Spencer, you already know that you're both interested, he isn't a catfish, and he has some good things going on in his career. No, you don't know everything about him just yet, but that's the purpose of dating. Get a feel for the guy. If you aren't feeling him, then at least you know, and there's no hard feelings."

"But what if there are hard feelings?" she blurted out. "What if things don't work out and then I have to avoid my favorite coffee shop after that? I don't want to make things weird." Her body tensed up, shoulders kissing her earlobes.

Joanie watched. "What are you really worried about, Savs?"

"Okay, maybe I'm worried that he'll get to know me and then wish I was different." She shrugged. *Maybe.* "I don't think that I can handle that again."

Joanie held up a hand. "What Jason said and did to you was pure asshole behavior. He didn't know what he had. And, yes, there are other guys in LA that are like that. They're chasing a mirage, like most people in this city. Spencer isn't Jason, and if Jason ends up chasing some empty vessel, he's a fool."

"Seriously, girl." Maggie studied her face. "There's going to come a time when you realize exactly what you are worth. Jason traded in a lifetime investment for some magic beans."

"Facts," Joanie agreed. "There's literally nothing else to say. Just ride the wave."

Savvy cubed the red potatoes, tossing them into boiling water with whole cloves of garlic. As the olive oil reached its burning point and began to smoke in a cast-iron skillet, she set the first ribeye seasoned with kosher salt and fresh-cracked pepper seasoning-side down. Its sizzle was drowned out by the doorbell. Savvy grimaced as she added the second steak to the skillet.

Joanie raised a church finger. "I'll get it."

Savvy sipped her drink and began chopping the spinach, watching the steaks carefully so that she knew when to turn them.

"Hey, ladies. Wow, it smells good in here." Spencer waved at her, giving Maggie a hug. "Hey."

"Hey." Savvy nodded. "Hungry?"

"Who in their right mind would say no?" He cocked his head to one side. "Need any help?"

"Nah, but pull up a seat and let's go over the samples. I can multitask."

"Oh, we want to see!" Joanie sidled up to the kitchen island.

"Okay, here are some countertop samples. All quartz." He set four square samples on the island. "And these are glass subway tile options for the backsplash. All herringbone patterns, per your request, Savvy."

"Wow, these are all so pretty!" Mags gushed.

Savvy seasoned and flipped the steaks, tossing butter into the hot oil, along with a clove of garlic and a sprig of rosemary. Savvy quickly basted the steaks before setting the pan in the preheated oven. She moved another pan onto the burner in its place to start the creamed spinach. After peering over the samples on the island, Savvy turned back to her spinach. "Twenty bucks to the person who guesses which samples I want."

"Okay, okay!" Maggie clapped her hands. "I got this." She pulled the blue glass subway tile and a white quartz with flecks of gray.

"Hmmm… What would you choose, Kotter?" She tried to keep her best poker face.

Joan tapped her finger to her lips, as she scrutinized the samples. She pulled a clear glass subway tile and a white quartz with gray marbling. She looked over at Spencer. "What do you think?"

His hands planted on the counter, he leaned forward to look at all of the pieces. He picked a graphite blue glass subway tile and an all-white quartz with bright white flecks. He looked up at Kotter and winked. "So who wins?"

Savvy took a slow stroll around the island, eyeing each of their choices. The samples no one chose had brown undertones, and they were right to leave those alone. "Hmmm…"

"Did one of us get both samples right?" Kotter asked.

"Yep."

"Is it me?"

"Nope."

Maggie raised a fist in the air. "I won?!"

"Nope."

Spencer grinned.

Savvy pulled a twenty from her pocket, but he stopped her. "I'm already taking enough of your money. It's my job to understand your tastes."

"Mmm-hmm." Mags stepped between them. "Especially before your date."

"Mags."

"So you saw my message?" He watched her navigate the kitchen.

"I saw it," Savvy said casually, pulling the steaks from the oven.

"So what do you think? Would it be weird for you?" He leaned with his back against the island.

"Why would it be weird?" Joanie piped up.

Savvy gave Joanie a death glare, and she retreated, grabbing Mags by the arm. "We're going to go wash our hands."

"I don't think it's weird per se," she started, trying to choose her words carefully. "You saw it all go down, so you know I just recently got out of something. I'm not looking to rush into something else. Plus, if things don't work out, I don't want it to mess up our current business dealings."

He held out a hand to slow her. "Whoa, listen. It's just dinner. There's no rush, and we could wait until after the reno is done if it makes you feel better." He looked at her for a long moment.

Damn, he looks good tonight. It's just dinner. Savvy considered his offer, thinking of her friends' encouragement to get back on the scene and start figuring out what she wanted. *A girl's gotta eat…*

"Just dinner. We can try dinner," she said slowly, and Spencer's lips curved into a smile. Out of the corner of her eye, Savvy saw Joanie and Mags doing a happy dance. "You can come back now," she called.

"So where are y'all going for dinner?" Joanie didn't bother to hide her ear hustling.

"And when?" Mags chimed in.

"Savvy's choice. I trust her judgment." He winked at Savvy as Joanie handed him a drink.

Savvy turned back to the check on the steaks as a different kind of heat began to build in her chest. She didn't want the meal to be about the two of them going out, even though she racked her brain to decide on a location for dinner. "Mags, are you joining our next tennis session?"

Maggie's shoulders slumped. "It did look fun, but I don't want to sweat out my hair. Maybe once I get braids."

Savvy turned back to eye her friend. "Nice try, but you run four miles three times a week. You only sweat out your hair in yoga."

Maggie shot her a look. "Right…"

"Come on, Mags," Joanie pleaded. "It would be the three of us playing tennis together. Plus, you are the most competitive person at this table. You know you would feel some type of way if we said that you opted not to come because you thought you might lose."

"Shots. Fired." Savvy laughed. She set out creamed spinach, garlic mashed potatoes, and ribeye steaks sliced off the bone basted with butter. Savvy handed everyone a plate to help themselves. When she got to Spencer, his hands grazed her fingertips as he accepted his plate and nodded his thanks.

His eyes held her gaze for a long moment, until Joanie erupted with teasing laughter as Maggie's lips tightened into a straight line.

Spencer waved finger pistols at Maggie, making little laser gun sound effects. "Pew-pew-pew." Joanie cracked up.

Mags reddened. "No one at this table would believe that I opted not to play because I was worried about losing."

"I don't know, Mags. Maybe you saw how hard we played last week and now admit that we have some skills." Savvy lifted her hands and shrugged, purposefully triggering her best friend's inner Hulk. "We might be too much for you now."

Maggie's cheeks flushed further, and they relished every minute of it. "Come on now. None of you want to be embarrassed like that."

"Girl, you gon' have to put your money where your mouth is, because I think we will work you." Joanie leaned forward, looking Maggie in the eye with a steady gaze. "You ain't ready."

"Oh, really? I'm being kind when I say that if Beth puts me up against any of you in singles, I'll school you two out of three."

"That's being kind?" Joanie goaded. "Come on, Mags, say how you really feel." Appealing to Maggie's competitive nature was the button Joan and Savvy loved to push. Maggie Hulk-smashed on anyone who doubted her ability to win.

"Y'all ain't ready for this work. You'll see tomorrow."

Joanie and Savvy exchanged a glance. *Checkmate.*

"Oh, don't think that you Jedi mind-tricked me into playing either. I'm going to come, just this once, and I'm going to beat you so badly that you won't invite me to come to any more sessions. We'll knock this out tomorrow, and then

I can get back to my usual Pilates schedule." Maggie's game face made Spencer chuckle.

"Mmmkay, Mags. I guess we'll see tomorrow." Savvy never considered herself as competitive as Maggie, but it was fun to rile her up. She took one last sip of her cocktail and leaned back in her seat. Joanie made another round, handing one to Spencer.

"You have to tell me the outcome of this epic tennis match," he teased.

Maggie shrugged. "I'll win, nothing new."

Joanie and Savvy made faces at each other and burst out laughing.

"What? It's true. Not like either of you really stand a chance. I was trying to stay out of it to save your feelings, girl."

"Go ahead and give me her cocktail, Sis. She has clearly had too much to drink," Savvy laughed. She raised her glass. "To Mags and her Hulk Smash."

"To Mags!"

15

Bump. Thwack. Bump. Thwack.

They started the session with a warm-up jog around the courts, some high knees and jumping jacks, and then went straight into drills. Maggie was on the court, while Joanie and Savvy formed a line to the left side of the doubles sideline.

Bump. Thwack.

Beth had the ball machine on the opposite side of the court, shooting balls to the corners, forcing Maggie to sprint back and forth. From where they stood, Maggie's sprints were effortless, her backhand one-handed and mean. "Can you believe this shit?" Joanie muttered.

"She's really killing it," Savvy admitted. "It's going to take a team effort to take her down."

"Agreed. Okay, her turn is about to be up. Hands in." Joanie thrust her hand out. Savvy put her hands on top, they thrust them down, and lifted their arms into the air waving spirited fingers. "Team," Joanie whispered.

"Great job, Maggie. Excellent form. Okay, Joan, you're up," Beth called, grinning at their exchange. "Hurry, don't miss that ball! Yes! Well done."

Joanie ran to the far side of the court, hitting a clean winner straight down the line. Maggie stood on the opposite doubles sideline from them, breathing hard, hands on her hips. She watched Joanie's movements like a hawk, scrutinizing how dexterous she was on her feet, the confidence with which she swung her racket. Joanie changed directions and ran back across the court, bringing her left hand to her racket for a two-handed backhand. Her follow-through impeccable, she powered through the ball and hit it across the court. The ball landed just inside the baseline.

"Yes, Joanie!" Beth cried. "Now cross and give me another ball up the line. Then follow your shot and come up to volley." Beth watched Joanie with something more than admiration, taking in the way that her muscles tightened, how quick she was on her feet, and how she would step forward and get low to catch a ball early on her backhand side. Joanie hit the ball straight up the line perfectly, hauling ass to get to the T for a volley. Savvy let out a whoop as Joanie rushed forward.

Beth used her remote to adjust the planned trajectory of the ball machine, forcing the ball to shoot right a second time, in an attempt to throw Joanie off balance, but she was too quick on her feet. She stepped forward and swung hard, pounding the ball straight toward the machine. It bounced off the base, and Savvy cheered. As she reset toward the center of the court, Beth forced the machine to shoot another ball toward the right. Joanie sprinted forward, reaching her racket as far out as she could, deftly flicking the ball just in time to return a low shot down the line. She reset herself quickly, as Beth shot a ball quickly toward the left side of the court. Joanie rushed over and sliced at the ball, sending it just over the net, where it abruptly dropped, barely bouncing due to the spin.

Savvy let out a low whistle, and Maggie glared at her. "I didn't hear you cheering like this when I was up, Savvy."

She laughed, raising her hands out to her sides, "You brought this on yourself, Mags."

"Exactly," Joanie breathed as she hit another return. "We're united against you. You're coming back for Thursday's session."

Beth smiled brightly. "That's what's at stake today? Okay, now I understand the vibe. Alright, Joan, last ball. Give me a forehand ball across the court."

Joanie ran left, around the ball, and hit it so hard that her follow-through brought her racket quickly to her left and up over her head. She looked like a pro, complete with her old-school pleated tennis skirt and a dry-fit tank top. Her thin sporty headband held back the flyaways from her ponytail.

"Damn, girl." Beth shook her head. Joanie walked off the court slowly toward Maggie, looking at Beth over her shoulder, a sway in her hips. Beth licked her lips, as Joanie gave her a seductive half smile.

Even Maggie soaked in the moment. She snapped her fingers hard in support of her girl getting her grown woman on, catcalling her approval. "Yessss, Joanie. You betta work!" Maggie cheered, smacking her on the ass as she got closer. "She ain't ready for this work right here!"

Joanie broke into a quick little dance, Milly Rocking to her own beat. They burst out laughing, whooping it up for their girl.

"Okay, Savvy, you got this. Hey, batter, batter!" Joanie called.

"Uh, Kotter?" Maggie said slowly. "Wrong sport."

Joanie broke into a grin. "Savs gets me. Come on, girrrll!" Joanie cheered.

Savvy ran across the court, and Beth immediately tried to jam her with a body shot. The ball came right toward her midsection, and she backpedaled just in time to catch the ball with her forehand. The ball flew back across the court, dropping just inside the service line.

"Okay, girl, OKAYYY!" Mags yelled.

"Not so fast," Beth muttered.

Savvy readied herself, pushing her shoulders back. The ball machine swung left, shooting a ball toward the deep corner. She ran toward it, catching it with a swinging volley before it could hit the ground. The ball clipped the net and landed on her side.

"Damn," Savvy whispered, clapping her hand against her thigh with frustration.

"It's okay, Savs," Joanie coaxed. "Stay focused."

Savvy tried to shake it off as Beth swung the machine toward center court, shooting a ball right down the T. Savvy moved forward, remembering to move her feet, swinging an inside-out forehand that curved and landed in the right corner.

"Keep moving," Beth called. The machine shot a ball farther right, and she hit a shaky forehand up the line. "Get across that court, Savvy, go!"

The machine shot a ball toward the opposite corner, and Savvy sprinted back for a double-handed backhand. Savvy got there just in time, bending her right knee to get closer to the ground, swinging her racket and rotating with her hips. The ball crashed into the machine. "Yessss!!" Mags yelled. Savvy inhaled deeply to try and catch her breath. Sweat was building on her forehead.

"Move forward, Savvy, let's see it." She raced to catch

the ball with a swinging volley, wedging the ball machine. Beth turned it off with the remote. "Great work! You're definitely moving those feet more."

Savvy jogged the last few steps to her friends before leaning forward to stretch her lower back. She took a few deep breaths, patting her forehead with the edge of her tank top. Beth tossed her a bottle of water, and she took a big gulp before passing it on to Mags.

Joanie turned brightly to Beth. "So what's next?" Their eyes caught in an electric gaze for a brief second.

Beth smiled at Joanie. "I think we're going to do a round robin. Maggie, you take that side. Joan and Savvy, you two on the other side." Beth gestured to the court next to where they just completed their drills. "Maggie, they'll have you serve first."

Maggie grinned, strutting over to her side of the court.

Savvy rolled her eyes and picked up a ball by wedging it between the outer edge of her shoe and her racket. "Here we go," she breathed.

"Okay, ladies," Beth said. "Are you all ready?" Each of them nodded, gripping their rackets a little tighter. "Okay, Maggie, you are up to serve first. Joan will receive. Savvy, you come up to the net to volley."

Everyone took their places and Maggie prepared to serve. Joanie leaned forward, her legs in a wide stance, knees bent. She swayed from left to right, cradling her racket in both hands.

Maggie served a ball toward the far corner, which Joan returned easily down the line. "Nice, return, Joan! Savvy, don't be afraid to step in there and cut off that line," Beth encouraged. Savvy nodded, retreating to the service line.

As Maggie prepared for the next serve, Savvy took a deep breath. Beth stood at the side of the net watching all of them, ready to call out pointers to them as they went. Maggie's first serve went into the net, and each of them took a moment to reset. Savvy leaned forward, watching Maggie as she tossed the ball into the air, trying to guess which direction she would choose for her serve. She swayed right, anticipating that her friend would serve down the center of the court. She took a deep backswing and powered through the ball, pulling her racket across her body to follow through. The ball ripped straight down the center of the court, and Maggie's jaw dropped.

"Ooo, Savvy." Joanie walked toward her to give her a quick high five. "Out here channeling Serena."

"Moving on," Mags spat. They continued playing, Maggie's frustration growing. The last straw came when Maggie was able to get in a position to volley, but the sun got in her eyes, and she missed the ball. Before she lost her shit, Beth called the game and told them to take a couple of laps.

"Good job, everyone. How are you all feeling? Anyone need ice?" They all shook their heads, so instead, Beth passed cold water to each of them. Savvy took her bottle gratefully, chugging down half of it before she set it on the ground next to her. Beth handed her a second bottle, smiling. "You're really improving, Savs. Can you tell?"

She nodded. "It's beginning to feel easier to move around."

"Same for me," Joanie said. "Those sprinting drills are great. How are you, Mags?"

"Oh, I'm fine," she said. Her voice sullen, she looked down at the ground in front of her. "Thanks for today, this was a good session." Her face contorted between a frown and a grimace.

"You have a pretty serious game face there, Killer." Beth smiled at her playfully.

Kotter huffed. "Serious is an understatement."

"I know," Maggie groaned. She looked around at all of them and then back at the ground. "I'm a work in progress, fam. Please don't hold it against me. I'll try to do better next time," she muttered.

Joanie and Savvy slow-clapped for Maggie because this was the first activity where she didn't need to be told about herself. "Our baby is getting so big now!" Joanie wailed. Savvy snickered.

Mags had an arm crossed over her chest, her other arm pulled it tighter toward her body to stretch out her shoulder. She turned. "So are you ready for your hot date with Spencer?"

"Oh, when is that happening?" Beth asked, squatting next to Savvy with furrowed brows. "Want me to meet this guy?"

She laughed. "You already offered to meet him! Nah, I think it will be okay. I have no doubt that he will be a gentleman." Her girls nodded in agreement.

Beth raised an eyebrow. "Those are always the ones that end up getting a little too fresh on the first date. Where is he taking you?"

Maggie hollered, "You sound like my grandma. 'Don't you let that boy get too fresh, now!'"

Joanie fell out laughing. "Them boys always want the milk for free, baby—they don't want to buy the cow!" she drawled in her best Big Mama impersonation.

Savvy giggled, placing a hand on Beth's to pacify her third degree. "We're going to meet up at a Korean spot that I love. They do the usual bibimbap, but they also do this version with raw fish and spicy sauce. It's delicious and it keeps me on track."

Beth nodded. "Okay, that sounds relatively harmless. Kudos for being mindful in your meal planning."

Joanie turned to her, poking her thigh. "So what are you going to wear for this hot date tomorrow?"

Everyone perked up and looked at her, Beth included. Savvy blushed. "I don't know. I guess I hadn't thought much about it."

Maggie threw up her hands. "How is that even possible?"

"I do know that I will not be wearing my glasses."

"You can barely see four feet in front of you when you aren't wearing your glasses. How is that going to work?"

She'd begun wearing glasses in the fourth grade, when her teacher caught her straining to see the board from the front row. She smiled ruefully. "I have an appointment to get contact lenses tomorrow. Project Upgrade: New Look, remember? I've always wanted contacts, so I figured now would be the time to try them out."

"Wait, what?" Maggie squawked. "Why?"

"What if Jason—"

Maggie's voice dropped two octaves deeper, her forehead creasing tightly. "Do NOT speak his name."

She shrugged. "I mean, he's not Voldemort, Mags. I'm just saying. What if he was just a pinch justified in what he said?"

Joanie sucked her teeth, looking away. Beth cocked her head to one side, waiting for Savvy to complete her thought.

"Not about him deserving some kind of upgrade. But what if," she continued more quietly, "what if I really did let myself go for a while? What if I had forgotten who I was or what I was bringing to that relationship?"

Beth remained silent, though Savvy could sense that she had something on her mind. She took a deep breath. "I was lost in that man. I never changed anything about myself because I never really looked at those decisions as my own. I don't even know if I recognized my own opinion while I was with him."

"What is your opinion of yourself right now?" Joanie asked slowly.

Savvy shook her head, tears welling up in her eyes. Beth scooted closer to her, putting a strong arm around her shoulders. Savvy leaned into her and let the tears fall. Beth stroked her hair, and the contact made the tears fall harder. "Honestly, I'm not completely sure. I'm trying." A sob caught in her throat, and Savvy took a deep breath. "I want this revenge body to raise my confidence level."

Beth pulled away from her slightly so that they could look each other in the eye. She wiped a tear from her cheek. "No, Savs," she said quietly. "Let's make the goal for you to love yourself exactly where you are right now. No matter what change you make to the exterior, Savvy, you are who you are on the inside. The outsides are just window dressings."

"That's right." Joanie nodded. "You could stay exactly the way you are right now, and everyone sitting here would love you regardless. Just as you are."

16

As Savvy exited her car, she saw him first. He wore a pair of dark jeans with a black button-down shirt, his sleeves neatly rolled up, exposing his forearms. "Savvy?" He smiled in surprise. "Where are your glasses?"

Savvy blushed. "I decided to try contacts." She gave herself a little Vanna White display, showing off a faded denim jacket over a royal blue dress flaring at her waist. "What do you think?"

"You're beautiful." He regarded her slowly, apparently savoring the sight.

Her stomach fluttered. He gave her his arm, leading her toward the restaurant. His arm emanated heat while the familiar scent of citrus and cedarwood invaded her nostrils. "I've never been here, but I am excited to try something new."

"I love this place. It's not pretentious. Just simple, good food." Heady from his cologne, Savvy's hand tingled in the crook of his arm, her fingers lightly gripping his biceps. *Why does this feel so natural?*

Spencer turned his head to look at her. "Not everyone would share one of their favorite restaurants right away."

Savvy smiled shyly at the ground. "This place allows me to stay in my comfort zone."

The hostess led them to a quiet booth against the windows, handing them menus with Korean writing and big pictures. She returned with plastic cups filled with hot barley tea. Savvy held her cup between her hands, closed her eyes, and let the steam waft up to her face. "I love this tea."

"I've never had this before." Spencer sipped the tea carefully, brows furrowing, as he looked down at the clear brown liquid.

He pursed his full lips to blow on the hot drink, and Savvy sipped her tea as she watched. An image of those lips trailing down her neck flashed across her mind and made her choke. Spencer's eyes shot up, and Savvy held out a hand. "I'm okay. It was hot." *Very hot.* Savvy cleared her throat. "So what do you think?"

"It's nice. Not sweet at all."

"Are you a tea drinker?" Savvy asked, sipping slowly.

Spencer smiled. "If I'm at the coffee shop, I usually switch to tea in the afternoons. I try to limit my caffeine intake, or I won't sleep well at night." He gestured to the menus. "So what is your favorite thing on this menu, since it's one of your favorite restaurants?"

"Do you eat raw fish?"

Spencer pretended to gag, but broke into a wide smile. "I'll eat pretty much anything, or at least I can say that I will try anything once. I love sashimi, so this should be fine."

"Perfect. What about spicy?"

He chuckled. "How many questions are you going to ask before you answer mine? Do you need a list of food restrictions?"

She colored. "I'm sorry, I'm just such a foodie. My grand-mother helped me discover my love for cooking at a young age, and I'm so into trying everything that I tend to ask a lot of questions up front to learn what limitations people have on food."

"I get that." He nodded, amused. "Don't worry, I don't have food allergies or aversions. I'm probably not on foodie level yet because I'm such a creature of habit. This can be the start of my foodie adventures."

Savvy grinned. "So then you're saying you trust me to order for you?"

He leaned forward, nodding faintly. The way he held her gaze unnerved her. "I trust you."

Heat spread up her neck and rested in her cheeks. "Okay, well then, I think you're in for a treat."

Spencer's smile spread across his face, igniting his dimples and crinkling the corners of his eyes. "I have no doubt."

Savvy pushed a button on their table, alerting a server that they were ready to order. They ate bites of banchan, small side dishes set in front of them before the entrées. Spencer's eyes lit up as he sampled fresh kimchi, fried fish cake, marinated cucumbers in a spicy chili paste, pickled radishes, and a potato salad that included broccoli and slices of fresh apple. Their server topped off their barley teas from a steaming pitcher, and Savvy smiled contently, holding her cup of tea between her hands.

His eyes closed, cheeks full of pickled radish. "How have I never tried this?"

She smiled knowingly. "This isn't even the entrée. You'll see."

Spencer grabbed the last piece of fish cake with his metal chopsticks, happily plopping it on his tongue. "You're like the Yoda of good food. What other restaurants do you consider favorites?"

Savvy shook her head teasingly. "Nope. Experience this place first. The last thing you want to do is be thinking about a food you can't have here. It sullies the experience."

"Sullies?" Spencer teased. "You really take this seriously." Looking around at the restaurant, which was now filled to capacity to the point that people stood outside waiting for tables to open, he nodded. "I get it, though. I can already tell this is a great choice."

She bit her lip, taking in his compliment. "So what made you ask me out?"

He laughed, caught by surprise. "I could ask you why you're on Tinder..."

Savvy waved the question away. "You know what I mean. Half of the time, when I see you at the coffee shop, you seem to have a throng of followers who would happily date you. Why did you decide to venture into online dating and ask me out?"

Spencer sipped his barley tea thoughtfully. "If you want to find something different, you have to try something that you've never done, right? I've gone on a few dates with women that I met at the gym or the grocery store. After it doesn't work out, I continue running into these women, and it's awkward."

"So now you're trying to avoid connecting to people who you feel are too close to home? I get that." Savvy nodded, tilting her head. "But shouldn't that exclude me?"

His eyebrows furrowed. "Shouldn't what exclude you?"

"Don't I fall into the category of being too close to home? Patron of the same coffee shop and gym. Low-key going steady with your chocolate Lab."

He laughed.

"You would still run into me after this date, wouldn't you? So shouldn't you have excluded me?"

Spencer leaned forward, catching her off guard. His dark brown eyes crinkled at their corners. "Maybe you're not like the others. Maybe every time I run into you at the coffee shop or the gym, I want to."

Savvy swallowed, her heart beating faster. "You...you want to run into me?"

"Maybe." He smirked. "Don't be so surprised! Out of curiosity, what would be the downside?"

She shrugged, Jason's laundry list of reasons on the tip of her tongue. "I'm just not everyone's cup of tea."

Spencer cocked his head to one side, exploring her face, but was interrupted by the arrival of their food. Deep bowls of greens, rice, and veggies topped with cubes of fresh raw tuna. The server gestured to the bottles of spicy sauce on the other side of the table. Savvy nodded and thanked her. After she grabbed a bottle of sauce, Spencer watched her season her food, carefully mixing it together so that spicy, savory sauce was on every bite.

He followed suit, mixing his food together, and guided a big bite to his mouth. "Oh my God." He chewed, shaking his head as he savored his first bite. "Mmm. I will never doubt your food choices."

Taking a triumphant bite, Savvy nodded. "I'm going to hold you to that."

They talked and laughed through the rest of the meal, the bustle of the restaurant never reaching them. They agreed to walk to a bubble tea shop two doors down for dessert. Surprised at how comfortable she felt being out with Spencer, Savvy ordered them each a cup of her favorite warm weather indulgence.

Stepping outside with their strawberry watermelon slush drinks, each with lychee jellies concentrated toward the bottom of their cups, they laughed about Teddy's growing and undying love for Savvy. They walked toward her car, then leaned against the door as they talked, Spencer's back angled toward the entrance of the restaurant.

Savvy was so engrossed in their conversation that she almost choked when her eyes landed on Jason standing near the restaurant entrance with Chloe. Chloe spoke to him with a big smile on her face, making emphatic gestures to get her point across, but he wore a dark expression, looking directly at Savvy. Tiny hairs rose on the back of her neck, as her mind raced, wondering whether he was over there picking apart her appearance.

She clenched in anticipation of his scrutiny. Shaking her head, she refocused her attention on Spencer, who shared with her some mischief that sweet Teddy found for himself. She looked up at him, sipping her slush.

Spencer put his hand on her shoulder. "Hey, are you alright? Something in your face changed. You look like something is bothering you." He gave a quick glance over his shoulder and saw Jason and Chloe in the midst of a conversation, though Jason made frequent glances in their direction. "Or is it someone?"

Savvy looked down. "I'm so sorry. I wasn't expecting to see him here."

"Is that who I think it is? From the park?"

Savvy nodded toward Jason. "That's my ex and one of the new girls he is dating. It's a long story."

Spencer squeezed her shoulder lightly and let his hand travel up her neck. His thumb rested on her cheek as his hand held her head in place, looking up at him. "Listen, I don't know what happened between you, but I do know that I want to keep getting to know you. If you're not ready for that, I completely understand, Savvy. I'm not going to rush you."

Looking up at Spencer, she relaxed into the warm hand

cradling her face. "I want to keep getting to know you too, Spencer. Let's just take it slow."

Spencer looked down at her with eyes so warm and welcoming that Savvy felt a heat begin to build deep within her belly. He pulled her closer. Still holding her face, he leaned forward and kissed her cheek slowly. As he pulled away, his lips brushed against her forehead, and he wrapped his arm around her shoulder. "Slow is just fine. Too fast, and Teddy might steal you away from me altogether."

Savvy giggled, pushing against his chest. He grabbed her hand and held it there against his heartbeat, looking at her. "I'm glad to see your smile is back."

"Well, Teddy does that to me, I don't know what to tell you," Savvy teased.

Spencer tossed his head back and laughed. "Touché, Ms. Sheldon. Well played."

Savvy grabbed either side of her flared skirt and gave a little curtsy. "Why, thank you."

They joked for a few more minutes, sipping on their boba drinks, and then Spencer wrapped an arm around her shoulder. "Have some free time this weekend?"

"I have my first cooking class on Saturday, but maybe Sunday after my tennis session? Lunch or early dinner?"

He nodded. "Sounds good to me. Can you think of somewhere else that you'd like to show me on this new foodie adventure?"

She grinned. "I already have something in mind."

He raised an eyebrow. "Should I be scared?"

She shrugged, making him laugh. Spencer opened her car door for her, and waited for her to get inside. He closed the door lightly, and Savvy turned on the engine and rolled down the window. "Thank you, tonight was a lot of fun."

He smiled, leaning his face down through the open window frame. "I had a great time. Let me know when you make it home?"

Savvy nodded. "Will do. You too?"

He nodded. The air crackled with chemistry as they stared at each other. Spencer weighed his options and leaned into the window, pressing his lips firmly against hers before moving them close to her jawline. "Talk soon," he murmured into her ear. Savvy took in his cologne and nodded, devoid of air, feeling the lightest stubble graze her cheek.

Savvy watched him walk away, still entranced by the fullness of his lips. *Get it together, girl!* Putting her car in Reverse, Savvy looked through her windshield at the restaurant before backing out of the parking spot. Jason and Chloe sat at a booth just inside the door. She let out a deep breath before she pulled out of the parking lot. "It is what it is."

Savvy pulled up to a restaurant along the Santa Monica Pier, sailboats and small speed boats docked along one side. The sun shone brightly, dancing along muted waves. From the restaurant's front door, every table appeared to have a view of the ocean. Folding glass patio doors opened wide, welcoming a cool breeze in from the water. Strings of small Edison lights hung overhead. The hostess greeted her, directing her to the second floor where the teaching kitchen was located. Overhearing, the restaurant owner came out from the kitchen to introduce himself and walk her upstairs.

"Hi, I'm Savvy." She smiled.

"Savvy, it is lovely to meet you. I'm Paul Morales. Trust me when I say that you are in very good hands today." Paul put on all of his charm, holding one of her hands in both of his. His tanned complexion and slight accent made Savvy wonder where his family was from, though she'd guess Spain. "We have a small class today, and you'll be

learning some of our signature dishes." He took her hand
and looped it up around the crook of his arm, leading her
to the teaching kitchen.

They walked into a room with six kitchen islands facing a larger island in the front of the room. "You can pick
any of the six islands, Savvy. What can I get you to drink?"

"What do you have with gin?"

Paul smiled, his dark eyes shining. "I have just the cocktail for you. Be right back."

Always wanting to hone her skills, Savvy made it a habit
to take cooking classes all around LA to learn different techniques. When Savvy heard about Chef Sarah, a renowned
Black chef and owner of one of the hottest restaurants on
the water, she'd jumped at the chance to sign up for cooking lessons with her.

At the end of her island there was a hook for her purse and
jacket. An apron was folded on the butcher block countertop,
along with recipe cards. Various ingredients were packaged
and placed inside of a wooden basket. Thumbing through
the recipes, she saw they were set to prepare the restaurant's
signature clam chowder and their lobster and avocado salad.

Paul returned with another guest and her special cocktail, which had a large square cube of ice, a lemon wedge at
the rim, and a sprig of rosemary. He introduced her to the
guest, who took the island behind her. They clinked their
glasses together. "To trying new things. Salud."

Savvy smiled at him. "Cheers." Savvy took a small sip
of her drink, savoring the honey, lemon, and rosemary that
blended so well with the gin. "Oh, yeah, I'm going to need
this recipe."

Paul grinned. "I'll make sure they write it down for
you. In the meantime, I'd love to introduce you to today's
instructor—our executive chef here at the Dockside Oyster

House." A smiling woman in a starched white chef's coat approached, directing two other guests to their islands. "This is my wife, Sarah."

Sarah's dark skin was smooth and supple. Her high cheekbones and forehead stood out proudly, her eyes framed by dark curly lashes. Sarah's natural hair had been woven into a halo braid, which crowned her beautiful features. She'd rolled up the sleeves of her chef coat, exposing tattooed forearms. *Hot.*

"Hi, I'm Savvy. I'm really excited to take your class! I love cooking."

"I'm so glad! It's always a better class when we have someone here who knows what they're doing. Others will follow your example."

"Thank you for this opportunity. I've taken a lot of cooking classes, but I've been wanting to come to this restaurant for a while. I'm such a fan of your work—I saw it highlighted on *Best Seafood Bites*—and learning to cook some of your signature recipes is such a treat!"

"Just wait until you taste these dishes, Savvy!" Paul beamed at his wife. "These are two of my favorites."

"I can't wait. Are you a chef also?"

Paul shook his head fervently. "I dabble in the kitchen, but my wife has all of the talent. I am the lucky taste tester."

Sarah smiled and took her cue to head up to the front of the class as the final two guests arrived. "Hi, everyone! Thank you for joining us today. Now let's get started."

They tied on their aprons, opened up packages of food, and set to prepping the soup ingredients: minced garlic, sliced leeks, diced potato, and cubes of fried bacon, along with chopped clams and littlenecks still in their shells. Savvy brought one of her own knives from home and made quick work of the mise en place. As the chowders came together, they marked the broth with cream, and ladled themselves a bowl. The woman at the island across from Savvy's had had a mishap with the clams, so she came and enjoyed a bowl of Savvy's. Paul came by to sprinkle some fresh cracked pepper over the top and brought them crusty French bread with butter and a smoky black salt to sprinkle on top. He returned with another round of cocktails for them and complimented the consistency of Savvy's knife skills.

"How did you enjoy your drink, Savvy?"

"Heaven." He stood by as Savvy brought a spoon of chowder to her lips. "Oh. My. God." Savvy closed her eyes and hummed, savoring the hot broth, which burst with the flavors of fresh clams, garlic, the crisped fat of the bacon, a touch of heavy cream, and the velvety potatoes. "Mmmm. This doesn't even make sense." The food was so good, Savvy didn't care who watched her eat it.

Sarah and Paul exchanged a knowing smile.

Savvy smoothed a bit of butter onto a corner of French bread and then sprinkled a bit of the black salt on top. Taking a bite, her eyes rolled back, and she blushed, remembering her seat in front of strangers. "I can't even tell you how good this is, Sarah. Wow."

"I'm so glad, Savvy. And your chowder looks just like mine. Good job."

"Seriously, Paul," Savvy said with full cheeks. "Don't ever let her go. I might snap her up myself. Then I can be fat and happy forever."

Paul chuckled. "I'll be careful now that I have some competition. Do you have any special recipes up your sleeve?"

"Mmm-hmmm. I make a mean rack of lamb with a savory bread pudding, and nobody beats my strawberry tiramisu. I will gladly make that to win her heart." Savvy didn't even look up, as she grabbed another slice of bread. "She might decide that she's ready to make moves."

"Oh, so what you're saying is that we're coming over for dinner sometime soon?" Sarah lovingly propped her elbow on Paul's shoulder.

Paul smiled, entwining his fingers with his wife's. "She's got a mean sweet tooth."

Savvy took another spoonful of chowder, a big clam right in the middle, and closed her eyes. "Sarah better watch out. I'm coming for her." Paul's smile grew bigger, and he squeezed her shoulder.

"Let me know if you need anything else."

They packaged the rest of their soups and set about to make the lobster and avocado salad. By the end of the class, Sarah and Savvy had exchanged numbers and promised to get together soon for a potluck. Something about Sarah and Paul felt special. Sarah cooked the way Savvy's granny had cooked—with love and respect for the ingredients and an openness to improvise based on the freshest sustainable proteins. Savvy couldn't wait to pick her culinary brain.

"So how was the date, Baby Girl?" Savvy rolled her eyes at the amusement in her uncle's voice. On the phone, her uncle sounded like a radio deejay for a smooth jazz station.

"It went well. He's a really nice guy." She turned off the burner under her whistling teakettle, then poured hot water into a mug of green tea as she cradled her phone on her shoulder. The fragrant scent of the leaves wafted up, calming her senses, as she added in a slice of lemon.

"So you're finally moving on from Jason."

"I guess so. At least, I'm trying." Her voice held a question mark.

"Mmm-hmm." Savvy pictured him sitting back in his recliner chair, waiting to hear her out. "Tell me what's wrong, Baby Girl."

"It's just hard, Uncle. I loved Jason for a long time. It's not easy to walk away, even after how awful he's been." She walked into Joanie's living room, trying hard to avoid spilling hot tea all over herself. "I still miss him. He was part of my life for so long, but I know I can't go back to that."

"Now, you know I don't like that guy, but I will say that maybe he doesn't know what he wants. Maybe that's what he's trying to find out."

Savvy sat down on her couch, thinking it through. "So what do I do?"

"Exactly what you are doing. You can't stand by and wait for him to figure it out, especially because he seems to have no concern for the fact that he's hurting you. That's not a man you wait for, Savvy. He needs to grow up."

"I needed to hear that. I just don't want to feel guilty for going out with someone else."

"What's there to feel guilty for, Savannah? You've seen that boy out with several others before you even considered going out with someone else."

Savvy chewed on her lip. "I just feel like I'm moving fast."

"You didn't marry the fella, did you?"

Savvy covered her eyes, laughing. "Oh, Uncle. No, I didn't marry the guy. It just feels fast to get out of something and already go on dates."

"Move at your own pace, Baby Girl. You ain't gotta rush for nobody. And if he's a worthy guy, he'll meet your pace."

Savvy ran her fingers over her hair, pulling her swoop behind her ear. "Okay, Uncle. Thanks for that."

"I gotta ask you a question. See, Mabel and I— I'm taking her out to dinner next week." Her uncle chuckled bashfully.

"Y'all are finally making it official?" Her lips twitched with amusement.

"Come on now, Savvy. We ain't official. We're going on our first date, just like you."

"Oooh, a Saturday night date? So what's the question?"

"What the hell do I wear for something like that?"

Her heart melted. "Uncle, why are you so cute? Can I come to take pictures of you guys?" she gushed.

"Now, Savvy," he warned.

"Fine, fine. How about some slacks and a nice button-down shirt?"

"I ain't gotta wear a tie, do I?"

"Nah, that's okay."

He grunted. "Been a long time since I been on a date. I'm nervous. But your date was good?"

"Yes, he was a perfect gentleman."

"Good, he don't want no problems." Her uncle's gruff voice held a warning tone.

"Uncle…" Savvy groaned. "What am I going to do with you?"

"I love you, Baby Girl."

"I love you too, Uncle. I'll give you a call later this week. Tell Ms. Mabel I said hello."

"Sounds good. Now go have some fun tomorrow."

"I sure will." As they hung up the phone, Savvy smiled. Uncle never had his own kids, but he took seriously his role in helping to raise her and her brothers. *I need to do something special for him.*

She started researching potential gifts for him, but the work she'd brought home for the weekend pulled at her. Her meeting with Warren on Monday morning would mark the start of her new role, and she wanted to be ready. She couldn't wait to move into her new office. Closing her laptop, she picked up the outlines for new products that Warren had sent her to review. *Better get to work.*

17

Bump. Thwack. Bump. Thwack.

Their Sunday morning session consisted of Beth guiding the ball machine to move Savvy all around the court, forcing her to sprint from one side to the other, trying to trip her up. The courts around them filled up. Tennis coaches put kids through warm-up sprints, one man set up a ball machine for his son and daughter, a pair of mixed doubles couples started a leisurely match on a far court. Savvy was excited to get in this full session before starting her new position tomorrow—she had no idea how often she'd be able to play once she settled into her new role.

"Good, Savvy. Now I really want you to go for these next few. Run hard, move your feet more, bend your knees. Right, now where's that follow-through? Yes!"

Savvy's breath labored, but she didn't want to stop. She sprinted toward center court to reset, but the ball machine powered down. "Really? Already?" she whined.

"Session's not over, but we're done with the ball machine. Let's do a ball pickup, and then give me four laps."

She nodded and got to work. While she jogged, Beth chatted with one of the tennis coaches a couple of courts down, who put three teenage boys through drills. A couple of guys took the court directly next to Beth's, conspicuously eyeing Savvy's journey around the courts. *Oh lawd, here we go.* They went over to Beth and the other coach, dapping each other up with handshakes and hugs. They nodded and laughed, one of the men pointing in her direction. *Who are these guys?*

Her awareness of her curves jiggling to the beat of her stride made her panic inwardly. *Maybe today wasn't the best day to try out a smaller size in my workout clothes.* Acutely aware that there were eyes on her, she pushed herself to keep going, ignoring the tiny hairs prickling the back of her neck. Once she finished her fourth lap, she walked toward the benches, hands on top of her head with her elbows splayed wide, pulling air into her lungs.

"Hey," Beth called from behind her. Savvy turned and caught the water bottle thrown in her direction. Savvy took a quick sip, dabbing her face with the sweatband around her wrist. Beth came closer with the two men from the next court and the coach, who called out to his three charges to take themselves through rounds of sprints. "Savvy, these are a few of my friends." She gestured to the coach first. "Rob's always here coaching." They shook hands. "And Shawn and I went to school together."

Shawn smiled and shook her hand. "Been homies since middle school." Shawn's rich voice was fit for smooth jazz on the radio.

She smiled. "Nice to meet you."

"This is Matt. We grew up together too. He went to

school with me and Shawn. We lived next door to each other through most of our school years."

Matt shook her hand. "Our parents are still neighbors." Matt had short curls and a solid build. "This chick kept me out of trouble more times than I can count."

"She's a good egg. It's nice to meet y'all." Savvy nodded to them. She nudged Beth with her elbow. "I thought we weren't allowed to meet your elusive friends?"

Shawn's eyebrows perked up. "We? You mean there's more of you?" He peered around the courts.

She smiled. "Three of us. I started out as Beth's client, but then I brought two of my girls along. Now we all do training sessions together."

Rob chimed in, gesturing around at the empty court. "So where are they? How did I miss these sessions?"

Beth looked at them sideways. "Just Savvy today, fellas."

"You didn't want us to meet them, huh?" Matt questioned. "What's up, man? You holding out on us?" He threw a playful punch in Beth's direction.

Savvy laughed. "Uh-oh." She held her hands up in surrender, taking a slight step backward. "So you guys all come out here to play tennis?"

Shawn nodded. "When we were kids, there was a park that had courts in our neighborhood. They would hold a tennis camp over summers, and our parents sent us there to keep us out of trouble."

She nodded. "That's cool. I met my girls at a tennis camp in middle school and played on high school and college teams, but I got injured and stopped. I've been wanting to get back into it for a while, so Beth has been helping me. And now my friends too."

Beth grinned, gesturing toward her. "They're mad funny too. Ridiculously competitive."

Matt tilted his head, sizing her up. "Word?"

Beth nodded, and Savvy blushed. "We have one in particular who is extremely competitive. We usually all end up rising to her level of petty to keep her in line."

Rob looked at her thoughtfully. He licked his lips. "Savvy, are your friends good-looking too, or do they just have really nice personalities?"

Shawn squeezed his eyes shut and dropped his head to look at the ground.

Beth looked at her friend with dismay. "Come on, man," she warned.

Rob held up his hand. "Hold on, now you never said that you were training anyone who looks like Savvy. And she has two others that she brings with her? So there are *three* of them, my dude?"

Hearing Rob's comments made warmth spread from her chest up to her cheeks. Savvy hadn't heard someone openly admire her like that in years. She stared at the ground, fighting to hide a smile.

Matt jutted his chin toward Beth, a playful look on his face. "What's going on, man? Why you blockin' blessings over here?"

Rob put an arm around her shoulder. "Right? I mean, we're just trying to get to know your friend here. See if your friend can be our friend, B."

"Right," Matt chimed in. "Savvy, when is your next group session? We wanna be out here. Meet the squad."

She grinned, looking over at Beth. "Tuesday evening. We'll all be here."

Rob smiled triumphantly at Shawn and Matt, all of them turning to her. Rob pointed in her direction. "Bet. We'll see you then."

Beth had had enough. "Okay, let's all get back to our sessions. Some of us have places to be."

Savvy turned to Beth. "Are you meeting up with Joanie later?"

Matt moved back toward the court next to them, but he stopped short. "Hold on, who is Joanie?"

Savvy laughed. "She's one of my best friends. You'll meet her Tuesday."

"Oh, word? So you were just gonna keep them all to yourself, B? See, that's why you don't want us to meet them—she got motives."

Rob shook his head at his friends and smiled at her. "Hey, Savvy, I will see you on Tuesday."

Grinning back at him, Savvy chuckled. "I'm looking forward to it. Maybe we can all join together to play a few rounds."

Rob jogged back to his court, immediately having the boys drop down for push-ups. Matt and Shawn muttered comments about Beth's betrayal, making sure that she heard each one.

Beth put her arm around her shoulder. "So now you've met my friends."

Savvy grinned at her. "Are you dreading Tuesday? I think this is going to be hilarious."

"Are you kidding? I was intentionally trying to avoid this!" She shook her head. "You better warn the others."

"Why? They seem nice."

Beth deadpanned, "They're still men, Savs. Fuckery is inevitable."

She laughed. "Go into this with an open mind!"

Relenting, Beth nudged her in the ribs. "Okay, now let's get back to it. You and I are going to play a set, so why don't you take the far side of the court?"

She walked to her side of the court, gathered a couple of stray tennis balls, and shoved them into the waistband of her leggings. When she looked up, a ball was already sailing over the net to her side, so she sprinted to catch it. Off balance, Savvy hit it right at Beth, who blocked her face with her racket.

"Ohhh! She's got skills!" Shawn cheered, hitting a hard forehand toward Matt.

"Get it, Savvy!" Matt called, powering through a return.

Beth smiled big. "You know, you're better than you think."

"You think so?" she asked.

Beth hit a ball deep into the court, brushing the line, and Savvy returned it to her backhand side. "I've been meaning to ask you, how was the date?" she called.

"It was actually really nice, but there was an awkward moment at the end."

"Awkward how?" she asked, hitting a ball down the line on her forehand side.

"At the end, my ex showed up with that girl we saw at brunch."

Beth stopped, standing up straight. "You're kidding me. Do you two frequent *all* of the same restaurants?"

Savvy pulled a tennis ball from the waistband of her leggings, dropped it to the ground to let it bounce, and hit it toward Beth on the rise. "If there was one thing we for sure had in common, it was good food."

"Wow, so what happened?" Beth hit a ball just short of the service line, forcing her to run forward.

Turning back to Beth, Savvy stopped. "He didn't recognize me at first. I was wearing my new contacts." Savvy gestured toward her face. "That, plus my hair, and I was wearing a dress. He kept staring at me."

"So your plan is working?" Beth asked, hitting a ball toward her. "Operation Revenge Body in full effect."

"Should I just walk away from the whole revenge aspect? I mean, he's moved on. He was out with someone else."

"Not to be a dick, but so were you, Savs." She half smiled, and Savvy rolled her eyes.

"But I never thought about going out with someone else until I saw him out with three different girls. I figured if he was moving on, I should try too, otherwise I'd just fixate on him all the time."

"I get that. Did Spencer catch on to what was happening?"

Savvy nodded. "I didn't want to tell him, since he was so focused on me, but he noticed my distraction, so I pointed out that Jason was on a date at the same restaurant. He knows who Jason was because of an encounter at Griffith Park, but he doesn't know the reason for the breakup. What if Spencer thinks I'm damaged goods?"

Beth stopped, letting a ball sail past her. She walked closer to the net, so Savvy followed suit. "Savvy, you're not damaged goods. You're hurt. You're just barely out of a relationship that meant something to you."

"But does that mean that I should stop seeing him? Spencer, I mean. I'm not sure I'm even really ready to be seeing another man. What if it's too soon?"

"Aren't you supposed to see him today?"

She nodded. "We have lunch plans."

"Well, I don't think you should cancel them. You like him, he likes you. It's not like you have to rush into anything." Beth shrugged. "Hell, bring him for next session so that we have an even number."

Savvy laughed. "True."

"But you're right. This whole journey isn't about revenge. It isn't about Jason at all. It's about you feeling good and

doing the things you love because you've gotta love you before you can love anyone else. Only you can decide when
you're ready, Savs."

She looked to the sky, trying not to tear up. She hit another ball toward Beth. "You're right."

"I don't want to be right, Savs," Beth said softly, letting
the ball pass her once more. "I want for you to be happy.
You deserve that, whatever that looks like."

"I'm just not sure what that is right now." Savvy sniffled.

Beth tilted her head to one side thoughtfully. "Well then,
just take your time. There's no rush to make any decisions.
See who's there once you know what you need. Could be
Spencer. Could be someone you haven't even met yet."

Savvy nodded again, gazing at a fluffy cloud to try to get
her tear ducts to calm down. "Sound advice."

Beth smiled. "Good. So, then let's stop procrastinating
and let's get this set started..."

Savvy met Spencer outside of the Boiling Crab, a place
known best for boiled seafood by the pound and a cloud of
Cajun seasoning. Butcher paper and plastic bibs lined each
table, and bags of hot buttery shellfish were delivered to
groups along with pitchers of beer.

"This should be interesting." He grinned as he approached.

Savvy opened her arms to hug him, and he stepped in
close, wrapping his arms around her waist. His mouth
loomed close to her ear, sending a tingle down her neck.
"How are you?" she murmured.

He stepped back and smiled. "Hungry. You smell really
good, by the way."

She blushed. "You always smell good."

"Well, thank you. How are you doing?"

"Hungry for sure." Savvy smiled. "I had tennis this morning."

"When do I get to cheer you on in the stands?" He smiled slyly, opening the door ahead of her.

There was a wait inside. "Tournaments make me nervous, but actually, we need an extra person at our next session. Do you play tennis?"

Spencer smiled. "I might be able to do a little somethin'." The hostess advised that the anticipated wait was forty-five minutes. Spencer turned to her. "Is that okay with you?"

Savvy nodded, giving the hostess her cell number so that she could text her once their table was ready. "I'm not in any rush, plus, the perfect place to pass the time is right upstairs!" Savvy turned back toward the door, looking at Spencer mischievously over her shoulder.

Spencer raised an eyebrow with curiosity. "Really? What's up there?"

Savvy grabbed his arm and led him to the elevator. "You'll see."

Minutes later, they set up a pool table for a couple of rounds. Savvy told Spencer to break first, and he walked around the table confidently in his black Ralph Lauren sweater, dark wash jeans, and loafers. *Definitely not homeless.*

He leaned forward, broad shoulders squaring as he rested the pool cue on top of his knuckles. In one fluid motion, he thrust the pool cue forward, and the triangle of balls clacked and scattered, bouncing off the padded walls. Two striped balls went into pockets at opposite corners of the table. Her stomach fluttered. There was something sexy about the way this man handled a stick. "Nice shot."

Spencer smiled at her. "I guess I'm stripes?" He moved around the table to get set for his next shot.

"I guess you are," Savvy breathed back. "You seem like you're pretty good at this."

"We had a pool table in our dorm hall in college. We

got in a lot of playing time when the table wasn't covered in cups for beer pong." He smiled, shaking his head at the memory. He had set his sights on the nine ball, hit the pool cue carefully, and grimaced when the ball just edged out of the pocket by a hair. "What about you?"

"My stepdad had a man cave in the basement. When he and my mom started dating, he would invite us over all the time to get to know us. Pool table, darts, air hockey—our family is pretty competitive. And we had a pool hall right down the street when I was in college. They had the best juke box."

Spencer laughed, watching her face light up as she spoke.

"We played all the time. I made a lot of money off guys who underestimated my skills," she warned.

He raised his hands. "I have no doubts that you know what you're doing."

Savvy chalked the tip of her cue and walked around the table once to survey.

He chuckled. "You're like a wolf preparing to attack your prey."

She smiled. "Just getting an idea of where everyone is on the table." She aimed first at the ten ball, hitting the pool cue at an angle so that the ball would drop smoothly into the side pocket.

"Nice shot. You know, Savvy, you are just full of surprises." He watched her closely as she moved her hair behind her ear.

She half smiled at him, setting up for her next shot. "You're not going to be a sore loser, are you?"

Her phone buzzed, and Spencer smiled. "Guess we'll have to wait to find out."

Savvy walked over to the table where she'd set her purse, then stared at her phone screen, puzzled.

Spencer stood straight. "Everything okay, Savvy?"

The text came from Jason. Three little words felt like weights dropping onto her shoulders. Can we talk?

"Savvy?" Spencer asked again, concern clear in his tone.

"Um." Savvy bit her lip. Before she could respond further, her phone pinged again. It was the restaurant. "Our table is ready." Savvy looked up at him, seeing the questions in his face. She brandished her phone. "I just heard from my ex. Strange."

Spencer gathered the balls from the pockets and set them back onto their tray. "I take it you two haven't been in touch?"

Savvy shoved her phone into her purse and shook her head. "We've run into each other a couple of times, but purely by chance. We don't keep in touch. It wasn't a clean break, as I'm sure you remember." She thought back to the moment that Jason drove off and how she yelled at Spencer. "Not my finest moment."

"I can listen if you want to talk about it, but I won't press you," he said softly. "It's rare that breakups go smoothly, at least in my experience."

"Yeah." She wrestled with the idea of talking about it, but she didn't want to bring down the energy of the date.

As they descended the stairs, Spencer put his hand at her back. "Whatever reason things didn't work out, it made an opportunity for me to get to know you."

Savvy smiled weakly. "Yeah, you have definitely been the silver lining for me."

"So this breakup wasn't something that you initiated, I take it?" He led her into the restaurant, and they were seated near a window and given their bibs.

She shook her head wistfully. "I didn't initiate it, but if you listen to him, I caused it."

"How exactly does that work?" He raised an eyebrow as he glanced at the menu.

Her face burned. "He didn't like that I had gained weight. Thought I needed to update my appearance. There was a list."

The server came, and Spencer ordered a pitcher to share. Puzzled, he looked at her. "Wait—so he broke up with you because he didn't like how you looked?"

She nodded, looking down at her hand on the table, her fingers tracing over lines on the menu. "I would understand if you decide you don't want to stay. I'm sure this isn't what you signed up for."

Spencer reached his hand across the table to rest it on hers. "I signed up for you, Savvy. Just as you are. You're beautiful."

She smiled slightly. "I should tell you, I don't do well with compliments."

"Why is that?"

"Most of the time I feel like they're undeserved."

"Then I'll compliment you until you believe that I mean it, because I do." He leaned forward, and the scent of his cologne wafted across the table.

She inhaled deeply, caution written on her face. "I believe you. I think it's just hard to reconcile what you think with what someone I was in a long-term relationship with thought. He thought I had to change to be worth his time."

"Savvy, I noticed you long before I got up the nerve to speak to you. Long before you started making all of these changes. Even before you thought I was homeless."

Savvy laughed, shaking the memory from her head.

"You are beautiful. If you didn't change a thing, if you grew out your hair and put your glasses back on, I would think the very same thing." The matter-of-factness of his voice made her exhale the anxiety she'd held.

A weight lifted from her shoulders, and she let herself sink back into her chair a little. "Thank you," she whispered.

"No, thank you," he replied, smiling coyly. "I get the sense that maybe you're beginning to believe me, just a little."

She smiled back. "I am. Just a little bit." She squeezed her thumb and index finger close together.

He reached out and pushed them farther apart, her fingers tingling from his touch "Better." He grinned. "So what do you like to order here?" He returned his gaze to the menu.

"You're letting me order again?"

"Like I said before, I trust you." Setting his menu down, he gestured to the one in her hands.

Savvy smiled. "Okay. Level of hunger?"

"Two notches from hangry."

"Excellent." She grinned.

They feasted on king and Dungeness crab, shrimp, red potatoes, smoked sausage, and corn on the cob. Savvy told their server to load them up with all of the seasonings. They clinked their pint glasses together and eased into their date, reminiscing about the last seafood boils they'd experienced. He shared stories of his family's backyard boils in New Orleans.

Savvy crinkled her nose. "Well then, this might be a disappointment to you. New Orleans boiled crawfish is incomparable. Plus, this might feel overseasoned to you."

"I'm sure I'll be just fine, Savvy. I promise. I like trying new things with you." His easy confidence was contagious.

She watched him, watching her, and smiled a little.

"What are you thinking?" he asked.

"I'm wondering if you're too good to be true." She bit her lip, coloring when his eyes trailed down to watch.

He cleared his throat and took a sip of his beer. "I'm wondering the same about you."

She clinked her beer against his and took a long swig,

maintaining eye contact. A flutter in her stomach began to travel south, and she licked her lips. "Stay tuned."

He smiled, his gaze drifting to her lips and returning to meet her eyes. "I will. Hey, do you want to come by, get an update on the house? There's been a lot of progress."

"Progress." She bit her lip again, nodding. "Can't wait."

They parked their cars in the driveway, butterflies churning in Savvy's stomach as they neared the door. "I—I can't wait to see what you've done."

He held out his hand to help her up the front porch stairs. "I think you're going to like what you see." A muscle in his jaw flexed, and he pulled her close. Savvy wondered if he could feel her heart pounding in her chest.

He pressed his lips against hers, her back against the door, then hunched down for a deeper kiss. Tasting the sweetness of mint on his tongue, Savvy pulled him closer, running the tip of her tongue lightly over his, biting his lower lip. He moaned against her lips, wrapping his arms around her as Savvy fumbled with the doorknob behind her, willing it open, her voice nearing a whimper as Spencer's tongue traced a trail toward the nape of her neck. For a split second, she wondered whether they were moving too quickly, but everything in her body screamed to let it happen.

"I— Shit. This door." Savvy turned around slowly, and Spencer nudged her gently against the door before Savvy could turn her key.

Her face pressed against the red lacquer, Spencer's breath blew warm against her ear. "I've been wanting to do this since you cut your hair." His fingers traced from her temple to her jawline, pushing her hair back to expose her neck. Her eyes fell shut as his lips tickled her neck and shoulder, his other hand moving the strap of her dress, revealing more flesh.

"We should go inside," Savvy said, finding her voice. "My mother has half of these neighbors on speed dial."

Spencer kissed her temple, breathing into her ear. "You want me to come inside?"

Savvy squeezed her eyes shut, nodding as the butterflies migrated further south. "Yes. Come inside. Now." Turning the key, she unlocked the dead bolt, stepping forward into the foyer.

Spencer stepped in behind her, grabbing her arm as he shut the door. "We're inside." Savvy nodded and pulled him close as he nudged her against the wall, maneuvering a knee between her thighs as he kissed her, running his tongue over her front teeth. She'd forgotten how good it felt to have someone this hungry for her. He held her face in one hand, crooking her chin between his thumb and forefinger, gently turning her face. She buzzed with anticipation, melting into the warmth of his touch.

Her mouth dropped open as he nuzzled her neck, still holding her face. His other hand brushed against the hem of her dress, fingertips grazing from her thigh up to her hip. Hooking a finger under the leg of her panties, he followed the seam over her thigh to the warmth between her legs, tracing circles with the pad of his finger so lightly that Savvy wanted to scream. Synapses firing, bursts of light erupted behind her closed eyelids.

"Mmm." Savvy opened her eyes to Spencer looking at her.

"You want me to come inside?" His fingertip continued to barely kiss her exposed skin; the contact slowly carried her close to climax.

Unblinking, Savvy nodded. "Right now."

"Right now, what?" His finger dipped farther between her legs, and Savvy gasped.

"Please. Come inside, Spencer. Right now," she said,

panting. She couldn't wait any longer and began to reach for his hand.

He thrust his hand forward, gliding inside, as he kissed her collarbone. His other hand dropped from her face, down the side of her body, eventually curving behind to grip her ass. "You are so beautiful, Savvy. So soft and sexy."

She bucked, grinding against his hand, pulling her dress up and over her head. She didn't want to hide herself from him. He grunted approval as Savvy reached for the hem of his shirt, stopping him just long enough for her to tug his shirt over his head. "Come here." He pulled her into the kitchen, the floors and counters covered in white paper.

"Wow." Savvy gawked at the changes. The room where her kitchen stood had been transformed into an open, expansive space covered in butcher paper and tarps.

"We'll talk about the kitchen later, if that's okay with you." He lifted her onto the island, her butt barely on the counter, and she didn't even think about how much she weighed, just how strong he was and that now he was tugging her thong down past her ankles. "Mmm-hmm, go ahead and relax, Savvy." He rubbed between her legs with his knuckle, and her head fell back. Pressing his fingers inside, he guided them in and out slowly, bringing her to the brink.

She gasped, writhing under his touch. He watched her, running his free hand over her breasts. "Mmm, can you take this off for me?" he whispered, tugging at her bra.

Reaching behind her, she unhooked the closures in one smooth motion, and he dragged the straps off her shoulders, then tossed the bra aside. She propped herself up on her elbows, watching him admire her body. Still guiding his fingers slowly, he stepped forward to kiss her lips, then dragged his mouth from her collarbone across her nipples, his tongue pulling one into his mouth as he looked at her. He grazed her nipple with his teeth.

Savvy moaned softly, wanting to lie back, but not wanting to take her eyes off him. He trailed down her belly with his lips.

Holding a hand at her waist, he kissed just above her belly button, continuing lower until he ran his tongue slowly over her clit. His fingers still inside, he slowly wound her up until she cried out.

The pressure from his tongue intensified and she shuddered, legs shaking as she cursed the high heavens. Spencer waited patiently to deliver wave upon wave, as she moaned against him. Her thighs resting on his shoulders, he kissed and bit at the soft inner flesh until her spasms calmed. Removing his fingers, he buried his face between her legs, sticking his tongue where his fingers had been, igniting another wave of spasms.

Spencer kissed and licked his way back to her mouth, guiding her legs around his waist, as he removed his belt. "You okay, Ms. Sheldon? Is the surface too hard for you?" He brought his hands back to run his palms over her breasts, her stomach, never shying away from her curves.

"Never too hard, Mr. Morgan." After pushing herself back up to a seated position, Savvy kissed him, unbuttoning his jeans and pushing them down off his hips. Reaching into his boxers, her eyes widened. "Hard indeed." He squeezed the flesh at her hips.

He grinned. "Lean back for me." He slipped on a condom, running the tip against the moisture between her legs. He rubbed against her slowly, reactivating all of her nerves, before he pushed himself inside. "Okay?"

Savvy nodded, moaning lightly. "Yes," she breathed. He moved back and forth at a glacier's speed, holding one of her legs behind him while he pulled her other knee over his shoulder. He kissed the inside of her thigh as he pushed farther inside. Savvy sucked in a breath, feeling him fill her up, digging her fingernails into his shoulder.

"You are so fucking sexy." He leaned forward, gripping the sides of the island as he moved deeper. Moving his hands to her hips, he pumped harder, turning to kiss the inside of her knee.

Savvy watched his face, forehead creasing each time she lifted to meet him. He smiled at her, leaning forward to trace circles around her nipples with his tongue. With each stroke, he brought her closer to another wave of orgasm, and as he got close himself, he pressed his thumb against her clit.

"Fuck, I'm about to—" Savvy cried out, and he sped up, grabbing onto her hips to pull her toward him as he finished. They panted, smiling shyly at each other. Savvy giggled into her hands, then reached out to wipe the sweat from his brow. "Wow."

"Want to know something, Ms. Sheldon?" He stood back, pulling out of her gently, helping her off the counter.

"What's that, Mr. Morgan?" Savvy stretched her arms above her head, basking in his admiring gaze up and down her body.

"The sun hasn't even gone down yet." He took off his shoes and removed his boxers from around his ankles, then kneeled at her feet to help her out of her shoes. Savvy rested a hand on his shoulder for balance. He grabbed her hand gently as he stood, leading her back toward the bedroom. "We have all night."

Hours later, Savvy woke, reaching for him. The space he'd occupied in her bed was empty. He was gone. Looking at the alarm clock on her night table, Savvy groaned. One minute to six. Monday morning.

18

"So you were out on a date with Spencer when Jason texted you?" Mags asked incredulously. "Hold on a second, I need to hear this." Savvy heard her shutting the door to her office.

"Uh-huh," Savvy mumbled in the direction of her speakerphone. Her new desk was buried under a mountain of files, but the distraction kept her from thinking about Spencer. She had her first Monday morning one-on-one with Warren, and she'd received a warm welcome from her new team.

"So what did you do? I need details, Savs!" Maggie was beside herself. Her closed door barely muffled the projection of her voice.

"Spencer and I went back down to the restaurant, and I told him the truth—that it was a message from my ex, and that I hadn't heard from him for a while." She sighed. "He asked a few questions, and then he let me change the subject. We had a nice time after that, though in retrospect, I think

I made it awkward. The food was good, and we laughed, but I think that now he's feeling some type of way."

"What makes you think that?"

"I haven't heard from him at all today. That seems odd to me since we had a date yesterday."

"Maybe he's busy. He does have a job, Savs. You know that better than anyone, since he's currently working for you."

Savvy put her head down on her desk. "We sort of slept together last night," she said, her voice muffled by the file in front of her.

"Okay, OKAYYYY!!! Yes, honey. Someone slipped my girl some prime penis, and now she's searching for his ass with a flashlight." She cackled. "A FLASHLIGHT, you hear me?!"

Savvy covered her face with her hand. "Dear God…"

"Why are you so worried that you haven't heard from him, girl? What's really going on?" Maggie's tone calmed; the concern in her voice palpable.

"What if I scared him away telling him the reason that Jason broke up with me?"

"Wow, you two got into the details?"

"Yes, but he didn't seem fazed by that."

"Then, again, what are you worried about?" Savvy listened to Maggie type at her computer, her nails clicking against the keys.

"He was gone before I woke up this morning." Savvy chewed her lip.

"Mmm-hmm…"

"No, seriously, he was gone. No note, and I haven't heard from him." *Why doesn't she think this is a big deal?*

"Interesting," Maggie said, slurping her coffee. Savvy pictured her sitting back in her plush office chair, holding her coffee mug in two hands, thoughtfully assessing the details of her date.

"Are you paying attention?"

"I am, but I'm more interested in all of the sexy details. You're worried that he freaked out?"

"Well, why the hell else would he leave? I mean, we had sex twice, and fell asleep. He's working at my house, and we were already there. So where did he go?"

"Y'all did it twice? DAMN, GIRL!"

Savvy rolled her eyes. "Is that all you heard? You're worthless, you know that?"

"Okay, Savvy." Mags sighed. "I need you to listen to me carefully."

"Okay…"

"He could have needed to run errands, or pick up tools, or maybe he didn't feel comfortable going number two in your house. There could be a perfectly logical explanation. But in any event, y'all are dating. Ain't no commitments or rings on the table just yet. Now let that man live."

"Ugh, I hate that you're right." She fingered the next file to be reviewed.

"Of course I'm right! Listen, Spencer's a good guy, and even if he isn't the one, at least this means you're well on your way to moving on from Jason."

Savvy thought about that for a moment. "I think that I need to clear my head. Whatever Jason is thinking, he just confuses me, and what does that mean for Spencer? Maybe I should plan a mini vacation or something."

Maggie tsked. "But what does getting away accomplish? Isn't that the same as poking your head in the sand? I'm not seeing how the ostrich effect really helps you here."

"Maybe it doesn't help, but maybe it does? I need some time alone to think. I don't know what I really want, but I feel pressure right now. If I'm away, maybe the weight of the pressure is off me for a little while so I can think."

"But isn't this pressure self-imposed? No one is rushing you to make a decision. You've been on two dates with Spencer. Jason might want to talk, but he's currently MIA. You don't even know what he wants. So what is the source of the pressure you currently feel?"

"It's probably self-imposed." Savvy blinked with irritation.

"So, if you go away to think about this, aren't you still imposing the same pressure?"

"Why are you trying to go all Spock on me right now?"

"'It's only logical,'" she mimicked. "I mean, logic works in this instance, so I'm Team Spock. I'm trying to understand where the relief from the pressure comes from, when the pressure is self-imposed, and self is the one going on this trip."

Savvy sighed.

"I know when you're veering off into the dark place. Spencer isn't Jason, Savvy. He's not going to do what Jason did."

Savvy hated the way Maggie read her, but she was spot-on.

"Don't run and hide, Savs. Face this shit head-on. You can do this, and while we all know that I have my opinions, I think that you ultimately have to decide what it is that you want and need right now. We don't have to live with the ultimate decision in the same way that you do, so this is really about what you think. Take your time. If you don't start putting yourself first, we're going to be right back here in the future."

"Easier said than done."

Mags ignored her. "Maybe go on a couple of dates with other guys from the app and see what all is out there. This isn't a situation where you have to make a choice about a man. This is about what makes you happy, what makes you

feel valued, what you no longer intend to put up with, and
what you want out of your next relationship. That's why we
set up that Tinder profile in the first place. Once you figure
that stuff out, then you can figure out who you might want
to focus your energy on. But don't do anything serious until
you put yourself first and figure out what you really want."

"That doesn't sound unreasonable, I guess," Savvy con-
ceded. "So I guess that means I'll find someone to take me
out to dinner tonight. Or maybe just drinks."

"You got this, Savvy. Happy hunting!" Maggie giggled.

"Bye," Savvy muttered.

Surveying the folders around her, Savvy made a list of
tasks to complete by the end of the day and set to work re-
viewing the files piled on her desk. Her phone pinged, and
a notification popped up on her screen that a guy named
Braden had liked her profile. Savvy unlocked her phone,
curious to take a look at her potential date.

I am never fucking listening to Maggie again.

Braden sat across from her, arms stretched across the high-
top table, closing the distance between them. Savvy sipped
on a glass of old vine zinfandel, glad that she'd opted for
a drink and not dinner. They sat close to the bar at a local
dive located within walking distance of her house. Savvy
had gone to the bathroom to tell Kotter that an emergency
text was necessary to get her out of there.

Braden reached forward and stroked her wrist. "I would
love to know what you are thinking, beautiful."

Savvy eased her hand away, attempting to smile. "Oh,
nothing. I'm just enjoying the company," she lied.

Braden smiled broadly. He was attractive enough, and
had a nice build, but his home training lacked boundary
markers. When Savvy arrived at the bar, he'd immediately

pointed out another girl who he'd hooked up with recently, and he was far too quick to try and touch her. *No more online dating for me.*

A text notification zinged her phone. "Sorry, I need to check this. My friend is watching my dog for me—I had to take him to the vet earlier today."

"Oh, I didn't know you had a dog? What kind?"

Shit. Savvy hadn't thought through details. "A corgi?"

He nodded. "Nice. I had a border collie with my last girlfriend. She got him when we split. Now I only get to see him when she calls for a little reunion, if you know what I mean." He grinned at her, raising his eyebrows suggestively.

Ewww.

Savvy shuddered inwardly. "Oh, wow." Looking down at her phone, Kotter's text read, Come home now! Sparky needs you. Inwardly, Savvy rolled her eyes. Sparky? "I'm so sorry, but I'm going to have to cut this short. She's saying my dog is still getting sick, so I'd better get home to take care of him."

Braden threw back the rest of his vodka soda. "No problem, I'll walk you back." He gestured to the bartender for the check.

Savvy stammered, "Oh, that's really not necessary."

"Nonsense," he said casually, his eyes sparkling with motive. "It's dark out, and I'm a gentleman."

"Of course you are." Savvy forced a smile, taking a long sip of her wine. *How the hell do I get out of this?*

Only about three blocks from her house, Savvy cringed when Braden grabbed hold of her hand. "Such a nice night out." His thumb stroked her wrist, and her insides screamed. Snatching her hand back, she shoved it in her pocket, wanting to run for it.

When they reached her front door, Savvy turned to thank

Braden for the date, but he was too close for comfort. He stood just inches away before leaning down and pressing his lips against hers. Trapped, Savvy squeezed her eyes shut, turning her head to the side, when she realized that he wasn't quite finished. She hinted gently that she was done. "Okay, thanks for the walk." *Big mistake.*

Braden slid a hand up to tilt her face to the right, his lips pressed tightly against hers again. His tongue slid forward, breaking the seal of her closed mouth, launching itself against her teeth. Savvy put a hand on his shoulder, pushing against him to break away, but he took her touch as encouragement. He stepped forward to close up the space Savvy had created, pinning her against the front door, his tongue slowly delving forward again to wrestle with hers.

Overwhelmed, Savvy put both hands on his chest and pushed him backward. He blinked with surprise, smiling down on her. He put his hands on her waist, trying to pull her closer, but Savvy kept her hands against his chest, maintaining a semblance of her bubble.

"I see how you like it," Braden said, leering. "Playing hard to get." He tried to advance forward again, but Savvy held him back.

She shook her head with a conciliatory smile. "I play no games."

He scratched his head. "Don't you want to invite me inside?" He gestured toward the door.

"No, I don't think that's a good idea. I really need to attend to Sparky."

His left hand returned to her waist and traveled down to the curve of her hip. "Well, I think it's a very good idea," he murmured, looking at her beneath heavy lids. "Come on, just for a little while."

Savvy smiled. "Thanks, but I have an early morning tomorrow." Savvy removed his hand before he could grab her ass and then patted him on the shoulder. "This was...nice. I'll call you, okay?" He nodded slowly, and Savvy turned to unlock the door. She stepped inside, shuddering hard as the door closed behind her.

"Hey."

"AHHH!" Savvy fell to the floor, stifling her cry with her hands.

Spencer stepped back with his hands raised. "It's me. You're okay."

"Oh my God, Spencer. You scared the SHIT out of me."

"Yeah, well, you surprised me too. You'd better attend to Sparky. Make sure he's alright." He raised an eyebrow at her, still on the floor, and walked back into the kitchen to collect his things. He left a minute later.

Shit.

19

Savvy wasn't paying attention as she rushed into line at the coffee shop the next morning, until a hand landed on her shoulder. She turned to see Spencer's handsome face smiling down at her. "Good morning."

Savvy inhaled sharply at the sight of him. "Good morning." They hadn't discussed Savvy's date with Braden after Spencer left, and Savvy had spent a restless night worried that she'd ruined everything.

"So how are you?" he asked.

"I'm okay. Work is busier, now that I've taken on my new responsibilities, but I am up to the task." Savvy laughed awkwardly.

A weird expression crossed Spencer's face before he returned his normal smile. "I didn't bring Teddy with me today. I have some deadlines to get through too," he said. "Maybe when the week calms down, you can let me know if you're interested in getting together for dinner? Maybe we can talk about what happened last night too."

She gave a quick nod. "Of course, that sounds good! I know that we were talking about that great Ethiopian restaurant you mentioned, and I'm really interested." She tried to sound genuine, but instead her words came out overly enthusiastic.

Spencer nodded his acknowledgment. "You look beautiful today," he said slowly, taking in the features of her face.

Savvy smiled. "It seems like a lot of people think that lately," she quipped, thinking of Braden and the guys at the tennis courts. Project Upgrade seemed to be garnering real results.

Spencer's smile flattened. Her face flushed. "Right, well," he said slowly, "I should probably get back to work. I just wanted to say hi and see where things stood for later this week. Just let me know."

Before Savvy could respond, he walked away. *I'm a complete fool.* Savvy ordered her almond milk latte from Jessica at the front counter, adding quickly that it was to go. Jessica gave her a big smile and got started on her order. "Cinnamon on top, right, Savs?" she asked.

"Yes please." Savvy knew her face was flaming red from embarrassment after her fumble. While she waited for her drink, she glanced in Spencer's direction. He'd put on noise-canceling headphones and was bent over his laptop, staring intensely at his screen. "Don't Bother Me" was written across his face.

Damn.

Jessica handed her the latte, and Savvy grabbed a lid from the self-service kiosk. She ducked her head and headed out the door, her foot too far in her mouth to say goodbye to

Spencer, but she stopped herself. She turned on her heel and marched over to his table.

"Listen, I'm sorry. Work has been chaotic, I've been really stressed, and I was so confused the other morning, because you left without saying goodbye. I took that to mean that you didn't have a good time, and my friend basically warned me that I was catching feelings too fast. So I went on that really awful date for drinks and used a fake pet emergency to get out of it." *I sound like a complete lunatic.* "Anyway, I apologize."

He watched her for several seconds. "It's okay. Honestly, the whole pet emergency was pretty funny. You had nothing to worry about—my phone was dead, and I needed to rush home to walk Teddy."

Of course, Teddy!

Savvy closed her eyes. "I'm such an idiot. It's just that I'm out of practice with this dating stuff."

Half of his mouth curved. "I get it, Savvy. There's no rush, okay? Seriously, we can take our time. I'm not going anywhere."

"So you'll still come to tennis?"

He squeezed her hand, and the fluttering returned to her stomach. "I'll be there."

Savvy showed up early to the tennis session to get some one-on-one practice time in before her friends arrived. A ball moved toward her forehand, and she ran to get into position. The ball machine bore the brunt, as she aimed her frustrations at it, daring it to try her. *Why did I have to say that to him? Like throwing Braden in his face is something to be proud of...* Ball after ball returned back to the machine, slamming against its sides, until Beth turned it off and told her to take a couple of laps.

She had her hands on her hips, watching Savvy put her

racket down to get started on her laps, giving her a tough side-eye. "You good, Savs?" she asked.

She grumbled something noncommittal and started her jog. Beth matched her stride, taking the jog with her. Savvy sucked in a stubborn breath.

"What's going on? Is this about that guy, Spencer? The fellas and I can pay him a visit, you know." Beth shook her head.

"No, it's not him," Savvy said, her breath starting to quicken. "Not exactly anyway. Besides, he's our fourth, so you're meeting him shortly."

"So what happened? I need an explanation as to why you're trying to break the ball machine." She glanced at her with a half smile.

"I saw him this morning, and I acted a complete fool."

Beth's face scrunched up into a suspicious frown. "You acted a fool? How?"

"He was being sweet and complimentary. He told me he thought I looked really beautiful today." Savvy breathed deeply, giving pause for effect. "And then I told him that was a popular opinion lately. And this is after he caught me at the tail end of a bad date last night."

Beth tossed her head back and gave a high-pitched sigh. Chuckling softly to herself, she shook her head. "Oh, Savvy."

She half smiled, trying to keep her breath even. "Those two words are extremely loaded, Beth."

"It's not unsalvageable, but that was kind of a low blow."

"It was a dick move. You can say it."

Beth nodded in agreement. "It was a dick move, Savs. And trust me, I appreciate that you are willing to admit that it was a dick move."

She nodded, looked at the ground in front of them as they jogged. Beth nudged Savvy with her elbow.

"He wouldn't have gotten under your skin, and you wouldn't feel how you do right now, if you didn't like this guy, Savs. You wouldn't be so bothered about making a dick move unless you liked him."

"Maybe I'm just a nice person?" She looked at Beth, trying to keep a straight face.

"Right, Savs, that's it." She laughed.

"But you're right. I like him. But now Jason wants to talk. I don't know what to think." She shrugged. "I think I need to get away for a while. Give myself time to think."

"That doesn't sound like a terrible thing, as long as you aren't trying to hide."

Savvy rolled her eyes. "It's like you've been talking to Maggie, I swear."

Beth laughed. "Maggie's a smart woman."

She nodded. "That other date I went on the other night? The guy was a total skeez. No sense of personal boundaries." She shuddered, thinking of his sloppy kisses. "It was supposed to be to try something different—get my mind off Jason and Spencer. I don't think I'll be trying that again for a while."

"That's fair, considering you're still having a visible reaction." Beth laughed. "Do I need to go looking for this guy?"

Savvy chuckled. "Only if he shows up outside my house."

She nodded. "Bet."

The girls arrived a short while later, and Savvy was glad she'd gotten in some good quality time with Beth on and off the court. Still, it did her heart good to see Beth pull Joanie into an embrace. When she dipped her head for a quick kiss, Savvy made a mental note to catch up with her girl, because she'd neglected the customary follow-up for all-of-the-details of their budding relationship.

As they pulled away from each other, Joanie looked at

the empty court next to them. "I thought you were having some friends join us today?"

"Yeah, I was really interested in meeting them after Savs filled us in," Mags started. "I'm so curious to meet these handsome friends you've been hiding from us, Beth."

Savvy smiled. "Trust me, you won't be disappointed." She rubbed her hands together mischievously. One of the guys was a hundred percent Maggie's type.

"Ladies." Spencer jogged toward them in a T-shirt and basketball shorts, a racket bag slung over his shoulder. He looked damn good. He extended a hand to Beth. "I'm Spencer. Savvy speaks very highly of you."

Beth smiled. "I could say the same. The others should be here any minute. They were probably in the parking lot when you three arrived." Beth shook her head and looked at Savvy, the gravel in her voice dipping lower. "Total fuckery."

Spencer turned to Savvy, wrapping his arms around her shoulders. She circled his waist and he leaned closer to whisper in her ear. "What have you gotten me into?" he teased.

Savvy giggled as he released her, throwing her hands up in the air. She couldn't wait for shenanigans. From a distance, they heard catcalling and all turned to see Beth's friends sauntering over.

Savvy's girls got into formation around her. Mags propped an arm up on her shoulder, intently watching the approach. Spencer laughed, jogging in place.

"Hey, Savvy," Matt called out to her. "I see the squad's rollin' deep today!"

Matt stood at six foot six, with his soft curls and a groomed beard. His glasses sat on a trail of freckles roaming the bridge of his nose. Savvy grinned at him. "Hey, Matt, how are you?"

He leaned down to give her a quick hug. "I'm good. You good, Sis?"

"Damn, she's Sis already?" Beth glared at Matt.

Matt shrugged. "We all received the threatening text you sent. You told us to leave Savvy alone. I'd say that puts her in Sis territory." He turned to her. "We need to take care of some clown for you, Savvy?"

Savvy's smile broadened. "Nah, I'm good right now. Thanks, bruh."

Matt pursed his lips and nodded. "Cool."

Shawn shook his head and dipped forward to give her a quick hug and a kiss on the cheek. "How you doin' today, Savvy? Please excuse my friends."

Savvy made general introductions, ignoring the cheesy looks the guys gave her friends. She stood next to Spencer, bumping her hip against his. He squeezed her waist.

Rob stepped forward in tennis gear and a baseball cap. His dark chocolate complexion was smooth and well-groomed. "Ladies," he said, his velvety voice reverberating as he shook hands with each of them. Mags took to Rob right away, the way Savvy knew she would, and he looked at her like she was a whole snack. Savvy saw her blush a little, as Rob tilted his head to the side, watching.

Matt and Shawn followed suit. Shawn had a broad frame and thick arms, but Savvy liked him the most because of his chill personality. They all shook hands with Spencer, who was standing near Savvy, but not crowding her. Showing up, but giving her literal space, and she thought she might love him a little bit just for that.

Matt stood between Savvy and Joanie, putting his arms around their shoulders. Joanie hid a smile, watching Beth's reaction. "So these two are both off-limits, B?"

Beth nodded toward Savvy. "That's Sis. Plus, she brought

a date." Then she nodded toward Joanie. "That's me." Joanie beamed up at her, and Savvy caught looks of surprise from Spencer and Maggie.

"DAMNNNN!" The rest of them reacted simultaneously.

"Like that, bruh?" Matt turned, eyeing Joanie more closely. "I see it, actually. Yeah, this makes a lot of sense right here."

"I can't believe you just made a public declaration!" Maggie nudged Beth with her shoulder.

Beth turned to Mags. "So you approve?"

Maggie looked to Savvy, and they looked at Joanie, who was glowing and still smiling up at Beth. "We approve," they said together.

Rob raised his eyebrows. "It's like they're of one mind. Beehive mentality."

Savvy wrapped her arms around Joanie's waist, her friend reciprocating immediately. "When it's about our friends, that's exactly right."

Maggie nodded, stretching her arms up over her head. "So we're beating you guys in tennis today?"

"Oh," Rob recognized quickly. "You're the competitive one."

Joanie snickered. "Guilty."

Mags rolled her eyes, ignoring looks from all of them. "Yeah, whatever. Let's warm up so y'all can get this work."

"Whoa!" Matt exclaimed. "You didn't tell us that she would go this hard, B. I am so ready for this." He put his bag down and started jumping in place to warm up his calves. He leaned into a lunge with a serious face, and everyone burst into laughter.

Beth shoved him over to one side of the court. "Okay, clown. Get moving. Fam, you're going to start on that side.

Ladies and Spencer, this side." She gestured toward their side of the court. "Let's get warmed up."

Savvy moved everyone's gear to the benches to get it out of the way. She knew Beth's plan for the group workout, and had already warmed up, so Savvy ran around the court with the tennis ball hopper to pick up the stray balls while Beth ran the group through their warm-ups. The girls snuck looks at the guys, whispering their observations to Maggie. The guys were a lot more obvious in their observations. Spencer wore a look of amusement. Savvy grabbed her racket, smacking him on the butt with it before joining the line so that Beth could run them through drills.

Beth assigned everyone a spot on the court. Matt slapped his arms and legs, getting into a low squat, imitating all of the meatheads they'd seen at the gym and channeling Kevin Hart's stand-up routine.

Joanie grinned.

Maggie already had her game face on, sizing up everyone on the court. "Let's go, ladies," she called out, rolling her shoulders back to show that she meant business. "And Spencer."

He nodded in her direction, his legs wide as he held his racket in both hands.

Beth looked at her, and Savvy rolled her eyes. She called out, "Everyone ready?"

They all grunted. Rob gave Mags a quick wink as he bent his knees and got into position. Savvy couldn't see her face, but she imagined her smiling just enough to ignite her dimples, which would completely be an advantage as long as those two were in that position.

"Do me proud, girl," Savvy whispered, to which Maggie gave an almost imperceptible nod.

Beth tossed a ball. "Savs, you're up. Once a team gets to

ten points, you'll rotate positions. You don't have to serve—
I just want you to get the ball over the net and into play.
Part of the drill is getting to the ball, the other part is being
mindful of where everyone on the court is situated. This
drill requires communication. You don't want to hit your
teammates, and you do want to be strategic in your ball
placement."

Savvy nodded. "Got it." She grinned over to Matt, who
was going to be on the receiving end. "You ready?"

"Let's get it." Matt dipped into a low squat in jest, and got
a playful smack in the back of the head from Rob.

"Pull it together, bruh." Rob shook his head. His deep
voice was so rich that it sent a shiver down her spine. *That
man was fine.*

Savvy heard Maggie exhale. "Whew, chile," she said
softly.

"Alright, y'all, let's go get 'em," she said, as she held out
the ball to let the guys know they were starting.

"We got this, Savs," Kotter called out.

Thwack! Savvy hit the ball just inside the T, giving it everything that she had. Matt blinked, swinging his racket
hard, but missing the ball as it whizzed by.

"Damn, girl!" Matt called out.

"Nice, Savs." Spencer clicked his racket against hers, giving her a wink.

"One point for Savvy's team." Beth smiled confidently.
"This is going to get interesting really quickly."

She tossed a ball to Maggie to serve next. Shawn squatted into a ready position, gaze steady on Mags, swinging
his racket side to side. Maggie served hard toward Shawn's
body, but he stepped out of the way and hit the ball with
his forehand across the court. Joanie leaped toward the ball

with a swinging volley, which Rob missed because he'd set his feet to go in the opposite direction.

"Well, well," Rob said. "Looks like we have to play a little catch-up now."

"Be careful over there, Savvy," Matt called. "This dude comes with the heat on serve."

Savvy put on her mean mug to defeat her nerves. "Bring it."

Her friends cheered, and Beth was all smiles. "That's right, get 'em, Sis. I want you to focus on body shots."

Savvy nodded, setting her sights on Rob, tilting her head slightly as she bent her knees and squared her shoulders.

"Damn," Rob said, watching her. The rest of the fellas chuckled. "No one better mess with Savvy if she gives you that look!"

Spencer peeked at her from the corner of his eye.

They played on, putting their all into it, rotating spots, and punishing the guys for thinking that they had anything on them. Spencer was smooth on the court. Quiet, focused. Savvy admired his technique, thinking that all of his competitiveness must be in his head, because he didn't talk smack. After five or six rotations, the other guys were ready to throw in the towel. Matt plopped down on the ground, catching his breath. "Y'all came to play today."

"If we're here, we came to play." Maggie said it simply. "Mama didn't raise no punk."

Shawn pointed at Mags, smirking. "You weren't lying, Savvy!"

"So where are y'all heading for dinner?" Rob asked, looking squarely at Maggie. "Maybe we can join you? We need to make plans for the next time we can all get together."

Maggie nodded slowly. "Let's go to Savvy's house. She can really burn."

"And I just had my kitchen renovated, so there's space for everyone." She stood next to Spencer, catching her breath. The scents of his natural musk and cologne combined to create an intoxicating fragrance.

All of the men perked up. "Word?" Matt asked. "Just tell us what to bring."

"Don't worry," Savvy smiled. "I got this. Just be careful around the construction."

20

Savvy left the tennis court before the others to get the food started. Spencer had to get home to walk Teddy, but he promised to stop by after. Rummaging through her old refrigerator, which was still on the back patio, she found she had everything she needed to change the ingredients into something that would be well received by the guys. She pulled the white paper off the island countertop, allowing only a brief thrill to run through her as she remembered what she and Spencer had done there.

Savvy turned the dial on her new six-burner stove, excited to see parts of her kitchen coming together so beautifully. The new flooring was still covered. The backsplash wasn't up yet, and they hadn't painted the kitchen yet, but the bigger, open space was inviting. The island faced the dining and living area, with new built-ins and crown molding. The furniture was covered with tarps from fresh painting.

Savvy coated some chicken thighs in olive oil and jerk

seasoning, threw them into a pot on high heat to brown the sides, and then poured a bottle and a half of lager and a cup of orange juice in to cover the meat. She turned the burner up to high and let that get to work while she pulled purple and green heads of cabbage out of the refrigerator, along with a couple of carrots, green onions, and cilantro. She grabbed white miso, white pepper, sesame oil, rice wine vinegar, and a bag of dry-roasted sliced almonds from her new pantry.

Everyone arrived then; Savvy heard Joanie let them in with her key. Mags took bags and coats, while Joanie removed tarps from the furniture and began mixing drinks. Mags connected her cell phone to the Bluetooth speaker, put on a chill playlist, and came into the kitchen to offer help.

"So." Savvy lowered her voice. "What do you think of Rob?"

"Girl, he is so fine. I don't know. And that voice!"

"Right? That voice is something serious." Savvy took a swig from her bottle of lager and then handed it to Mags, who followed suit.

Grasping the bottle, she shook her head. "Seriously, he could talk me straight out of my clothes."

"Well, damn, girl. Don't deny yourself. I say just let it happen." Savvy chuckled, beginning to slice up the cabbage and carrots for slaw. As she finished, she threw the vegetables into a bowl, then chopped up the fresh cilantro and green onions and threw those on top. She whisked together the dressing, squeezing in a little bit of lemon juice.

Mags looked around the kitchen, taking in the changes. "Spencer's done a great job. You look really close to having a finished kitchen!" She noticed that Savvy had already set out sweet Hawaiian rolls, some sliced red onion, sweet pickles, a tray of sliced cheeses, and two kinds of barbecue sauce. "Damn, girl. How did you do this so quickly?"

She shrugged. "I already had everything I needed for this potluck at work. I can just get more. This is an easy one. I'm doing a pulled chicken instead of pork, but it's dark meat, so the flavor should be good. Hey, grab the tongs and check the meat for me, will you?"

Mags lifted the lid and the scents of beer, citrus, and jerk seasoning wafted up. "This smells amazing." She used the tongs to lift up the chicken, and it was just starting to fall apart.

"Keep doing that. It'll continue to soak up the flavors from the liquid as you pull."

"Mmmmm." She snuck a piece to taste. "I miss your cooking, and it really hasn't been that long."

"I'm glad Beth came through."

"Yeah, she's good people."

"I heard my name. What are you two doing over here?" Beth walked over from the living room area, taking in the sights in the kitchen. "Damn, Savvy. You've been holding out on us!"

"I need to see this." Matt pushed his way into the kitchen, head craning over Maggie's to see the pulled chicken.

"Do any of y'all have nut allergies? I should have asked earlier." Savvy turned to their kitchen intruders.

"We eat everything, Savvy. Don't even worry about it. Matter of fact, don't expect to have any leftovers." Matt tried to sneak a piece of chicken out of the pot, but Mags playfully slapped his hand.

"Cool." Savvy poured her fresh dressing on the cabbage slaw, tossing it with another pair of tongs, and then sprinkled a handful of sliced almonds on top.

"This girl's a gourmet," Matt observed to Mags. "Y'all work out together and then eat well, I see."

Mags grinned up at him. "You have no idea!"

"You might have to fight me for this chicken," Matt

joked. Mags stopped what she was doing and snapped the tongs at him. He jumped back laughing, hands up. "You know what, I'm going to go back over there where it's safe and grab a drink. Just let me know when we can come in here and make a plate."

"That's what I thought," she retorted, giving him a sly smile and turning back to her assigned task.

Savvy turned to Beth. "You know, your friends are really something."

She cracked a smile. "You know I tried to tell you, right? Your friends are pretty unique themselves." She tapped Mags on her left shoulder and stole a piece of chicken from her right side. Mags nudged her toward the door.

"Okay, Sis. You just lost your pass too. Out you go!" Mags shooed her out of the kitchen.

As she rounded toward the dining table, she turned to grin at her. "You just gon' let her do me like that, Savs?"

Savvy hooked an elbow around Mags's shoulder and smiled over at Beth sweetly. "Every time, love."

With everything ready, Mags helped her carry the food to the dining table, which Joanie had uncovered and set. Joanie had drinks ready for them, and the fellas dove into the food like they hadn't eaten all day. Just as Savvy went to reach for a Hawaiian roll, her cell phone rang.

"Excuse me for a sec, I need to take this."

Walking into the other room, she answered the phone. "Hey, Unc. Everything okay?"

"Come to the house, Baby Girl. It's on fire." The strain in his voice told her everything she needed to know. She rushed into the living room to grab her purse; everyone looked at her in surprise.

"I have to go. You guys eat. I'll call you." Savvy was out the door before anyone could respond.

★ ★ ★

She stood next to her uncle feeling the warmth of the flames kissing her cheeks from two hundred feet away. Savvy put her arm around his shoulder and felt him tremble. Their refuge was burning to the ground. Home to all of their memories. "What happened, Unc?"

"I don't know, Baby Girl," he whispered. "I was coming home from the doctor's office, and the firefighters were already here. Ms. Mabel across the street saw smoke and called them."

Savvy leaned toward him, pulling him into a hug, as tears flowed down her cheeks. "Thank God you are safe. I can't lose you, Uncle," she whispered.

Their foreheads met for a moment of silence, and she closed her eyes to say a silent prayer of thanks for his safety.

"You ain't done with me yet, Baby Girl." Uncle Joe's voice caught, and he had to step back to compose himself. He covered his mouth. Unable to meet her eyes, he turned away from the fire. "This is my fault."

She looked at her uncle in surprise, his eyes squeezed shut like he wanted to push something from his memory, the weight of responsibility anchoring his shoulders. "How is this your fault, Uncle? You didn't start the fire."

"No, but if it started because of those damn electrical issues, it's my fault." He sucked his teeth, shaking his head. His arms were out at his sides, splaying widely, as he made his case. "I thought that I had more time, that I could take care of all of the issues in the house. I knew they were there, but the cost was too much to handle all at once. And now look at it." A tear escaped his eye; his voice barely above a whisper. "What would your granny think? She left me to care for their home. Look at their home now."

The fire raged throughout the entire house. The front

door stood wide-open. They could see nothing inside but fire illuminating the hallway toward the kitchen. Flames spread over the rooftop. They stretched out like arms reaching for the stars from the windows.

Water forced its way into the house through the broken windows, and Savvy thought about Granny's quilts, the old photographs of her grandparents dancing or hosting their beloved neighborhood cookouts. Her uncle's new instruments. Nothing would be salvaged.

She pulled her uncle to her. "Granny wouldn't blame you, Uncle. Remember how she used to crack jokes about the stairs creaking? How they had to take down the porch swing? The house always had problems, but we loved it anyway."

He nodded slowly, watching as the blackened steps of the porch warped under the force of the water. "We sure did." He cracked a sad smile that touched only half of his mouth. "She used to joke that someone could fall through the floor of that guest bedroom and land right on the stove." He chuckled slowly. "Oh, Mama. She never cared about stuff, you know. She wouldn't let this worry her one bit. The only thing she'd try to salvage would be—"

"Her big pot," Savvy finished, smiling. "That's so true. That pot is magic."

"Mmm-hmm. Good thing I gave that to you after she passed."

She slid her hand into his, leaning her head onto his shoulder. "I'll keep it safe, Uncle. I promise."

He kissed the top of her head, squeezing her hand. "There's no one else I'd trust to do the job, Baby Girl." He smiled ruefully. "I can only imagine what your mama will have to say about this."

Savvy tugged at her uncle's hand, and they sat on the curb.

They stayed like that, watching the firemen work, sharing old memories, trying to laugh through the loss they both felt. Eventually, Uncle sent her home, saying he was going to stay to talk to the firemen. Ms. Mabel had already offered for him to stay in the in-law suite on the back of her property. She liked the safety of having a retired cop in the neighborhood, though Savvy suspected she wanted his proximity for other reasons too. She gave him a tight squeeze, promising to call him in the morning. "I love you, Uncle."

"I love you too, Baby Girl. Go get some rest—you have work in the morning."

"You sure you're okay?" Spencer rubbed her shoulder, rhythmically kneading his thumb into her back. His head propped up in one hand, he used the other to ease some of the tension out of Savvy's muscles.

She lay with her back to him, appreciating the contact, but feeling numb inside. "Yeah, I'm okay. Thank you for staying to check on me." She hadn't said much since she returned. The girls had sent Beth and her friends home with care packages, exactly as Savvy would have done. When she got back, she promised to keep the girls updated as they left.

"Of course. I got here right after you left. When the girls told me about the fire, it just seemed right to wait." He ran his fingers up her arm, and she shivered. He pulled her closer against him, kissing her shoulder, running his hand over her hair. "Just relax, Savs. I got you."

He continued to run his fingers over her hair, and Savvy felt herself relax. She opened her eyes hours later, hearing the lock on the front door click. *Again.*

21

Savvy pushed through her file review with huge resolve to be done at a decent hour, though she was completely inundated by her new clients. She made a list of things that had to be tackled that day and decided everything else could wait. She had plans to meet the girls for dinner in Little Tokyo. She had been dreaming of an uni dinner tray for weeks. Fresh sea urchin was something Savvy could never turn down.

Her phone pinged with a text message from Spencer.

Hey, beautiful. I hope your day is going well. Give me a call when you have a free minute.

Butterflies began to flutter in her chest, but then she remembered him leaving before she was awake again and she stared out the window. The sun had begun to set, but there was still another hour or two before dark. A hazy orange glow spread across the horizon, and Savvy thought again about having a little escape. Maybe a spa trip would do her some good.

I'll respond to him later. Once she made it through a critical mass of files and reviewed a strategy memo for an upcoming meeting with Warren and some of senior management, she looked at her calendar to find a window of time that fell after a big presentation she was scheduled to give their new clients. She was barely keeping her head above water in this new role—deadlines were coming to her fast, and she wasn't able to stay ahead like she had in the past, but she was sure it was just because she'd been distracted with the breakup and the renovation. After her presentation would be the perfect time for a long weekend. By then, the renovation would be done too, so she would have the house back to herself. She could use the time to get her head right for the job. Convinced, she sent an email to her boss requesting three days of vacation time.

Warren emailed her back almost immediately, marveling at how much paid leave she had stored up over the last few years. When Savvy replied, telling him that she was rewarding herself with a getaway, his immediate response made her laugh. About damn time.

After another hour, she surveyed the mountains of files on every flat surface of her office. She easily had several hours more work to do, but she was too distracted to focus. Switching gears, she researched more cooking classes offered at Paul and Sarah's waterfront grill. *A staycation could be everything.* Before Savvy could overanalyze the whole thing, she booked three different classes with Chef Sarah, and texted an invitation to have her and Paul over for dinner.

Savvy met the girls in front of one of their favorite sushi spots. Joanie left work early to position herself in line, since no reservations were accepted.

They settled in at their table and ordered a bottle of sake. "How's your uncle?" Joanie wiped her hands with a hot towel.

Savvy took a deep breath. "He's really shaken. He feels like the fire was his fault. It's a total loss." She shook her head. "We're devastated."

Joanie squeezed her shoulder. "I'm so sorry. Please let us know if there's anything we can do. Literally anything."

Maggie nodded, reaching over to grab Savvy's hand.

"Thanks, guys. I will," she assured them, reaching for her menu.

"How are you holding up?"

"Honestly, I've been better, but I have some news." The girls looked up at her from their menus expectantly. Savvy put on her brightest smile, ready for the inevitable. "I've decided to plan a little solo retreat."

"Savvy." Mags sighed. "Not this again."

Joanie looked at Maggie and then back at her. Maggie jumped a little, like she'd been kicked under the table. "So where are you thinking of going?" Joanie asked.

"I'm going to take a few days off, have a staycation. The time is already approved, and I booked some cooking classes already. I just want to hole up in the house once the renovations are done. I feel a little disjointed right now."

"What's going on? Did something happen with Spencer?" Maggie frowned.

Her shoulders dropped. "He did it again. He left without saying goodbye. He just sneaks out in the morning before I wake up."

"But didn't he say he had to get home to walk his dog last time? Are you wanting him to wake you up?"

"I just don't like the way it makes me feel. I mean, we didn't have sex last night, but still." Savvy didn't want to feel like she was being needy, but she wanted him to be there when she woke up.

"He stayed the whole night, though, Savs. He waited for you to come back to make sure you were okay," Joanie pointed out. "Have you told him how you feel?"

She shook her head. "I know I'm doing the most right now, but I just want someone who will stay. Maybe it's too soon to have these expectations, or maybe he's just not that guy for me."

"Girl, you should tell him how you feel. Men are not mind readers. Or better yet, just have him bring the dog over to your place."

Savvy smiled at the thought, looking off in the distance.

"I know that this retreat wasn't planned because Spencer didn't stay until you woke up, so what's really going on?" Joanie propped her head in her hand.

"I just feel like committing to some serious self-care. I never did anything for myself when I was with Jason, so I thought it was high time I tried. It's just an extended week-end of pampering. No dating..." She shrugged.

"I love that!" Joanie grinned. "We could all use more of that."

"Couldn't you just do a spa day?" Maggie questioned crossly.

"Do I tell you the right way to pamper yourself? I haven't even gotten my nails done in two years! Let me live, Mags," Savvy snapped.

She shook her head. "Seriously, Savvy. You deserve the time off, but don't use this as an excuse to avoid Spencer. Just talk to the man."

"It's not all Spencer. I'm still annoyed with Jason. He asked to speak with me, and then he decided to ghost me again when I asked what he wanted to talk about. I just don't understand the mind games. And work is busier than ever. I'm overwhelmed by the pace I'm supposed to keep. I need to unplug."

"Just block Jason! Heffa, I need you to understand why your friends might be concerned! Besides, we talked about this. You can't run away from your problems, Savvy. You need to face them head-on. Ow, stop kicking me!" She winced from the impact.

"No one is running, Mags. Seriously, breathe."

"I actually think this is a great idea," Joanie said. "I was a little worried, because you haven't done this before, but I think it could be really good for you. A little mental health break."

Mags shot Joanie a murderous look. "Seriously, you're going to support this?" She gestured toward Savvy like she was a problem and not a person.

Joanie leaned forward. "If by 'this' you mean our best friend, hell yeah, I'm going to support her."

Maggie sat back in her seat and sucked her teeth. "I can't believe you've been drinking the Kool-Aid. I blame Beth."

"Maggie, now you know I love you," Joan started slowly, her voice lowered through gritted teeth, "but you need to choose your next words very carefully."

Savvy lowered her head slightly, as if she were the kid at the dinner table who wasn't yet in trouble. Joanie maintained her cool most of the time, but she was not the person that you wanted to piss off.

That tone must have triggered Maggie because she immediately tried to temper the conversation. "Look," she said slowly. "I want what is best for Savvy, but I think that this trip only delays the inevitable. She's ducking her head in the sand and pretending like there aren't decisions to be made. This is all a hot mess."

"What decisions would you have Savvy make right now? Let her make her own damned decisions when she's good and ready."

Savvy raised her hand peevishly. "Um, can we act like Savvy is actually at the table?"

Joanie turned to her. "Of course."

Maggie sighed. "Yes, Savvy, you're here. But I don't feel like I can reason with you right now."

"But what is there to reason away?" she asked. "It's not like I'm on the lam. I'm trying to get some peace of mind, focus on some self-care, which I have been needing for a long time now. I want to come back, hopefully with fresh eyes, and see things for what they are. I'm not hiding from making decisions—I just want to be sure that I'm making the right decisions with a level head."

Maggie bit her lip, nodding slightly. "I just want you to see in you what we all see. I don't want you to be overwhelmed by the nonsense that people like Jason spew, because all it's meant to do is break you down and make you doubt yourself. You're gorgeous, revenge body or not."

"Well then, give me time to see that. I have to work my way there."

"I think this could be good for you, Savs," Joanie offered. She observed the steam coming out of Maggie's ears. "Sometimes you can't see the forest for the trees when you're right in the middle of it. Taking a step back helps you get a view that you might have missed otherwise."

"See." Savvy gestured to her. "I'm sayin'. Maybe not as clearly, but that's what I mean. Now let's enjoy this food before Joanie pops you one good time, Mags."

"She did get the momma voice real quick," Mags laughed.

Joanie nodded. "Everyone best act right round TT Joanie!"

Savvy grinned at Joanie. "Kotter, give the people a jingle for that 'Act Right.'"

"Keep your teeth from clicking with Act Right. Act Right, from the makers of Backhands by Big Momma." Joanie put on her best advertisement voice.

"I know that's right!" Mags cackled. "One more!"

Joanie cleared her throat. "Okay, okay. Do you ever get sent into the backyard to pick switches? Are relatives constantly threatening to put hands on you? This patented, extrastrength formula is an attitude changer in a bottle. Pick up a bottle of Act Right today. Act Right: kid tested, momma approved."

"Okay, now let's eat. I am too ready for this uni dinner." A server appeared with their trays of uni and sashimi, bowls of sticky rice, and plates of nori and shiso leaves.

Joanie raised a piece of uni between her chopsticks. "To Savvy and self-discovery. To finding clarity and growing into our best selves so we can live our best lives."

"To living our best lives!"

22

Lina followed Savvy into her office after her first strategy meeting. "So how did it go?"

"Better than I thought that it would. I was so worried that I wouldn't have anything to contribute, but they liked having a fresh perspective in the room. The new client they're bringing on is a really big one, and they need to plan out the division of work. Plus, they offer products that none of us have been underwriting here, so everyone will need to go through a couple of training sessions to get up to speed."

"Are you sure they're ready to take it on? You're pretty inundated right now." Lina took in the massive piles around the office.

Savvy grimaced. "Well, it's already a done deal. We've got the lead on it. Nation's Mutual will be moved off our plates so that we have the bandwidth to handle this one. They're called People's Trust."

"Oh, cool! I've heard of them. They're really popular

right now. And moving Nation's Mutual will help allevi-
ate some pressure."

"Yes! I have a presentation with People's Trust before
my vacation, where I'll walk them through the training
modules I have to create. They want to make sure we have
a strong grasp on the features of their products before the
team is trained."

"Well, if we're expecting a huge amount of work from
this client, we'd better get those new underwriters up to
speed. You're carrying their workload right now."

Over the past week, she'd hired two junior underwriters.
They'd completed medical terminology classes and HIPAA
training, and they'd been studying their current products
for the past few days. "Agreed. Let's schedule time in the
conference room for tomorrow morning, and then see if
Karen can offer them some systems training now that she's
back from vacation."

Lina nodded. "You think about two hours for the conference room is enough?"

"I think so. I want them to start with doing the file
screenings, ordering the telephone interviews and medical
records, and getting a sense of the rates based on health con-
ditions. Ana can lead the training and audit their files, since
she's open to working a little overtime. Once she feels like
they're up to speed, assign them each to a product to clear
out some backlog."

"You got it, boss." Lina smiled. "You were made for this
job, you know."

"I still feel like an imposter in this office," Savvy laughed.
"But we're getting there. It will be nice to have a full team."

"It will be a huge help. I'm still amazed that you're finally
giving yourself some time off!"

"I cannot wait. In the meantime, I'm going to work remotely this week. Try to catch up on some of this backlog."

"I'll email you lists!" Lina called over her shoulder.

"Thanks!"

On her way home, Savvy thought about her issues with
Spencer leaving in the morning and wondered whether she
was making a big deal out of nothing. But it felt like something to her. Jason was forever walking away from her. In
the end, it seemed like he was there only for the meals she
made. She wanted Spencer to feel different, and maybe com-
paring the two was unfair, but she couldn't help it.

Spencer's truck was parked out front when she pulled up.
"Hello?" she called as the front door swung open. "Wow!"
she breathed. She clasped her hands beneath her chin as she
stepped into the house.

All of the protective paper and tarps were gone. She admired the slabs of slate on her kitchen floors, the reddish-
brown hardwood throughout the rest. Her L-shaped kitchen
with a farmhouse sink, the giant island facing the rest of the
living space. The recessed LED lighting reflected off gleam-
ing white counters and cabinets, and the polished stainless
steel appliances shone. A tall wine fridge stood next to her
double-door refrigerator. Three leather stools sat on the
other side of the island.

A bottle of wine with a red bow sat on the island with a
card. "Welcome to your new home kitchen, Savvy! Cheers
to many new memories and amazing meals!—Spencer and
Teddy." She smiled.

"So what do you think?" Spencer leaned against the wall
leading toward the bedrooms.

"Hey, I was wondering if I'd missed you." She had the
urge to give him a hug, but she remembered that she had
been upset with him that morning.

"Just clearing away the last of the tools and materials."
He lifted a power drill in one hand.

"It's beautiful, Spencer. Beyond all of my expectations."
Her farmhouse table was set under a new fixture of Edison
lights. The new sofa and chairs framed an intricately woven

rug topped with a square upholstered ottoman. New built-in bookcases covered an inner wall. "I don't even know how to thank you. I'm so overwhelmed," she gushed.

"I was a little worried when I didn't hear back from you." His head tilted to the side, as he watched her, stepping closer.

She wanted to tell him how she felt, but she couldn't find the words. Savvy ran her fingertips over the counters, searching for the right thing to say.

"Savvy?"

Nervous energy bubbled over. "Work's been kicking my ass," she blurted out. "I'm really behind, so I'd better get back to it." She gestured toward her office.

"Okay, sure." He came closer, squeezing her hand. "You sure there isn't anything else going on?"

"Nah, I'm just anxious about catching up. Want me to call you later?"

He eyed her suspiciously.

I am a terrible liar.

"Sure." His eyes held questions, but he didn't press her.

Savvy stood on her toes to kiss his lips. "Seriously, thank you. This space is everything."

He kissed her again, nuzzling her cheek. "I'm glad you like it, Savs. Don't forget to call me, okay?"

"Promise."

Savvy arrived at the tennis courts a few minutes early, but Beth was already there and set up. "What up, Savvy? Man, I need to thank you again for that meal the other night. You have some serious skills!"

Savvy grinned at her, giving her a customary high five and a hug. "Anytime, love. How is your week going?"

"I can't complain. Picked up a couple of new clients. People have seen some of our group workouts and want to do something similar. I'm thinking of putting on a clinic this summer."

"That's great! You already know you can sign me up."

"I hoped you would say that. How's your uncle?"

Savvy shook her head. "He's devastated and staying with one of his neighbors, Ms. Mabel. I offered to help pay for repairs, but he refused. He's waiting to hear back from the insurance company."

"Wow, I know that's heavy. That was your grandparents' house?"

"Yeah." Her voice caught, and Beth wrapped her arms around Savvy. "I planned to buy that house someday, you know, just to keep it in the family. Now it's gone."

Beth gave her a squeeze. "Did you make any decisions about the vacation you wanted to take?"

Savvy nodded. "I booked it already. I'm going to do a few extra lessons with you and take some cooking classes."

Beth nodded thoughtfully. "That's what's up. Everyone needs a few days here and there."

"Yeah, I'll have a five-day weekend."

"Damn, Savvy. That's going to be so good for you."

Savvy looked up at Beth. "That's exactly what I'm hoping it will be. Thank you for being one of the few who haven't immediately tried to talk me out of doing it."

"Why should I? Besides, you can help me plan different drills for the summer clinic."

"Bet."

Beth gave her another high five and her expression transitioned into coach mode. "Alright, Savvy, give me a few warm-up laps while we wait for Joanie. You really should work on your friend with her timeliness."

"There's no way in hell I'm going to have that conversation with her, and you would be wise to embrace her timetable." Shaking her head, Savvy dropped her bags on a bench and took off a new track jacket she'd found online. She started her jog, observing the other courts, which filled up with the after-work crowd. She waved big at Rob, coaching the same teenage boys from before. They were doing sprints across the court, pumping hard and then lunging down to touch the lines. Rob waved back, and gestured that he would come by the court later.

Continuing her jog around, she saw Joanie sprinting toward their court from the parking lot. She was in a short tennis skirt with kick pants underneath and a racerback tank top with a built-in bra—something Savvy could never get away with wearing. "Hey, girl!" She immediately dropped all of her stuff and joined the jog.

"I see you made it."

"Safe and sound, mama. How was your big meeting today?"

"Productive. I've got a lead on a new client's product, and it's a really big account. Probably going to take up even more of my time, but I'm excited about it. I just need to get through this backlog."

"Well then, this vacation is just what you need before you bury yourself under even more work. I'm proud of you! People at your job are finally starting to see in you what we see."

"Enough talk! Let's get to work, ladies." Beth ran them through some sprinting drills before setting them up on one side of the court facing off with two ball machines.

Joanie grinned at her. "This is going to be fun!"

"Okay, ladies. I want you to work on your communication and movement as a doubles team. Tell each other when you're going for something, declare it early, and move together so that you can be in position for whatever comes next."

Joanie and Savvy each stood at the baseline, essentially in a sumo squat position, swaying from side to side. Savvy gripped the base of the racket in her right hand, steadying it with her left. They could hear beeps from the controller as Beth fired up the machines one at a time. One machine shot a ball toward her on the baseline, and Savvy reacted. "I go!"

As she hit through the ball, the other machine shot a ball toward midcourt, in front of Joanie. "Mine!" She sprinted forward to catch the ball on the rise, and then started to backpedal when she realized that the next ball was also in her direction, but harder. She moved her feet and got into position, hitting a swinging volley that slammed against the machine.

"Hey, ladies!" Rob called. "Can you please not break the ball machines?"

"Shut up, Rob," Savvy yelled back as she ran forward for a short ball. "More outbursts like that, and we'll tell Maggie not to respond to your texts."

"Carry on, ladies," Rob called back.

Joanie cackled. She was back on the baseline in time to sail a one-handed backhand up the line. They worked on moving back and forth in tandem, yelling when a ball came close to the center of the court, as Beth changed tempo and trajectory to trip them up. Rob jogged over to watch the action.

Feeling light on her feet, Savvy ambled forward for a ball angled toward the midcourt sideline. As she hit that return, she saw the other machine start to shoot a ball toward the same spot on the opposite side. Knowing that Joanie had been pushed back behind the baseline, Savvy ran for it. "Switch!" she yelled.

As she ran left, Joanie ran right, and just in time. The other machine shot a ball deep into the right corner. They both connected at the same time, making a loud clang as the balls connected with the machines. Rob whistled, and Beth turned off the machines.

"Now that's what I'm talking about." Beth tossed each of them a water.

"Savvy, you are a beast." Rob grinned at her, giving her a fist bump.

"You're just saying that," she laughed, sipping the cold water slowly. Her chest was still thumping hard, but it didn't hurt trying to catch her breath.

"I'm really not. You're way better than you think you are."

Beth and Joanie both nodded, Beth's arm slung around her shoulder. "Your fitness level is way up, and you're going for shots that you wouldn't take before. You took four or five that were meant for Joan because you knew you could get there."

"My girl killed it." Joanie had the wide smile of a proud mama on her face.

"Well, I have an idea," Savvy said slowly. "Rob, are you done coaching over there?"

Rob shrugged. "Not really, but I have them playing a set right now. I've got time."

"What do you have in mind?" Beth raised a brow at her.

"I'm thinking battle against the coaches. Let's move these machines."

Joanie immediately started moving toward the other side of the court. "Let's get it."

"Can you imagine if Mags were here right now?"

"Man, if Maggie were here, she'd be going all wild with the insults and the stares," Beth told Rob. Beth started to pace back and forth quickly, imitating Maggie on one of her tamer days. "We got this! They ain't ready!"

They played six games of a set, and the score was tied at three games apiece. "Okay, Savvy, your serve," Beth called.

Savvy nodded, heading to the baseline. She and Kotter maintained their communication, ultimately beating the coaches in four games before Rob had to return to his clients. He gave a wave and jogged back over to his students, who had finished their set.

Two guys took over the court next to them, and as Savvy returned to the benches separating the courts, she caught a glimpse of one of them who seemed oddly familiar. Her pace slowed and she locked eyes with Jason, who did a double take when he saw her. She turned away, giving Beth a high five and a hug before nudging Joanie. Seeing Jason, Joan pulled Beth close for a quick kiss, whispering into her ear.

"It's cool, you guys," she said quietly, her back to him. She reached for a bottle of water, grateful for something cool after all of the activity. "I don't want to deal with, or even acknowledge, his presence."

Beth ran her hand over her hair thoughtfully. "Okay, Savs. Do you want to do drills, laps, or we can work on volley techniques?"

"Volleys."

"Cool. Both of you stand a couple feet back from the net. I'm going to hit balls to you. Please try not to hit your returns at me directly."

"No promises." Joanie grinned, smacking her on the butt as she moved to pick up the ball hopper.

She nipped at Joanie's nose and walked away.

"You two are annoyingly cute."

"I know," Joanie whispered back. "I'm gushing, Savs. Literally gushing."

"I'm so happy for you. Mean it." Savvy looked meaningfully at her friend. They slapped each other five and got into position.

Beth started to hit balls across the net, and they continued to yell out to each other, moving quickly, getting their feet into position, and taking a hard swing whenever possible. Joanie whooped gleefully when she hit Beth in the shin with a ball.

Beth didn't look amused, but she was proud of their progress. "Very funny," she said. "Just remember that later."

"Uh-oh," Savvy teased. "Don't get yourself into trouble, girl."

They hit a round and Beth told them to move back, as she started to float balls to them, working their shoulders. Savvy loved those; they felt like serves with less pressure. She aimed each one at Beth, and soon Joanie followed suit.

"Y'all think you're funny, but I got you. Just wait till next session," she threatened.

They kept at her anyway, laughing and whooping when they connected with her or the ball hopper. Soon they were just peppering balls back and forth with Beth. Joanie worked on her backhand, and Savvy worked on her forehand follow-through.

"Okay, Savvy. Give me a ball down the line and another into the opposite corner, and then you can stretch and be done for the day."

She nodded, immediately hitting the next ball down the line with ease. Savvy pivoted a little, ready for her corner shot, but the first one clipped the net. She ran across the court to get into position for the next ball, which she backhanded with two hands on the racket, gently kissing the inside of the corner.

"Damn, Savs. Your placement is killer!" Joanie marveled. She gave each of them a high five, picked up the ball hopper, and jogged around to pick up the stray balls. When they met back at the bench, Beth handed them each cold water, and Savvy sat on the ground to stretch out her hamstrings. As she reached forward, gripping the heels of her shoes to pull herself farther, Joanie pressed her hands on the middle of her back, and Savvy could feel her hamstrings lengthen.

"That feels great, thanks," Savvy sighed happily. When she came up, bringing her legs into a butterfly stretch, Joanie plunked down next to her, contorting into a pigeon stretch. "Today felt really good."

Beth nodded. "I could tell. You should be really proud of your progress, Savvy."

"I can tell you're feeling it," Joanie said. "And you look amazing!"

"Thanks," she sighed. "I wish the scale would catch up with me, though. It's moving so slowly even though I'm starting to see some definition in my arms."

"You're building muscle," Beth offered. "Numbers on a scale don't mean a thing. Just keep doing what you're doing."

Savvy nodded. "As long as it feels good like this, that's easy." Crossing her legs, she started to stretch her arms and shoulders. "Are you going to join us for yoga tomorrow night, B?"

Beth grinned. "Wouldn't miss it." She stood up, leaning forward to offer her and Joanie either hand. Pulling them to their feet, she smiled. "Maybe you guys can get Maggie to come?"

"I wouldn't hold your breath on that." Savvy smiled. "She just got her hair done."

"Oh, yeah, you can count her out for a couple weeks." Joanie laughed. "Never get between a woman and her 'do."

Savvy reached out and gave Beth a hug around her middle. When she stepped back, Joanie gave Beth a quick kiss and said she would see her a little later. Beth winked at her, and Savvy made little kissing noises as they headed toward the parking lot. The guys on the court next to them slowed, but continued their game. Tired at the thought of him, she didn't bother to look.

Kotter couldn't stick around to rehash their Jason sighting, so Savvy went home and jumped in the shower. She'd just stepped into her robe and wrapped a towel around her hair when the doorbell rang. She pulled off the towel as she trudged down the hall barefoot, squeezing more moisture from her hair. "Coming!"

Savvy peeked through the peephole and reached for the doorknob when she saw Spencer.

"Hey, you." She leaned against the door seductively.

"Wow, hey." He took in her robe and the towel in her hand, running his hand over his head. "I, uh, caught you at a bad time. Sorry, I should have called." *Why is he being awkward?*

They stood, still on opposite sides of the door. "Aren't you going to come in?" She looked behind him and noticed his car still running.

"I just came by to drop off your keys and the warranties for your appliances. I'm headed to the airport."

"Oh? Headed out of town?" She rested her head on the door.

He shook his head. "Not me."

Puzzled, Savvy looked him over. He looked good; a pullover sweater and dark wash jeans. Over his shoulder, she saw movement in his passenger window and went cold. "Wait, is there someone in your car? Is that...a woman?" *Oh, hell no.*

The woman had her hair pulled back into a honey-colored topknot, accentuated with big hoop earrings. They made eye contact, and she gave a slight nod. "What is this, a date?" she accused. *Looks like a trophy to me.*

Spencer fidgeted. "No, it's not what you think. Savvy, I swear I—"

"Have you slept with her?" Savvy crossed her arms over her chest.

He looked at her, opened his mouth to speak, but no words came out.

She blinked, feeling her heart fall into her stomach. "Wow. Okay, well, thanks for the warranties. Your check's in the mail." She snatched the papers from his outstretched hand, closed the door, and locked the dead bolt. "Ain't nobody got time for this bullshit," she muttered.

"It's not what you think! Come on, Savvy," he called through the door. "Let me explain." She heard his hand press against the door. "Please."

"Go away." Savvy stalked back down the hall, turning the hot water on in the shower again. Her hands shook as she reached to unlash her robe. *Fool me twice, shame on me.*

23

Savvy broke into a cold sweat the moment they entered the conference room. Between the fire and Spencer showing up with another woman, Savvy's backlog had only grown. In her attempts to catch up, she'd neglected to adequately prepare for her presentation with their new clients and now her nerves had her tongue-tied. "Uh, h-hi, I'm Savannah Sheldon, I'm managing the transition of the administration of your product. Thank you for taking the time to come and meet with us today." *Fuck, what do I do?*

Warren nodded. "Have a seat, everyone. Josh, so glad you could make it." Josh, senior VP of People's Trust, hadn't confirmed that he would attend the meeting. Warren rounded the table to shake his hand. The rest of the People's Trust team took their seats.

"Thanks. I was able to delay another meeting. Good to be here." He nodded in Savvy's direction, and all of the facts and figures she'd prepared at the last minute fell out of her head.

"So let's get started. We've got about an hour and a half of presentation to get through. Please feel free to ask questions at any time. At the conclusion of the presentation, we'll have a break for refreshments, which will be followed by a debrief with Warren and Josh." Savvy aimed a small remote toward the laptop at the front of the room, moving the slides from their agenda to an overview of their administration plan for their new product. Her hands shook as butterflies navigated patterns of chaos in her stomach.

"So this product comes with standard riders for long-term care, carrying the options for both home health care and assisted living facilities. The biggest difference is…uh…"

"That we aren't charging a deductible or limiting these riders to our preferred select tiered clientele," Josh finished.

"Right. Uh…" Savvy reached for words out of her grasp, using the remote to move to the next slide. She hoped that it would jog her memory. Instead, she read straight from the slides. Sweat beaded on her forehead. *Pull it together, Savs!*

Slide after slide, she read the language. "So, as you know, presence of the following diagnoses automatically drops a client from preferred select to preferred…" The People's Trust team whispered to one another as Savvy limped through her plan to implement training modules for her team and the timeline she'd planned to have everyone prepared to take on the administration of this new product. She smiled tightly. "So, let's open up to questions."

Everyone, including Warren, raised their hands. Savvy's eyes widened, and she took a gulp of water before calling on a People's Trust rep.

"But shouldn't this particular rider include a requirement that all clients undergo the additional screening?"

"Um...yes?"

"Are you asking us or telling us, Savvy?" Warren raised an eyebrow.

"Telling? Telling! Telling." She nodded, her cheeks hot with embarrassment.

She limped through the rest of the question-and-answer portion, with Warren jumping in to field some of the answers. The tightness of his jaw and the shake of his head hit Savvy right in the gut. Disappointment in his eyes, Warren asked to speak with Savvy privately before his scheduled debrief with Josh.

Warren followed her back to her office, closing the door behind them. "Do you want to tell me what the hell happened in there?" He came close to her, confining her to the far side of her office. "You couldn't even answer basic questions for the client!"

"Warren, I'm so sorry," Savvy stammered, her heart beating out of her chest. "I prepared for the presentation, I swear to you. It's just that the volume of files has been so much, and my new underwriters aren't up to speed yet, and with the strategy meetings I've fallen behind. I underestimated how much preparation was required, and my focus was elsewhere."

"You think?" he snapped. "Savvy, your output has decreased since the promotion. Did you think you could just skate by?"

Shit, shit, shit. "Decreased, sir?" He caught her by surprise. Savvy didn't think he watched that closely. "I've been trying to stay on top of my files, but—"

"Trying, Savannah? You told me you could handle this!" He slammed his fist down on her desk.

Savvy sat, willing herself not to burst into tears. "I did. I'm so sorry. It's just that—"

He raised a hand. "I don't want excuses, Savvy. I need performance. Get your people up to speed. You shouldn't still be in that same holding pattern covering for everyone when you have a dedicated staff. You have to be able to balance management, files, strategy sessions, and your new client. If you can't do that—"

"But I can!" she blurted out. A tear escaped her eye, and Savvy pushed it away. "I'm up to the task."

He shook his head, pinching the bridge of his nose. "You said that before. Now, I don't want to crush you here, Savvy, but you need to make some decisions. You're distracted. You used to stay late without being asked, you took files home on the weekend. You stayed ahead on your deadlines." He surveyed the mountain of files in her office. "Where you stand right now, you won't make your deadline to close out Nation's Mutual, and that client is smaller than People's Trust."

What do I do? "So." Savvy took a deep breath. "How should we proceed, Warren? I want to prove to you that I can do this job. I'll cancel my vacation time. I'll limit my evening workouts so that I can get in more hours."

Warren looked at her for a long minute. "No, don't cancel your time off, Savvy," he said gently. "You need to take some time to decide where your priorities lie. Either you're committed to what it takes to do the job, or I need to find someone else."

Her stomach dropped. "Are you going to fire me?"

He shook his head. "You're an excellent underwriter, Savvy. And I can't blame you for prioritizing your own wellness—you look happier and healthier than I've seen you in years. If you were still in your old position, you'd be managing your deadlines without an issue, but the stakes are higher now that you're in a supervisory role.

"If you can balance everything you're doing with the new role, great. It will be yours to keep. But you have to decide how much you're willing to commit. If you want your old job back, you can stay on this same team as an underwriter, but I'll put someone else over the strategy and client development. It would be a demotion of title and pay, but I'd be willing to meet you halfway between your old salary and where you are now, given the volume you typically take on."

Her mouth went dry. "Is there anything that I can do to make it up to the clients? Did I ruin that relationship?"

He shook his head slowly. "It's best that you don't have any contact with them right now. I need to smooth that over, but they'll be fine."

She dipped her head, squeezing her eyes shut. "Warren, I can't even begin to tell you how sorry I am. And I mean it—I can cancel my vacation plans, really."

"No." He tapped his fingers lightly on her desk. "Your vacation is supposed to start this weekend, right?"

Savvy nodded, clearing her throat. "Yes, I am supposed to return to the office next Thursday."

"You should take some extra time. Go now, and take the full week next week." He stood.

"Sir?" Savvy rose, following him to her door.

"Consider the additional days administrative leave. You've got two weeks to think about what you want, Savannah. What are your long-term goals? Do you want to be in management?" Warren ticked questions on his fingers. "Are you committed to this volume of work? Take these extra days to think, so that you can try to recharge during your planned days off. When you come back that following Monday, we'll meet and you can tell me what you want to do."

She nodded, flinching when he rested a hand on her shoulder.

"I will respect your decision, Savvy. See you in a couple of weeks."

Savvy spent several days making excuses, avoiding her friends. She needed time to think, and didn't want anyone worrying about her.

The presentation blunder played repeatedly in her head. She'd failed big. The first two days after Warren sent her home, she didn't eat. She left her bed only to go to the bathroom. Her phone was set to Do Not Disturb.

On the third day, Savvy had groceries delivered along with several bottles of wine. Losing herself in a bottle of zinfandel and a fresh jar of cookie butter, she rehashed her argument with Spencer. She hadn't responded to any of his phone calls or texts, but she wondered if she should have taken the time to hear him out. Fighting with him had played into her distraction at work, which led to her bombing the presentation. Everything had fallen down like a cascade of dominoes.

When she woke the next morning with a dull headache, Savvy forced herself out of her room, padding to the kitchen to guzzle down some water. Twisting open the blinds, she squinted out the window at a clear, sunny day. She popped some ibuprofen, donned a pair of sunglasses, and took her phone into her backyard for some fresh air. She lay on a lounge chair and reconnected with the world, starting with the girls.

After a Saturday morning hot yoga session, she, Beth, and Joanie showered at the studio and headed over to the coffee shop to toast to Savvy's planned time off. Of course, Maggie met the rest of them at the coffee shop. She refused to sweat out her hair and thought hot yoga early in the morning was torturous. She preferred to do her runs at night.

Joanie, Mags, and Savvy occupied the big center table while Beth ordered drinks for everyone. While Joan tried to get details out of Mags, who had a date with Rob that night, Savvy went to the iced water dispenser. Savvy poured an extra glass, quickly guzzled it down, and poured another one to help her cool down from class.

"Hey, Savvy. I didn't expect to see you here today." Spencer stood behind her with a large to-go cup of iced tea and Teddy at his side. When she turned around, Teddy whimpered and came forward, pressing his nose against her thigh. Spencer gave her a tight smile, his jaw flexing.

Savvy set her cup on the counter next to the dispenser and kneeled, gathering her fingers behind Teddy's ears to give him a good scratch. He licked her chin to show his appreciation. She focused her attention on his owner. "Hey" was all she could muster.

He nodded. "You know, I've been trying to reach you. I should have made the effort to come in and explain." He cocked his head to one side. "I'm sorry."

"So who was she?" Savvy hugged Teddy's neck, and they both looked up at Spencer.

"That was Hailey, my ex. We—"

"You know what? I don't want to hear this. Not yet." She held up a hand to stop him. *Of course she was his gorgeous ex-girlfriend.*

Caught off guard, Spencer protested. "But—"

"Just give me some more time, okay? I just can't right now." Overwhelmed, she let go of Teddy and took a step back.

Concern was etched between Spencer's brows. "Savvy,

whatever is going on with you, I'm here. We can talk and figure this out."

She shook her head. "Hear me when I say that I want to, but I need to get my head right first. I have a lot on my plate right now."

"I can respect that." He smiled cautiously. "I told you that I was a patient man. I figured something was going on with you, but I wish you'd just told me."

She nodded. "I'll reach out when I'm ready."

"Okay." He leaned forward and kissed her cheek. "Good." As he and Teddy walked out of the coffee shop, Savvy turned back toward her table and had three pairs of eyes trained on her.

"So I take it you didn't accept his apology?" Joanie called loudly. Beth and Mags tittered, but Savvy was too through.

She flipped Joanie off, refilled her cup, and carefully carried back four cups of cold water. "Astute observation, heffa. Thank you." Turning to Mags, Savvy promptly changed the subject. "So where is Rob taking you tonight?"

Mags ignored her. "We got you something for your stay-cation." Before Savvy could protest, she continued, "It's not anything big, it's just a journal. This time off is a big deal for you, so we thought it might be fun for you to log some of your memories and reflection."

Joanie handed her a brown leather journal, which had a flap to close the cover and an elastic to pull around the flap to hold it in place. Branded into the front cover were her initials with a chef's hat and a whisk. Savvy ran her fingers over them in surprise. "You guys!"

"You used to write all the time. That used to be your favorite way to express yourself. Maybe this can give you a chance to start up again."

Savvy reached out her arms to pull them close. She gasped, surprising herself when she burst into tears.

"Whoa, are you okay?" Joanie pulled her onto the sofa.

She shook her head. "I bombed that presentation at work. It couldn't have gone any worse. Of course, Warren was there to witness the whole thing, and now I have to choose whether I want to keep the promotion or go back to being a regular underwriter. I've been on administrative leave since Monday afternoon."

"Wait, what? Savvy, it's Saturday. Why didn't you tell us before now?"

She shrugged, wiping her eyes with a napkin. "It's my fault. There isn't enough time to get into it right now, and the more I think about work, the less I want to have this time off."

Mags put her arm around her. "Oh, no, you need this. You need time to think."

Joanie stood before Savvy could protest. "I second that. You've got to decide what is best for you. We're here for you—we'll listen or help you brainstorm—whatever you need. But this time is good for you to figure things out. You ready to take this show on the road?"

Savvy nodded, rising from her seat. "Okay, you're right. Yeah, I just need to think everything through. I'm gonna head home and get myself together."

Beth squeezed Savvy's shoulder. "Enjoy your time. You'll figure this out. I'll see you tomorrow for tennis."

"I'll be there. And don't forget that dinner on Tuesday."

Savvy waved as she left the coffee shop, slowing when her phone pinged. She fished it from her purse and Jason's name appeared on her screen. I'm sorry.

Savvy stopped in her tracks so abruptly that the person behind her bumped into her, jolting her forward. Savvy apologized profusely, then, regrouping, she shoved her phone back into her purse. When Savvy reached her car, she got out her journal and penned her first entry.

I will not allow myself to feel guilty for self-indulgence or self-care. I will live in the moment and spoil myself if I so choose. I will not be concerned with anyone's timeline or expectations but my own. Before Savvy takes care of everyone else, Savvy takes care of Savvy.

24

Beth nudged her playfully. "Okay there, McEnroe. Ready for set two?"

"Very funny."

Beth finished her water and jogged to the baseline and prepared to serve. "Yeah, you're not ready," she called. Tossing the ball high in the air, she served before Savvy was completely set.

"Damn, girl. That's not fair!" Savvy grinned, racing across the court for the next ball.

Beth made quick work of her in the second set. "You're doing great, Savvy. I'm really impressed with your progress!"

"Yeah, but you still whooped my ass."

"Yeah, but I went full-out today. That match was way closer than you think. Plus, your recovery time after hard sprints has decreased substantially. You're killing it!" She stretched her arms behind her. "Listen, I'm going to run

over and talk to Rob for a second. Why don't you fire up
the ball machine?"

"Cool." After jogging over to the bench, Savvy grabbed
the remote and hit the power button, getting herself to
midcourt before the first ball shot out. Backing up toward
the baseline, she allowed the machine to dictate direction,
and she focused on hitting balls toward the sidelines or at
the machine. She worked up a light sweat, moving her feet
quickly, changing directions, focused on meeting the ball
early and following through.

Once she hit the machine three times in a row, a deep
voice called out, "You really have it out for that machine,
don't you?"

Savvy grinned, waving at Rob, hitting another ball at the
face of the machine. "Beth and I joke about that. I usually
aim my cross-court shots at the lower half of the machine,
and then I'm aiming down the line for others. Just trying
to focus on controlling direction."

"Well, your accuracy is on point!"

"Thank you!" Savvy raced across the court to catch up
with a change in direction, clipping the ball. It landed on
the painted line.

"Well, that couldn't have been a better shot," Beth sur-
mised. She turned the ball machine off, stretching out her
shoulders. "How do you feel?"

Savvy chugged some water. "Good. Still have a lot of energy. Are you joining Kotter and me for yoga?"

Beth shrugged slowly, poking out her lips. "I was going
to give y'all some alone time in case you wanted to confide
in your bestie. I know you're still figuring out your work
situation."

She waved away the thought. "There's nothing you don't
know. You should come!"

Beth nodded at her, squinting in the sunlight. "Okay, I will! Thanks, Savvy. But first, I need you to run eight laps for me."

"Eight?!"

"Because you can, Savvy. You're in great shape. You've built some muscle, your core is stronger. And you just told me you still have a lot of energy."

Reluctantly, she put down her water bottle. "Here we go." Savvy set off, thinking about what Beth said, remembering her first time on the court. She'd asked her for a lap, and Savvy had walked and wheezed through half of it. Rounding her fourth lap now, her breath even, it hit her. *I'm not winded.*

"Keep pushing, Savs!" Beth clapped.

Savvy picked up the pace as she finished lap seven, sprinting the last leg.

"Yes! Almost there!" Beth stood at the end with her water bottle.

Crossing the finish line, Savvy smiled at her, breathing hard but still not winded, not on the verge of collapse. "Okay, now I see what you mean. That actually felt good."

"Excellent! So next we'll work on those moments when you doubt yourself, because I saw your face when I said eight. You didn't think you could. We'll build up that confidence, Savvy. You're almost there."

She guzzled down her water, feeling the coolness travel toward her belly. "You're right, I didn't think I could. But with what you said, I'm realizing the improvement, even if there aren't major changes in the mirror."

Beth looked her up and down. "What do you mean? You don't see a difference?"

"Little things here and there." She shrugged.

Beth smiled wide. "You'll have an aha moment, Savs. This is just denial. You'll see it soon."

"You see a change?"

"Inside and out, girl. You'll see."

In her second cooking class of the day, students were tasked with making their own pasta for lobster ravioli. On her countertop, Savvy combined semolina and all-purpose flours into a mound. With her fingers, she created a well in the center of the mound, where she dropped raw eggs, a pinch of salt, and a little water. She mixed the dough by hand until all of the ingredients combined, watching its composition change as she kneaded the dough to a firm consistency. After wrapping the dough in plastic wrap, Savvy let it rest for the next thirty minutes, while she prepared ravioli filling.

In a sauté pan, Savvy melted butter before tossing in garlic and shallots. After a minute, she added in cups of lobster meat, seasoning the protein with fresh chives and parsley, salt, and pepper, sautéing the ingredients for another minute. She poured in a little cognac, giving the alcohol time to cook out before turning off the heat, then poured the contents of the sauté pan into a large mixing bowl. Using tongs, she removed the larger chunks of lobster to a cutting board to dice and returned them to the bowl. As the contents cooled, Savvy squeezed fresh lemon juice over the mixture, spooned in fresh ricotta, and stirred to finish the filling.

Sarah came around the room to show everyone different techniques for rolling out the pasta dough and for cutting the ravioli, gesturing toward Savvy's table, where Savvy ran long strips of dough through a pasta roller, laying them out in rows. Next, she added tablespoons of filling on top of the strips, leaving space between each spoonful. She brushed egg wash around each mound and laid another long strip of pasta dough over the top, pressing the pasta together with her fingertips. A ravioli cutter wheel rolled patterned lines for square pockets of filling. They all carefully cooked their ravioli, praying they didn't burst in the boiling water, and finished the dish with a browned butter, lobster, and sage sauce.

In her journal, Savvy wrote down ideas for other ravioli fillings, wanting to use that sauce with butternut squash or ricotta with buttery leeks.

Later on, in the restaurant over grilled seafood and a citrusy sangria, Savvy joked with Paul and Sarah about relationships and movies. "This has been such a fun day. I feel rejuvenated!"

Sarah grinned. "Cooking does that for me too."

"What should we bring to your place?" Paul nodded toward her.

"If you want to, you can bring fixings for a charcuterie board and something for another starter."

"Hmm." Sarah's hand rested on Paul. She tapped him. "What about the croquettes?"

His eyes rolled upward, crinkling at the sides. "They're so good, Savvy." He admired his wife. "So good."

"Oooh, I can't wait to try them! By the way, my friends are pretty silly, so just prepare yourselves."

"I'm just so excited to see your new kitchen. Every time you mention it, your eyes light up. I might need you to connect me with your contractor." Sarah sipped her sangria conspiratorially.

Savvy smiled sadly. "I have no doubt he would be excited to meet you."

"Savvy?"

She was returning from a hike, and didn't see Spencer until she walked up the driveway. "What are you doing here? Did you forget some tools?"

"I just want to talk to you. Please." Spencer stood on the porch, Teddy at his feet.

"I told you I wanted space."

"You did, and I want to respect that, but I just needed to get this off my chest. And if you still need space after this, I promise to give that to you." He held up his right hand, brows knitted together. "I promise," he whispered.

Savvy jogged up the steps and unlocked the front door, leaving it open for him to follow. "Come on," she huffed. She grabbed a glass and filled it with cold water from the door of the refrigerator.

Moving farther into the house, she stepped out of her shoes, carrying them with her to the new sofa. She sat cross-legged at one end and waited for Spencer to sit. Teddy whimpered, waiting by his master's side. "Oh, go on."

At an instant, Teddy made his way to Savvy, sitting in front of the couch, resting his chin on her leg. She blew him a kiss, turning toward Spencer, who sat opposite her in a leather armchair. "Nice furniture."

"Thanks." *Get on with it.*

Spencer leaned forward, resting his elbows on his knees. "Listen, Savvy. I'm so sorry for all of the confusion. Yes, Hailey was my ex, but I swear to you that nothing is happening between us."

"If nothing's happening, why is she riding around town with you? And why was she twiddling her little fingers at me through the window?" Savvy imitated her wave. "I don't have the time or the patience for bullshit, Spencer."

"I promise you, I'm not bullshitting. I was just giving her a ride to the airport. She called me last-minute—her car broke down not far from my house."

"Well, why didn't she call an Uber?"

"She thinks the car services are suspect at night. Doesn't

trust them." He spoke quickly, his eyes pleading with her. "I swear to you, we broke up years ago. It was never going to work out."

"Why's that?" It irritated Savvy that she agreed with Hailey—that car services at night made her nervous.

"She cheated. I forgave her, but I couldn't forget. I couldn't stop picturing her with another man." He shook his head, looking down at the floor. "We decided we'd be better off as friends. She's in a long-distance relationship now with some dude who works up in Seattle. That's where she was headed, and she just panicked when her car stalled. I thought that by coming by with her in the car, being open with you that I was driving her, you'd see that Hailey's just a friend, but clearly that backfired." He laughed nervously.

Savvy's shoulders released and she blinked hard, putting the pieces together. "Yeah, I'm not sure that was the best logic. So after you left…"

"I dropped her at Burbank Airport and drove back here, but all of your lights were out. I should have knocked on the door anyway." He wrung his hands. "I wanted to."

"You should have. And I should have let you explain, but I've been completely dropping the ball at work, and it's all sort of falling apart now. I was projecting on you. I'm sorry."

"What's going on with work?"

Savvy pinched the bridge of her nose. "Honestly, let's talk about it later, okay? Even thinking about it raises my anxiety." She waved it away, her voice small. "I'm glad you came."

Spencer looked at her, closing the space between them in an instant. Teddy moved out of the way, watching the two embrace. On his knees, Spencer wrapped his arms around Savvy, who leaned forward to rest her head in the crook of his neck. She brought her hands to his sides, his taut muscles jolted at her touch. He pulled back to see her face, hands cradling her head. "I missed you."

Looking into his dark brown eyes, Savvy's heart fluttered. "I missed you too. Both of you." She gestured to Teddy. She tugged at Spencer's T-shirt, tilting her head as she pulled him closer. They kissed and she parted her lips, gliding the tip of her tongue gently across his.

He moaned against her mouth. "I want you."

"I need a shower, love. I just came from a hike and I'm all sweaty," she laughed.

Spencer softly kissed her cheek, pulling the straps of her tank top and sports bra to one side to trail his tongue lazily down her neck to her shoulder. "You still taste sweet to me."

She sucked in a breath, leaning toward his mouth as he traced her clavicle with the tips of his fingers. Before he could return his lips to hers, she stood and grabbed his hand. "Come on."

"We don't have to go anywhere, Savvy."

"But...that's a new couch, and I'm already all sweaty," she blurted out. Looking into Spencer's eyes, they burst out laughing. "Oh my God, I'm turning into my mother!" she shrieked.

Spencer chuckled. "Well, I can't wait to meet her. In the meantime, why don't I give you a bath?" He took her hand and led the way.

The claw-foot tub in Savvy's bathroom was one of the features her mother loved about this house. Savvy rarely took time to enjoy it, but she could never resist stocking up on luxury bath products. She'd installed shelving to display bath bombs and salts, bubble baths with soothing scents of lavender, eucalyptus, and coconut milk with honey.

As she reached out to select a bubble bath, Spencer grabbed her hand. "Let me do that. Go ahead and take off your clothes—take off your makeup." He dipped forward, pressing his parted lips against hers gently, whispering against her, "I want to see you completely naked. All of you." Kissing her again, he cupped her ass in his hands.

A shiver ran up Savvy's spine as she nipped at his lower lip. "Whatever you say." She moved toward the bedroom, peeling off her clothes. The sound of running water in the bathroom was followed by the sound of "Kind of Blue" by Miles Davis. "Nice." She dropped her clothes into the hamper and wrapped herself in the silky kimono robe that was wasted on Jason.

When she stepped back into the bathroom, the scents of coconut milk and honey filled the air. Savvy stole glances at Spencer in the mirror. As he lit candles, she rinsed cleanser from her face, then patted it dry with a soft towel. She hummed along to the music, closing her eyes to apply her favorite moisturizer. She swayed her hips to the music, and warm hands gripped her waist, tugging at the sash of her robe.

"Let me help you out of this, Ms. Sheldon," Spencer whispered. Gently, he curled his fingers around the collar of her robe, allowing it to fall open, as he lifted it from her shoulders. The robe fell to the floor softly, and he led her to the tub. Steam rose from the bubbled oasis, and he held her hand as she lifted one leg over the edge of the tub to test the water with her toes.

He continued to hold her hand until she sat comfortably. The water was deliciously hot and scented with notes of cinnamon and honey. Savvy smiled up at him. "The milk and honey bubble bath is my favorite."

He smiled at her, placing a kiss on her lips before she settled into the frothy tub. She rested her back against one end, the nape of her neck against a towel rolled into a pillow. Several warm vanilla candles cast soft flickers in their direction from the counter and shelves.

"Are you going to join me?" She looked up expectantly.

He pulled a teak bench from against the wall and sat close to the edge of the tub. He crossed his arms over his front, gripping his T-shirt to pull it over his head—smooth brown skin hugged the chiseled contour of his chest and stomach, his bulky arms lined with tattoo ink. He shook his head, intent on her face. "No, this is just for you, beautiful. Let me take care of you tonight, help you relax." He ran his fingertips over her skin, from her shoulder down the length of her arm, brushing his fingertips against the center of her palm. "Just relax."

The heat soothed her muscles, and Savvy sighed blissfully, closing her eyes. "I haven't done this in a long time."

He grinned at her. "You've never done it like this, I bet."

"No, I've never had an audience." She giggled.

"Think of me as an interactive experience." The tips of his fingers ran back up her arm, across her collarbone, and down the center of her chest. Gently, he cupped one of her breasts, squeezing her nipple between two of his fingers. "Just relax."

He kneaded her breast, his touch becoming barely a kiss on her skin. His fingertips trailed farther down, drawing circles around her navel. "You have a beautiful body, Ms. Sheldon."

Savvy sighed as his fingers went farther still. The width of his hand gripped her thigh, massaging her leg down past her knee to her calf. He held her foot in his hand, applying pressure to her arch with his thumb. She hummed. "This is the best bath ever."

Spencer laughed. "Good."

He rubbed her other foot, massaging his way up the other side until he reached her navel again, tracing it gently. He traced his fingers down, resting them at the apex of her thighs, circling his middle finger around her most sensitive spot.

"Mmm." As heat built low in her belly, Savvy's cheeks grew flush, and she wiggled as her body reacted. She bucked against his hand as he pressed his fingers farther, entering her. He continued to circle her clit with his thumb, moving his hand smoothly in a circular motion to penetrate and also massage. *My God, this man's hands are magic.*

Savvy gasped, squeezing her thighs closer together and gripping the edges of the tub. He sped up the motion of his hand, keeping his thumb firmly pressed against her pulsating bundle of nerves.

"Don't hold back," he whispered.

Waves of pleasure crashed over her and she arched her back, shuddering against his hand. He continued to massage, and wave after wave rocked her, her eyes squeezed shut, her breath ragged.

As her body calmed, Spencer brought his hands to knead her shoulders and the base of her neck, rounding again to trail down her arm, across her collarbone, past her navel, to the juncture of her thighs. By the time he returned between her legs, Savvy panted, anticipating another round. Before he could rev her up, she opened her eyes to grab his hand between her thighs.

"It's my turn," she breathed, looking up at him.

"What do you mean?"

"Come closer." She pulled herself up onto her knees in the bathtub, iridescent bubbles running down her smooth skin.

His eyebrows rose like question marks, but he did what he was told, inching the bench closer to her.

She unbuckled his belt, staring into his eyes. "Spoiling should be mutual."

25

Sarah's eyes widened to the size of saucers when she and Paul stepped into Savvy's home. She gushed about the six-burner stove, placing two bottles of vintage red wine into her wine fridge. She introduced Paul to Spencer, and they immediately headed toward the bar cart to pour themselves drinks before going out to the patio to relax and be out of the way.

Since their makeup, Savvy had seen Spencer daily—one day he brought her flowers and her favorite strawberry watermelon slushie, and the next day they watched movies and cooked together. Savvy still hadn't broached the topic of him leaving her house in the early-morning hours, but she knew that she wanted to have that discussion. That he agreed to help her host this dinner was a big step in the right direction.

"So, Savvy, I am really excited to try this tiramisu. I've never had a strawberry version. Do you mind if I keep you company in the kitchen?"

"Please! I'd love to pick your brain about that lovely chowder of yours."

"Paul still tells me that he has some competition," Sarah joked. "You know, once in a while, he'll make me a beautiful omelet, but he prefers to watch me in the kitchen. And then I make him do all of the dishes."

Savvy laughed. "Oh, I'm going to convince you. Paul's no competition." Savvy waved away the thought with a smile. "And you're so lucky! One thing I've always hated is washing dishes."

Sarah laughed. "Truly." She looked around at the pots on the stove and the ingredients laid out on the island. "Great. So tell me where you need me."

"Darling, it's your day off, so kindly sit right here on this bar stool and relax."

"Oh, see, you are already in the lead. We brought stuff for the charcuterie tray and the croquettes. Just let me know if you need me for anything else." Sarah wore a bright orange wrap dress that cinched her waist and flared over her wide hips. She adjusted the skirt as she climbed onto the stool.

"That's a beautiful dress, girl."

"I love me a wrap dress! They are so flattering on women with curves." Sarah's eyes lit up. "When I find something that fits right, I buy every color."

Over the next hour, Sarah and Savvy chatted about food, recipes, their favorite restaurants, bucket list travel destinations, and pampering. "I really love that you're taking this time off just to do you. I don't know that I've ever done that."

"Honestly, I don't think I'll ever let another year go by without some kind of solo retreat. I'm not sure that I really planned out my time wisely, but so far, it's been exactly what I needed."

Sarah checked on the lamb, while Savvy used a hand mixer to combine fresh whipped cream with mascarpone cheese. "Mmm, Savvy, I never thought to use Dijon as a part of the lamb marinade. That smells delicious!"

Savvy beamed at her, feeling slightly less intimidated by this professional chef in her kitchen. "That really means a lot coming from you. Thank you."

"So what else do you need to do?"

"If you can blend that strawberry simple syrup on the stove with that cup of orange juice, I will have all of my components together for assembling this tiramisu." Savvy pulled the last of the ladyfingers out of the oven and set the tray on a rack to cool.

Sarah snagged one of the ladyfingers that had come out of the oven earlier and took a bite. "These are so light and they have the perfect amount of sponge. I need the recipe."

"I will trade you my tiramisu for your osso buco."

"Deal." They shook on it, and then Savvy set up her assembly area. "Are you sure that's not too many strawberries?"

They'd sliced about six pints, and she needed one more. "Nope, this looks just right. Trust me." Sarah sat back on her stool and watched intently as Savvy set her cast iron baking dish with a red enamel coating on the island counter in front of her. Slowly, she dipped each ladyfinger in the strawberry simple syrup mixture. She transferred each cookie into the dish, lining them up tightly along the bottom. She put in a layer of fresh strawberries followed by a layer of the mascarpone and whipped cream mixture. She repeated these steps two more times, using the remaining slices of strawberries to make a mosaic rose design on the top.

"Okay, Savvy, you are an artist." Sarah marveled at the finished dish, her eyes bright with anticipation as Savvy set it on a vacant shelf within the refrigerator. She went back to clear off the tiramisu mixing bowls and checked on the savory spinach and artichoke bread pudding when the doorbell rang. "I'll get that. You keep making magic over here."

Savvy smiled to herself, pulling the lamb out of the oven, then standing the racks on a platter so that the frenched bones stood resembling a crown, then covering the racks with a tent of foil to let the meat rest. The pride of a great presentation swelled within her. The extra touches and buildup to unveiling a beautiful meal were her favorite parts of cooking.

"Something smells good in here!" Joanie called as she walked through the front door. She went right over to the tented lamb to peek. "Hey, girl! Mmmm. I am starving!" From the corner of her eye, Savvy peeped Sarah pointing into the fridge. "Wow! You just made that?"

"I sure did."

Spencer and Paul came around the counter to take a peek. "Everything looks and smells amazing, Savvy. We're in for a treat," Paul declared.

Savvy smiled up at him. "Thank you! The girls are getting some cocktails together if you want to give them a hand." She gestured toward Maggie and Beth.

"I'm on it."

Spencer gave her a quick kiss on the cheek, retreating to a stool at the island to watch her and Sarah work.

Sarah took brioche rolls from the bread warmer and placed them into a basket lined with a red cloth napkin. She pulled plates from the cupboard and other dishes from the fridge that were made ahead of time. Feta and watermelon salad. Marinated olives and Marcona almonds. The charcuterie board with toast points, raw honey, sweet cantaloupe, Calabrese salami, and thinly sliced prosciutto. She grabbed a tray of potato croquettes from the fridge and put a Dutch oven on the stove to fry them.

"What's in those?" Savvy raised her eyebrows.

"A little bit of chorizo and queso fresco."

"That's going to be delicious." She pulled the savory bread pudding from the oven.

Sarah dropped a few croquettes into hot oil, letting them get crispy and brown on the outside, heating the mashed potatoes and cheese on the inside. When she pulled out the first batch, Joanie and Savvy each dove for one, laughing at their burnt fingers and savoring the garlic of the mashed potatoes, the salt from the cheese, and the spice of the chorizo.

"Wow."

"I can't believe y'all are sneaking food before we even make it back here!" Mags reached for a croquette, and Joanie slapped her hand away playfully. Paul and Beth both craned to catch glimpses of all of the food.

Spencer shook his head in awe. "You ladies are meticulous."

Savvy pulled the foil away from the lamb, letting the steam and scent waft up toward the skylights. She closed her eyes and breathed in the smells of the kitchen. Potatoes and cheese croquettes, her savory bread pudding. The remnants of strawberries. Lemon hand soap. A flash permeated the other side of her closed lids, and Savvy opened her eyes to Beth smiling smugly. "Had to do it."

She came around the counter to show her the shot on her phone, and Savvy was instantly glad that she'd captured the moment. She had a look of contentment on her face, her eyes closed and hands resting on the island, with a peaceful smile starting to reach her lips. Steam from the pan of bread pudding traveled upward around her, with the dishes spread all over the counter. "Wow, can you send that to me?"

Sarah leaned over. "That looks like the cover of a cookbook!" Beth passed her phone around and everyone agreed.

"Before you put your phone down, Beth, you should take a picture of Savvy with her beautiful dessert." Sarah nudged her toward the refrigerator, and Savvy laughed.

She opened the refrigerator carefully, feeling six sets of eyes on her back, and reached in with both hands. Joanie held the fridge open for her, and as Savvy turned, a chorus of oohs and aahs greeted her. Mags closed the fridge and stepped to the side as Beth took another picture. Savvy smiled big, tilting the dish toward the camera for a better view. Once the tiramisu was on the counter, Sarah and Savvy high-fived. Sarah passed out plates, grabbing a bowl for herself. She wanted dessert first.

Paul watched Sarah take her first bite, and Savvy imagined a reenactment of her clam chowder reverie. She closed her eyes, swayed side to side, humming to herself. She guided another bite toward her mouth. "Oh my God."

One by one, Paul, Beth, Mags, and Joanie each reached for a spoon to push through the layers of tiramisu. Joanie's eyes rolled so far back in her head that she might have achieved full orgasm. "Girl, I can't even really have dairy like this, but Beth will have to live with it tonight."

Beth went back for a second bite, though her mouth was already full. "Worth it."

Sarah regained consciousness. She opened her eyes, pressing her spoon against her lips. "What else do you like to cook, Savvy?"

She shrugged. "It depends. I make a really pretty frittata. Or a perfectly arranged apple tart," Savvy offered. "My grandmother's curries. I like to take old family recipes and make little tweaks to them. Make them more my own."

She nodded. "What if we did a cookbook together?"

"Seriously?" Butterflies churned in her stomach.

"I've been thinking about making one for a while, but

what if we did some sort of comfort food cookbook where we highlight fresh ingredients that are staples in our favorite family recipes?"

Savvy's mouth dropped. "That sounds incredible. I'm not sure my recipes are good enough for a real book, though."

"If the rest of them are in the ballpark with this tiramisu, you're far better than you think. Watch." She grabbed a chef's knife, slicing two lamb chops from the rack. Her fork dipped into the savory bread pudding, and she closed her eyes as she tasted it. She sliced a piece of her lamb chop, then brought it closer to her eyes for inspection before placing it delicately on her tongue. "The bread pudding is light and flavorful. You have that brie and spinach in there, but it doesn't weigh you down. The lamb has good caramelization of fat, is a perfect medium rare, and packed with flavor from your marinade and the rosemary. You have the gift, Savvy."

Making wide eyes at Spencer, her smile grew from ear to ear. "Really?" Her eyes welled with tears. "Y'all, this past week has been such a difficult time for me. I can't even tell you. And a cookbook is so outside of the realm of possibilities that I saw for myself."

"Well, we've been waiting for your food to be recognized," Joanie chimed in. "You've been making us drool over your cooking for over a decade." Maggie nodded in agreement.

"You really mean it?" Savvy turned back to Sarah.

"I'd be a fool to pass up on an opportunity like this, Savvy. Your food is so comforting and full of love—it should be shared."

She sighed contentedly, thinking of the proud look on her grandmother's face after feeding the neighborhood on a Sunday afternoon. "Then I'm all-in. Everyone, let's enjoy this meal."

Joanie blessed the food and their new venture. Mags gushed, and they made plates to take out onto the deck to enjoy the sunshine. Beth forwarded her the two pictures plus shots of the food and of them bowing their heads for prayer. "Really, you were taking pictures while we prayed?"

"I thought it might help give you guys some direction. Plus, how cool if some of my pictures end up in your book!"

Savvy shook her head at her, smiling. "Everyone's looking for a come-up."

She burst out laughing, wrapping an arm around her. "Okay, Savvy. I see you."

Savvy beamed, looking around at her friends and their feast. Spencer wrapped his arms around her waist. "I think I'm starting to see me too."

On day three of the second week of her administrative leave/staycation, Savvy visited a traveling yoga retreat near the beach. Choosing to remain on the periphery, she joined some of the classes before heading to the meditation room to savor extended periods of solitude. During these moments, she took in her surroundings, listening to the sounds coming from outside the center. She heard birds and frogs, the breeze, the water. She felt the breeze as it came in through the slatted windows, gently nudging the white gauzy curtains, which muted the clear blue skies.

She quieted her mind and looked internally, listening to the systems of her body. With closed eyes and a straight back, she rolled her shoulder blades farther back, placing her hands on her knees, as she sat cross-legged on a zafu in the middle of the floor. Inhaling deeply through her nose, she followed her breath inside, aware of her chest and her belly expanding like waves. Savvy parted her lips softly, exhaling out slowly, feeling her diaphragm contract. After focusing on her breath for several minutes, she let her mind cycle through thoughts that played at the edges of her peace. Savvy let each thought come to her slowly, as if for permission, and then followed each thought down their respective rabbit holes.

She thought about the last Savasana of the day's class, during which the instructor encouraged them to tap into their heart's desires. "Think about the one thing that your heart desires most. What is your heart yearning for?"

Deep down, her heart whispered, "Peace."

But what would peace entail for her? Thinking about returning to work, Savvy could already feel stress tightening her shoulders. She could feel herself being pulled in different directions, but most roads included Spencer. She felt the pressure from her friends to make a decision, pressure from her mom to succeed, and pressure from Warren to pick up the pace with their new client and get on the ball.

If I decided to take a chance on Spencer, would I find peace? Would I create chaos? If I choose to begin a relationship, am I at peace? Am I making things more difficult for myself? Am I making myself the priority?

In her heart of hearts, nothing was more important than finding peace. Her heart wanted her to be at peace with herself. At peace with accepting herself, for better or worse. At peace with owning exactly who she was in the present moment, irrespective of what she perceived to be her flaws.

The more that Savvy thought about it, the more comfortable she felt in the present moment, balanced. Savvy felt clarity within herself, as if her heart nodded at the idea of being a little selfish. She ruminated on her heart's message, slowly coming out of her meditation, first by wiggling her fingers and toes, followed by movement in her wrists and ankles. She brought her hands together in front of her chest in a sign of gratitude, sending it out to the instructors who taught her, the time she had to think about her circumstances, her body for cooperating, and inwardly to her heart for guiding her. Bringing her thumbs to rest between her eyebrows, her hands still together, Savvy whispered, "Namaste." She sat with the vibrations of that one word for a long moment, and then brought her hands back down to her knees. Rubbing her hands on her thighs, Savvy let her eyes slowly flutter open. Her heart told her what it wanted, and in that moment, she had it.

Peace.

Later that night, Savvy sat out on her patio with a glass of wine, looking up at the stars. She reached an arm up toward the sky, playing connect the dots with the stars. Opening her journal, Savvy turned to the last blank page to jot down some resolutions.

Savvy's Self-Care Plan:
1. Meditate daily.
2. Tennis and yoga as often as possible.
3. Be kind to yourself.
4. Give yourself a day of pampering each month.
5. Journal more.
6. Let yourself be a priority.
7. Live in the present moment.
8. Work smarter.

Looking up at the stars once more, her heart swelled with contentment. "Thank you," Savvy whispered out into the universe.

"Okay, so we talked about the strawberry tiramisu, and the rack of lamb, and the clam chowder, but what else?" Sarah asked. They'd finished another cooking class, and after helping to clear away the mess, they sat down to brainstorm for the cookbook. Savvy still couldn't believe it was really happening.

"Well, are you entirely sure that you want to include the clam chowder recipe? I mean, it is the signature recipe for your restaurant. If you put it in the cookbook, others will be able to replicate it and potentially take business away from you." Savvy tapped the cap of her ballpoint pen against her lips. "I think we have to reserve the very best recipes. Gives us something to wow folks with in the next one."

"Nice—I like where your head's at." Sarah grinned. "Should we reserve the strawberry tiramisu? I mean, it's a thing of beauty, Savvy."

Lifting her hands, she shrugged. "But mine is just something I share with people on special occasions. I don't cook for a living."

Sarah mulled it over. "Okay, fair."

"Besides, my best dessert recipe is my granny's apricot lemon cake. And no one gets that recipe."

"Mmmm, tell her more." She rested her chin in her hands.

"So it started as a lemon drizzle cake recipe, but it changed over time, and now it's an apricot lemon drizzle cake with an apricot syrup over lemon and butter pound cake." Savvy pictured her grandmother patting her Bundt pan as the cake dropped onto a cooling rack.

"That sounds divine! I'd love to try that sometime." She looked at her curiously. "I know Beth's shots are with her phone, but I love the photo of you holding up the rack of lamb for the cover. The others could be candid shots throughout the book."

"Oooh, including the prayer. That was a great picture."

"This might be weird to say about a picture including prayer, but your boobs look great in that picture."

Savvy laughed. "Girl, it's so annoying! I love the cut of a V-neck, but I swear it always looks like I've put everything out for display."

Sarah empathized with a nod. "If I'm not wearing a turtleneck, I have some cleavage showing."

"Okaay!" They slapped five, turning back to their list of recipes when Savvy looked back at Sarah, feeling a connection. "Can I tell you something?"

"Of course!"

"I had the worst thing happen at the department store the other day, and I didn't tell the girls because they'd flip out and want to burn the place down, but it really pissed me off."

"What happened?!" Sarah leaned forward, resting her head in her hands.

"So I walk into this place, and I ask where the plus-sized section is—"

"Ugh, was it up on the second floor where no one ever goes?" Sarah rolled her eyes, shaking her head.

"Of course it was! And the store clerk had the nerve to get an attitude about it." Savvy frowned, as her feelings from that day washed over her.

"What did she say?"

"She told me to take the elevator 'cause she didn't want me to overexert myself." Savvy threw her hands up in the air while Sarah's jaw hit the counter.

"Are you fucking kidding me? She's lucky you didn't throw hands." Sarah's brow furrowed as she laughed in disbelief. "Wow."

"That's exactly how I felt. Then when I was checking out, chick pipes up again to take credit for helping me with my purchase. And when I said she didn't, she said, 'she asked me where the fat clothes were, and I told her.'" Savvy pursed her lips and turned her head at an angle, like she hadn't heard what was said to her.

"So what you're telling me is," Sarah started slowly, steepling her hands. "This chick woke up and chose violence."

Savvy rubbed her face with her hands. "I just don't understand why people think it's okay to come for us."

"Right, cause she said that with her whole chest. I've had similar encounters. These folks need to choose life, because I am not the one." Sarah's eyebrows rose as she shook her head.

Savvy grinned. "They need not try either of us. Just thinking about that makes my heart beat faster. The way people think they're entitled to share their unsolicited opinions."

"That part! But you know what, I have a thought." Sarah tilted her head. "What if we add some personalized elements to the book to connect to people looking for healthier options?"

"How do you mean?"

"We can include little hacks to make some of our favorite recipes lighter in calories. The full-fat version would be pictured for the most part, but we can leave a note on how to change up the recipe."

"Oh, I like that idea! There are definitely times where I'll cut back on full-fat cheese for a lasagna, or substitute a leaner protein. Or use squash or eggplant instead of noodles. I have a coworker who is gluten-free, and so I suggest those options for her."

Sarah's eyes narrowed, and she looked up toward the ceiling. "Yes, actually, that's even better. Recipe hacks to meet with dietary restrictions where possible—whether they're gluten-free, vegetarian, vegan. I love the thought of an egg-plant lasagna! We should make that."

"Love that! Now I'm hungry, though." Her stomach gur-gled.

"We can fix that, girl." Sarah snagged some ingredi-ents from a double-door glass reach-in refrigerator. Grab-bing apples from the counter, she set about making grilled cheese sandwiches with fresh-sliced bread, a triple-cream brie, sliced apple, and thinly sliced prosciutto.

"Sarah, that looks divine." She marveled at the chef at work. Her mandolin sliced perfect, thin slices of apple as butter toasted to a nutty brown in a pan. On one slice of bread, she layered the ingredients. After spreading fig jam on the other slice, she pressed that on top and placed the sandwich into the pan, the butter sizzling. When she flipped the sandwich with a spatula, the bread was a perfect toasted brown, and Savvy's mouth watered.

To distract herself, Savvy pulled out her journal, flip-ping its pages to find her list of recipes she wanted to offer for the cookbook. "Okay, so I want to add my savory bread pudding, Granny's Massaman curry, a lasagna from scratch, an apple tart, my family's favorite baked mac 'n' cheese, a braised lamb ragù, and the rack of lamb. What about you?"

"The fresh pasta dough, the lobster ravioli, osso buco, a corn and crab chowder, blueberry scones, a perfect holiday turkey, and my grandmother's oyster stuffing." Sarah ticked off the recipes on her fingers. She turned off the heat, using the spatula to lift the sandwich out of the pan and onto the butcher block counter.

"Ooooh, I can't wait to test out your recipes!" The thought of oyster stuffing made her stomach growl again.

"We should test them out in the cooking classes. You can teach with me!" She sliced the sandwich in half with her chef's knife, and used it to scoop up one half and deposit it in front of Savvy. She picked up the other slice.

She shook her head. "I couldn't possibly." Lifting the slice to her face and biting into it, Savvy savored the crunch of the buttered bread, the saltiness of the prosciutto, the richness of the brie, and the sweetness of the apple. "This is heaven."

Sarah took a bite, nodding as she chewed. "You absolutely can teach with me. There are no limitations here, Savvy. Only the ones you put on yourself."

"You should be a motivational speaker, you know. That was deep, Sis." She took another bite. "I'm in, and these sandwiches are a requirement for all planning meetings moving forward."

26

As a finale to her staycation, Savvy planned a whole day committed to pampering. She visited the salon to update her hairstyle, which had grown out a bit, coming out with some textured waves. Nearby, she found a new boutique by a local designer specializing in maxi dresses with bold colors and fresh prints. She perused rack after rack of vibrant, shimmery fabrics and creative prints, and decided to get a dress for each of her girls. She scoured the store to find something fitting each of their personalities. Joanie got a backless navy blue dress sure to stop Beth's heart. Maggie's featured watercolor flowers and an off-the-shoulder ruffle to show off her sculpted arms.

As she prepared to pay, she spotted a dress in blush-and-gold tones that would hug her waist and fan out with a full skirt and knew she had to have it. She picked out one more; a black one with little cutouts in all the right places. *Wait till Spencer sees this.*

As she walked down the street, Savvy noticed that she was receiving a lot of attention. As she entered different shops, men took the time to open doors. Women smiled, but a couple watched her curiously. *Odd.* A car drove by, and a man leaned out the window to whistle at her. She panicked. *Was the back of her dress caught in her underwear?* Puzzled, she swiped her hand across her backside to make sure she hadn't exposed herself to the public.

Approaching a gift store, Savvy caught her reflection. Her skin had deepened into a bronzed brown from her tennis sessions. Her hair's fresh, beachy waves barely kissed muscular shoulders. Her big, Audrey Hepburn–style sunglasses covered half of her face, floating above defined cheekbones and a jawline. She looked *good.*

She stood straighter, pulling her shoulder blades farther down her back, thinking of her yoga postures. Her collarbone, covered only by the thin straps of her dress, protruded proudly above her full breasts. She could see the start of some muscle definition in her arms. Her curvy figure looked back at her, but something was different. Savvy marveled at herself, reaching up to touch a lock of hair, wanting to see her reflection follow her just a little bit more. "Wow," she breathed. *I look strong.*

She'd forgotten about her revenge body plan weeks ago, but now she stared into the reflection of a beautiful woman with curves to be celebrated. Savvy silently made a mental note to write about this revelation in her journal. *I'm exactly where I want to be.*

Savvy stared at the phone, not wanting to pick it up, but knowing she needed to get it over with. Sighing, she dialed and lifted it to her ear. "Mama."

"Savvy, are you okay?" Her voice had an edge to it.

"Yeah, why would you ask that?" she laughed nervously.

"Because I always call you."

"Well, you always beat me to it," Savvy offered.

"I'm not buying it. Something's wrong."

"Nothing's wrong, per se. It's just…"

"Just what—spit it out, Savannah."

"Mama, I don't think I want this promotion." Savvy squeezed her eyes shut, waiting for the fallout.

"Of course you do," Mama said matter-of-factly. "What do you mean? We always aim high."

"Well, I have been aiming high, and I got what I wanted, but I'm not ready for it. I'm distracted. There's just too many other things that I want to do." Savvy's feelings of being overwhelmed sounded in her voice.

"Like what? What could be more important than solidifying your place with the company?" Her voice held frustration.

"Mama… I've been kind of rejuvenated by everything that I'm doing with fitness, cooking, with the renovation—I can't wait for you to see it—it's beautiful. I'm even doing a cookbook with this chef that I met recently," she gushed.

"But what does any of this have to do with you having a job, Savvy?" Her stern tone wiped the smile off Savvy's face.

"I want to be able to do all of these things. Warren knows how hard I work, but I don't want to spend my whole life in that office when there's more to life than that."

"But—"

"No, Mama, I can't. Believe me when I say that I want to make you proud, but I want to do it my way."

The phone went silent, and Savvy bit her lip. As with every kid she knew, she believed that her mom could snatch her through the phone if she wanted to. She always had the ability to know that Savvy was doing something wrong, even when Savvy was behind her. Sometimes, Savvy swore she could read her mind.

"Savvy," she said softly. "I know that I push you to have security, but I just want to make sure you're taken care of."

"Mama, I know. It's not about being taken care of now. I've done everything that you taught me—I have a great job, they pay me well, I have savings, I own a home, right? You did that—we did that together. I just want you to be proud of me."

"Well, what made you think that I wasn't proud of you?"

"We were always talking about these promotions and getting more security, and I just felt like I hadn't reached what you were hoping for yet."

Her mom sighed. "Savannah. All I want is for you to be happy, healthy, and secure. If you are all of those things, I want for nothing, you hear me?"

"Yes, ma'am." They sat in a comfortable silence. "Well, I should get going, I have to go tell my boss what I just told you."

"You told me first?"

"Mama, come on," Savvy laughed. "I'm not scared of him, but I'm scared of you!"

She chuckled. "I'm proud of you and I hope that your boss is a reasonable man."

"Thank you, Mom, I have my fingers crossed that he is too."

"He would be an idiot if he let you get away, and I say that for your new gentleman as well. You know, I've been in touch with Mrs. Walker, and she speaks very highly of him."

"Yes, Mama," she laughed. "That's a conversation for next time."

"Alright, Babe."

"Love to Max, and I love you."

"I love you, Savannah Joy."

★ ★ ★

Standing in her office, Savvy looked around at all of the empty file bins. When she started her administrative leave, Lina had reassigned all of her files to the rest of her team. They weren't told why she was going to be out, but Savvy was certain they'd heard how terribly she bombed the presentation. She looked out the window, down to the park. *The view isn't that much better on the executive floor.*

Looking around her office again, she took a deep breath to quiet the butterflies in her stomach. Down the hall, she knocked on the open door to Warren's office. He took off his glasses. "Savvy? You're not supposed to be back until Monday."

"Hi, Warren. I wanted to try and catch you today, see if you had a minute to talk. I figured this way, when I come in on Monday, we already have an understanding of my role here."

He leaned back in his chair. "Sure, come have a seat. You can close the door if you want."

Savvy shut the door gingerly, taking a chair opposite Warren's desk. "First, I want to thank you for giving me the opportunity to grow professionally. I've loved working here, and more than anything I appreciate that you recognized how hard I was working."

"I have to admit, I am relieved that you said you were coming back on Monday. I'm sorry if I was too hard on you. I just look at you and see so much potential. You're one of our best underwriters."

"I appreciate that. I want to keep learning and growing, but I think I'm not quite ready for the senior position."

He raised his eyebrows. "Are you sure?"

"Not completely," she laughed. "But I think that we may have a piece missing in our organization."

He rested his elbows on the armrests of his chair, steepling his fingertips. "I'm listening."

"You mentioned during our last talk that you knew I'd been putting more time into an active lifestyle, which took away from work?"

"I did."

"I think that we need to have wellness workshops here. Help people to balance this work life with their home lives. All of those deadlines I took on for others were related to either health challenges or people simply needing mental health days." Savvy looked at him. "They're burning out. It's not sustainable to maintain performance with this volume of staffing without support to help folks balance."

"So what kind of workshops are you proposing?"

She couldn't read his expression. "I think we could add lunchtime workshops on nutrition and healthy eating, workout routines, stretches for tired muscles, strategies to address stress, injury prevention and safety guidelines, tips on creating a work-life balance, building boundaries for home life, quick and easy recipes for meal prep, brown bagging to save money. We could be bringing in a yoga instructor once a week, a certified financial planner once a month, maybe a meditation instructor and a nutritionist. I have a chef friend who teaches cooking classes—maybe we can commission her to host a corporate cooking class for us.

"The point is, if we care for the whole person, production levels go up. If we're not expecting them to give up their weekends after putting in forty-plus hours during the week, we show them that we're respecting their time too. Over time, I do think that each team still needs an additional member to address our growing client list, but these changes would make for a great start. I've also been researching programs to become a certified wellness coach."

Savvy looked at him expectantly, fully prepared for him to laugh her out of his office.

"Hmm." He pursed his lips. "We've never done anything like that."

"True, but we could do a trial year. If the staff sees that a commitment is made and it doesn't work out, they'll appreciate the attempt. If it is successful, I bet that you'll see improvements in productivity and more ideas flowing in our staff meetings."

"What about the senior underwriter position?" He cocked his head to one side.

"I know that I'm capable of doing the job, but that role requires me to give up things that are priorities to me right now. I'm comfortable going back to my old position." She folded her hands in her lap, waiting.

Warren exhaled deeply. "You had me on board until now." He shook his head. "I can't let you step all the way back to where you were."

Savvy sat at the edge of her chair. "Warren, you saw how badly that meeting went. I was underprepared, behind on my files, and now the team has had to absorb my work. Right now, I'm just not willing to put in the number of hours it would take to succeed in that role."

"Just because you don't want that role doesn't mean you're not ready for a more senior position," he said thoughtfully. "What if we take your old role, add in the strategy meetings and this wellness project, but give someone else the new client transition projects?"

"Does that equate to a partial demotion?" She frowned.

"As opposed to the full demotion? Yes. Though a much smaller pay cut."

Hmm. "Are you sure you want me in strategy meetings?"

"You have a fresh take on things that the others can't bring. And I know the reason you weren't prepared for that meeting is that we overextended you. Next time you'll hit it out of the park." He smiled. "Plus, what do you think this whole wellness project is? It's a retention strategy."

"True…"

"Think about it over the weekend and tell me yes on Monday. I'll prepare an email to send out that assigns Karen to new clients and announces you as our senior underwriter and wellness officer. We'll fund your certification, you keep your office, and Lina stays with you to help facilitate these workshops."

Her mouth dropped open. "Warren, I—"

"Get out of here, Savvy." He waved her toward the door, putting his glasses back on. "I'll see you Monday."

She grinned. "Yes, sir!"

27

The girls cackled on her tablet screen. Savvy had them on video chat while she rummaged through her walk-in closet.

"So what are we doing in the closet?" Joanie peered around at Savvy's meticulous organization.

"I have a date with Spencer tonight. The only problem is, he won't tell me where we're going."

"That's right. This should be good! What are you going to wear?" Mags asked.

Savvy grinned, holding her two maxi dresses. "I got myself a couple dresses the other day, so I need you to help me pick."

"Just looking at these, I already know which one I'd choose," Joanie said, eyeing the fabrics. "Put that black one on first."

Leaving the tablet propped up in the closet, Savvy walked back into her room with both dresses and did as she was told. When she returned, the girls met her with collective gasps and a rousing catcall. The black dress had thick straps and a plunging neckline, the waist had a thick band across it, which was accented with geometric cutouts that exposed areas of bare skin. Turning, they could see a thin racerback strap run down a generous scoop, baring most of her back.

"Okay, Savvy, you might kill him in that one," Beth said, her face close to Joanie's. "He'd die happy, but maybe it's too soon."

Savvy shook her head, smiling, and went back to the bedroom to put on the other dress. She added her cognac leather sandals for height and a thin gold braided leather belt to accent her waist. The thin straps of the blush-and-gold maxi dress were barely there and led down to a feminine V shape. The open neckline showed off her collarbone and the belt cinched her waist. From there, the skirt became full and flowy, with multiple layers of the airy fabric, barely showing the bottom third of her shoes. She kept her hands in her pockets and turned, showing that the back had a deep V cut with strips of fabric at the bra strap line and at her waist, right where the belt wrapped around her.

No one made a sound. Maggie's jaw was next to Joanie's on the floor. Beth's head tilted to one side, her lips pursed.

"I think you should go dancing," Joanie finally said.

"Showstopper," Beth added. "But you still might kill the man."

"Yeah," her girls agreed.

"Well, I have one more surprise." She picked up the tablet and carried her friends back to the bedroom, then sat on the upholstered bench at the end of her bed.

Maggie shook her head. "No. I don't think I can handle any more. You are doing too much now, Savvy."

Joanie rolled her eyes. "I think she's PMSing. That's the only explanation for all the dramatics today. Tell us, Savs."

"Remember Paul and Sarah?" They nodded. "Sarah already had a proposal accepted for our cookbook!"

"What?! That's amazing!" Joanie shouted.

"Congratulations, Savvy. If you need anyone to taste test your recipes, I got you," Beth added.

"Savvy, we all got you on that one." Kotter put her arm around Beth.

Maggie burst into big, ugly tears.

"Mags? Are you okay?" Savvy held the tablet closer.

"I'm just so proud of you!" she wailed. "I feel like a proud mama."

"Lawd."

Savvy heard the doorknob turn, and Uncle peeked his head in slowly. "You here, Baby Girl?"

She rushed over to give him a hug. "Hey, Uncle. How are you doing?"

"You shouldn't leave your door unlocked, Savvy. But wow, look at this dress!"

She twirled for him, and he laughed. "Come on, Uncle. It wasn't unlocked for long. I knew you were coming." He grumbled as Savvy led him to the sofa. "Want some iced tea?"

"Is it sweet tea?" Her uncle looked up at her hopefully. "I never understand how you drink that unsweetened crap." He took in the kitchen, nodding. "Wow, you really changed this place. Finally making it your own."

Savvy gave him a playful eye roll and turned on her heel. "Well, both you and Mama pushed me to make some changes, you know. And I made some sweet tea just for you, because you know I can't drink that stuff. I end up diluting it to the point where it doesn't even taste like tea anymore." She grabbed two glasses from her new cabinets.

"Your mama likes that unsweetened crap," he called.

"Yeah, well. We were bound to agree on something eventually."

He chuckled at her response as she poured two glasses of tea. She handed him the sweet one, and he took a sip to test.

"Could still be sweeter, you know. When you order it in the South, it hits that spot on the end of your jaw." He pointed. "That's how you know it's right."

"Mmkay, well, I won't be responsible for giving you diabetes."

"Mmm." He took another sip, a smile in his eyes. "Well, I have some news, Baby Girl."

Savvy sat down, turning to face him, trying to read his facial expression. "Good news?"

His eyes widened, and he shrugged slowly. "It's somewhere along the spectrum of good and bad, I guess. Not great, but not terrible."

Savvy frowned. "Okay." She waited, nervousness boiling in the pit of her stomach.

"I've decided to sell Granny and PopPop's land."

"The insurance company won't rebuild?"

He pursed his lips, shaking his head. "They found me to be partially liable for the fire. The wiring issues were far worse than I knew, and they're saying that the outlet issues should have been enough for me to hire someone to take a look. An electrician would have recommended rewiring for the entire house."

"So what does this all mean?"

"They've agreed to pay for demolition of the house, but they're not going to help rebuild."

"Wow." Savvy struggled to process what this meant. "So you're going to sell it?"

He nodded. "You know, I've lived in that house almost my entire life. It's time for your uncle to travel and really enjoy being retired. Plus, I want to pay you back for all that you put into the house. It wasn't on you to keep that place standing, but you sure tried."

She stared at him. "Well, Uncle. You know I'd do anything for you. And I loved that place. I grew up there too."

"Mmm-hmm. Well, the neighborhood has been changing, you know. Lots of the folks we grew up with have moved away. New folks all around."

Her eyebrows shot up. "Someone approached you already?"

He toyed with a button on his jacket, eventually placing his hands in his lap. "Mmm-hmm. One of those development companies. That's a good-sized corner lot. They want to turn it into a coffee shop."

"Really?" She thought about the property, in the midst of residential. "Does that work there?"

"They bought the house around the corner and are making that area storefronts with communal office space up top. The neighborhood is changing, Baby Girl."

"Changing via gentrification, Uncle. I mean…we could rebuild!" she stammered.

"Savannah Joy," her uncle said sternly. Savvy shut her mouth immediately, so rarely chastised by her uncle. "Neither one of us can afford to build a new house. It's time to let it go."

"Ugh. That's what Mama said." She sat back on the couch, crossing her arms.

"Yeah, well, don't tell her I said this, but she's right. It's time. You got to do more for yourself. Stop trying to take care of me. I'll be just fine." He set his iced tea on the coffee table, grabbing her hand. "They made me a good offer, and when I told them what that land meant to me, they upped the ante. We will be just fine." He squeezed her hand.

She wasn't ready to let go. "But what about Ms. Mabel?"

"She's a strong woman. Can't nobody push her out if she don't want to go. Besides, I'll be there with her if she needs some backup." He smiled, and Savvy thought she saw a twinkle in his eye.

"You and Ms. Mabel are living together?" Savvy grinned. "For real?"

"Mind your business, young lady," he warned, attempting to hide his smile.

"Mmm-hmm. We're going to talk about that later." Her mouth twitched.

"Mabel ain't selling quite yet. Her property values are about to go up with these additions to the neighborhood."

"Wow." Savvy propped her elbow up on the back of the sofa to rest her head in her hand. "So where are you off to first?"

"I'm going up to the Bay Area to see my bull-headed little sister. I want to take her something." He turned to pick up a bag he carried in with him. From it, he pulled out a worn album.

Her eyes widened. "How did you save the photo album? All of those photos of Granny and PopPop!" She ran her fingers over the leather cover, knowing exactly what was inside.

"Every once in a while, I do something right." He tapped on the album with his fingers. "I had a fireproof safe installed for important documents. I kept this in there."

Savvy hugged the album to her chest, feeling her eyes brim with tears. "This is all we needed." She turned to her uncle, her face pinching, as she fought back the urge to cry.

He put a hand on her shoulder, squeezing gently. "That's right, Baby Girl. This is all we need. They're in these photos, and more importantly, they're in our hearts."

Savvy nodded her head, overcome with relief for the salvaged photos. "Mom won't show it, but she is going to be so happy to have this."

"I know it. Now if I remember correctly, you have somewhere to be tonight."

Savvy shook her head. "I do, but it's okay, I'm not in a rush."

He eyed her for a long moment. "I see, since you're already dressed. So you made some decisions about your job?"

"I did. And I think I'm at peace with them."

"You want to talk about it?"

"Not yet. But soon."

He nodded. "Okay, Baby Girl. You go on ahead and get ready. I'm gonna get going. I promised Mabel I'd take her to the movies tonight." Savvy grinned wide, and her uncle rolled his eyes. "All right, now, calm down. It's just a movie."

He got to his feet, and Savvy wrapped her arms around him. "As long as you're happy, Uncle, I support all of it. Doesn't mean I won't still try to take care of you."

"Oh, I know it. And you know Mabel wants your granny's apricot lemon cake recipe."

"Yeah, well, she's got a long way to go before she earns that."

"Mmm-hmm." His amused smile was all Savvy needed. "I'll call you this weekend, Baby Girl. I love you."

"I love you too, Uncle." She kissed him goodbye.

Spencer's jaw dropped as Savvy opened her front door. "Savvy. You look... I can't... Wow."

A wave of crimson crept up her chest and washed over her cheeks as she gave him a little twirl. "Thank you. You look handsome."

He wore a light sweater under a blazer with dark jeans. Flashing a quick smile, he offered his arm. "Thanks. Shall we?"

She nodded and took his arm, turning back to close the door behind her.

"Did you cut your hair shorter?"

"Just a little. I think the waves make it look shorter than it really is."

"Well, you look phenomenal, Savvy. You're going to turn a lot of heads tonight."

"So where are we going?"

"We have a dinner reservation out by the water, and then I think we could maybe go grab a drink, listen to some live music?"

"That sounds perfect." She beamed up at him.

They set out for a quiet seafood restaurant near the Santa Monica Pier, which had some of the best shellfish in town along with a killer view of the sun setting over the water. They shared an order of grilled oysters, and then Savvy had sea bass while Spencer enjoyed a bowl of cioppino.

"So after all of that, you landed the job you wanted? That's amazing, Babe." Spencer leaned in to kiss Savvy's cheek. "You must feel a sense of relief."

"I was so worried," she admitted. "I thought my boss was going to fire me—that presentation went so terribly that I honestly wouldn't have been mad at him if he did."

"You work too hard for them to let you go, come on now." Spencer's reassuring tone made her reach for his hand under the table. She interlaced her fingers with his.

"Thank you for being so supportive. I have more good news." Her excitement shone on her face.

He leaned forward, eager to hear it.

"Sarah's proposal for our cookbook was accepted!" She waved her fists in the air.

"Savvy, that's amazing. Congratulations! It's like everything is falling into place. Getting settled at the new job, taking time for yourself, meeting personal and professional goals."

"Yes, all of that. Thank you! It's been exciting. I'm extremely happy with where things are going right now."

As they waited for dessert, he toyed with her ring—a rose gold fox with emerald stone eyes had its tail wrapped around her index finger. Though the contact was minimal, Savvy felt little zings of sensation coursing from her hand through the rest of her body.

"I'm really glad things are working out for you, Savvy."

"Me too. It's good to be getting back to normal." She rested against him.

"It's good to be here with you." He leaned forward to kiss her shoulder.

She felt a flutter in her stomach. "It's good to be here with you too, Spencer."

They held each other's gaze for a long moment and settled into a comfortable silence as their dessert arrived. He continued to play with her ring.

From dinner, they made their way to a popular lounge, but the entrance was roped off. "What's going on?" she asked one of the bouncers.

"Special listening party tonight. Do you two have tickets? We're expecting a full house."

Savvy started to say that they didn't, but Spencer stepped forward and produced two tickets. He winked at her, leading her into the main room lit by hundreds of candles. Booths framed the room, and smaller tables curved around a piano at the center. A huge crystal chandelier hung above the piano, catching light and sparkling from all of the candles.

"What is this?" She turned to Spencer, who led her by hand to a booth.

"Did you hear how there were musicians in town who

TAJ McCOY

had decided to hold some smaller, more intimate shows over at L.A. Live to feel closer to their fans?"

"Sure, didn't John Legend start that trend?"

"This is his last show." His sly smile grew wider.

"Oh my God, Spencer, are you serious? This is too much!" Stunned, Savvy looked around. "How did you manage this?"

He grinned. "The owner here is one of my clients, so I can't take the credit for these tickets, but I'm glad you could come with me."

"Me too!"

They enjoyed a cocktail and got settled into their booth. Savvy sat close to Spencer, his hand over her shoulder along the back of the seat, his other hand holding hers in his lap. He snuck little kisses as people around them were seated. A hush spread over the room, followed by an outbreak of applause as John Legend walked out to the piano and immediately began playing. Three backup singers flanked one side of his piano.

A few songs in, Spencer turned to her and reached for her hand. "Wearing a dress like that, you have to dance."

A smile grew across her face. "Do you know Joanie said the same thing?"

There wasn't a ton of space, except for the area just in front of their booth, but Spencer spun her around and brought her hand to his heart, as they swayed together to "Overload."

Out of the corner of her eye, Savvy caught a quick glimpse of Jason on the other side of the room. *Seriously, how the hell did that man manage to follow her everywhere?* But she decided not to give him another thought. Not about what he was doing there or who he was with. Not about whether he'd spotted her too.

"Hey—" Spencer slowed "—is that your ex over there?"

"Yep."

"Did you two talk after our last date?"

"He's reached out, but I don't feel that there's anything to say. It's over." She shrugged. "I've moved on."

He looked at her for a long moment, and then he pulled her close again, keeping her hand against his heart. Savvy rested her head against his chin. They danced another couple of songs and then took their seats, sipping cocktails throughout the rest of the show.

They were quiet on the way back to her apartment, but Savvy was grateful, because she had to think about what she had been wanting to tell him all evening.

They reached her doorstep, and Spencer took her face in his hands. "You are so beautiful, Savvy." He leaned forward and kissed her softly.

He started to lean in again, but Savvy stopped him by placing a hand on his chest. "Wait."

His eyebrows knitted together with concern. "You okay?"

"Oh, yes. I just—I think we should go and pick up Teddy."

"Teddy—are you sure?"

Savvy nodded. "I don't want you to have to leave before I wake up. It always make me feel like some sleazy hookup when you sneak out. Let me walk Teddy with you in the morning. Besides, I can finally see proof that you're not homeless."

He laughed. "You know Teddy will want to be wherever you are."

Savvy grinned. "Oh, Teddy just wants me all to himself."

He looked at her for a long beat, unblinking. "I know the feeling." Her stomach fluttered, and Spencer grinned. He leaned down and kissed her again, their lips locking gently. "Let's go get Teddy, Ms. Sheldon."

28

When they returned to her place, Spencer took Teddy for a walk, and Savvy went inside to make her obligatory call to the girls for a date recap. She grabbed a bottle of water from the refrigerator and settled on her couch with her laptop. She called Joanie and Maggie for a video group chat. Their faces appeared on her screen, and Savvy waved to both of them, quickly sipping some water.

"Savvy, you look so pretty! I love your makeup. Very natural." Joan was sitting on the couch and she could see the outline of Beth's shoulder next to her. She dipped her face into view and gave her two thumbs-up.

"Did you end up using the gold clutch?" Maggie shouted into the screen.

"Jeez, Grandma. Maggie, you can speak like a normal person, and I promise you, we will hear you just fine. And yes, I used the gold clutch." Savvy lifted the purse in her hand to show them.

"Oh, that goes perfectly!" Joanie nodded her approval.

"Come on, get to the good stuff. Did y'all do it yet?" Maggie was alternating between popcorn and Hershey's Nuggets with almonds.

Savvy put on her best imitation of Old Hollywood glamour. "A lady never kisses and tells."

"Oh, he kissed you, then. He clearly hasn't put it on you yet though, 'cause your hair is still bangin'."

"Shut up." Savvy sucked her teeth at her, and then turned when she heard her phone ping. It was Jason. "Whoa. Hold up a second."

"What? Savvy, what happened?"

"I just got a text from Jason."

"You what?!"

Savvy leaned back from the screen, laughing. Maggie, Joan, and Beth were all in view on her screen waiting for more details, looks of horror across their faces.

"You guys really have the best reactions."

"Well, what the hell did he say, Savvy?" Maggie's face scrunched in anger.

Joan looked into her camera giving a wide-eyed expression complete with a grimace. In her next life, she could be an emoji. Savvy bit her lip to keep herself from laughing.

"I'll read it to you. He said, 'Hi, Savvy. I'm not sure if you saw me at the show tonight, but I saw you. You looked so beautiful.'"

"Stating the obvious, but mmmkay." Maggie waved away the message.

Savvy eyed the camera on her laptop. "It continues. 'I'm sorry for how I acted. Tell me what I can do to make this right.'"

Maggie's voice lowered to a register Savvy never heard before, a guttural tone that would be perfect for a scary movie voice-over. "Nooo!"

Joanie covered her face. She was laughing so hard that there were tears in her eyes. She gasped for air, wiping away her tears. "What are you going to say to him, Savs?"

"Not a thing." Savvy took a slow sip of water. "There's nothing to say." The conflict that used to churn in her stomach over Jason was gone.

"Wow, girl. I'm proud of you."

"I'm so glad that you figured that out for yourself and moved on to better things. We really like Spencer for you, Savs." Maggie's tone had calmed to something more encouraging.

"I do too. He's walking Teddy right now." Savvy leaned closer to the screen to whisper, "And I saw his place! He's not homeless!"

"Oh, Savvy. I cannot believe you ever thought that man was homeless. What does his place look like?" Joanie leaned in. "Sounds like you've decided to keep him."

"Cute little bungalow in Silverlake. Can I tell y'all something? You know, these past two weeks have been full of emotions, but I had a lot of time to think. The biggest difference that I feel between Jason and Spencer, aside from the fact that Spencer is obviously a decent human being?"

"What's that, Savvy?" Beth asked gently.

"I don't have to change for him. I can be one hundred percent myself, flaws, curves, rolls, and all. I don't flinch when he touches my stomach or second-guess whether he actually finds me attractive. I can just be."

"Well, I'd say he's a keeper." Maggie smiled wide. "You deserve, Sis. We're so happy for you!"

Savvy heard the front door open and paws tapping on the hardwood floor. "Okay, y'all, I gotta go."

"Well, don't do anything we wouldn't do!" Mags arched her back a little, making a kissy face. "But don't forget to arch that back, ho!"

Joanie and Beth erupted into howls and screams.

Savvy stifled a laugh with her hands. "I can't with you people. Bye!"

"Bye!" they yelled.

Spencer stepped into the living room smiling ear to ear. Teddy rushed to Savvy on the couch, laying his head in her lap.

"Did you say hi to the girls for me?"

"I did! They're all incredibly jealous."

He placed a dog bed near the patio doors for Teddy, who immediately stepped into it, circled twice, and lay down. Moving toward the couch, he reached out for Savvy's hand.

She placed it in his, allowing him to pull her up and into his arms. He kissed her jawbone, running his fingertips lightly across her back, making her shudder. His tongue trailed down her neck to her shoulder and back again as she dug her fingernails into his back.

"You gonna arch your back for me?" he whispered into her ear, lips curving into a smile.

Savvy cackled, color rising to her cheeks. She playfully slapped his chest, laughing. "You weren't supposed to hear that!"

He chuckled in response. "I couldn't help it. I'm intrigued. I feel like I need to see this in action." He leaned down and kissed her lips softly, then more urgently, parting them with his tongue.

Savvy tilted her head for more access to Spencer's mouth as his hands traveled the length of her back, squeezing her backside. Kissing him hungrily, she grabbed his hand to lead him to the bedroom, the apex between her thighs throbbing.

Leaning him against the bed, she kissed him slowly, savoring the scent of his cologne as she unbuttoned his shirt. He lifted his hands to help, but she pushed them down to rest on the bed. After opening his shirt, she ran a hand down his chest to his belt, trailing kisses from his mouth to his neck, playfully nipping at his ear. As she unbuckled his belt and the waistband of his jeans, Spencer stood, smoothly stepping around Savvy so that he stood behind her, facing the bed.

"My turn," he murmured into her ear, running the tips of his fingers over her collarbone and down to her breasts. She whimpered as his fingers slipped beneath the rose gold fabric and grazed a taut nipple, circling slowly. As he rolled it between his fingers, she arched her back, her soft ass pushing back against his erection. "You're teasing me now."

She nodded, mesmerized by his fingertips. He slid his hands behind her, unzipping her dress and lowering it so that Savvy could step out of it. He knelt, running his fingers down her thighs and calves to her ankles to unclasp her sandals. She leaned forward, hands resting on the bed, as Spencer pulled off each shoe and kissed the backs of her thighs. Standing, he unclasped her bra, licking the nape of her neck. "I want to see all of you."

She expelled a low moan as his lips moved down her spine, using his knee to widen her stance. He wrapped a hand around the front of her thigh, squeezing her soft flesh as she arched her back in anticipation. His other hand found the wetness between her legs, the pads of his fingertips grazing lightly over her most sensitive spot. "So wet," he whispered. He grabbed a condom from his pocket and moved quickly to put it on.

Savvy gasped as Spencer rubbed the tip of his thick erection against her wetness, slowly thrusting back and forth over her clit before he entered her. As he glided in and out, she leaned forward, hands on the bed, arching her back on the tips of her toes.

His grip on her thigh tightened. "Oh my God," he grunted, picking up the pace. He brought his hand farther in front of her, drawing circles around her clit with his middle finger as he pushed deeper into her.

"Shit," she whimpered, biting her lip, bringing one leg onto the bed for support. She dropped down to her forearms, rocking back against him.

"No running, Ms. Sheldon," he quipped, stepping closer to her, his fingers moving deftly over her bundle of nerves. "Come for me."

She arched her back again, closer to orgasm, as she turned to receive his kiss. "Oh, my—" she gasped as her body convulsed.

He slowed, letting wave after wave rush over her. When she became too sensitive for his touch, she moved his hand away. "Wow," she breathed. Turning to look at him, she smiled at him seductively. "I think it's your turn, Mr. Morgan."

He slowed his thrusting further, toying with her as he glided into her with delicious deceleration.

"What do you propose?"

"Lie down on your back," she whispered.

"Yes, Ms. Sheldon." He nestled his head into the pillows as she crawled onto his lap, grinding against him. He moaned, pulling her face to his, her lips swollen from his kisses.

She kissed him deeply, licking his lips before she sat up. As she guided him into her, she grabbed the top of the bed frame to steady herself and took in his full length. Riding him slowly at first, she leaned forward slightly, her breasts inches from his face.

He lifted his head, taking one nipple into his mouth, running his tongue between her breasts, bucking against her when she wound her hips in a circle. "Damn, Savvy."

She said nothing, smiling at him as she tightened her grip on the headboard. Something about him made her not want to hold back. She moved more quickly, back and forth and in a circle, driving him right to the brink. He gripped her hips, pushing his up to meet her as she moved.

He clenched before he came, Savvy watching in satisfaction. He thrust into her, grunting and exhaling deeply. "Holy shit."

Savvy leaned forward, resting her chin on her hands over his chest. His heart pounded against her, and he lifted his head to kiss her. She climbed off him, resting her head against his shoulder. Smiling, she drew circles on his chest. "That's what happens when I arch my back."

They both burst into laughter.

"I'm glad I asked." Spencer smiled, kissing her forehead.

"Me too," she laughed, wrapping her arm over his chest. "You should consider asking more questions."

"Yes, Ms. Sheldon."

29

One year later

Everyone crowded around the kitchen island. Savvy looked around the room at the people she loved. Beth and Joanie, Maggie and Rob, Uncle Joe and Ms. Mable, Mama and Max, Paul and Sarah, Lina, Spencer, and Teddy.

Spencer lifted a box onto the kitchen island, and Sarah stepped forward to stand with Savvy.

Savvy cleared her throat. "So everyone, thank you so much for coming today. I know it may have been an odd request, since the book isn't officially published yet, but these ARCs will give you an idea of what Sarah and I have worked so hard on. We're so excited to share this with all of you."

Her voice caught, and she paused to regain composure. "The past year has been a roller coaster for me. Y'all know, because you all talked me off of the ledge when anxiety ran high."

Mags and Joanie nodded, proud smiles on their faces.

"Work drama, a breakup, a spiteful revenge plot, an amazing trainer, my support system, my love." She smiled at Spencer. "If you asked me then if I saw any of this coming, I'd say no. But everything happens for a reason."

Grabbing a pair of scissors, she cut through the packaging tape on the box.

"Spencer once likened my recipes to his renovation blueprints, and it makes a lot of sense. You need to have all of the components before you start building, you need all of your ingredients to make a successful dish, you find all of the necessary pieces to build a strong foundation. You all are my foundation, and this—" she pulled a book out of the box "—this is a result of your support."

Everyone clapped and cheered. Maggie and Joan poured champagne for the group, passing glasses to everyone. Savvy's mother moved close to give her a hug.

"I'm proud of you, Savannah." She smiled, squeezing her hand.

"Thank you, Mama." She kissed her mother's cheek. "Oh, I forgot, there's one more thing, y'all!" Savvy moved to the dining table, and carried a covered cake stand back to the kitchen island. "This is going to be included in our second cookbook!"

She uncovered her grandmother's special apricot lemon drizzle Bundt cake, a dusting of powdered sugar on top of the lotus-patterned cake.

Uncle Joe smiled, tears in his eyes. "Your granny would be so proud of you."

Grateful for the squad who stood by her, Savvy looked at her friends raising glasses of champagne in her direction. Self-doubt gone, she prepared to tackle the next big project: moving in with her boyfriend and his adorable chocolate lab.

Spencer stepped forward, handing her a glass and raising his own. "To Savvy, may this venture be the first of many opportunities to come that bring you joy and allow us to celebrate just how special you really are. We love you." He winked at her. "I love you."

Savvy beamed up at him, her eyes glistening.

Everyone clinked their glasses together. "To Savvy!"

★ ★ ★ ★ ★

ACKNOWLEDGMENTS

First, last, and always, I give God thanks for another day and another opportunity to connect with, and love on, others.

Savvy encompasses so many of the uncertainties that I've had about my own identity, so I'd like to truly thank you, readers, for giving me the space to express myself and shed that skin.

To Veronica Park, my incredible agent, I am grateful for #BeMyLI and the cast of *Lost Girl* for bringing us together. I can't imagine navigating publishing with anyone else. Thank you for being my advocate and champion, my sounding board, my plot bunny wrangler, and my friend. To film agent Debbie Deuble and foreign rights agent Heather Shapiro-Baror, thank you for your enthusiasm and for believing in my projects. I'm so lucky to have a kick-ass team of women supporting me. To Laurie and Gordon, and everyone at Fuse Literary, thank you all so much for the love and support! To Skellie, Bo, and Jake, thank you for providing me with a space and opportunity for a writing retreat!

To my editor, April Osborn, thank you so much for believing in Savvy and for helping me bring her to life in ways I didn't know were possible. Each step in this process has taught me valuable lessons that I will continue to carry with me. To the incredible team at MIRA, Gigi Lau, Laura Gianino, Ashley MacDonald, Ana Luxton, Tracy Wilson, and others behind the scenes, I am so grateful!

To Noa Denmon, thank you for breathing life into Savvy for the cover. I get emotional every time I look at her, and I will stan you to infinity.

To my family, thank you for being my foundation. Mom and Pop, thank you for always pushing me to go for broke, to try new things, and to be confident in the strengths and values that you instilled in me early on. To Uncle Stuart, thank you for always, ALWAYS, being there. To Uncle Kirk, Kira, Jess, Mykel, Grett, Yvette, Ariana, the McCoys, the Welches, the Adams, the Harts, the Grimes, the Batistes—I am blessed. To my niece, MacKenzie, and my godson, Lucas, I don't want y'all reading this book, but I want you to know that this is possible and that I am so very proud of you both.

To Alaysia Jordan, Tylar Thacker, J. Elle, Yasmin Angoe, Ka-Ton Grant, Michelle Grant, thank you for being early readers of my work, for providing me with invaluable feedback, and for loving Savvy just as much as I do. Savvy and I wouldn't be where we are today without each of you.

To the writing community, thank you for inspiring me, for helping me grow as a writer, for teaching me about pitch contests and querying and social media promo, for helping me learn about beats and agents and synopses. Thank you to Beth Phelan, Eric Smith, Kiki Nguyen, Ashley Herring-Blake, Michelle Richter, Jill Mansell, Kyra Davis, Ryan

LaSala, Shannon Doleski, Kimberly Ash, Rachel Mans McKenny, Kellye Garrett, and countless others, THANK YOU.

To Talia Hibbert, Mia Sosa, Adriana Herrera, Morgan Rogers, Denise Williams, Charish Reid, Sarah Smith, Farrah Rochon, Catherine Adel West, Jasmine Guillory, thank you for reading my work! I am in such awe of your talents and am honored to get to know (and stan) each of you.

To my Canon Crew, Better Than Brunch crew, DInk Squad, Yay Squad, 99 Dead, Mer-Peeps, my Shut Up & Write crew—words can't describe the blessing that you all have been to me. Thank you for the Zoom writing sessions, the coffeehouse sessions, the Slack talks, the phone calls, the boosts. Thank you for encouraging me, nudging me to keep going, sitting with me, procrastinating with me, crying with me, and just being incredible friends. Lane Clarke, Andrea Williams, Catherine Adel West, Charish Reid, Cass New-bould, Denise Williams, AJ Sass, Naz Kutub, Anna Gracia, Robin Wasely, Ayana Gray, John Clarence Stewart—words can't describe what y'all mean to me. To Traci-Anne, Gates, Paul, Rosey, Jeida, Robin S, Tee, Kyla, Pammie, Terry, Allie, Regina, Destiny, Sonora, Stephanie, Clem, Jen, Hector, Diane, Christopher, Jay, and so many more, I love y'all!

To Bianca Berdiago and Farley's East, I hella love y'all. Thank you for supporting local writers and repping the Bay the way you do. I will always come back.

To the Clubhouse crew, especially AJ, Harper, Melody, Alex, Hannah, Ariel, Racquel, Dante, Kristin, Ines, thank you for the writing sprints, the panels, the procrastination rooms, and the encouragement.

To the Buzzsaw in DC—Everett, Amir, Matt, Sayyid, Octavius. Thank y'all for supporting me and always having my back. Thanks to Stretch for writing with me and to the Civil crew for all the love.

To my law school admissions tramily, my higher ed family, my students, my community—words can't describe my love and gratitude. Tracy, Michelle P, Shani, Camille, Stephanie, Lisa, Mae, Maya, Brenda, Michelle A-S, Jannell, Carol, Traci, Margie, Shawn, Reggie, Allana, Kelly, Alicia, Joseph, Alice, Elena, Thembi, Eric, Whitney, Anne, Miri, Abby, Darius, Olivera, Finney, Yusuf, Linda, Tyler, Traci, Heidi, Katya, Gina, Kristina, Kott, Elizabeth, Nicole, David, Keshia, and countless others. Sarah Moody. Emily Lee-Escher. You've seen me through some of my highest highs and lowest lows, and I wouldn't be who I am today without your example, guidance, support, love, confidence, humor, or company.

Lastly, to Lizzo, thank you for being the positive inspiration for young people that I needed twenty years ago. Your confidence and joy, your body of work, and your platform are a beacon to so many, and I thank you for helping folks to feel GOOD AS HELL no matter where they are in their journey. I hope that Savvy and I bring that feeling to people as well.

<3 TJM